ZONA

PRINCESS OF LATIUM

Also by Nick Berry:

A Bit of a Shake-Up
Diadem Books, 2009
ISBN 978-1907294266

Zona: Princess of Troy
Diadem Books, 2011
ISBN 978-1908026057

Hunting God
Diadem Books, 2012
ISBN 978-1908026378

Pardon: Pirate Ben Long and Crew Face Trouble
Memoirs Publishing, 2013
ISBN 978-1909544284

ZONA

PRINCESS OF LATIUM

by

Nick Berry

Published by Memoirs

MEMOIRS
PUBLISHING

25 Market Place, Cirencester, Gloucestershire, GL7 2NX
info@memoirsbooks.co.uk www.memoirspublishing.com

ZONA: PRINCESS OF LATIUM

Artwork by Carly Edge

ISBN: 978-1-909874-43-5

'...where there is life,
there is the chance for new ideas,
tolerance and understanding...'

– *Wonder Woman.*

ACKNOWLEDGEMENTS

My thanks go to Charles Muller especially. It was you, Charles, who came up with the idea of a sequel to *Princess of Troy*. Here it is. Who knows if it measures up to that first book, but it was a whole lot of fun to write.

Once more, thanks are due to Carly Edge for some great artwork.

As before, my brother Tim, his lady Shirley and my sister Vicky should all take a bow. The flat and cats are lovely too, Vicky. As for your trip to China, bring on the photos!

This couldn't be done without a nod to my cats Winston, Elektra and Pentha. You rock, guys, and always will!

Gratitude has to go out to Sheila Miller. You put up with, even quietly encouraged, this eccentricity of writing. As ever, you're a person who lightens all my days!

To Stanley Lombardo for a translation of the Aeneid which brings Virgil's old poem to vivid life. Sorry about the liberties!

PREFACE

✣

If you enjoy reading about the legendary adventures of Ulysses or Odysseus, and stories about Aeneas, the Trojan hero who survived the sack of Troy following the Greek trick of gaining entry to the city inside a wooden horse, and the aftermath of this legendary war, then this imaginative novel, *Zona: Princess of Latium*, is for you! If you are not familiar with the legendary history of Aeneas as recorded by Virgil, then this book is a very palatable introduction to the events of that ancient time that preceded the establishment of Rome. Mind you, the events and facts, if facts they were, are magically filtered through the kaleidoscopic lenses of Nick Berry's rich imagination, thanks mainly to the introduction or implanting into the scenario, of a female Amazonian warrior that transcends all warriors, a super hero that causes Superwoman to pale into a two-dimensional flat comic book figure. With her magnificent thighs, skimpy strapless garment, and her overriding sense of justice, she charges through the old legends, throwing a new light on ancient legendary history. Next to her, Aeneas is no longer a victorious godlike hero, but is diminished into a small-minded selfish murderer, an opportunist intent only on his self-glorification, assuming the role of a god merely to manipulate his followers.

The author's narrative technique easily captivates the reader. There is good use of parallel montage, with different chapters picking up different strands of the story as the strands gradually come together in the final climax, the astounding battle between Zona and Aeneas. The opening chapter, the sack of Troy, is the 'Big Bang' that pushes the various actors of the story into different, far flung places of the old world, a north African desert, Carthage, Latium, and we follow with mounting interest their journeys as they gravitate to the final denouement, bent on revenge, justice, or (in the case of Aeneas) simply riding the wave of overweening ambition and pride.

Not just the main characters, or actors in this drama, are drawn in the round, convincing because of the internal monologue that conveys their innermost thoughts—as in the case of Deiphobos, the unseated prince of Troy who nurtures his dream of revenge against Zona who, through her bravery as a warrior, thwarted his conniving ambitions:

> *That's one more thing to be added to her account,* he went on reminding himself. When he caught up to her, she'd die slowly, not in a duel. *I'll build a rack, stretch her on it. Such wonderful tortures. A knife blade heated in a fire'll be tame. She'll be naked, of course.* About then he'd catch himself licking thick lips and drooling. *I'll savour each moment...* and he kept himself going by thinking things like that – in tight circles, round and around.

As we see in this extract, the author has written a novel with three dimensional characters—for we do not just see them externally, from the outside, involved in lucid actions; we also know them from the inside: the repeated use of internal monologue puts us in touch with their thoughts and, as in this case, base desires and motives of revenge, tainted with lust. A little bit of James Joyce here, foregrounding the real sweaty characters of the author's creation against the legendary heroic figures of the Odyssey scenario. In this way the author brings these characters down to earth and we know them, warts and all.

In Zona the author has created a real, convincing woman—not just a vital, dynamic warrior but a woman capable of sympathy and empathy, as we see when she commiserates with Alissar or Dido, Queen of Carthage, who, used and betrayed by Aeneas whom she loved, nearly committed suicide:

> "It happens." She [Zona] laid a hand over the other woman's. "When you're in love the way you were, you always want to believe the best."

Zona is a super hero, but with a real woman's heart. In Virgil's version, Dido does commit suicide, but Nick Berry's story takes a new twist through Zona, who saves her at the last minute. A silvery sheen or radiance gradually envelopes Zona's magnificent limbs as she fights for justice against Deiphobos and later, Aeneas, and it is clear that the force is with her. This is in keeping with the tradition of Greek mythology, where the gods often support and give power to their protégés. There's a very powerful scene when Zona, only dimly aware of this support, heals Camilla, her companion in arms, from a mortal wound, the sheen of light flowing over and enveloping the two women in this magical moment.

Perhaps the greatest power of this author is in his evocation of dramatic descriptions or scenes of nature, as in the graphic seascapes and storm scenarios, worthy even of Joseph Conrad:

> More lightning sizzled though curtains of
> rain; in its flare the sea was heaving like
> a giant cook stirring a soup. Even before
> darkness like Hades flapped back, thunder
> was a shattering blast.

Or perhaps it is the portrayal of rapid, unexpected action that the author seems to do best—especially in the scenes of combat:

> The squad had crept into position while
> the guards were diverted. He saw the huge
> shape of Dares rise, just caught the jut of
> his beard. A crack came through the night
> as Dares broke a man's neck. There was a
> gurgle, stink too as the soldier voided his
> bowels. At the sounds, the other gate guard
> spun. A member of the squad took him
> down, a knife blade gleaming as it thudded

in his back. Aeneas heard the limp body fall forward. *A good start,* he exulted.

This is just a small sample of the dynamic prose that follows when the author dramatizes the triumphant fights of Zona, the author's own, original creation. This is not the first book he has written that embodies the heroic exploits of this magnificent woman, for she first appeared in *Zona: Princess of Troy*, which is the prequel to this novel which, if the reader has not yet read it, I also strongly recommend.

Virgil, the original author who recorded the exploits of Aeneas, makes a brief appearance in this latest book on Zona, as a soldier who charms his listeners when he reports on the proceedings of a battle; Nick Berry, I would venture to say, has equally charmed the readers in this latest account of the events that followed the demise of Troy—but especially through the towering, majestic, yet compassionate character of Zona.

Charles Muller
MA (Wales), PhD (London), DEd (SA), DLitt (UOFS)

CHAPTER ONE

❖

THE LEAN, DARK MAN was knuckling sleep out of his eyes, his black mop mussed.

As a dagger pierced him under his ribs he cried out. When the burly soldier jerked it upwards, cutting a lung, he caught at the knife and gurgled. With blood running from his mouth, another assassin slashed his throat. They stabbed him again repeatedly. As he fell, more blood splashed.

Aeneas was cleaning up, Troy bursting into flames all around. What he looked forward to after getting free of the city couldn't include Polydamas.

With a sigh, Aeneas watched his old comrade on the floor spattered and gushing blood. Clean-shaven, not unlike his victim in build and swarthy colouring, he rubbed a now-bristled chin as his troopers left the dying man. He'd hoped all along that a time like this wouldn't come but Antenor had been right to advise caution, Zona too... He felt chills ripple all over him under his soldier's tunic and kilt. Those eerie amber eyes... When Troilus went down to Achilles she'd said they had to talk. Aeneas hoped it would never happen, but who could have foreseen the wooden horse which would bring Troy's ruin?

Rubbing tired eyes, he wished none of this was happening. *Like everyone else in this city.* His old friend had often been useful but not now. There was no point regretting anything, and he'd more to do. He had to be hard, see what was needed and do it – as he had all his life... He was in bed with his comely wife Creusa when awoken. Not for him clouding his mind with wine like so many others in the celebrations before the Greeks broke into Troy. In their room Ascanius the baby was asleep in his cot, his wet nurse bedded down beside him. The shouts and screams, smells of fire and blood had Aeneas tumbling out of bed, cold all over with his belly tightening. He cursed as he dragged himself awake. At thirty-five, hair speckled white, he wasn't as up for this kind of thing as in the past. Now there was this; looking down at the gore-splashed remains of his friend and fellow general.

Aeneas sighed again. They'd known each other so long, were practically brothers well before the battles for Troy. Of course, he would kill his own brother as well if necessary but still it was a loss. *Oh never mind; Ares would see the necessity here.* As he should; it was for the war god he was acting, himself as well.

Mikhail, the captain of his guards, broke in on him. "Where now, Sir?"

The surviving Dardanian commander set his chin. This man, like the others, would have to go when he'd done – as soon as possible. They would know too much... and a brief vision of the warrior Zona's face glared in his mind. He couldn't take the slightest chance of what he'd already done, let alone the stuff to come, getting through to her of all people.

Having finished wiping their blades on the dead man's tunic, the captain and his men looked at Aeneas expectantly. He reminded himself that these men were from his picked Household Guard. They would stay, fight their way out beside him and do as they were told. *Until I take them out*.

Clearing his throat, he met the cold grey eyes of the blocky, granite-featured man. "Home. We've business to take care of there now this is finished."

Aeneas' guards closing round him, they left the house, shutting the front door carefully. The night air was chill, full of the smoke of fires lit during the celebrations, and by the Greek invaders. In the lower city and working their way up the hills, fires were sending out leaping flames. As the marauders came nearer, Aeneas could hear hoarse shouts, screams and wailing. It couldn't be long before the first enemies arrived; he could clearly hear the clash of weapons, running feet. The need to hurry was growing; it wouldn't be long before this part of the city was overrun.

Another thing made him break into a trot as he and his men of the Household Guard jogged up the streets towards his home. In the east still-intact houses were silhouetted in a ragged line against the air. Soon it would be dawn; what poets might call a rosy blush would spread up from there. When the sun rose he and his men would be conspicuous, the work they were about more likely to be interrupted and dangerous. And at any time they could meet a Greek force too big to handle.

Out of breath – *too much good living* – he pushed on faster. On the right Prince Deiphobos' house was ablaze, throwing out clouds of sparks and smoke. Women, some clutching children, ran screaming from it. His guards shoved a few roughly aside. It was all too likely there were still Greeks around.

The air now hot and thick, Aeneas was panting. Perspiration in his armpits trickled down his sides. Licking salt off his lips, he caught the odour of himself and his guards and wrinkled his face. A painful stitch drilled under his ribs. In his mouth it was dust-dry and there was a vile taste like down a cesspit. He still managed to push himself faster. The banners of flame, curling shadows from the burning Heir's house mixed with the near-dark of the coming day. Unless he was mistaken the shadows of men were over on the left. For a ragged heartbeat he wondered where Deiphobos was, then decided it didn't matter. There had been times he thought of joining with the man, but maybe it was better if the prince knew nothing of what Aeneas was soon to do. If he had done, he would only have had to die.

The party reached his home. It was intact, candles burning behind the drapes of the lower rooms. As he drew it, he was pleased his hand was steady on the hilt of his sword but this would have been easier if he'd felt nothing for any of them.

He and his men passed through the ornate gateway. There was no sign of Greeks – unless they were already inside. In which case they might already have saved him some work… At the thought of them still there, Aeneas felt perspiration stick his things to him as his heart beat swiftly, raggedly. If only this was all over and he was clear of Troy and building his new life.

The guards' captain must have seen something in his face. *I must be the colour of the melting ice they use to cool wine*, Aeneas thought. *I wish we'd cleaned up here and were away.*

"Would you like me to do this, Sir?" The man's voice gravelly, his square features were expressionless.

Behind the captain loomed the giant Dares who lived only for killing, and it was tempting to use him but only with complete ruthlessness was Aeneas going to get through this. Already the soldiers had killed his fellow general for him. This one had to be his job.

When it came to it, he still drew back. Even though he remembered that Achates was also there and could see him in the thinning night.

The band of Aeneas and his guards had gone all the way through the trees and flowering shrubs of his garden. The winding drive behind them, the men tramped up to the front door. The burly guards climbed the three steps to the door. Aeneas came with them, heart stuttering in his throat. A fresh light film of sweat broke out under his clothes. Away to the right and down the hill they'd climbed to get here, the night sky was red with more fires. His nose screwed up as he stifled a sneeze; his lungs seemed full of smoke and ash. *How many times have I cheerfully come home to this place?* Now, along with the shouts, wails and screams which pierced the thick air, Aeneas could pretty well hear the heavy thuds of his heart. He really didn't want this; if only there were something else he could do. His stomach was a cold, gaping hole; the general so wanted this over.

A picture of Deiphobos flitted in his mind, the coarse dark hair flopping over his forehead; heavy blue jowls, his features otherwise clean-shaven. Aeneas disliked the prince and Heir of Troy. The man was tricky, cruel and brutal. If anyone survived the city's fall it would be him. People like him were born on their feet, swift and cunning as any cat. The man almost certainly had no imagination to get in his way. He wouldn't see, almost feel what was about to happen, and what a gift that would be.

He caught at his captain's arm. There was no reason he'd got to do this himself; what a silly idea.

"You do it," he said.

He thought it sounded craven but at least his voice was firm.

The man's eyes travelled expressionlessly over him. Perhaps there was a hint of something in the officer's face, but maybe it was Aeneas' imagination. *It is; I need these men a while.*

"Very well, Sir."

Just that, nothing more, *but is there more?* He put it aside. With Troy in flames, Greeks likely on their way, he reminded himself again how he needed these men – *for a while at least.*

"Let's get on then." His mouth was dry, tongue swollen.

Mikhail's rocklike fist hammered the thick, dark

oak door. Silence behind it was broken by a woman's quick steps.

"Who's there?" called a timid but resolute voice.

"My Lord Aeneas," rasped the Guards' commander. "Open the door."

There was relief in the woman's voice. Aeneas tried to recall her name but it danced on the end of his tongue, just out of reach.

"Oh thank the gods you're here! Greeks are everywhere."

Mikhail's face was creased by a grim smile which came and went. Bars rattled being drawn back as the door was unfastened.

When the heavy door swung back, the maid's face was a pale blur in the darkness of the hall. A candle shook its flames in her hand, throwing shadows to fight their way up the walls and lie in corners. Aeneas could see lit chandeliers further back. The guards' captain jerked his head to the other soldiers. They crowded past the general into the hall.

The captain didn't speak as the maid stared at him and his men. Comprehension, terror and incredulity widened her dark eyes and she spun to flee down the hall.

"Stop!" commanded the captain. His voice was flat

and hard. "Are my Lord Anchises and the Lady Creusa here? What of the babe Ascanius?"

The maid's mouth opened and closed. She was shiny-faced with perspiration and no sound came out. *Like one of my fish in the backyard pool,* thought Aeneas.

"Y-y-yes Sir," she finally whispered. "Upstairs in my lady's rooms."

"That's good," replied the hard-voiced soldier.

He didn't say any more, just stared with cold eyes.

"All of them?" asked Aeneas.

"Y-y-yes Sir."

"Ask them to come down here," he ordered. "And to bring the baby."

"Y-yes Sir."

Silence fell like a cold damp blanket. A couple of troopers shuffled their feet, and stopped at a look from Aeneas. He found himself sheathed in yet more sweat. *Where does it all come from? Things are happening outside but even so* – Fighting in battles on Troy's behalf was much easier than this. Even when he and Polydamas – he shut his mind to the images which floated like rank weeds in a pool – let Troilus die under Achilles' blade.

Followed by Anchises, Creusa came gracefully down the stairs. She wore a pale blue gown and had her black hair piled on her head. The baby was sleepy but quiet in her arms. Her brown eyes were puzzled, swarthy olive complexion pale. Aeneas felt a moment of doubt. Fear, presumably of marauding Greeks, gave way in her face to pleasure at the sight of him. She probably thought he'd come to take her to safety… Until she saw the guards' drawn swords and grim expressions and her colour drained completely away.

Yet she was still a princess. Her chin was up, shoulders back as she addressed the men.

"What's the meaning of this?"

"I'm sorry," Aeneas said. "This has to be."

"Why? I've always been a good wife to you!"

The lean, grizzled Anchises laid a hand on her shoulder. "It's no good, my dear."

The guards captain didn't speak; no-one did. He waved the two biggest of his men, Dares and Achates, forward. The hulking killers' swords whistled in the hot air. As blood erupted, spattering the nearest wall, heads flew.

The baby began to wail.

CHAPTER TWO

✜

CONSCIOUSNESS oozed back, like dawn in a cloudy sky.

Not that it was in any way light. Pain throbbed, waves in his head from the back to the front behind his shut eyes, and started again. Nausea twisted in his guts and he was cauled in chill sweat. Shivers chased over him and the taste in his mouth defied description; it surpassed even the manure of donkeys. *Why is it so dark? Is this Hades? Maybe my eyes are stuck; Gods, am I blind?*

The sickness swilled in him like a breaking wave and he clamped his teeth against it. More cold sweat. Someone moaned; there were fresh combers of pain in his head. He groaned once more – which brought the acid back into his mouth. In a new sweat, he fought it, and the taste *was* worse than donkeys. His treacherous innards went on squirming.

Breathing heavily through his nose, he tried sitting from where he seemed lying on his back. His back ached as if steel had been shoved into him behind his

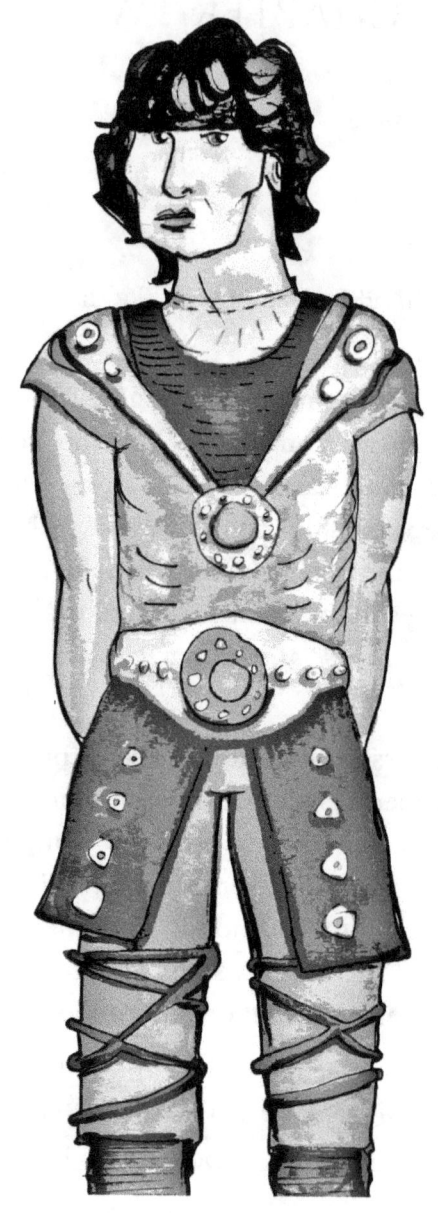

shoulders. Watery limbs failed him and he slumped back down. Once again his head opened and shut. He cried out hoarsely; there was fresh icy perspiration, and another battle with his belly.

OK, wait a while, then try again. Without warning a scalding burp ripped out of him. *Something I've eaten? Too many marinated songbirds' hearts, or was it the wine? Ares, it sure disagreed* – Whatever it might have been, his insides were off another time.

Crying with weakness and pain, he went on fighting to hold it in. This sweaty battle with himself was the most basic and humiliating thing. At length he won but he was trembling all over.

Shouts and screams exploded in the darkness.

The men's voices sounded hoarse, exultant and savage. The screams were those of terror and despair. Was this the clash of weapons, the smell of fire growing? Unable to stop himself, he sneezed violently. It burst through his head and set his stomach off some more. He went into the whole messy cycle a new time – and another sneeze juddered through him.

Awareness struck. His sticky eyelids were torn open.

Instinctively his left hand flexed. The thing he'd been clutching rolled away on a muffled surface, then hard wood. He could see and for an eye-blink he wished he couldn't. Fear washed away the other feelings in a black torrent.

The room was dimly visible, a glow shining through closed drapes. The men's voices went on but closer and the fire smells ramped up. He could hear the flames too.

Now fully aware of where he was, the prince nearly cried out. Something heavy and cool was pressed to his brow and gingerly he touched it. The movement dislodged the crown of Troy; Priam's Lion Crown and terror wiped out the other symptoms of his weakness. The crown thudded on the floor and this time he made it, sitting up.

In jagged bursts like lightning flaring, it all came back to him. Finally Helen was his! He was going to do her right here in her chambers. Her high-flown ways wouldn't help her. She could yell herself hoarse. When he'd finished, the prince was going to take her – or maybe her head alone would be better – to the Greeks. That should convince Odysseus and the others he was on their side.

If only something hadn't gone wrong.

"By all the gods!"

Deiphobos hardly recognised his own voice because he was reeling at more flashes of memory. They made him feel stronger but…

The men were louder, sounding as if just outside

the door. Feet pounded and all the noise drilled into his skull.

"In here!" a soldier shouted.

This was no time for worrying about dignity. The Greeks were sacking Troy and he was alone with the stink of his fear. As the door crashed open against a wall, he slumped back to play dead. He'd no idea how he stopped a groan as his head bonked on the floor, punishing itself and his roiling belly. He heard men spill into the room.

"By Athena, look at this!" crowed a rough voice.

Another spoke. "Crowns!"

There was an excited babble, words so fast that he missed them and feet stomped nearby. He could smell the men's perspiration, the smoke of fires. The Lion Crown and the tiara with which he'd been mockingly endowed were picked up. Probably turning one of them over in his hands, somebody sucked in his breath. There went the funds with which the prince planned to escape – if he lived. He ground his teeth, wished he'd not done because of what it did to his head – and had anyone heard?

"We're rich!" said a man, sounding clogged with greed.

"Well don't you look dainty!" jeered another.

Deiphobos guessed one of them wore the tiara or crown but dared not even slit his eyes open to look. Anger at his own helplessness gnawed him. *If only I could stop these thieves!* He'd get them in his dungeons, think up something really special, do it himself, but that was all over. For now he had to focus on surviving.

"Quite the princess, aren't you," added the man.

"I'll have your balls," growled a fresh voice. "What are you men at? Torch the place and let's go, and give those to me!"

"Aw Serge," complained the man who the prince thought wore the tiara

"What about this guy?" asked another.

There was a two-drumbeat pause; fear was ice, stopping his breath. They'd see his chest rise and fall –

"Put a sword in his guts and leave him," ordered the sergeant. "I told you; I need you guys now."

The Trojan prince went on playing dead; it was all he could do. Every nerve screamed at him to get up and run. With all he'd got, he overrode the message. He was too weak for running and the same went for fighting his way out. These were professional soldiers. He thought there were four, including the sergeant but could be there were more who'd not spoken yet. As a prince, then Heir of the Trojan Lion Crown, briefly

King, he wasn't famed for martial exploits. Not like his brother. *Till Achilles killed him...*

Sweating, he waited for someone to obey the sergeant. His belly quivered, pretty well able to feel the sword punch in. All his muscles were locked tight as if they could fend off the cold bronze. Hideous pain would flare in his vitals as the metal twisted and gore flowed hot on his skin. Why was he cursed with such imagination? But maybe it was the side effect of a healthy concern for one's own hide.

Feet tramped but Deiphobos still didn't risk cracking his eyes open. If anyone saw him watching...

"Ah!" A voice came from right over him. "I don't want to mess up my sword."

He was certain the man would see him shrink away. When he did, the trooper would change his mind, make the thrust.

Over the prone King of Troy, the man muttered but incredibly still no blow came. Instead boots scraped the floor as they tromped out; against all logic he was alone once more.

Gasping, he couldn't believe it, they'd left him, he was still alive. For some time he was unable to do anything but lie, sweat and tremble. Maybe, in spite of all that had gone down, Ares still favoured him.

Thoughts of the dark, seductive god led him to how

he'd got here. Lying in Helen's boudoir while the city burned and its people were slaughtered like pigs or cattle. Now he'd to get out – quickly.

Bitterness scalded through him like indigestion, mixed with even more potent ingredients of hate and misery. For so brief a time he'd had it all; even Helen was in his grasp.

Until Zona went and spoiled it all.

The Trojan prince, Heir and King pushed himself up to sit. His eyes briefly stayed shut as memories played behind them. The pictures were too bright and vivid, in garish colours.

There he was, gripping Helen by a wrist. The long-awaited sweetness of possession was at hand.

Until Zona came.

From the way she burst through the door, she must have heard or seen what he was about.

Zona!

Deiphobos had hated her before, but now…

He saw again how light she was on her feet, in spite of being solidly built, with generous curves, over six feet tall. Her blade flickered at him like a snake's tongue; it was all he could do to keep out of its reach. A heavy man, he was soon perspiring as in a soft, deep voice she taunted him. Sometimes she merely circled him, sword pointing at the floor – and he still couldn't catch her. In strapless vest and short kilt, she was fire-smudged and smelled of the flames. She'd doubtless been in at least one fight before coming to him; her near-black hair was tangled with sweat above broad shoulders. The bare, shapely arms that wielded her sword with terrible skill, her chest, shoulders, long, muscled legs in short boots shone only lightly in the heat. She wasn't even working at it. Her breathing was even as she pushed him to exhaustion.

She broke through him. The prince's growing fear ballooned into blood-freezing terror. He saw light on her sword as it darted out, was reeling away, certain he'd feel its ice in his neck. Something cracked his chin agonisingly –

Now here he was.

He was no longer King of Troy, no Lion Throne for him. The reverence and luxuries that would have been his were forever lost. When the Greeks were done with the city, Odysseus and his spymaster would no longer need him. Even the crown and tiara which could have been sold in Egyptian markets were gone; he was near-destitute. No more marinated songbirds' hearts, herb-seasoned lamb for him. He was certain scented baths, mute slave girls and the rest were lost as well.

He'd to reckon up his assets but the trouble was

there weren't many. Zona hadn't killed him; he was still alive during the sack of Troy, and that was it.

Zona!

This was all her fault. If she'd never come to the city none of it would have gone down. A bit of his mind recognised that the Greek spy he'd ordered killed was right. The prince was obsessing over the lady warrior but he paid it no attention, except to note it was there. Odysseus would have stayed by him if not for her; Troy wouldn't have been burned down around him. He would be King, Helen his queen. It beat inside him like a fevered drum. Everything was the cursed warrior's fault. He'd tried many times to arrange her death but she always wriggled away. Now he knew that, after downing him, she'd successfully left the city. It was as certain as drawing his next breath. Well, this time she wouldn't get away with it. He'd dedicate himself to tracking her down and making her pay.

Only then could he take back his life, have what was rightfully his. The thinking did not hang together all that prettily but to him it made a lot of sense.

She had to die.

From somewhere he'd get at least a knife. When he finally caught up to her, there'd be such tender, drawn-out joy. He'd savour, cherish every moment.

He would make it at night. She'd have stripped,

would maybe wear nothing at all for sleep and have put aside her weapons... Darkness always threw people off, made them disoriented, vulnerable, even someone like her. She wouldn't know he was coming.

He could scarcely wait.

CHAPTER THREE

ZONA stirred her fire.

Maybe Hades was telling her something in her sleep. She wasn't normally subject to nightmares and visions. That was more the lost Xanthia's thing but of all people she thought maybe she'd dreamed of Deiphobos, and it wasn't the first time. Somewhere in the darkness he was coming for her.

The warrior wasn't afraid of the darkness any more than she was of dreams. She'd met some things along the way – Furies, for instance – and stood her ground. *OK, maybe it was because I had to,* she told herself, but it was different now.

Swarmed with shivers, as always since leaving Troy she wore only a dark, strapless vest and matching kilt. Rubbing the chill off her arms, she wrapped herself, dragging her lion blankets to cover herself. She was dismayed the shakes went on.

"Maybe it's the dream I keep having, got to be."

In the starlit clearing her voice sounded unnatural. Hearing it Lina, her golden horse, pricked forward her

ears. It was a comfort that the mare was with her –
but it made her uneasy. Before her lost partner, she'd
always been alone with just her horse. And until the
aftermath of Troy's fall, she never had this particular
dream.

Xanthia again. Her thoughts were more circuitous
than a labyrinth. She'd heard minotaurs, whatever
they were, lived in them. *Maybe it isn't surprising,*
she told herself as often before, *that my thoughts and
dreams went along this particular trail.* Blue-eyed,
corn-haired, her friend had been a bard so maybe the
dream, like a story – *prediction? I hope not!* – wasn't
surprising. *She did change me, all kinds of ways.*

With a pang like a knife cut, the blonde woman's
ghost seemed to be there in the clearing. Grinning as
she launched into one of her wild stories. The warrior
could hear merry laughter, the bubbling stream of
her friend's talk. This was no good and she set herself
against tears. Prickling her eyes, they wet her cheeks.
Some time there had to be a way to stop being like this.
It was ironic the number of times round campfires like
this one, she'd wished her friend would stop talking
quite so much. Now, if only she could hear that voice
once more. *Might as well wish I could ride to the
moon,* she thought. It was never going to happen
again. Their parting was as unalterable as this night.
It happened, can't be turned back, get over this. If she

could just figure a way to do it.

There wasn't one; Xanthia was with Andres who'd ridden from the ruin of Troy with herself, Helen and Rupros. Shaking her head like a horse plagued by flies, Zona batted irritably at her eyes. Her friend was better off this way; there was hardly a future with a killer like herself.

The dream... With a near physical ache, she went on sitting. If her friend were here, she'd think of an explanation. As the woman wasn't, perhaps she could work out a meaning.

First step: confront the thing, what she'd say. By Athena, she'd got to stop this. Already, in the manner of dreams, its wisps and tendrils were fading like mist as dawn strengthened.

The warrior caught onto it, held it, and wished she hadn't.

The dream... If this one would only behave as so many others did, shredded away more quickly when she'd woken. Because what or who was after her? Of course it was a 'who'. It was Deiphobos.

Wasn't it?

Go through it, analyse and move on. It was the only way to get past it because dreams were things of the mind. What had the bard called it? *P, no psycho something or other. Trust her to find a word for it.*

Once more tears pricked the warrior's eyes at the thought of the other woman. Brushing them away, she tried to ignore how they came back. Her throat and sweat-glossy chest ached with emotion.

Focus! she ordered herself, and worked at it. The dream was the thing, and what in Hades did it really mean?

Sitting by her fire in now-sticky heat, the warrior clasped her arms. She felt the blankets slip all the way off her shoulders but cold was no longer a problem. It was everything else, the feeling something was on the way. *Maybe that was what woke me? Could be something/one is really out there.* Looking carefully around, doing it once more, she could see nothing out of place.

Zona listened to the sound of crickets in the brush and dry grass around her. There was the distant twit of an owl, a strange birdcall in apparent reply, breezes coming and fading in the scrub. Her golden mare shifted and blew through its nose in the darkness outside the light of her fire. She smelled the familiar odours of horse and dry vegetation around her campsite. Wind blew again, stirring the near-non-existent smoke of her fire, tossing its flames. Having roused them from embers, it ripped them into tattered banners before they came together again.

Shifting, she gave twigs, then a couple of logs to

the blaze. An attempt at telling herself the rising wind had woken her made the warrior wrinkle her nose. Her friend would have called it avoidance. *It was a miracle where she got some of these words. From the gods themselves, I guess.*

"Yeah, I guess."

A sigh went along with a frown. She hadn't realised she'd spoken aloud – again. She guessed it happened when you were alone, and the voice had been her own.

Not noticing she was rubbing fresh cold from her arms, she went back to the dream…

… She was in a dark, cramped space, curled almost in a ball. It might have been a cupboard, a forgotten one by the damp, musty smell. Her knees drawn right up to her chest, she was unarmed. As she did in her normal daytimes, Zona wore only her vest and kilt and she was hot, hair straggly round her face and shoulders.

It was growing harder to breathe and she knew she had to get out soon. She didn't have the name claustrophobia but it was close to what she was going through. She forced herself to breathe steadily, taking big mouthfuls of the close air.

This isn't going to help, being this way, she told herself. *I'm stuck in here, I don't know why. Must keep my nerve* – She cut off the trail of thought. For an instant it shifted, gave her bright sunlight, wind in her face, lifting through her hair as she rode her horse… The vision left as quickly as it had come. There was still the gods knew what or who out there. She remembered she had no blade of any kind – and why was that? It just wasn't like her, any more than being trapped in this cubby like a rat.

Along with other things it told her, the dream said the cupboard was in a city. Like Troy it was a ruined one. The sky would be grey, heavy and ashen, if it was even daylight out there. The streets were littered with trash, much of it burned and tattered. Everywhere the smells of burning and decay hung. Buildings were falling down and many appeared victims of fire. When a warrior crept outside, she was met by empty, broken windows with blackness behind them, gaping door spaces which were also dark. It was as if the eye sockets of fleshless skulls watched her passing. Other things also studied, sized her up, and they were slowly clumping together. Each time she went out, she needed to return to her hole quickly. Grab what food and water she could ferret out and run.

Somehow, another titbit the dream serves up, I know this hot, desolate place isn't the ruins of Troy. Often the warrior picked at the questions of where and when she was like a hangnail but never got near any answers.

She was back in her cramped wooden space. The air was almost moist, dense and fuggy, pressing in. She knew she'd been discovered. Any time they would be coming for her. They were getting swiftly nearer; she could practically feel them.

For long-drawn moments everything seemed to hold its breath, or be unable to suck in air. *Like me* –

The assault began.

First came the noise of something sniffing the flimsy wooden door. Whatever the thing was, it was big and heavy. Zona thought of griffons, and wished she hadn't. Or maybe it was a creature Ares had made, especially for her.

The snuffling and prodding was done. After a moment a tentative rap on the door was followed by a fresh short silence, but it seemed she could smell a wild, musky odour. The warrior dared to hope she'd not been found because, wherever this city was, here was the thing or one of them which had destroyed it.

A more definite bang on the wood shocked her out of that. It was succeeded by a storm of blows which shook the door in its frame. Another silence, sniffing once more and louder. Savage blows rained on the old timber. With wide eyes, she saw it bow inwards. Puffs of dust came from it with mildew smells. The lock was a simple bronze bolt. Abruptly it flew off, just missing one of her feet, to clatter on the wooden floor. Zona thanked the gods that the thing, things or men out there didn't appear to grasp raising latches.

"In Ares' name, what's that creature?" Her voice was a strained whisper. *If only I had a weapon - of any sort.*

Another silence was quickly filled by more snuffles and what could have been a whining. Her thoughts flew to hounds the war god had once set on her. Since she was no longer a bloodthirsty bandit leading a gang of marauders, he was rarely pleased with her. Next came a fuzzy mutter of sounds. So there were more than one of them – and what *were* these things?

Whatever they might be, the warrior knew she'd got to do something, and fast. *Any time now those creatures are going to be in here with me!*

The attack on the door was renewed with even greater ferocity. Again it bent inwards. With a sharp crack one of the planks split and barely stood in place. More dirt and sawdust trickled and Zona sneezed. A second door timber fractured loudly. There was a scrabble of claws and she almost made out the whining speech which gabbled with it.

Not pausing for images to glare in her mind, she scooted nearer the door. As blows hammered it, she shot out booted feet to brace the sagging boards.

Mingled with snarls and spitting, the voices outside were excited. Blows pounded the splintering planks; she was shifting her feet hurriedly to brace them as they split in more places. It did no good. Pieces of broken wood fell around her legs. The door went on coming apart. Soon it wasn't any more than a few fragments she held up with her feet.

A large chunk of door flew onto the floor with a cloud of dust. Through the jagged hole it left, an impossibly long, black-haired arm scrabbled. It was muscular; there were horny claws...

Sweating hard, Zona shrugged off her blankets which at some time she'd pulled back round her shoulders. The dream was so vivid; it kept repeating over and over. Having confronted it, she was certain something was coming along the trail.

The question was who or what would it be?

CHAPTER FOUR

✤

HAVING PUT HERSELF through the dark cupboard, the warrior shivered convulsively. Almost reaching for the blankets she'd shrugged off, she paused; soon she would be hot again and the night was pressing in. Something was very out of line; it was her sheathed sword she stretched out for.

On the face of it the silence of the North African night was unchanged. The air had gotten cold but Zona paid it no mind. It was just how night was in these parts. She could hear crickets at their thing, the scuffle of a small animal in the surrounding brush. Breezes whispered in grass and in the leaves of the trees which overhung the place. The nearby stream which had caused her to stop here chuckled softly in the darkness and not far off an owl called. Above her the night was crowded by the bright points of stars –

The air was torn by a scream.

The warrior froze. Her eyes flicked right. She just made out her horse contentedly munching grass. No, she wasn't; the horse had stopped and her ears were pricked forward. Zona began to relax, mind catching at the hunting owl and its prey, but her mare didn't.

She and her mount had been together long enough to form close bonds. The warrior was too good at what she did to ignore the warning.

Moving quietly but swiftly, she drew her sword, careful to make sure there were no tell-tale sounds of steel through leather. Coming to her feet in a crouch, she moved to her bedroll. Making sure she wouldn't be silhouetted against firelight, she arranged blankets. It wouldn't pass close-up inspection but she aimed to stop whoever or whatever stalked her getting near enough to see the mound wasn't her. She had a melon. It did to simulate her sleeping head. Hopefully, if her opponent was a lion, the breeze would carry her scent from the bedroll to it. Slipping her sheathed dagger into her left hand, the warrior merged with the shadows under the trees.

Whoever was on her trail was good, but she was better.

The faintest rustle that wasn't a breeze reached her. As she held her breath, a little closer there was the snap of a twig. It was followed by a muffled curse from across the clearing.

A blade in each hand, Zona moved in the shadows. Her horse was still, then began chewing grass as she flitted past. It was as if the animal was playing her part in this, acting like everything was normal. The warrior ghosted on round the clearing.

A burly shadow was in her fire's light. Unable to see what he wore, she saw the wink of flame-light on a blade.

"Zona?" a man's voice called softly.

She slid behind the man who she saw wore a soldier's gear. The edge of her sword rested on his throat.

"Who wants her?" she breathed into his ear.

The man held perfectly still. Her fire crackled; there was the noise of the crickets but otherwise silence. She smelled fire-smoke, his sweat, the odour of the horse he'd been riding.

"My name is Mikhail," he told her, "and would you mind shifting the sword so I can breathe properly?"

"I was thinking of cutting your throat," she murmured.

"Ah, if I explain – "

"Sounds a good plan," she answered silkily. "Starting with why you sneaked up on me."

"The sword?"

"Move into the light so I can see you better."

"I wouldn't have thought you needed to – "

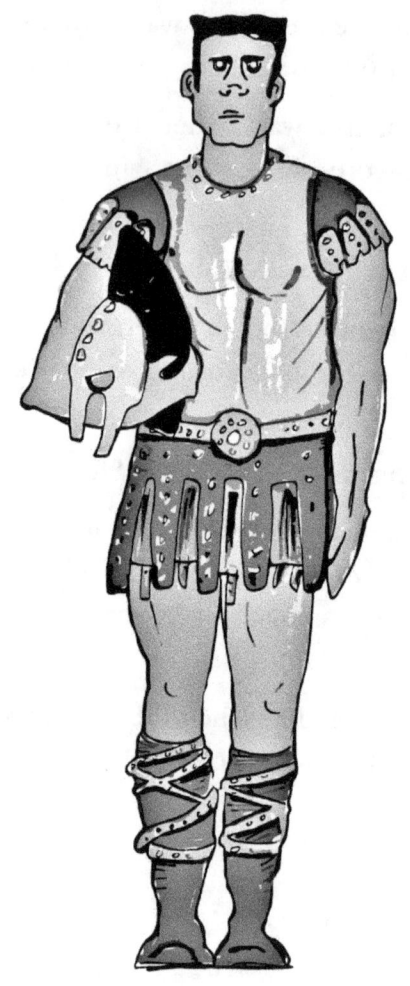

" – Just do it."

"I want to see your face, look into your eyes," she added.

His throat bobbed against her blade. "Before you

take me down, and if that owl hadn't caught something, I was hoping to meet you on better terms."

"Maybe."

"Murder's not your thing, my lady, which is why I was seeking you."

"Into the light, I said." The warrior took her blade away from his skin. Stooping, she laid the weapon aside. In her other hand, she still held the dagger and she switched it to the right hand. Through his armour, she prodded the soldier with its tip and he flinched. "Move slowly. Don't even think of trying anything."

"One tough chick, aren't you?" he growled unexpectedly.

"You better believe it."

Carefully Mikhail began to walk, slowly and smoothly as she kept the point of her dagger pricking through his leather armour. She slipped past him to seat herself on a log she'd drawn up to the fire earlier. Her long-bladed knife stayed in her grip. She turned it, inspecting the steel in her fire's glow for nicks. Across the flames the man who'd come to see her hunkered in a squat. With him in such a position, the fire between them and her knife, it was as safe as it got. Like she'd said she would, Zona gazed at him steadily while the flames crackled and spat. The fire started burning low. She moved to put on a couple of branches from her store of fuel nearby and sat once more.

Reluctantly, she found herself liking the man. Since Troy fell and Xanthia left with Andres, his friend and Helen, it had been better keeping herself alone. She didn't want any more trouble of whatever kind; she'd gone through enough and was ready to hang up her sword. She needed the time to heal from her loss but now this. Instinct was yowling at her that trouble had found her. Maybe this was what the dark cupboard dream was about, not Deiphobos – or was it something else?

Chilled in spite of the fire, the warrior held and rubbed her arms. Narrowing her eyes against its smoke, she waited for the fizz of cold to pass. Her Palomino mare blew through her nose and stamped a foot. The horse went back to chewing, and everything seemed normal, except for the night-time visitor.

As she went on searching his face, the warrior sighed to herself. She really didn't want this, whatever was on the way, but saw no means of avoiding it. Unless she killed the man, but she couldn't do it. Her lost friend had changed her too much, and Mikhail had gambled right in that.

The soldier was blocky but wasn't a midget either. Somewhere he'd lost his helmet, unless he'd left it with his horse. In the military way, his hair was cut short, a brown and grey fuzz on his square skull.

Although his face was beard-shadowed, he favoured clean shaving; his jaw was craggy in the firelight and shadows which flickered over it. He was tanned by sun and wind. Dark eyes which might have been brown or violet in daylight, looked at her steadily, and she knew she couldn't take the easy way out of this.

"Want some coffee?" she asked.

His voice was deep, with a rasp. "What's that?" A sergeant or a captain was her guess. "Will it poison me?"

That had come with the trace of a smile on his bluff features. *Ares, you pig. Why did I have to like him?*

She shrugged. "It's bitter, an acquired taste. They drink it in these parts. Zeus knows where they get the beans. You sweeten it with goats' or asses' milk, if you can get any."

He hesitated, then, "Yeah, why not?"

"Don't worry." A grin lit her stern features. "To the Arabs there's quite a ritual in this. It means, 'I trust you and now you're safe in the hospitality beside my fire.'"

"Where do you get all this stuff?" The man was curious and she felt their wariness shredding slowly away.

She shrugged again. "Oh, it was from a tribe along

the way. There was a lion, well, a pride, bothering their cattle, taking the odd one. I helped out. They showed me and parted with a bag."

He shook his head, and she was back remembering the lion hunt. The heat, dust, herself on her mount flanking the great cats, driving them to the Arab hunters… Her blankets were made from lion hides.

"OK." She smiled some more. "You asked for it, let's go."

He grinned back, and they were silent. As the warrior worked at making the coffee, she felt him study her.

As ever unaware of her dark beauty, she ignored him looking as much as she could. As she pounded coffee beans with a smooth stone in a bronze bowl, she focussed on the task. She'd known other guys be like him but she couldn't understand him any more than those men. Where it was exposed, her skin was a rich, deep and creamy honey from the North African sun. Mikhail licked his lips but she took no notice of it. The near-black, ragged hair swayed over her shoulders as she worked. In her black, strapless vest and short kilt, her athletic body moved easily in its rhythm. The scent of the coffee added itself to that of wood-smoke. He'd not seen her in combat at Troy but he thought she was all he'd heard and then some. Last, there were the chill amber eyes that had warmed to him briefly.

He was grateful they had; this was no person to have against you.

She looked up, smiled briefly. Mischief shone in those eyes. "What?"

"Ah, nothing," he replied.

The warrior carried on her coffee-making.

As the soldier watched light and shadows on her face, she took water that had been set to boil over the fire while she crushed beans. Pouring it onto them produced more appetising scents. She sat back on her heels watching the coffee.

"What's next?" he asked.

"I rather thought I'd be the one with the questions."

CHAPTER FIVE

✤

"ASK AWAY," said Mikhail.

"OK, let's start with a big one." She stirred the drinks pot. "What's a Trojan officer doing here?"

"That's indeed a tale."

Zona got up, went to her roll of possessions and fetched a small piece of translucent material. She spread it over a mug.

"The Arabs make this," she explained. "Something to with camel gut, I think."

"What's a camel? I, ah, haven't been in this part of the world long. I got lucky finding you so soon."

The warrior smiled as she picked up the pan and began pouring. Steaming dark and aromatic liquid pattered through the fabric to the cup below.

"Easy to see you've never ridden one," she chuckled. She pointed in the direction of her horse in the darkness. "Even before I started asking questions. A camel has one or two humps on its back."

"What?"

"They store water in there. Camels are very good over long distances without drinking."

"A tactical asset."

"Yeah." She passed him the first of the mugs and began to work on the second. "Drink it. Don't worry. I've already said it means you have the hospitality of my camp around here. I can't put a sword or dagger in you till you leave. And camels? Revolting animals; they spit green cuds, bite – you should see their teeth. They barge you, tread on your feet, you name it."

He pulled a face as he sipped at his coffee and made another.

She tossed her head, laughing. Black hair swirled around her shoulders, gleaming in the firelight. "It's not that bad, surely, though Arabs do it better."

"I think I'd sooner you cut off my head!"

The warrior looked fierce, drawing her brows together. "That can be arranged, but I guess this stuff's an acquired taste."

"I agree there."

She'd finished pouring out her own coffee and sniffed it, smiling again. "Could be worse. What's wrong with you?"

"You drink it then. Go on."

"I'm going to." She set her mug aside. "When it's a little cooler. Now, why are you here?"

Mikhail hesitated. Her expression was serious as she studied his face, the amber gaze thoughtful.

He sighed. "You know my name, and you'll be able to see I am, was, a Trojan officer. I fought my way out when the city fell to that sneaky Greek trick with the wooden horse."

"It was easy to see the horse couldn't be trusted. I tried to warn you guys. So did Cassandra."

His lip curled. "Cassandra!"

Zona was back in the great hall of Priam's palace. Sunlight laid white bands along it from high windows. Courtiers and officers, their ladies as well, thronged it and the king wanted to bring the horse into the city. His Heir certainly didn't object. Only Antenor, the king's most trusted councillor, and her sounded notes of caution. Until Cassandra threw herself wailing prophecies into the hall. Joined by the aged councillor, the Heir ordered her manhandled from the hall. But she'd been right…

"Yeah, Deiphobos was all over her." She lifted her cup from the ground next to her and sipped at it. "But I fixed him."

"You might think so, and maybe you did, but I suspect not. The guy may be a bottom feeder but he's a survivor."

She pursed her lips, sipped more coffee. "You're likely right there, but what else?"

Mikhail looked dismayed, guilty too. Wondering what could be on the way, she stayed quiet. Now he was started, if she waited, the man would tell it his own way. She couldn't help wondering what he might be ashamed of, just how the ex-officer had escaped Troy.

He looked ashamed some more, desolate in fact. "You will never be able to talk with Polydamas."

"Why not?" The warrior had a bad feeling about this.

"I killed him."

There was a long silence.

The fire burned with a few crackles, its smoke invisible in the dark air. Zona smelled the mingled, comforting aromas of it and the coffee filling the mug she cradled in her hands. Her horse shifted and went on placidly chewing. She listened to the sounds of crickets and cicadas as they got on with their lives. There came the lonely cry of an owl, another kicking in. All normal sounds like any other night, and this man certainly had a lot to tell her. He'd been right about that. Mikhail was staring into the fire as if remembering. She was herself.

The warrior cleared her throat and drank coffee. The fire popped and a spark flew out. Mikhail moved a foot to crush it.

"Why?" she asked.

"Aeneas ordered it," he replied heavily.

"I thought he and Polydamas were good with each other. They *were* the Dardanians. Although," she finished, "Clearly not anymore."

The Trojan officer flicked her the hint of a smile. It turned into a grimace when he drank some more of his coffee.

She repeated her question. A large blue-black fly was hanging around; she waved it off. The warrior had always wondered about Aeneas, his fellow general and their men. On the face of it, they'd been strongly for the city but what had they really wanted? Recalling the scene in the king's personal chamber, she pulled a face at herself. It was the Heir-ship, ultimately the crown. Yet, although a good soldier and tactician, Aeneas was always a very clever politician. She'd even wondered if he might do a deal with the Greeks if he thought he could gain from it. *He wasn't the only one there,* she thought. *And wait till I see him again!*

"Why?" she asked a second time.

"Not my concern," the man replied stolidly. "I am a soldier, I follow orders."

"Oh, come on! That's the excuse of killers down the ages." Her voice was exasperated.

"I didn't like it."

"Oh yeah?" She softened her tone. "It's just that you remind me of myself."

There was real puzzlement in the soldier's tone. "You?"

"That's right, me. You must know I was a bandit chief once. I've done things which can never be forgiven."

"Most of Troy knew. It didn't stop folk from calling you 'Princess.' But – "

"I've never understood that."

He went on. "But you've gotten over it. You're not that cutthroat anymore."

The warrior stared broodingly into the rippling veil, the reds, golds and oranges of the inside of her fire. She took a long draught of her coffee. It was cooling off. *I so wish this man hadn't come out of the night to rake up my memories.* Her lost friend was there. *As if I could ever forget, it was her who worked to change a killer and marauder.* Wondering where the blonde woman, the two men with her and Helen were, what they might be doing now, she sighed heavily. When Mikhail gave her a questioning look, she shrugged.

"So is there more?" she asked.

"Oh yes." His face looked as if chiselled out of stone. "There're Creusa and Anchises."

"What?" her eyes widened, leonine in the firelight. She shook her head at the man. "Did you take them down too?"

"Yeah."

"I guess you must have trouble living with yourself, like me. Disturbed nights, and so on."

Mikhail shook his own head. He slugged at his cup, like he was punishing himself. The fly or another was round them again. Frowning, she waved it off.

"You should hear what they were saying about him, Aeneas and the old man," he said. "It made me sick! How he begged Anchises not to die on him, carried his father out of the ruined and burning city on his back. That was only a bit of it – "

" – and people *believed* this?"

"When they're in trouble, being slaughtered and panicking, they'll go with anything if a strong leader turns up and gets them out. He's being called 'The Father of Troy' now. Anyhow, the ones who knew different are all dead, or on the run like me."

"The warrior drained her coffee, brushing off the fly some more. She looked and said nothing.

"Do you know, the only reason he didn't kill Ascanius, his baby son, along with his mother, was because I said the kid might come in useful! Not that it excuses me at all – "

"Oh Aeneas," she broke in quietly but intensely. "You and I have some catching up to do."

CHAPTER SIX

❖

MIKHAIL looked sickened. Whether it was at himself, Aeneas, both of them or her, Zona couldn't tell.

"You should have heard what he said about his father to the first person who asked where Anchises was. And his wife? She just 'disappeared', and he searched everywhere for her. The lying sack of – "

The warrior cut in gently. "Back up a bit. You said about his father?"

He looked at his coffee, then seemed to change his mind. "An acquired taste. You said about Anchises. Well, listen to this, and don't forget we murdered the old man. As far as I can recall, he said to we few who got out something like this. 'I carried him out on my back through collapsing buildings, fires, women and kids being massacred. The Greeks were even killing the cats and dogs, anything which moved! What else could I do? Warriors were all around, stabbing, cutting. The noise, you wouldn't believe it. The stinks of blood and innards! But there he was, my own old man, crippled with arthritis. I was OK till I fell over a body. When I turned round he was gone!' Tears came;

Aeneas can turn them on and off like a spring."

Mikhail was pulling a face, looking disgusted. She chipped in.

"What about his wife, did you say her name was Creusa? I don't recall her but I remember you talking of his son."

"Didn't I say about them? The boy, Aeneas thought he might be useful, burnish the image like Hector's breastplate. Do you know, those thousands of refugees were calling him 'Pious Aeneas' when I got out, and 'God Aeneas'?"

She made a face of her own, laying aside the mug she still cradled in her hands. "What about his wife? Wait a moment, you said – "

Mikhail poured out the dregs of his coffee onto the fire which sputtered vilely. "You are going to kill me before this is all done. I wouldn't blame you. Aeneas, 'Pious Aeneas', hadn't the guts to do his cleaning up himself. She was no longer useful to him. So my men wielded the blades. He needs to be able to marry again, make a high-born alliance when and where it suits. So Creusa had to go. I told you, it was me!"

"Mikhail," she said quietly. Sympathy for the man cut at her like a dagger. "Don't beat yourself up. People change. Look at me. You've already done enough, putting aside an officer's career, setting out to find me."

"Believe me, that wasn't so tough," he said bitterly. "I can't stick him anymore, the tacky hero act. I'm used to politicians, him included, but he's colder than snow on the peaks of Mount Ida. Do you know the worst? I think he half believes the good guy stuff himself!"

"So his wife? Mikhail, you need to get this stuff out properly, and I'm not gonna kill you."

It was nearly a groan which drifted from the soldier across her fire. "I told you he got scruples. Damn near grizzled like a baby after the teat. Along with doing his father, we beheaded her. It was quick – "

"So what did he say to put a spin on that?"

"Claimed she just vanished in the sack of Troy." He looked frustrated with himself. "Oh, how much of this have I already blurted out? Naturally, he searched everywhere for her. Yeah, and my squad did the servants as well. That's the full list of my crimes. Then we fired his house and got out of there."

"Not a pretty tale, but then Troy's fall wasn't. And believe me, I've done enough of that kind of thing myself. What made you run? I'm guessing it was something big; you're a soldier."

Mikhail cursed under his breath. Getting up, his knees cracked but he seemed not to notice. Hands clasped behind himself, he took a swift, angry turn round the fire, then another. What she'd said to console him as best she could was true. She sat by her crackling fire which showed their faces in light and shadow too well for a story like this. The warrior waited patiently, feeling for him in his self-dislike keenly until he sat again, this time with a thud.

"OK, not much gets past you," he gritted. "And you're right about running. Several of my men had accidents before I caught on. Two were killed before we got out of the city, but at length even a simple soldier got there. I couldn't trust my commander. I figured it was more of his clean-up, no witnesses to what really happened. So I got out while I could."

"And you looked for me."

"I just knew somehow you'd listen, and I had to confess, be judged."

Zona pushed hair out of her eyes. She got up to throw him one of her lion's pelt blankets.

"We need some sleep. Tell me the rest in the morning."

"I was a coward but I stayed till after Crete. I thought I'd find a way to kill him, my commander. Cleanse the earth of this stain – "

"Tell me in the morning, and tomorrow we'll go hunt him."

The next morning, as was her habit, the warrior rolled out of her blankets early. Sunlight angled through the leaves of the nearby trees. Flies and stinging insects were up and it was already hot. Her horse was grazing placidly, flicking her tail at the flying things. The soldier was still asleep, snoring on his back with his mouth open. His breath wafted a fly away every time it tried to settle on his face.

Heading to the stream, Zona shucked out of her vest and kilt and scooped water over herself. Rubbing it in her hair, wiping it over her torso, she was soon refreshed, the last of her sleep washed away. Back in her black things, she returned barefoot to the camp. Mikhail went on snoring, keeping the fly off himself. She coaxed their fire into fresh life, dropped some trail sticks into her battered cooking pot, added water and waited for it to boil and soften them. While she was waiting, she used twigs to comb the snarls from her locks, then to do the horse who wandered to the stream to drink. *All very homey,* she thought, pulling on her boots.

Prodding at the guards' captain with a toe just made him roll over onto his side. The guy obviously needed sleep and she wondered what things he might have gone through and seen to reach her. He'd told her some of it but she was sure there was more. She'd leave him a bit longer. Plucking fronds off a nearby bush, she went to his mount to groom it. The rangy black and her palomino had been all squeals and bared teeth when he tried to bring his animal into camp the previous night. Her lips quirked as she went to work on the creature. *Can't blame Lina. They'd not met before and she wasn't in the mood.*

Back in their camp from the tree she'd left the black where he'd tied it a way down the trail, the warrior put on some more of her precious coffee. When it was ready for straining and pouring, she shook the man's shoulder.

"On your feet, soldier!" she said crisply. "Rise and shine."

"Huh, what?" Blinking, he shook his head.

"Go wash in the stream," she told him. "Then come back for breakfast. And after this morning it's equal shares of the chores."

Mikhail knuckled at his eyes, saw her crouching beside him, lips tugged by the beginning of a smile. His face cleared.

"Oh, yeah."

When he came back from cleaning up in the stream, the man was fresh and alert. He passed his hands back over wet hair. His stubble was thicker but the warrior shrugged mentally. *He could use a knife to shave but it's not a matter for me,* she told herself. *His business.*

At least he didn't smell.

"My horse," he said.

"Taken care of," she answered. "Want to risk my breakfast? It's only jerky and coffee, I'm afraid. My friend used to say I couldn't even do that well enough to eat."

"I'm sure it'll do, and your friend? Ah, the blonde woman. Some men used to say…"

"Don't go there, and surely I told you of my partner last night?"

He was chewing jerky, sipping coffee. "You did, I know of her anyhow. Most of the army knew of you two. And, hey, I could get used to this coffee."

"Blots out the taste of my trail sticks anyhow." She was smiling and it lit up her features, reaching her catlike eyes so they sparkled.

When they'd finished breakfast they cleared away the camp. Mikhail fetched his black horse. It and her palomino looked at each other, ears back and eyes rolling, but there was no further hostility. Perhaps the mare had staked out boundaries and the horses would accept each other.

As they mounted, she asked, "So, on along the African coast?"

"Works for me. As I said last night, there are stories

of Aeneas being here somewhere. At least there's a big host so I guess that's him. He might be travelling by sea, although close to the coast. We should still see him, a large, near-in fleet. As long as the weather stays OK."

"It usually stays fine and clear, this time of the year, or so the locals say." She clicked her tongue to her horse which began walking. "Let's go."

It was some time before either spoke any more. The country was hot and scrubby with scattered trees and bushes. Sand rose in thin beige clouds round the horses' feet. Insects did their thing, pestering ceaselessly. The sky was deep blue and only a few seagulls and buzzards called. On the riders' right the sea washed rocky, then sandy and more rocky beach. It was a lonely, deserted place but Zona liked it that way, finding it soothing. Ahead a low range of hills in the distance angled to the coast.

She broke the travellers' easy silence. "What about Crete then, what did Aeneas do there?"

The soldier hesitated. "Yeah, we never got to that, did we?"

"No." She reached back, wiping sweat from between her shoulder blades. It went on, cool and tickling. "We didn't."

Mikhail sighed. "Are you sure you want to hear all

this?"

She shrugged. "It passes the time."

A deeper sigh. "All right, here goes."

The warrior kept silent.

"When we hit Crete the weather was like this," he began.

"And?"

"It all looked so peaceful when we sailed in using ships stolen from the Greeks at Troy. It was easy enough; they were off sacking the city. No guards were there, and where was I?"

She smiled. "Sailing into Crete."

"Oh yes." Mikhail waved off flies. "Well, no problems when we beached the ships, except some black rats came ashore. Black rats, can you imagine that? They had rats aboard. I mean, what are those Greeks like?"

"Where you've a lot of people you're always going to have vermin. And careful; I'm Greek."

As they rode on through the hot sunshine, the soldier looked at her narrowly. Insects stayed around, plaguing the riders and horses, feeding off their sweat. The land went on being dry, alternate patches of reddish sand and, gravel and parched dun rock. There were sparse, patchy and tough-looking grass, a few bushes, even some trees, but it was an inhospitable landscape. The low hills ahead scarcely seemed to creep nearer and buzzards still floated in the blue dome of the sky. Surely nothing good could happen in such a place.

"So you are, but you fought with us," he said.

"I was there to help my friend Helen, and what we wanted was peace."

"Yeah, I heard about that – which of us didn't? Pity the gods didn't see it that way."

"I just think they like to see us suffer, fight and bleed, especially Ares."

They walked their mounts on a while in a new silence. Zona took a drink from the water skin hanging from her saddle. The captain watched her, light gleaming on her dark mane in rainbow flashes, the bob of her long neck as water went down. Aware of his gaze on her, she hitched the water skin back at her saddle, wiped moisture from her chest and met his eyes, her lips quirking.

"So what happened? You haven't told me all of it. And same as before; it'll help you to say it."

Mikhail pulled a face. "I don't like to keep dirtying his name. Don't forget; he was my commander."

"But you left," she pointed out.

"Yeah, well."

The horses plodded on until he spoke some more. "We'd drawn up our ships on the beach. Nobody paid the rats any mind. Aeneas was busy making laws and rules because a lot of people liked Crete and wanted to stay. So he was laying out a colony. We parcelled land among the colonists, and at first everything looked OK."

"What about the local people?"

"What about them?" Mikhail took a drink from his own water skin and fastened it back in place. "You know how these things go. When someone, a little old lady, raised it, he said only the strongest survive."

"Yeah. I see."

He looked at her. The chill in those golden eyes. It might not be good to be Aeneas when they caught up to him.

"So anyhow. It was like from nowhere this plague appeared. People broke out with fevers, running hot, then icy. They begged for water and there were great dark swellings at their necks, armpits and groins. The swellings were so painful they couldn't be touched. Then they burst with a lot of pus and other stuff. Folk staggered around crying, fell where they were and were left in the sun to die."

"Like the gods were punishing them."

"What for?" he asked sharply. "Us?"

"Taking over the land, and I mean the gods had it in for you guys."

"But the locals too, they hadn't done anything. They were just there."

"Yeah. You know how these things go. The gods just lash out."

There was another silence as the pair rode on. The sun kept blasting out of a cloudless sky. The hills must have been drawing closer, although they didn't look it. As the warrior shaded her eyes under a hand and studied them, the hills seemed mere lumps in the land. Around the riders pinkish-red soil carried on with outcrops of rock and it was increasingly barren. Even the tough brush and trees of North Africa were having a job putting down roots. *Tartarus,* she thought, *must surely be like this.*

After a while Mikhail said, "Maybe you're right, but if it was them, the immortals aren't done with us. There was a – "

" – Quiet!"

Zona heard the sounds of battle.

CHAPTER SEVEN

✣

"WHAT?" the Trojan asked.

The warrior didn't need to point south; he was already there but she did so. The wind gusted and brought faint but unmistakable shouts and screams. She heard clashing blades, more cries and yells.

"It's not our affair. The sensible thing is to keep out of it," Mikhail said.

She looked at him, then shrugged. "You're likely right, but what's that got to do with it?"

"It's not going to help us find Aeneas. It'll likely slow us up."

"Come on."

She squeezed her mount with her knees. Although they'd been plodding most of the day, the horses jumped forward towards the battle. Not having used up much energy during their travelling, the creatures enjoyed the run. Both were used to the sounds of combat and eager to be at it. The warrior leaned over her horse's neck and the air, cooled by their speed, rushed over her shoulders. She felt her hair stream and bounce. Mikhail was thundering after her, pulling up on her right. His face was split by a grin, and he'd found and put on a helmet.

With a wild yell, the warrior reached back. Her sword came into her right hand, sunlight flashing shards from the blade. She reached with her left for her knife. Dropping the reins for her horse to run free, she flourished the two weapons.

At a gallop they crested a low ridge. In the distance, still almost hidden by shimmering heat, dust boiled. A couple of buzzards floated high over it, little more than dark specks. With more screams, clashing blades, carried on the wind, Zona felt her mount's muscles surge beneath her. The joy of imminent battle sang in the beat of her heart and rushing blood, a new shriek that was torn from her lips. Neither she nor Mikhail heard as it was blown behind them. Now she could see milling figures on camels, a litter slumped on the ground. The fight grew swiftly closer, and this was so like old times.

A robed, hooded man on a pony was in front of her. In the shadows of the hood she made out a bearded face, the white of teeth in a dark skin. He was lean, hook-nosed. A dagger came her way. She ducked along her Palomino's side. He was slashing at her with a curved sword. Her nose stung at dust, the gamy stinks of horse and rider.

Avoiding the blow, she came upright. They were crammed together as they duelled. Sparks rang from their blades but neither could break the other's guard.

The pony tried to bite her horse's neck. Somehow the mare backed off, flailing with her hooves. When the other animal whirled, it left the rider exposed. Zona leaned to run him through. Her blade stuck on his ribs; she twisted it out. Blood flowed into the man's beard and he fell gargling.

She was surrounded by Arab riders. Curved swords and daggers flashed. The warrior ducked and weaved in her saddle, her mare helping out.

Mikhail was in trouble.

Two camel riders were on him, a third taking aim with a bow. Free of opponents a moment, she switched sword and dagger between her hands. She sighted on the archer. Without conscious thought, in a second her brain assessed trajectories and ricochets.

The dagger flew, knocking the bowman's weapon from his hands. In other circumstances his gape would have been laughable. The knife was still whickering, its blade flashing in sunlight. It struck a pair of swords, was back and she snatched it from the air.

Once more she was hemmed in. The fighting was hot. She was reacting without working out moves.

A man bored in from the left. When her horse

jinked, the warrior kicked out. Shearing away, the Arab wailed. Her boot had crunched a kneecap and his leg hung uselessly. She ducked over Lina's neck. As she pushed ahead she shoved past two assailants. The fight became a whirl of camels and ponies, robes, flaring blades. There were the smells of fear and excitement, the sweat of men and beasts. Clouds of choking dust part obscured targets.

The Arabs were tough but she and Mikhail were making progress towards the apparently abandoned litter. The two riders were helped by the bearers, four huge, bald and clean-shaven men stripped to the waist in gold-spun kilts. Being slaves, the men were unarmed. Impressive muscles were there, however, and their night-dark skins gleamed with perspiration. As the slaves dealt out blows to any Arab who came near them, white teeth glistened. Soon, closely followed by the Trojan, the warrior would join up with them.

From the sun's glare more Arabs on horses and camels boiled. They must have been hiding in a shallow valley or hollow. Part of a well-planned ambush, they waved curved swords as they came. Blood-chilling howls clamoured on the air from them and the men the pair were fighting.

Zona and her companion were tightly surrounded. The press got closer. It took all her blade-craft to stay alive. She saw Mikhail vanish and fought on, her mind ice. In the short time they were together the Trojan captain had shown himself a good man. He'd displayed genuine remorse over the things he'd done at Aeneas' orders. Mikhail had joined her decision to go after the man, ridden with her willingly. *Yeah, so he did wrong but he isn't the only one here.* Her own record wasn't spotless. However, people could change. It was what her friend now off with Helen always believed. The Trojan had started along that trail but now this, and it was all her fault. He'd not wanted this fight; it was hers alone. Now he'd likely died she would avenge him, even if it meant her own death. The warrior had lived by the sword. Now her end was going to come by it, as she'd always known.

Someone had gotten behind her. She felt it by the sixth sense which was ever hers in battle.

Whipping her mount round to face him, she slashed with her sword, followed up with her dagger. The man reeled back in his saddle as her long blade sliced his robe. A lean, swarthy, dirty face went pale at his narrow escape.

She pushed her horse on.

Something slammed the back of her head. She felt herself rock in her saddle, gripped harder with her knees. A sunburst bloomed behind her eyes with shocking speed. Trying to sway from the next blow, she couldn't see properly where it would come.

Everything was smeared together. Heat, smells, dust, the noise of combat, it all blurred.

With a fresh blow, more pain blossomed. *So this is how it feels –* She felt her balance go as she pitched off her horse.

Zona was awake.

Her eyes were stuck closed. Waves of pain throbbed from the front to the rear of her skull to the front and back again. She could feel perspiration sheathe her, stick her warrior garments to her, something rough to her back where she lay. Her mouth tasted as if rats had crawled in there, left droppings and died.

Memories pierced her like spears. There was the no-win battle, the loss of Mikhail. She groaned and thought of not opening her eyes, then sighed heavily, bitterness washing through her like the surf of pain in her head. If she'd just not gone into that battle! The Trojan captain hadn't wanted to. *He said it wasn't our fight, now look at us.*

This was no good; self-pity never was. She was a warrior who for some reason was still alive. She'd focus on escape and revenge for Mikhail. Beyond that was still Aeneas who had to be found and punished for the murder of his father, wife and servants, his partner too. Whatever he was at, he'd to be stopped.

Carefully the warrior worked her sticky eyelids

apart. At first her vision was swimming. *Hope those whacks on my head didn't screw up my eyes.*

Trying to hold back a tide of fear – *What good's a warrior who can't see right?* – she took it slowly. At length as she blinked to see, her surroundings blurred into hazy view.

Headache was back with the force of one of Zeus's lightning bolts. Her eyes flicked shut once more. When the pain wasn't rocking and thundering behind them, she prised her eyes open. There was more pain, she was slick with sweat, but this time she slogged through it. Fear stayed with her – *Maybe they broke my skull.* It would make her virtually helpless. The fact that she was here – *wherever 'here' is* – meant her captors had plans for her. She was under no illusion about what those might be, and didn't want to stick around for them. The Arabs would call it sport but it wasn't going to be running or boxing.

Once more her sight cleared. The tent with rough brown walls where she was a prisoner swam into view.

It was small, around six feet across, with curving walls sloping back towards her. A pole held it up near the tied flap and the floor was coarse sand, dried earth and stones. She saw that her ankles were tied and her arms wouldn't move from behind the small of her back. She wasn't gagged; she could shout but here it wouldn't help.

Slowly she turned her head, wincing at the fresh pain it caused. Propped on the tent wall, bound like her, was the unconscious figure of Mikhail. She was surprised and pleased to see he was still alive – his chest moved with his breathing. For her, as a woman, it wasn't hard to see why they'd kept her, but him? Better not to guess at what they were going to do to him. Escape for both of them was top on her list.

All she had to do was think of a way.

CHAPTER EIGHT

❖

THE FLAPS of the tent were untied. The Arab who ducked in wasn't bringing refreshments or aiming to wish her a nice day. He wore the grey robe of his people, was lean and dark-faced, bearded and hook-nosed with near-black eyes. An aroma of camel and old sweat came as he crawled quickly nearer.

Reaching Zona and Mikhail, he hunkered beside her. She caught the unpleasant waft of his breath as he spoke, a rapid stream of Arabic. She thought of acting like she didn't understand but could see no point in it. Playing dumb wasn't going to change his mind, what she could see in his eyes.

"Yes, he still sleeps," she answered in the same language.

"It shall not bother us, eh, pretty lady."

The warrior had caught sight of the shape of a dagger inside his robe. So maybe this could be less hopeless than it seemed.

"What is it you want?" she asked, voice level.

Maybe it would gain a little time, keeping him talking. He might also move a bit closer. From outside the tent she could hear birds and camels grunting at each other. A horse whinnied as if in pain, dogs barked and there was a rush of male voices. A shadow – maybe a tree or bush – fell over the fabric and swayed as if leaves were stirred by a wind.

Her voice lilted, "What can I do for you, how can I help?"

Still grinning, her and Mikhail's captor reached out. His lean, dirty hand with chipped nails was gripping roughly, hot and trembling on her thigh. Breathing faster, he began to push up her kilt till it was round her waist.

"Oh yes." His fingers were moving on up, poking. "You shall help me, pretty lady, and others of my friends. You have killed my brother, Salim, Rashid, others too, and you have no coin."

"I see." She fought to stay cool, show no reaction to him.

"Yet you and he have horses," he went on. "And these we shall eat, but more payment is wanted. One of the men you killed was my brother. I am sure you understand how these things go."

He took his fingers from under the kilt and sniffed them, looking disappointed. "You are not ready for me."

What do you expect? This isn't romantic.

The man still didn't move closer. In spite of the heat in the tent and the unclean smells, the warrior carried on her effort to keep him talking.

She jerked her head in the direction of the unconscious Mikhail. "What about him? OK, what you want from me is clear enough but – "

"Indeed we shall have much pleasure together." The Arab started grinning some more with his yellow teeth. "I shall be first, then the rest of our band will take turns with you."

"But what about him?" she persisted.

The Arab shrugged and bandit smells came her way. "Oh, it has been a good day. We have the Egyptian and you. Two of his men have been staked out for the buzzards and yes, we have lost men but these things happen, and Abdul will become rich."

"So you're going to ransom us?"

"Him, yes, and the Egyptian but, you, sadly no."

The Arab still didn't come that little bit nearer. It was frustrating but her curiosity woke at the talk of ransoms. Hoping he wouldn't notice, she shuffled a little closer to him. A few more moves…

"Who are you going to ransom us to?" she asked.

A false look of regret. "Not you, just them."

She held in a sigh. *There has to be a way to get him in range.*

Abdul did his own sigh. "There are many people travelling in boats a short way out to sea, but too far for us to get at them. Where there are so many folk like you and him riches will be carried. When they come ashore, as they must, we and the Egyptian, your man too, will meet with them. It is to the sea people we shall sell our captives. Soon we will break camp and catch them up."

The warrior was fascinated, hopeful too. *Who can the 'sea people' be? It's gotta be Aeneas. I've been after him long enough.* If it was him, where had he got what sounded a lot of ships and people? She wondered just what he was up to, then recalled Mikhail's story. A reckoning with the wily general was at hand if she and Mikhail could get free. She guessed they'd have to take the Egyptian along, whoever he might be. This time she did sigh and didn't try to conceal it. A flutter of the eyelashes came along too. She had to get him nearer.

Abdul missed the chill in her eyes. He put his fingers at the top of her vest, curled them inside and breathed hotly in her face.

"To it, eh, pretty lady."

"Right to it," she agreed softly.

Intent on his pleasure, he missed her tone. With a yank, he brought her vest down to her waist. His eyes glazed as he looked, then began to squeeze her. Zona pulled a face, eyes practically crossed. At last, he moved closer and in range.

Her head whipped back and forward.

The warrior's forehead cracked into Abdul's nose. With a startled cry, he grabbed at the injured part and reared back. Gore flowed through his fingers as he wailed.

Dropping a bloody hand, he scrabbled at his robe. The dagger which came to his fist glimmered in the dim light of the tent. He was going to strike –

Zona's brow crunched on his already bleeding nose. More blood erupted as he lurched and dropped the knife. While he sat crying, blood running into his beard, she head-butted him again.

Abdul slumped on her, mercifully unconscious. Not, with what he was going to do to her, that she felt like mercy. Huffing for breath, she wriggled under the weight and smell of him. *Now all I've got to do is get from under him, grab the knife and wake Mikhail. A walk in the park.* It was a lot better than what the bandit had been fixed on. Snoring and bubbling through his broken nose, he was a limp weight and she went on pushing at him.

At length she succeeded in shoving the knocked-out man off herself. He rolled loosely onto his back, arms flopping out. Where she'd butted it, his face was a red ruin. She was splashed with blood all over her torso.

"Sorry Abdul," she murmured. "But you left yourself open."

The knife was several feet off between her and the unconscious Mikhail. *Could have been worse.* It might have been the other side of Abdul. The less rolling about and humping herself she had to do the better. The Arab bandit was only going to be out for a while. When he woke, he was going to be sore and in a bad mood. It wouldn't help that she'd damaged his face. She'd picked up from previous contact with them that Arabs thought her unnatural, didn't rate women. This man was going to be hit in his pride as well as his nose. He'd be out for her blood.

It only took a short roll of her bound-up body to reach the knife. With her tied hands, she tried to get hold of it. Although she felt for it carefully, the blade skittered out of her reach. Swallowing curses under her breath, the warrior made another attempt to get hold of the weapon and managed it.

This was taking too long. Abdul was already stirring, bubbling through his wrecked nose. If he recovered consciousness before she was through, it would be hard to put him down a second time.

She dragged herself over to Mikhail with the dagger. *Now to wake him.* Zona didn't let herself think of how badly he might be hurt but he'd already been out too long.

Nudging him with a shoulder while keeping watch on Abdul, she tried to rouse the Trojan soldier. At first it didn't have any effect, and the bandit was beginning to snort. She stopped her efforts, keeping still, and the man subsided. She couldn't help being amused. *A half-naked woman tries to get him moving, and look at him. Mikhail, you ain't gonna forget this in a hurry.* The soldier coughed explosively, then grunted. Progress, but the downed Arab was stirring again.

The warrior manoeuvred herself so she could put her lips to the Trojan's ear.

"Mikhail! Wake up!" she whispered urgently.

Nothing. She wished she was able to hit him, at least shake him.

"Mikhail!" she snapped. Still nothing. *His dreams better be good, gods sent.* The warrior was amazed at herself, that she could find humour here and now, and tried once more. She bit his ear sharply as well. "Wake up, Hades take you."

The soldier grunted a second time. *At last!*

"Huh, what?"

"Keep your voice down!" she hissed.

"Ah – "

"Mikhail, keep it down, get yourself together. They captured us, and there's one of them here now. It's their chief, I think. I knocked him out but any time he's going to wake. I need you on the case – Now!"

"Huh?"

"Want me to bite your ear again? I won't be love-playing."

The Trojan captain's eyes almost creaked, opening. Abdul was still down but it surely couldn't be for much longer.

"What do you want me to do?" Finally the soldier was making sense.

"I've got a knife. I'll hold my wrists steady. Take it and cut me loose. Then we free you."

"Uh, yeah."

The warrior twisted herself so that her back was facing him. She held out the dagger so he could take it and start work on her. As the Trojan gripped it, the bandit leader was awake. Shaking his head, the Arab dragged himself to his knees. Blood was still welling from his nose into his beard and a lot was congealed there. She knew it would hurt like Ares had worked on it but couldn't afford to show sympathy. Mikhail's eyes widened as he registered her bare, with her vest down at her hips. She was blood-streaked but evenly and lightly tanned, all curves...

"Not now!" she rapped.

She scooted on her butt and her bound legs shot out. She was still wearing her boots; the heels slammed into Abdul's face. More blood jetted; he collapsed soundlessly as she thrust her wrists at Mikhail.

"Cut me loose."

Carefully turning his back to reach her, the soldier began. Neck craned round so he could watch his work, he sawed at the rope. After what seemed an age of grunting and huffing, she was free. Flexing her wrists to get the circulation moving, gritting her teeth at the pain, she cut the bonds on her ankles. Abdul stayed quiet and soon she'd cut Mikhail loose.

He took the dagger and shuffled to the Arab. "I'll cut his gizzard."

She pulled up and settled her vest in place. Grabbing his shoulder, she hauled him away.

"No you won't."

"Come on!"

"I don't work that way, Mikhail. There's no need."

"Well, what now?"

"You're going to watch him."

"Wait a moment!"

"One can move easier in this camp than two. I'll scout round, get our weapons back and your helmet, find the horses and be back here. Oh, and he said there's an Egyptian." She pointed at the prone Abdul as she spoke. "They were going to ransom him but I want him as well."

"Leave him, we don't need him, and they'll come after us – "

"You're likely right but we can use him as a bargaining chip."

"Maybe – "

"I'm not leaving him. Back soon."

CHAPTER NINE

✛

THE WARRIOR was soon back at the tent. With
her was a thin, dark, intense-looking man who had
drooping moustaches and wore a stained robe.
Earrings dangled from his earlobes and a chain hung
round his neck. From his battered appearance, the
bandits had evidently not been gentle with him. She
and Mikhail were soon to find out why.

The Trojan captain was seated with his back to
the tent wall and it was close and stuffy in there. He
gripped the dagger and was watching over a sullen,
blood-stained Abdul.

Grinning, he used the dagger to indicate the sword
rising behind her shoulder. "Mission accomplished?"

She hunkered beside him, smiling back. "This is –
Tell him who you are."

Her companion stayed on his feet but stooping,
arms folded. He spoke light-voiced but with a rasp
like a sore throat in cultured Arabic. "Hosni Sulaiman
Al Sabrahim Pebekkanun, Chief of the Chamber to
His Majesty Pharaoh Ramses III of All Egypt, Powerful

One of Ma'at and Ra, Beloved Of Amun, Ruler of Heliopolis."

Mikhail's brow wrinkled. "And you are? – "

"Hosin Sulaiman – "

"Not that," broke in the Trojan. "What are you doing, why are you here?"

The Egytian looked disdainful. "I have explained to her, the slut."

"Say it again," the warrior told him.

Although they hadn't been together long, her patience was fraying. Could be Mikhail had been right. The mouthy court functionary might be best left in captivity.

He started again. "It is really quite simple, even for such as you. I am here on an embassy on behalf of His Majesty Pharaoh – "

"Don't start all that again," cut in Zona. "Get to it."

A haughty sniff made her bite her tongue.

Hosni, as she'd decided to call him for short, looked at her down his beak of a nose. Disdain filled his voice. Plainly he felt like their captors about woman warriors.

"The answer, slut, is – "

"My name's Zona, not 'slut'."

"As you will." This came with a sniff.

"I do."

After a pause, he went on: "At any rate, the answer is right here, if you'd but the wit to see it."

Mikhail spoke up. "Zona, are you sure we need this?"

"I guess I'm a sucker for lame dogs."

"Yeah," he said.

An eyebrow raised for effect, Hosni looked them both over. He did it slowly, taking them in succession, beginning at their feet, going to their heads and back. The warrior marvelled at him and wondered how long she'd be able to keep Mikhail off him. She was far from sure the soldier might be wrong in saying they didn't need this and she shifted restlessly as perspiration ran down her. She was probably right in what she'd told the Trojan of her motives. Also, if she was honest with herself, her sense of humour was at work. She wanted to tweak the tails of Abdul and his men. There wasn't a better way to do it than by stealing the hostage they were about to ransom to the fleet off the North African coast.

"Tell your story, and be quick," she reminded the

envoy.

He sniffed once more, arranging his robes around himself. "I will make it plain."

"Yeah, do," growled the Trojan.

"Hurry it up," added the warrior. "They'll miss you, their leader too, and start searching. It won't take those bandits long to be here."

After another, slightly shorter silence – *I'll give him for effect,* she thought – the Egyptian said, "Very well. These Arab donkeys' filth are why I'm here. I'm sure I have previously said this. Never mind, I need to make allowances."

The warrior and the Trojan captain exchanged

glances, promises. The envoy affected not to see, or perhaps he really missed them at it. *He's so thick-skinned, likely the worst his king could have chosen for this job, whatever it is,* she reflected. The big cheese had to be dumber than a stone. Unless their companion had been sent for some internal political reason. Or maybe he was supposed to fail. *I guess they picked the right man there.* She shook her head. *Politics!* She'd never liked it, and she'd thought it was bad enough in Troy. Mikhail was glowering; she felt she must be herself. It occurred to her that maybe the envoy wanted them to be caught and that was why he was dragging his story out. If he was, he was crazy, considering what the bandits would probably do to them all. *They'll likely roast his feet over a fire,* but she and the Trojan would dish out a bit before they were overcome.

The Egyptian did his irritating sniff thing again, and it was louder. "I am envoy from the Light of the Sun to the new city which is taking shape in the West and is named Carthage," he said. "You are familiar with such a barbarian place, of course."

A second time the warrior and Trojan soldier exchanged looks. Gritting her teeth, striving to sound mild, she said, "We're strangers round these parts."

"No matter. The Lord of Light finds these Arab trash a distraction."

"A pain in his royal ass?" asked Zona, unable to stop herself. She just about managed to keep a straight face.

"Quite so." Though shorter than her and in spite of their now seated positions, the Egyptian functionary managed to peer down his nose.

Seeing it, the soldier growled, "Why don't we just cut this guy's head off? This ain't one of your better ideas. We don't need him. Let's leave his corpse as a present for the Arabs."

It's tempting, she mused, and the Egyptian sniffed another time, maybe to show what he thought of the idea. It grated at her nerves like a stone sharpening a blade, a habit she could so do without. *If he does it one more time…*

"I have been despatched to make contact with Queen Dido, Alissar as she calls herself of Carthage," the man continued. "Pharaoh Ramses III, May His Name be forever Blessed, of All Egypt, Powerful One of – "

"Don't start that again." The warrior drew and fingered her dagger.

The diplomat sniffed again. *– Maybe he can't help it but by all the gods –*

"Our Light of the Heavens wishes me to seek a treaty with the new city, eliminate these Libyan vermin. We shall burn their leaders alive, scatter their ashes in the streets of the empire and thus deny them the Afterlife. The rest shall be enslaved, sent to quarry copper at Timna, Canaan, you know."

"Remind me not to visit your Heliopolis," Zona said.

"That is my mission," said the Egyptian as if she'd not spoken. "And if the queen does not agree, I am commanded to say we shall send an army to crush her city like a beetle by a sandal."

"Well," commented the warrior and Mikhail together. She added, "Let's go."

"I'll bring up the rear, make sure he doesn't try anything," said Mikhail.

"I am envoy to – "

" – Yeah, yeah," said the warrior.

With her in the lead they left the tent. She had her dagger in her left hand, sword in her right. Outside it was blisteringly hot and there was a cluster of tents. Fires sent up plumes of grey and white smoke into the still, sunny air. She could see Arabs moving among them in their characteristic robes, a few sitting by the fires, and motioned for silence. Sweat trickled and there were the smells of men needing to wash, camels, horses and donkeys, and meat being cooked. If Hosni made a sound she'd kill him herself. So many Arabs were around, such a lot of open space, a change of plan was needed.

"Back in the tent, you two," she whispered.

In the prison tent once more, the warrior explained. The men listened, nodding in places.

"OK, so we need to do this differently from just sneaking out. I take it we're all agreed there," she said. "There's no proper cover and too many of them. So we walk out – "

"Walk?" That was the Egyptian, on a rising note.

"Yeah, and you have to play the bandit. We both speak Arabic but they'll know I'm a prisoner, and your Arabic's better than mine. I bet they can't wait to line up for me, once Abdul's finished. Take his robe, try and sound like him. Anyone enquires where we're going, make something up. Like Abdul wants us out in the country, and he's going to make Mikhail watch, before he kills me."

"Abdul?" enquired the envoy.

"Yeah, you need to be introduced," she said dryly. She pointed at the unconscious bandit chief. "This guy. Take his robe, let's go."

They stripped Abdul of his grimy robe and took three more knives the man had about him. When the Egyptian had the robe on, he sniffed. He clearly hadn't worn anything like it before during his pampered existence as head of the chamber or whatever to the king of Egypt. Zona took a turn round him, hands on hips as she studied him.

She was frowning. "Talk to me, and you still don't look like a tribesman with his prisoners.

He pulled a face; a stream of Arabic answered her.

"I know; these filthy things but it's the best we can do," she told him. She tugged at his robe, pulling its hood over to conceal his face. "Speak as little as you can get away with. They'll know their chief, and Hosni the – "

" – waste of space," commented Mikhail sourly.

Even though she didn't disagree with him that much, it got him an amber eyed look.

"Never mind him," she told the glaring Egyptian hastily. "And Mikhail, we need to do this as a team."

A look followed for the other man. "Take our weapons. We're your prisoners. Let's go."

CHAPTER TEN

A SECOND TIME they left the tent.

They walked openly, the warrior and Mikhail menaced by daggers the Egyptian carried. Feeling the tip of one prick her shoulder blades just above her vest, she wondered if he was enjoying this a bit too much. *I guess I should be nicer to him…*

It also occurred to her to wonder how much she and the Trojan captain were able to trust him. The enmity between him and Mikhail pretty well crackled in the searing air, one to the other and back again. It might be that Hosni would cut a deal with the Arab bandits if he thought he could gain by doing so.

They went on, the Egyptian guiding her by slight movements of his dagger point. Mikhail walked beside her scowling. The thing between the two men was already a problem, likely to get worse, hers to sort.

The little group reached, then threaded its way through tents, the sun seeming to get even hotter, the sky a deeper blue over them. Children ran about between the tents hide and seeking; there were a few veiled women who looked but otherwise ignored the three. So far no bandits. Dogs, lean, brown and hungry-looking, also watched from patches of shade. With the other aromas, the warrior could smell food cooking over fires which sent their plumes of smoke into the air. In a clearer space they passed several games with pebbles among small groups of lean, swarthy, bearded men in robes. A few glanced their way but, seeing the prisoners apparently menaced by Abdul with his blades, they went back to their games.

A corral was ahead; beyond it a wide pool reflected the sky and was seemingly clear. She guessed that because of it this was at least a semi-permanent camp for the nomadic Arabs. Horses, camels and donkeys filled the corral, some crowding to the rails as the trio walked steadily nearer. Lina was among them, and so far it was easy going. Perhaps the Egyptian could be trusted after all.

Until four Arabs came out of a tent. The warrior groaned under her breath. *Things are going to come apart any time now.* The tent was one of the last between the trio and the corral.

An Arab moved ahead of the others, his face suspicious. Zona could only hope the Egyptian behind her and the Trojan had his face well shadowed by the cowl of his robe.

"Ho, Abdul," said the man in Arabic. "Where are

you taking the prisoners?"

"Kasim, Akbar and him," a slightly burlier man added, "We thought we were due some knife practice, after we enjoy the woman."

Now was the moment it all hung on the envoy. If he could just pull this off... *But he's got to say something. These guys are gonna know he's not their chief, and what can he make up?* Maybe now he'd turn her and Mikhail in. She felt her muscles tense. As she poised for battle, there was a familiar emptiness in her gut, a dryness of her mouth.

The Egyptian grunted. As she turned her head to see him, he waved the men aside with a knife.

"Can't you see, idiots? He wants the woman to himself first. Can't you see, Moss?" the first speaker said. He grinned, showing broken, yellow teeth. "Excuse us, Abdul, and you will let us go at her when you are done?"

Another grunt answered this.

"I'm not so sure," said Moss slowly. "Something is off, smells like camel dung. And why can't we have fun now too?"

"I'm first, I am chief," the envoy told them. "You are less than the flies which eat the muck." Unfortunately, while he'd just about done what he could, the voice out of the robe was not Abdul's. *Did he have to say that last bit?* "I am taking them into the dried river bed where we ambushed them. When I return, you shall share the leavings of her."

There was a short silence.

It was broken by the fourth man. "Moss, you others, something *is* wrong! This is not our chief."

To Hosni: "What have you done to him?"

The attempt to bluff a way out was ended. Irritated even though the envoy had done the best he could, the warrior swiped back her hair. Now the whole camp would be down on the fugitives.

"He's got a sore nose," she said. "His dignity is ruffled too."

A shorter silence followed her words. Then everyone moved.

As the four bandits rushed them, Zona stepped ahead of her companions. Reaching out when they separated, she caught the two in the middle. With spread arms, she gripped robed heads. A quick jerk cracked their skulls together. Without a sound the men went boneless, slumping.

Mikhail was trying to get inside a third Arab's scimitar. Neither man could gain an advantage and they circled.

The Egyptian was hanging back, even though he

had daggers, her and the Trojan's blades under his robe. He was a man used to good living and political intrigues, not weapons. Zona felt an acid prickle of contempt, then pushed it aside. *He can't help the soft living of a courtier and diplomat. I guess I need to cut him a break.* He'd not chosen who he was any more than she had her own life.

The fourth bandit had almost reached him. The man was only held up by the fight between Mikhail and the other bandit.

The warrior spun. Her foot lashed out. She caught the Arab between his legs, bunching his robe. Colour ran from his cheeks, came back hectically, and drained, leaving him sand-coloured. He was gurgling, his mouth opening and closing, and his knees folded. She hit the back of his neck with the side of her hand.

Seeing the odds, the Trojan's opponent was about to call for help. Zona leaped. He cowered but her foot shot out. As his jaw crunched, it lifted him off his feet to drop him on his back.

"Good, aren't you?" Mikhail said ironically. "I guess some of the stories about you are true."

She smiled. "Maybe. But now we need to move. Any time now we could be stopped."

Approaching the corral, she shared a moment with her golden horse. As the mare laid her head on her shoulder, she scratched her behind the ears. The Palomino groaned with pleasure, her eyes half closed.

Releasing her, the warrior went to the corral's entrance and undid it. "We run their mounts off – it'll take them a while to round them up and start chasing us."

Mikhail agreed and they entered the corral. Flapping at the creatures in there didn't at first do it and she fumed with impatience. At any time Arab bandits might interrupt; it was only by amazing good luck they hadn't already done. She slapped rumps but several camels merely grunted and bared yellow teeth at her. The horses and donkeys were no better; it was only when Lina seemed to catch on and help that any real movement started. The horse bit a donkey in its withers. The normally placid beast let out a bray, jumped and headed for the way out, but only at a walk. While all this was going on, the Egyptian envoy stood and watched, hands clasped behind his back, a disdainful curl to his lips.

As the animals milled, the Trojan captain had saddled his horse and was vaulting to the black's back. "Catch a donkey or we'll leave you behind."

Hosni sniffed. He looked down his nose. "A donkey? I've never ridden before."

A distinct lack of sympathy took hold of Zona. At

this rate, if her companion didn't hit the Egyptian, she would. *Oh well. He'll be sore before we've gone far, and serve him right.*

She saddled her mount quickly, noted the water skin hanging from the saddle and leapt to the animal's back. "Get on one, like this."

The Egyptian functionary still looked dubious. "Where are my litter and my Nubian slaves?"

"Sorry to have to tell you this," she said. *I'm not sorry at all. I guess I'm, what was it Xan used to say? Incorrigible, yeah. That's me. Whatever, he's going to have to toughen up fast.* "But last I saw just before busting you out? They looked to have joined the bandits, though that Arab I knocked out did say about staking two for locusts or crows, something. Guess the guys who joined them went for it more than a life of slavery."

"I'll have them flayed."

"Gotta catch 'em first."

While they were talking, Mikhail on his horse was still trying to move the corral's other inmates.

The Egyptian climbed sulkily aboard a donkey. He did it rather more gingerly than the warrior had with her mount. Even so the animal flattened its ears and brayed loudly. It whipped round its head and tried to bite his leg. Only the loose folds of his robe saved him.

"That's done it," growled Mikhail. "Gods cursed Egyptian – trust him!"

She hid a smile, lips quirking. Once again she couldn't help agreeing with him, even if it hadn't been the man's fault. He couldn't help it that the donkey didn't like him, how he'd climbed on, maybe even the way he smelled.

"Never mind," she said, "Let's get these animals moving."

The three of them guided their mounts among the other milling creatures. Noise wasn't a problem anymore after the donkey's protest. Zona and the Trojan captain slapped rumps and yelled. Gradually the animals began to stir but she felt herself sweat in the intensifying heat of the day. A few camels turned and attempted to bite, spitting foul-smelling cuds when they couldn't. She wrinkled her nose. *These really are the vilest of creatures.* It could be that the bandits only rode them because they could go long distances without food or water. The Arabs had let her onto one once. *Never again; I thought I was going to be sick.* Perhaps they ran well. *If you can get them started.* Belting another rear, she just about managed to avoid the camel's kick.

Arabs were headed their way in a yelling cluster. Some threw spears, although the distance was too great for accuracy and the weapons clattered short on the barren ground. The men were getting closer; soon that would change. Others were brandishing their scimitars. Plenty of daggers were also on show but thankfully the raucous mob didn't seem to have any bows and arrows.

Mikhail suddenly roared, as if he was ordering his men to stand firm against the Greeks at Troy.

For a moment everyone stopped. She just had time to register that Hosni didn't appear to have done much to help so far. *Maybe he doesn't know what to do.* Again she was trying to be fair.

Everything four-legged jumped convulsively for the gate to the corral. The horses, camels and donkeys crashed into the oncoming bandits. Shouts became screams, cries of rage.

The Egyptian's donkey led the charge.

CHAPTER ELEVEN

ONCE THE WARRIOR and Mikhail dug Hosni and his donkey from the tangle of Arabs and fleeing animals, the trio rode hard into the West.

Soon they had to slow. Their flight was through more or less flat land with occasional stunted trees and bushes. As noon heat settled over the riders, singing birds lapsed into silence. Even flies and other insects appeared to rest, except round the Egyptian. Zona knew the riders had to conserve their mounts' strength and slowed to a walk. Every nerve sang a protest because the Arabs would soon round up their mounts and be on the way. She had no way of knowing how far behind the trio the bandits were, how long they'd pursue under the burning sun. Even the buzzards were silent; surely the Arabs wouldn't come far in this heat. Although the Egyptian diplomat was someone they were going to ransom, sensibly the bandits would cut their losses, avoid foundering mounts some time. *There's got to be a time, soon in sun like this, when the effort and losses of getting him back won't be worth it. Assuming those guys work on more than just injured pride,* she kept thinking, plastered to the back of her horse. But what else could she do, apart from ride as fast as possible while hoarding her beasts' strength? *All I can do is hope we stay ahead.* She went on fretting at their slow progress.

So did Hosni, loudly and volubly about everything.

First it was the heat which made his worn-looking, soiled grey robe darken on his back and under his arms. After a while he disliked the smell of himself, telling her while calling her 'slut' that slave girls would have bathed and perfumed him. Sitting heavily on his donkey, he was pestered by flies and some whining hornets, and told the other two riders all about it. *How dare they, and him the something of the chamber?* she thought ironically. He was thirsty, hungry and his head ached with tiredness and the heat. *I guess we should massage it with cool water. He'll be lucky.*

At length the warrior called a halt. They were all walking alongside their mounts through ever-dry country. It stayed flat, though hills were visible a long way off on the haze and dust-shrouded horizon. Almost no shade was cast by a few stunted trees and thorny bushes. Mirages of lakes shimmered around and ahead of the travellers while vultures and buzzards floated silently overhead.

Zona walked towards a tree not far off, her mare trailing after her with drooping head. Mikhail, the

Egyptian and their animals came too. Arriving at the tree, she unhooked a water skin from her saddle. The Trojan captain took it, poured a little into her cupped hands from which the horse drank eagerly. She returned the favour so that his horse could drink too. Back propped on the tree, the envoy watched, chin and moustaches wet with droplets. Looked at with large, dark eyes by his donkey, his own water skin lay at his side.

"You are foolish, slut. Water is for men, not animals," he said.

"I see," the warrior replied coolly.

"Not that this is good water," the Egyptian went on. "It tastes of the creature whose skin was used to make the bag. Also it is warm."

"I'd say you're lucky to have it." Mikhail laid aside his helmet to mop his brow. "You should be thankful Zona thought to bring some."

Watching them, irritated at their talk, the warrior reached behind herself to wipe sweat from between her shoulder blades. *What a pity this guy's with us,* she thought. Once more she reminded herself that if the bandits caught up, he'd be useful to barter for their freedom. *He's getting to be an expensive load, though.* She rubbed more perspiration from her chest and arms, then wondered why she bothered.

"This is brackish, not fit for the donkey," the ambassador stated.

"You better give him some," she advised. "Unless you fancy walking. Donkeys are tough – "

" – which is why we gave you one," cut in Mikhail.

"The water is for me!"

Impatience sawed at her; it was too hot for this. "And who are *you?*"

Although seated, the Egyptian managed to draw himself up. Perspiration rolled onto his nose but he ignored it.

"I am Hosni Sulaiman Al Sabrahim Pebekkanum, Chief of the Chamber to – "

" – You are a worm," she interrupted shortly.

"And if you don't stop your cackling, we chop you up and leave you for the birds," added Mikhail. He was lying stretched on his back with his helmet over his face.

A brief silence followed his words. The warrior blessed him. It seemed his threat might have at least temporarily put a stop to the Egyptian's bombast.

The man spoke up again. *No such luck,* she thought.

"Back in the Pharaoh's court you will be punished for such remarks. And she will be taught to know her place, as a woman should."

"Bring it on," said Zona.

Getting up, she took her water skin to the donkey. Mikhail came as well. From her cupped hands they allowed the animal to drink a little.

Watching them, the envoy curled his lips but said nothing. *Why didn't we just leave him for the bandits?* she asked herself, and wondered how many more times the question would come to her. Surely it wasn't worth dragging him around. She sighed. *I guess I'd no choice really. I couldn't leave him, knowing they might take it out on him for our escape. Wish I had, though.* She knew that if the time came, she wouldn't use him to dicker with the Arabs. Not that she'd let the supercilious bureaucrat know.

Turning to stand hipshot, she said, "Let's move or we're apt to have company."

"Why don't we leave him behind?" asked Mikhail.

"Like I said, I guess I'm a sucker for lame dogs, and he could end up useful."

Trying to look disdainful, the ambassador levered himself to his feet. He brushed stones and dust from his robe as if it was their fault the dirt was there.

"You would not do so to Hosni Sulaiman – "

" – Yeah?" said the warrior. "Want to bet?"

She pointed up at the vultures drifting and circling above them. "And don't forget those birds need feeding."

The envoy craned back his neck to look at the birds. He returned his gaze to the warrior, the Trojan officer, and his expression was dark. Seeing it, she repressed a shiver as coldness spread over her. The Egyptian diplomat would need watching. She wouldn't be surprised if he sold them out to Carthage up ahead or his boss in the East. *He's not going to fall in love with me, want to give me silks and perfumes.* Maybe she and the Trojan shouldn't be so hard on the man. If only the guy didn't attract it like spilled honey did wasps.

"Get on your donkey," she added.

The Egyptian walked stiffly towards his animal. As he neared it, the dun coloured beast flattened its large dark ears. She wondered if she ought to warn him – until she met Mikhail's eyes. Surely a donkey couldn't harm the priggish civil servant, and this might be fun, could be justice of a sort. Payback for what the pair had gone through with him, all the stuff which was sure to come in the future.

The lean, dark man in his soiled robe must have suspected all was not well. When he glanced back at her and the Trojan, they looked at him calmly.

"What?" the warrior asked innocently.

He stared a bit more, then gave some to the donkey. It looked back with its dark, liquid eyes. She saw a hint of its lip curling but the Egyptian seemed to miss it.

Gathering up his robe, he motioned to the donkey to keep still, although the creature almost certainly didn't understand him. It went on regarding him placidly. Hosni was maybe a little bit smarter then he seemed because his stern look projected threats. Cautiously he swung a leg over it.

In complete silence the donkey's head came round swiftly. Large yellow teeth clacked at the back of the envoy's robe. With a yelp, he shot over its head to land on his face. He came up dirtied and sweating, a large graze down the side of his cheek, clutching the seat of his robe. The donkey stood peacefully beside him.

The Egyptian broke into a truly impressive stream of invective. It called down the wrath of his king, their pantheon of gods on the donkey's head, the warrior and Trojan captain. It went on about their parentage or lack of it, which rats and snakes they might be descended from and more.

Eventually the man stopped for breath, perspiring and red-faced. His hand raised, he went to cuff the donkey. It bared its teeth at him, let him see the whites of its eyes and he began to swear again.

"Oh Great One, Hosni Sulaiman, blah, blah." Zona let out a most un-warrior-like giggle. She'd not enjoyed herself so much in a long time. "I should give it a rest if I were you. You're going to need that donkey."

Ignoring her, except that he didn't beat the donkey, the Egyptian went on with his tirade. He made to get on its back once more.

The beast wasn't having any. As soon as the envoy got within range of mounting, it showed him its teeth again. It might almost have been laughing at his expense. When the man tried to grab its ears so he could hold it still, the donkey bowed its head out of his reach. With a loud bray, it trotted off, leaving him swearing.

The ambassador picked up the skirts of his robe and hared off after it.

At the sight of the trotting donkey followed by the red-faced, cursing Egyptian, the warrior laughed so hard she thought she'd burst something. Perhaps she ought to bless the ridiculous envoy. This was the first loud, unaffected mirth she'd given in to since Xanthia had left her. Mikhail was chortling too and they clung together, holding each other up.

It couldn't go on. In the heat under the cloudless sky, although their shadows were lengthening east, the running man would soon dehydrate. The trio didn't need that extra complication. Reluctantly but still laughing, she pushed her horse to a walk and set off after the man and his animal.

CHAPTER TWELVE

✜

THE PRINCE, former king, thrust his loathing of Zona back into a dark cell of his mind. To catch up with her, there were some things to take care of before he left Troy. He needed to focus on them.

First he'd to get out of the palace. Helen's boudoir where the warrior had downed him, he was nearly framed and killed.

Once Deiphobos was outside the princess's quarters, the palace hit home to him. The air was thick with dust. Running feet, shouts and screams, the ring of clashing blades, and some of it was coming his way. The smell was off too, and he recognised the stench of death, like a butcher shop on a hot day. He could hear something creaking, a slam like the crash of shields coming together, as they had so often, on the plain outside. Fumes stung his nose, making him sneeze violently. With them came the crackle of flames, more smells of blood and death. For a moment he stood horrified at what was going down here.

Rage burst over him and helped. It was white-hot but like the Scamander, Simois and Xanthus rivers in flood as one.

The Greeks were tearing Priam's palace apart. Now that the old king and his trusted counsellor were dead the building was his. *How can Odysseus let this happen?* They'd had a deal. If he was able to get the Trickster King and the other one hundred rulers in here, he'd surely be King of Troy. He'd kept his end. Sneaking in Odysseus' and Diomedes' spies, plotting with that weasel Mikrekros. OK, he'd got rid of the guy but they accepted that Zona had done it. Odysseus had said so in his letter and the prince, briefly king, got their wooden horse into Troy. True the old man went for it as soon as it appeared but he, the Heir, would have done more if it was needed. Now this, they were going back on their bargain. Troy was being pillaged, wrecked before his eyes. Just because they thought he wasn't needed anymore. He'd show them, put a stop to this somehow.

Cringing, Deiphobos stole along the corridor. Soon he came to a downed Greek soldier and it sparked an idea.

Working quickly he divested the man of his armour, the leathers underneath which were soaked in blood and made him wrinkle his nose fastidiously. Soon he'd changed into the garments, blood and all. Worried that more enemies might catch him, he worked feverishly, often fumbling. The soldier's gear didn't quite fit his heavier build. Praying nobody would notice in the mayhem and carnage that were the destruction of Troy, he crammed the helmet over his ears. The Greek's sword belt and blade fastened round his thick waist, he took up the man's dagger.

His mind still clearing, he thanked Ares the enemy soldiers hadn't put a sword into him when they robbed him of the tiara and crown. It was time he got after her, but first a trip to his house. Of late as Troy's situation got worse and Odysseus had the wooden horse plan, even though he'd not known the weapon's nature, Deiphobos lived at the palace. It was safer that way, and he wasn't broke. If the Greeks hadn't already looted it, his home was filled with plenty to start the journey. Money, clothes, weapons, even slaves, it should all be there.

At last the prince made it out of the palace. As he skulked on, all the noises of its destruction kept going. In the gardens, now fully visible under a grey sky, towered the wooden horse. An open hatch on its back lit against the sky by flamelight showed what must have happened.

Warriors hid in there, likely several hundred crammed together. When the Assembly and the old man ordered the horse brought into the city, all they had to do was wait... Clever. He recalled Odysseus' offensive letter. *'I require you to make sure it succeeds…'* or some such. *Bastard! Son of one of his goats of Ithaca.* It would be a long time before the prince forgot that. The gods help the Trickster King and his slimy spymaster because he'd pay them back if they ever met again. *Yeah, the Grey-Eyed One better be there for them…But even Athena won't save them.* Unless, of course, they might be useful in helping to deal with his quarry. Oh, the exquisite pain he'd inflict!

While enjoying these thoughts, the wine better than any favourite of his, he was making a way along the streets through what was left of his city. Greek troops mingled with fleeing refugees, starting fires which threw plumes and streamers of grey upwards. Often they were throwing women to the ground, tearing at their clothes and taking turns at raping them. The clouds of smoke hung in the ashen stillness like the fumes of volcanoes. Here and there small groups of Trojans battled for honour rather than their lives. He passed the fights, hoping some zealous sergeant didn't draft him into one. It never occurred to him to help his fellow men; the Trojans were on their own.

As he got near his home, a building collapsed in dust and bricks. Fires shone red, orange and gold through the smoke. Even he flinched when a soldier dashed a baby against a wall and gore showered. A little further on was another rape. Men had a woman stripped and splayed in the road. While a bearded man went at her, others cheered him on. More men had almost finished stripping a shrieking girl of ten or twelve. The prince found himself shocked. It wasn't that he'd not expected things like this to follow his plotting with Greek agents, but he was a prince. By Ares they ought to have some respect in his presence, not do things like this in the open. He was king of Troy!

Finally, half choked by fires, sweating and dishevelled, he got home. When he'd crept through the trees of the grounds, he saw that his house was a smoking wreck.

Fresh anger flared. Someone, Greeks or maybe looters or thieves grabbing their chance, had started the fire. Almost reduced to its foundations the mansion still gulped out tongues of flame. He turned slowly around. Beyond his trees was the crackle and roar of other fires; the stenches of destruction and choking smoke seemed everywhere. Of his slaves there was no sign but Deiphobos didn't care; let the Greeks have their way with them.

He glowered at the wreckage, swiping coarse hair off his brow. His plan had been to get money here, food and drink, a wash, maybe a change of clothes. *Not much chance now.* Feeling the acid of indigestion, fear and annoyance, he burped and rubbed his belly. Not even a drink would be left here. *Odysseus and me, we got some talking to do all right,* he promised himself sourly. They just weren't meant to rip the city down like this. *It wasn't in the agreement, and this is my place.* He was to govern as king.

He listened to drunken yells of pleasure coming from the streets. *I bet they've been on* my *wine!* Coughing as a puff of a breeze wafted smoke his way, he wiped watery eyes. *Beyond getting even, what next?*

Rough voices were close. It sounded like a Greek sergeant and some men. Alarm jolted through him, until he recalled he was wearing a Greek uniform. *They'd better miss the blood.* He shook his head, blinking at more smoke and fumes. The way his thoughts were limping, his chariot had to be missing a wheel, its team of horses.

"Ho, Xixos!" The man who'd spoken appeared to have mixed him up with someone else. A coarse laugh followed. "You look as if you've been at too many of those slaves, especially the women!"

Another man slapped his shoulder. "Didn't get them all though. I had the little dark girl. Great they couldn't talk, huh?"

"It's a miracle he can walk straight!" a third guffawed.

"We all know what he's like. A regular goat. Bet he's got sore balls though!"

127

It was true what the last man had said. Deiphobos had always been a man of large appetites, and these bastards sounded like they'd had Miriam, his favourite slave. So this Greek soldier for whom he'd been mistaken liked women too. What puzzled him was that he was taken for the man. But perhaps it wasn't such a surprise. Everyone had to be battle-fatigued; he was himself. The Greek squad were all dirt, smoke and soot stained. The sky might be lightening but it was still heavy with a sheet of cloud and smoke. Ash and soot were added to that. Maybe the enemy soldiers were seeing the man they expected, of like colouring and build. Whatever was happening, the prince, no, King of Troy decided to ride his luck. Maybe Ares was at his side; if not, these men would have killed him in a moment.

"That's me!" he said, "And you're right about the walking thing. After all those women, famous goat that I am, my balls are like melons and I'm trashed. Serge, can I rest, then catch up?"

The sergeant looked at him narrowly but the prince's face was shadowed under his helmet. Although a couple laughed, the others of the squad looked too. The King of Troy's gut squirmed, his brow cold with perspiration. Had they discovered he wasn't their comrade? If they had...

"Yeah. Catch up," the sergeant muttered. "We'll

be down the road at some of the other houses. You great pussy, make sure you do catch up or I'll tear you apart."

Looting had been the Trojan ruler's plan as well. On the way he'd noticed quite a few of the rich looking mansions on this street were barely damaged or untouched. When he saw what had been done to his own place, looting one of them was his first thought. He'd need to be extra careful now.

The sergeant added, "Don't even think of deserting with your own stuff. If you do, I'll hunt you down and make you eat them. I've told you, or I'm telling you now, I'll eat them myself, puke what's left on your face!"

"Oh I won't Sir!"

"Poor old Xixos," jeered the soldier who'd first spoken. "He'll puke what he doesn't chew up in your face. Oh yeah!"

The prince scowled but was only acting. This had been easier than he'd ever have expected. The wonder was that the sergeant had agreed to leave him behind. Perhaps he and the other men were drunk on killing and looting, maybe weary themselves. The sergeant maybe wasn't thinking all that clearly. He was grateful, even remembered to thank Ares. The war god was surely on his side, which could mean he'd deserted

Zona. The prince enjoyed the vision of catching up to her, while he feigned tiredness and breathlessness.

"Get moving, you excuse for a trooper, or I'll be back for you like one of the Furies," promised the sergeant.

"Yes Sir!"

With a final suspicious look his way, the sergeant led his squad down the road, pushing a bawling child roughly aside. As the lad pelted off up the street, the prince watched the men until they rounded a corner, then let out a shaky breath. *Safe at last, if only for a while.*

Deipohobos changed his mind about staying at this place. It was time to get out of here while he could.

Giving the other men time to get well ahead, the King of Troy set off in their wake. He took care to ensure he was well back where nobody would see him.

When they came back into sight, he kept his distance and went on watching the squad. They entered a house like his own had been and he hung back till there was the smashing of crockery, a bellow of laughter. Sure the men were safely occupied, he crept past, then speeded up to the next intact house.

Entering cautiously, he found it empty. The *yellow-livered servants and slaves have all run. As soon as they knew the Greeks were in Troy. Trying to save their worthless hides; so much the better for me.*

Quickly he stole across the hall, checked out the other rooms. They'd been left disordered as the people ran. He found a bag into which he stuffed jewellery in the mistress's rooms. Gold, silver, pearls, sapphires in light necklaces, earrings and so on. The things were easy to carry and could be exchanged for other stuff he wanted whenever there was a need. In the great kitchen he found meats, cheeses, wine as well. The war might have been getting tough for common people but the rich like whoever had this house lived well. Regretting all that was past and must be left behind, he tore off chunks of cold lamb and stuffed them into his mouth. The prince crammed food into the bag on top of the jewellery which it would hide and left the building.

As he hurried through the grounds, he ran into the sergeant of the squad he thought he'd escaped. The burly soldier's eyes ran over the prince and his bag, narrowing.

"Why are you here, Xixos? Why haven't you joined up with us?" he rasped.

"Well, Sir… "

Then Deiphobos' mood shifted; he was more angry than afraid. This man and his squad were likely some of the people who'd burned his house down, the palace, everything. They'd taken away his privileged life as a prince, the Heir of Troy, its king, and turned him into a refugee. Disguised as a Greek trooper he might be, but it was what he was. They'd raped and murdered his slaves. He'd enjoyed cutting out some of the women's tongues himself and training them to serve his pleasures. Some he'd raped himself, going on to torture them when they didn't respond to him willingly enough. If anyone killed them it should be him, not soldiers of Agamemnon and the Trickster King. Everything caught up to him and fury, hot blood crossed his vision.

"… I've, uh, something for you," he grated.

The sergeant looked puzzled, his brow furrowed as the Prince of Troy put down his running-out bag. He'd see what there was inside in a moment, but first this man had spoken oddly, certainly not with the respect of one of his troopers.

"What is it?" the grizzled soldier muttered. "And I asked you a question. Why are you lagging behind?"

The Trojan prince stepped in closer and the sergeant looked more suspicious, fear dawning in his eyes. The disguised Greek soldier's sword was out of its scabbard.

The sergeant's hand went to the hilt of the sword

sheathed at his hip. He wasn't fast enough.

The Trojan ruler's blade stabbed out. Putting all his considerable weight behind the blow, he angled it up. The sword thudded into the man, went through his leather tunic. Panting, Deiphobos jerked it up again and blood ran. The blade grated on ribs as he tilted it still higher.

Mewling, the sergeant looked down. His cheeks were like dirty snow on Mt Ida. A look of astonishment came and went. Clapping his hands over the wound to hold in what came slithering out, the man cried.

Yanking his sword free as the victim's knees gave, the prince kicked him down. The soldier had voided his bowels and there was the stink of perforated insides too. Wrinkling his nose at the stench, he wiped the blade on the man's kilt and sheathed it with a satisfied grunt.

Without glancing back, he picked up his stolen supplies and left.

CHAPTER THIRTEEN

✤

AENEAS was fed up with being at sea.

As the voyage dragged on, he'd begun to call himself 'God Aeneas' or 'Father Aeneas' in the presence of his crew and the officers who'd sailed with him. In time the names would spread, add to his mystique. *I feel like the gods, Fates too maybe, are with me.* He'd seen himself progressively fitting into the role of Father, was certainly the commander, leader of his fleet – which was all to the good.

It was a blustery late afternoon, clouds racing out of the west low above grey-blue foamy water. The waves heaved under his ship, rolling it sharply so the crew had to keep bailing it out. It was cold as well. Aeneas was wrapped in a brine-soaked wool cloak which clung to him in sodden twists. His face was stiff with the wind, lips chapped, salty as he licked them too much.

Fortunately, he wasn't seasick. Some of the warriors rowing the ship were; a few hadn't been able to lean over the side fast enough. The stink of vomit mingled with the odours of himself, the rowers and salt spray and waves. *'Father' or 'Godlike' Aeneas I may be*, he thought. *I've told these men I was Priam's nephew, a prince in my own right. They should get that story round too, but heroic voyages are not my kind of life.*

He wondered when it would ever end and he'd feel dry land once more. He'd got to find or steal resources to build a new city – if he could fool someone into giving him his new start so much the better. As for working the smart politics, the con to bring it about, he'd make it up as he went.

As the ship rose on a wave that was bigger, he saw it. A wide, deep bay.

At first it was only visible in brief flashes but at least Aeneas and his fleet were being carried that way by the tide, blown by the wind. Through spray and a torrent of rain, he thought he saw an island with rocky sides in front of the bay. As the ship carried him and his people nearer, he could see more clearly behind it. It felt like a rip current was bearing his vessel to starboard of the island but for a while he still couldn't see what was there properly. Rubbing at red-rimmed eyes, he peered more closely but they watered and he still wasn't able to see fully.

Hills rose around the bay and they seemed to be wooded. A hole broke through the cloud cover and sunlight dazzled, leaping across the sea. Even the gulls wheeling over his ships, hoping for scraps, sounded more cheerful, less like forlorn children. Finally, after weeks of sailing, Aeneas and his band were nearing a shore.

They were past the island shielding the bay's entrance. In spite of his steady insides, the weather had been a bit too lively and he would definitely welcome dry land. In addition, as always, he was eager to get on with his project which would give him fame.

Past the island which went on taking most of the impact of the waves, the water scarcely rippled. Although it was clear green as the clouds broke further, when he looked over the side Aeneas couldn't see the bottom.

It was easy for the crews to row across the bay. As the stolen Greek warships ploughed on leaving creamy wakes of foam, the clouds thinned and tore further. Hazy sunlight which rapidly strengthened glittered over the water in fiery points. Soon the leading ships, followed by the rest of the fleet, grounded on shingle. Men leapt out and pulled them further up the shore.

The brawny warrior-sailors were followed by others. It had been a hard day's passage through the choppy seas and the high prowed and sterned galleys were heavy. A lot more time had passed reaching this place under cloudy skies than Aeneas realised. The men were tired and sweating hard. Many of them sprawled on their backs on a mainly sandy beach. Chests heaved as they dragged in sea winds and shifting sunlight with the warm air. Gulls wheeled overhead, crying out forlornly, a few sounding as if they laughed raucously. While the realist in him was grateful to have made landfall, the general was annoyed by his men's behaviour.

Aeneas went over the side of his own ship. The abrupt slap of waves on his shins made him gasp at the cold. Gritting his teeth, he waded on up the shallow beach, feeling shingle underfoot change to firm sand.

Clearing his throat, he barked, "Shape up, you men! Call yourselves sailors? On your feet!"

A bearded sergeant growled from the corner of his mouth, "We're what's left of the Trojan army, not sailors."

Aeneas heard the man, as he was no doubt meant to. For the time being, 'Father' and 'Pious' had to take a back seat. Not for the first time, he wished Mikhail hadn't deserted and wondered where the man could be. A few necessary killings and the guards' captain went to pieces. The trouble now was that the sergeant was a good deal bigger, tougher than Aeneas. Once Mikhail would have handled this; he'd have taken it for granted. The Trojans had always thought him a wily commander and politician. So he was, but he'd leaned unnoticed on such men and now couldn't afford to appear weak. He sighed, hoped nobody saw or heard it. He'd had more than his share of times like this. There was that time at Crete when he and his fleet barely escaped a plague… Aeneas hadn't found it so easy being tough all the time but compassionate too, earning and hanging onto the 'Father' title.

"Details like that are irrelevant," he said with the deceptive mildness which his men knew. Several, including the bearded sergeant, watched him uneasily. "There's a lot to be done here, as I'm sure you all know. This is indeed the Trojan army, and I am your commander!"

His voice rose. "So off this beach, let's go!"

Sulkily, deliberately not hurrying, the men heaved themselves to their feet. Perhaps he was being hard, overdoing it, but he reminded himself, *I can't afford not to be.* He dare not show any failings.

As they stood, he looked backwards. The ships were pulled up in a row along the beach. More which had been cut off by the storm that had preceded the afternoon's wind and cloud would hopefully join up later. The bay was now so calm, azure beneath the sun and cloud-dotted sky. Along with the big island at its entrance twin crags reared, forming each headland. He could see a line of waves breaking out there in foam. His gaze tracked along the wooded cliffs which towered green and lush around the beach. In spite of his men's unmilitary behaviour, peace came over him in a soft wash with the smell of salt, the cries of the seagulls. *My water's telling me that I've found a good place. Destiny's near, if not right here, and there's something else.* Up the golden beach on the right was a cave. A narrow stream bubbled out of it to vanish quickly in sand. It wasn't much but the fresh water meant a good campsite. His crews could rest up before whatever came next.

In a milder tone, as befitted the father of his people, he said, "This may be a good place to pass the night. We need to prepare, so this is what we do."

Women carrying children were getting set on the beach. Some of the kids were playing tag. Others had pieces of driftwood which would be good to burn later and were playing warriors, make-believing the timber was swords. Shouts, yells and laughter up and down the beach made Aeneas feel even better.

"Here's what we'll do," he repeated. "Some of you men gather brush and wood for fires. Women are to help, and you can rope in a few of the little ones. Pound some of our grain with stones and parch the kernels. You know the drill."

He sent off some men to scout the forest crowding up to the beach at a path through it near the cave. Others were to look inside and make sure nothing hostile was lairing in there. Then a perimeter with guards was to be set up round the camp. This place had a 'right' feel to it but 'Father Aeneas' was taking no chances. The sun was setting, westering behind one of the crags. The shadows of himself and his folk were moving, tangling and coming apart behind them. Light spilled colour onto the sea's flat surface as the sun lowered. Although seagulls hung around, wailing and crying, gliding over the Trojans, hoping to get lucky, it would be dark soon. Anything might happen then.

"Let's go," he finished. "I don't think we need tie up the ships or run out anchors with it so calm here and set to stay that way. Achates, Dares, with me. We'll explore up the trail by the cave."

With the two hulking men, he pushed up along the path. In the woods it narrowed with tree roots twisting across the way and the air was cooler. Insects weren't much of a problem. As the three men climbed the animal path, they only slapped at a few midges attracted by their sweat and were silent, except for their breathing.

At length they came out of the woods and were on a high, rocky point. Gulls wheeled and cried below and a cool breeze wafted, salty around them as they stood and looked at the darkening sea. They could see beyond the bay as the wine-dark surface dotted with whitecaps merged with the horizon. Gull wings were catching the light, shining pink, gold and copper-cream. *Hard to believe this was all so rough earlier on.* Aeneas inhaled the briny, refreshing air and sighed with pleasure.

For the first time in an age I can start to relax. He and his two guards turned back into the shadows of the trail through the woods. When they got back to the camp, he'd send out hunters. If they were lucky in apparently deserted woods like this, the men could shoot some deer. His mouth watered at the vision of some of the wine they'd taken from Sicily and the imagined smell of fresh venison.

The hunters found a herd of deer which had come to drink at another stream with the day's ending. Soon chunks of venison were sizzling on improvised wooden spits, the aromas mingling headily with that of the sea. The only thing that was wrong was the gulls which were shrieking as they dived at the camp.

Afterwards with full bellies, Aeneas did the friendly commander thing with some of his men, playing and gambling at dice noisily. When a few games had been played, he went off into the woods alone. The people would expect something good to happen in this place soon. He was after all nurturing his rep as 'Pious Aeneas' so he'd better give them something. *Cook up a nice brew to keep them happy and in line. Maybe a vision of a goddess, that ought to do it.* Aphrodite would fit; she was the goddess who came from the sea, and she was meant to be the Trojans' patron. Hadn't Paris strung her along before the war for Troy even began? Anything that pussy could do ought to be a walk in the park for 'Pious Aeneas', the Father of his people.

He settled himself comfortably in the hollow at the roots of an oak. *Spend the night meditating.* He grinned. *They'll go for that. I'm practically a god to them myself.*

Now put a spin on it... Perhaps he'd have the goddess disguise herself as his lost mother. They, especially Owl-Eyed Athena, were keen on that sort of stuff. She could prophesy; he'd make up something encouraging after he'd slept a while. *Folks will be right in my hands. Soft as clay as Artist Aeneas moulds them.*

In the morning, first dawn-light, he'd climb back up to the high place on his own. Mystics, Fathers of their people, did things that way.

This is going so well, easy as falling off a log. Aeneas shuffled his butt about among the tree roots, getting even more comfy. A broad grin split his face.

CHAPTER FOURTEEN

❖

IT WAS A COOL, clear morning when Zona pushed aside the two lion pelts under which she'd slept. She liked this time of day best of all. Later it would get hot. Flies and hornets, everything which flew and stung, would pester her, the two men and their mounts. For now Hosni the Egyptian and Mikhail still slept and she had the place to herself. Except for Lina, Mikhail's horse and the envoy's donkey.

She made her way towards the pool near which the trio were camped. This was an isolated green spot because of the water, with olive trees, brush and plenty of fresh grass. Hearing birds at their morning thing, the warrior smiled and stretched both arms over her head. *Life's pretty good on the road right now,* she thought. *If only that gods-damned Egyptian would stop his carping.* He wouldn't, though, and soon he'd be awake and starting. Peeling her vest off over sleep-roughened hair, she dropped it. Wriggling from her kilt and underwear, she strolled towards the pool. It was clear to a sandy bottom and deliciously chill. The warrior scooped up water, laved it over herself and cleared her hair of sweat before swimming. A twig cleaned her teeth and another combed her soaked and unruly locks. Back in her clothes, she went to the campfire and stoked it. She dropped pieces of jerky into a pot of hot water to soften it up. While she waited, she settled back, leaning on her elbows, her face turned to the sun, as she whistled along with the birds.

Zona didn't wake the others till the simple meal was ready. Even then, she fixed a little of their dwindling supply of coffee, before shaking Mikhail into life.

Soldier that he was, the man was instantly alerted. He put his hand to the sword beside him and had part-drawn it before it registered with him who she was. A sheepish grin came and went on his whiskery face. When he'd shaved with his dagger and washed up, they took their time over cups of coffee. In what had become something of a ritual, they shared a look, switched it to the snoring Egyptian.

"I guess we gotta wake him?" The warrior arched a brow, making a question of it. "Are we sure about this?"

"Sooner cut his head off," the Trojan growled.

Zona smirked. "Your turn today."

"It is not!"

"Is too."

"I'll comb the horses, throw in his donkey. Please!"

She laughed and he grinned at the sound, the way it lit up her features. She didn't fancy Mikhail as a lover but their relationship was increasingly easy, one of mutual respect and liking, one warrior for another.

"Please?" he asked again.

Shaking her head, she pointed at him. "Your turn, I did it yesterday. I never heard the last of it and him calling me 'slut' because I wasn't some pampered slave girl."

"You got ice for a heart."

"Yeah. Mikhail?"

Cupping his hands to his mouth, the Trojan captain roared, "Rise and shine! Up and at 'em!"

Hosni rolled out of his bedding swearing impressively about what he'd do to the soldier. His mood wasn't improved when, her eyes polished amber, Zona told him it was his turn to take care of the horses and donkey. They had breakfast and more coffee. Afterwards the Egyptian's language was rich and fluent when the donkey nearly bit him. As the trio broke camp and hit the road, he complained about everything. This was not the way for a high official of the Pharaoh, an ambassador, to approach Carthage.

Instead of the sun coming up higher, the morning

greyed over from the hills in the west. The travellers could have gone faster if not for the diplomat and his donkey. As the hills drew slowly closer, the riders saw mountains behind them but this day the peaks were hidden by low clouds.

There was muggy heat, together with an odd kind of stillness in the blanket of the air. Normally they were shadowed by at least one buzzard, an eagle or two. Other birds perched in olive trees and called out. Occasional creatures like scruffy dogs would watch, even cross the trio's path. Now it seemed the land itself held its breath.

They kept plodding on. It was midway through the ashen morning. A headache had built for Zona and she was sweating hard, the morning swim not even a distant memory.

In a narrow, rocky valley, they were following a dried-out streambed. The weather was carrying on with grey and hot and darkening. A few spots of warm rain began to squeeze from the sky, although it all stayed hushed. The warrior frowned at the silence as she wiped rain and perspiration from her arms and reached at the trickles on her back. The headache was tighter round her brow and her mouth was dry. After the Egyptian's initial complaints, it seemed no-one had spoken all that morning. For some time she'd been increasingly uneasy, drawing looks from Mikhail.

Sitting on his horse beside her, the Trojan was pale and shiny-faced, uncomfortable-looking as he sweated in his armour. Only the Egyptian rode on as if he suspected nothing wrong.

It was his donkey which stopped, so abruptly that he grabbed at its ears to keep from sliding off.

The donkey's big ears pricked forward. It stood, nose flaring, quivering all over. An eye was visible to the warrior rolling to its white as the creature pulled its lip back from its teeth. The envoy didn't notice its fear; all that mattered to him was the discomfort and lack of dignity he'd gone through. Swearing, he started to beat its withers.

Zona snapped as her horse jerked to a halt, the Trojan captain on his mount next to her. Both mounts were trembling, ears pointed forward.

"Stop it, you moron!" she rapped. "Can't you see the donkey's scared?"

"Yeah, it's got more sense than you," grunted Mikhail.

Ignoring them both, Hosni went on hitting the donkey. It refused to move, then started backing up.

"Something's wrong here. Look at our horses as well," she said more mildly.

It got through to the Egyptian. Glancing her way, he

left off belabouring the donkey.

"What?" he asked hoarsely.

Her eyes picked out what was troubling, *more like scaring,* their mounts. She pointed left at a long shelf of rock sticking out over the valley.

"Up there, they blend in."

Mikhail and Hosni followed the line of her arm to her index finger and beyond. The Trojan creased his brow when he caught the other man's quick look at her. It was as if he was sizing her up for a slave market. The envoy didn't notice him see because one of the creatures moved, flicking a dark-tipped tail.

"What is it?" the soldier whispered.

"It's big," added the other, "and it's a lion."

"The Arabs call them that." The warrior's tone was thoughtful. "They live and hunt all over Africa. Those with the dark ruffs, they're males."

"Big, all right," commented Mikhail. "A good part the height of our horses from the look of them. What do they eat?"

"Us, if we're not careful," she answered. "But if we're cautious, only move slowly, there's a chance they'll let us be. They don't look hungry but I wonder where the rest of the pride is."

"Pride?"

"Yeah. Usually they're said to live in groups called prides. Maybe these are outlaws on their own. I guess they could be scouts, though."

"I've told you, slut," the Egyptian said loudly, "we too know of these animals. Like all cats which are the Goddess Bast, also known as Maftet, they are sacred."

"Even though they're fierce predators?" The warrior couldn't help her irony, and the lions on the rock outcrop really were close. She could smell the big cat odour coming off them.

"What are we going to do, Zona?" asked Mikhail. "It sounds like you know of these things."

"Me and Hosni, but for me not that much. Only a bit I've been told by the Arabs."

"Who?" Even at a time like this he was curious.

"Just some guys I met." She was droll. "You know – the coffee? They wanted to make me – "

"To treat you as the trash you are," declared the Egyptian functionary.

They both looked at him, and held the stare. He returned it but finally dropped his own.

"OK. When they found it might be hard to make me a slave to their needs, the Arabs were friendly a while. Before we went our separate ways those men taught me their language and told me things, as well as sharing coffee and meals. Great honour. Among the stuff the men, likely bandits, said was something about lions. Oh, and once we went on a hunt, I think I told you."

"So what do you advise?" repeated Mikhail.

"We should run," said the ambassador, then looked ashamed of himself. The largest among the lions, a male, yawned, showing great white teeth, and he blanched.

The warrior thought a moment. "Wouldn't be a good idea. It might set them off. We could just sit tight a while."

Hosni sniffed. "I shall not tolerate this."

"Then what's your idea, O Great One?"

All the mounts had stayed restless at the close presence and scent of the lions. They shifted their feet, snorted and rolled their eyes. The warrior and Trojan officer calmed their horses by touches on the reins, leaning over and patting them. It was the Egyptian's donkey which acted up.

Throwing up its head, the dun coloured beast let out a strident bray. Seemingly on the verge of drowsing, the lions roused themselves. One stood and looked the interlopers' way and the others carried on lying but watched intently. The standing one flicked its tail, and the amber, dark-pupilled eyes were so like the warrior's own.

The envoy began swearing at his donkey, his language original. He whacked it round the ears which flattened. The lions watched, all now standing.

It seemed Hosni never learned. He screeched, "I am Hosni Sulamain Al Sabrahim Pebekkanum, Chief of the Chamber to His Majesty… I shall endure no more! Accursed by all gods, rulers of the sky and earth, spawn of carrion-eating flies, unutterably vile ordure – "

"It's a donkey." Somehow Mikhail held a straight face as he reminded the Chief of the Chamber.

Zona kept her eyes on the lions which were lashing black-tipped tails but she joined in. "And if you don't stop beating it up, he's going to make you regret it. You should know that by now, and I know donkeys."

She'd hardly got the words out when the donkey thrust down its head and bucked. Hosni Sulamain Al Sabrahim Pebekkanum grabbed at its long ears. They slipped through his likely sweat-greased hands. Swearing a fresh torrent, the Chief of the Chamber slid over its black-tipped nose. Sitting on his rumpled robe, he shook a fist at it. Ears flattened, the donkey trotted up the valley, followed by more curses.

The warrior and Trojan officer cracked up, laughing. Even in their peril they couldn't help themselves. Looking outraged, the Egyptian scrambled to his feet, tripping on his robe and nearly falling. He went on shaking his fist and sending imprecations after the receding donkey. Then, abruptly, he seemed to think better of it.

Thin, dark features flushed, he turned on the lions. His narrow moustaches bristled as he waved his arms at the creatures and screamed curses. The beasts watched quietly until one opened his mouth and hissed.

The diplomat wasn't put off. Zona could see that he was too mad to be aware of any danger.

"It is you made that product of a cat and dog misbehave!" He balled a fist at the lions. "By-blows of a camel and horse! What makes you think you have a right even to breathe? The Sun God will strike you down so that not even dust remains. Your souls shall be lost forever in shadows – "

The lions watched, golden eyes intent, until one opened its mouth in a more businesslike way. Funny this might be but the warrior felt it was about to get more serious and dangerous. A low growling came from the lions like a swarm of irritated bees. Very slowly and carefully so as not to upset them further, she dismounted and reached behind her shoulder to draw her sword. She wasn't sure what she might do but, annoying though he was, she knew she couldn't let the big cats maul the Egyptian. Seeing her moves, Mikhail got down from his horse and drew his own blade equally stealthily. They began to move up, aiming to flank the man and protect him.

The envoy either didn't notice or care what they were about. While they were still a few paces to the rear of him, he started into a run.

Still howling curses on the lions' ancestors, he gathered up his robe and broke into a charge. With it flapping round his legs he was stumbling forward quickly. For a moment the beasts carried on watching but at any time they could leap. They were down in a crouch on the ledge, tails lashing. Cursing under her breath, the warrior ran after him, Mikhail at her side. *Those lions are gathering themselves for a leap, any time… Why in the Furies' names couldn't that – Egyptian have let them alone?* Too late…

Abruptly the lions seemed to change their mind. Perhaps they were put off, distracted by the flapping, screeching man. They must never have seen or heard anything like him before.

Whatever might be going on in their minds, one lion got up, turned and leaped off the ledge and out of sight. The others followed him. Braying in triumph, the envoy ran on. The warrior and Trojan captain stood with pained expressions.

"Looks like we've got a hero on our hands," he said.

The warrior cast her eyes skyward. She couldn't help smiling as well. "Shall we ever hear the last of this?"

CHAPTER FIFTEEN

✥

THE THREE TRAVELLERS carried on along the coast. Ahead hills and mountains grew steadily higher each day.

There came a day when the trio had camped for the night beside a pool near the foothills. When Zona woke the next morning birds were cheeping in the surrounding brush and trees. The sky was mottled blue and white-grey cloud, an already hot breeze coming out of the west. She thought the weather could go either way, hot and bright or heavy and grey. It didn't bother her that much. Often she'd ridden through rain and could again if it fell, and the land needed it. Also if the Arabs were still tracking and trying to get the Egyptian diplomat back, it would wash out any sign of them.

Not that they can't have him, she thought as she approached the water for a morning bathe. *If they ask nice.* The Egyptian hero was becoming something of a pain. *But when wasn't he?* She was beside the pool on a slightly sloping, gravelled beach. When she looked back, the place was screened by thorn and olive bushes. Anyhow, the two men were still out to the world. She didn't mind Mikhail. He didn't have any thoughts about her; the man was a fellow warrior, even if he did think her bathing was weird. But the Egyptian, another matter.

Sighing blissfully, Zona stretched, feeling her back pop softly in the warm morning. *I'm getting old.* This morning, she didn't strip. *Everything could use a cleaning; easiest way is while it's on me.* Soon she'd left her sword and dagger within easy reach on the shore, wading into chill water. Quickly it was at her thighs. Scooping water over herself, she began to shimmer. She didn't notice how the pool glistened in the early morning sunlight. Neither did she see its odd sparkle as her splashing around flipped droplets into the air… It was as if a presence or someone watched over her. A voice almost spoke in her mind, although she didn't hear its words, and surely it was imagination.

When she stood, water swirling and shining round her, the Egyptian was there. Slicking cold, heavy hair behind her shoulders, she twisted and squeezed it to drain out water and scowled. *Trust him, to sneak up without me hearing.* Because she was irritated, the warrior failed to see the way sun and water shone together, glossing her all over like the thinnest of rainbows. A smile tugging at her lips in spite of herself, she folded her arms. Sleep-mussed, he was close to appealing to look at.

His burst of foolhardy heroics with the lions hadn't changed or improved the man's disposition. In addition to looking sleep-bedraggled, he was showing the effects of their journey. It kept her annoyance in check a while longer.

His thin, dark face was stubbly. In spite of frequent shaving with a dagger, the man's black beard shadow grew in fast. It seemed his nose was more hooked, the thin moustaches longer and ragged. The robe he clung to showed signs of travel, was sweat-marked under the arms and round the back. With no slaves to feed him, he'd spilled his meals down the front. The warrior thought she could smell him, even at a good distance from where he stood at the edge of the pool... But maybe it was just that after she'd bathed and before she ate, her senses were sharpened. After all she was used to him.

"Why am I not surprised you're here like a slave?" he demanded.

Her sympathies for him were evaporating fast as she clenched her teeth and knotted her brow. She reminded herself this man could provoke her even before he spoke. She answered his question with two of her own.

"What are you doing here? Isn't this a little early for

you?"

"Hosni Sulamain Al – " The Egyptian drew himself up, clasping the front of his robe. She began to wade out of the water and he backed up, keeping step.

" – Yeah, yeah, all that," she broke in.

About to answer her, the envoy goggled and she frowned a second time.

Gulping like a fish dragged ashore, he discovered a thin voice. "Look at you!"

"What?" It came out as a bark but she glanced at herself.

Her eyes widened.

Over her shoulders, down her chest and arms she glowed with a glaze of colours swimming into each other. It glimmered in the droplets of water on her vest and kilt too. She raised her arm, turned it over and it seemed there were the tiniest of sparkles in a coating of silver on her skin.

The lines in her brow deepened. "What? – "

"It would appear, unlikely though it is to me," sniffed the Egyptian, "that great Ra Himself blesses you, even like a slave as you are."

"Oh don't be so stupid! That's the wildest idea I ever heard."

The warrior looked at her arm some more, turning it one way, then the other. The silver 'it', whatever it might be, was still there and she couldn't help wondering

Why me? was the question which kept scratching at her mind.

No answer broke from cover.

A few days later the travellers came to a bay. On three sides it was hemmed by precipitous cliff topped by forests. The last side was the open, restless sea and opposite a rough trail snaked down the cliff face. They'd been following the coastline because somewhere along it to the west lay the new city of Carthage. Zona and Mikhail had decided to stick with Hosni on his diplomatic mission. That way both hoped to pick up a clue where Aeneas had gone, if they weren't lucky enough to find him there. For the time being at least there seemed no better way to catch up to him.

It was late enough in the afternoon for the warrior and Trojan soldier to decide the place was a good campsite when their mounts went down to it. Hot, coppery sun from a deep blue sky laid a metallic trail through light across the sea. Gulls wheeled, cried and laughed. A brisk, hot wind blew some along with the salt scent of the waves. Gravelled, as well as beige sand with a few rocks, the beach was gently sloping and wide. It had a good broad area above high tide mark, rock pools like molten gold in sunlight and she thought there might be shellfish. There was also plenty of salt and weather-silvered driftwood for a fire and both horses and the donkey were tired.

"We'll stop here," she announced, swinging off her horse.

"Why?" asked the Egyptian with a characteristic sniff.

Mikhail looked annoyed and the warrior was irked herself. *This is so Hosni!* Anything to show the slave girl and slut, as he persisted in calling her, that he was her master. *As if!*

Then she looked at him more carefully. Not for the first time, she felt sympathy for him bloom.

In the heat, late in the afternoon, his robe was perspiration and travel-stained, bunched around his knees. In spite of all the riding they'd done, he sat upon his donkey awkwardly, his thin, dark face dusty, sweat streaked and lined, near-black eyes hooded. The guy looked exhausted. He didn't do this kind of stuff well, and while irritation gnawed, sympathy for him didn't leave her. Biting off the sharp retort which danced on the end of her tongue, she told him why this was a good place to stop.

She finished up with, "And I don't know about you but I'm bushed."

"Good enough," the Egyptian answered. He didn't even sniff. "You may proceed."

"Glad you agree." Swinging off his black, Mikhail was dry.

From one of the cliff faces a streamlet made a shallow runnel, flashing and shining with sunlight on its way to the sea. Off over the beach near the cliffs tough but sparse-looking grass sprouted. Followed by the donkey with the Egyptian diplomat still aboard, the horses made a line towards it. She listened to birds in the trees atop the cliff and sighed and stretched, smiling.

"Gonna bathe in the sea," she decided. "Mikhail, why don't you come too? Hosni can fix us a camp."

The envoy looked mutinous and her sympathy burned off like perspiration in a sea breeze. As she laid aside her sword and drew her vest off over her head, a scowl emerged from it. She was about to speak sharply when he beat her to it.

"That is slave work, suitable for you," he declared, climbing off his mount.

As she bent to pull off a boot, the warrior looked at her sword lying in the sand. *Any time now I'll beat the flat of it round his ass.*

She sighed. "We have this discussion every night; you've got to do your bit. You know this."

With a sniff, the Egyptian jerked his head at Mikhail. "Let him do it, slut."

Boy is he asking for it!

The Trojan's brow knitted as well. "I'll throw you in the sea, Hosni Sulamain Al Sabrahim and the rest." As the two men glowered at each other, he added, "Go on, Zona, bathe, though I shan't, and he *will* make camp."

She sighed again, pulling off the other boot and sliding from her kilt. Since the Egyptian was watching, she kept the last undergarment on, running lightly towards the sea. *Let them sort it out between themselves.* Reaching the waves slipping up and down shingle, she shivered in delight as she dipped a foot in icy water. Wading on until she was chest-deep, the warrior began to swim lazily.

Much refreshed, her skin gleaming with droplets of seawater, she pushed wet hair from her cheeks.

The harpies came.

Ragged shadows rushing on the beach, three of them flew from behind the cliff tops. As Zona ran over shingle, wincing at the prick of stones, a harsh shriek sounded. Stamping into her boots, she bent to draw her sword from its sheath in the sand with a hiss of steel and leather.

What in the gods' names now?

When she braced herself, she looked up as the harpies swooped.

They came fast and she only caught flashes. Mikhail had his sword gripped two-handed. The diplomat, who'd made progress with the camp, was boiling jerky over a fire. Seeing the creatures too, he ducked.

The assailants seemed about twice as long as a tall man and were too thin. The bird-things appeared to wear tattered robes streaming around them. Pale faces twisted and wizened like knots in oak trees, there was something crone-like about them. Black eyes drilled into the warrior, rooting her to the ground. The creatures' wings like the torn ones of crows flapped, then closed to speed the raptor dive. Scrawny hands reached out with clawed fingers bent for tearing their prey.

With them gusted a stench like sewers on a hot day. Globs of shining stuff which were dark greenish-brown shot out their mouths. Grimacing, the warrior couldn't help ducking. The missiles rained past her and splattered on the beach. The creatures let out glottal, ear-splitting screams.

Straitened, she held her sword two-fisted and waited. At any moment the harridans would reach

her. Mikhail was beside her, the Egyptian sheltering at their backs. Glancing around, she saw no trace of the mounts. *I wonder where they are. I can so get them seeking cover. I'd do it myself if I could.*

Features sand-pale, eyes black holes, the whole mask greedy, the lead monster came at her head. She stepped aside, feeling the swish of its passage. *I just bathed, gods it stinks!* Its feathers ruffled by its speed, she thought she saw insects crawl. Her sword whooshed, glittering in the light of the setting sun. At the same time her target swerved sharply. The strike missed its dirty torso, ruffling feathers and cloak. Pulling up, the bird-thing jinked, coming in on a new dive.

Out the corner of her eye she saw the other two things. Pursued by the Trojan captain, they were diving at the abandoned fire and supper. As they flew in, beaky mouths spat globs of slime. A few fizzled and smoked vilely in the flames. Others landed hissing in the water pot. *That's supper ruined. I know someone's not going to be pleased.*

With Mikhail she got before the fire, blocking it off from more dives. There weren't any. As the creatures wheeled and flew off, Hosni was shaking his fist, spouting curses.

"Oh shut up!" The warrior was out of patience. The meal wasn't going to be much, just the usual, but it would have come after her washing off. She sniffed her shoulder and wrinkled her face. Some of the muck had hit her and a chill cud was drying on her skin. Flicking it off, she got a whiff and wished she hadn't. "Tip it out and start again."

The Egyptian glared at her. "You shouldn't speak to me like that. I am – "

Mikhail cut across him. " – going to end up over my knee with the flat of my sword on your ass."

"Make some more," repeated Zona. At his expression she only just kept a straight face. "We're hungry and it's your turn to be cook."

There was a tense silence broken only by the soft swish of wavelets. A gull wheeled, shrieked and laughed over the sea and the envoy moved reluctantly. She couldn't help feeling sorry for him – yet again.

She pointed at the cliff behind which the sun was setting. Shadows reached across the beach, blacker than before. "There. It's an overhang which ought to shelter you if they come back. Build your new fire under it."

Hosni grumbled but mooched off along the beach to gather driftwood for a fresh cook fire. Whether it was at her, a half-naked woman daring to give him instructions or the orders themselves eluded her. He muttered under his breath and it was Arabic. She didn't have enough of the language but she made out 'daughter of a camel grunting in labour' and scowled. He wasn't the only one who had problems here… She shook her head. *One of these days, pal.*

Eventually with her and Mikhail's help, the diplomat had a fire going beneath the overhang. A sea breeze blew, wafting away the smoke. The flames burned cleanly and it was a good place, as she'd said. More jerky was dropped into the cooking pot. Stomach growling, she went to retrieve the rest of her clothes. She was looking forward to the meal.

Until the bird women came back.

CHAPTER SIXTEEN

✥

THE AERIAL PREDATORS dived at the fire.

They were stopped by the overhang of the cliff face but didn't wheel away till the last moment. As they did, beaky mouths opened. What appeared cuds of slime were spat right under the overhang. The thought flickered in Zona's mind. *They sure can shoot.* The fire sizzled and the smell didn't have words to describe it. Vest now forgotten – only her sword mattered here – she took up a stance to hit the attackers if they came in again. With the blade clasped two-handed, arms extended, she glanced to the fire under the cliff face. Her features were scrunched at the stink, eyes slits.

Once more Mikhail had taken up a position next to her. His own sword held at the ready, he was sweating heavily. His face, also twisted, was greenish, eyes desperate.

The Egyptian screeched, spewing a shower of curses but neither looked at him.

"I've never – " the warrior began over the noise.

Shaking his head, the Trojan was unable or

unwilling to speak.

Their attackers hadn't finished.

As if the stench wasn't already appalling enough, the creatures evaded the swords when the fighters lunged together. As Zona leaped after them, first one then the others in line, the wheeling came. Their butts pointed below the overhang and streams of brown-black filth shot out. The fire smoked and spat some more and the stench was ramped up. Some of it splashed into the cook pot. Hosni jumped up and down and shook his fists. *I'm glad I'm not cook this evening,* the warrior grinned to herself. *Payback for what he calls me!* Curses such as 'flea-ridden spawn of toads and dogs' rained from his lips. She had a momentary twinge of guilt for her thoughts. Reckless as he'd been against the lions, the envoy sprang from his refuge by the fire. Sweeping her sword in a roundhouse blow after a ragged tail, she nearly beheaded him.

The diplomat pummelled her with his fists and as the creatures above were circling she pushed him back. *I wish I had cut off his head!*

"Idiot slut!" he hissed. "See what you have done. Were you not in my way I would have punished – "

Mikhail was there. A bird-thing was diving at them. She saw the white face, the jagged yellow fence of its teeth. The eyes were glittering; she could smell its charnel-house breath. The Trojan's sword was about to take off its lower jaw but Hosni knocked it aside.

"Get of a snake!" he hissed. "You are in my way."

Mouth sagging, the Trojan officer looked at him. Face reddened, he tried to speak, moving his lips, but no words came.

"I don't believe this guy!" The warrior shook her head and brushed aside hair, "Hosni, you're in *our* way."

The Egyptian jumped up and down again. He pummelled at her with his fists but she held him at arm's length.

"You wish me, Hosni Sulamain Al Sabrahim – to do a slave's work…"

She was still holding him away and her lips quirked.

"…to fix your meal," he spluttered.

"And yours."

"Me, me! To fix meals for a tramp and a slut!"

"Don't call me that," she said with deceptive mildness.

The envoy missed her tone and the warning in it. He shook himself loose from her grip. His face was sweat and dirt-stained, and he stank as well. *Some of that filth musta gone on him.* His fists waving, she pushed him away once more.

Staring at her, the Egyptian's eyes bugged. She noticed her arm; a silver film was clinging to it…

The creature pulled out of its dive and spattered the three of them from its mouth. *Gods! How can anything smell like this? At least it's not from the other end. Gonna have to bathe all night, and I still won't get rid of this.* She and Mikhail ducked but struck at the thing, the soldier gagging, her stomach like a ship on rough seas. Their blades passed through a wing and its chest without marking the thing.

The other two had followed in the dive, firing as they levelled out. Some of the ordure splashed the cliff, the rest put out the fire, leaving noisome clouds of smoke. Zona and Mikhail threw themselves flat to avoid the mess. Even the Egyptian lay prone, arms over his head.

Leaping up, the warriors spun after the bird-things, swords flashing in lowering sunlight.

Until Mikhail stood gaping.

Zona glanced his way.

He clutched her shoulder. She could feel his fingers dig in, hot and trembling. With their fight against these strange monstrosities what else could be expected? Blood up, she was likely the same.

"What?" she asked. "Mikhail, we don't have time for this."

"Your flesh," he got out. "You are – "

"What about me?"

He released her but didn't answer. It was the envoy who spoke, still flat on the ground. "Look! You must be – "

"What?" she barked, unsettled by them.

But she was looking at herself and couldn't say any more. Her shoulders, chest, both arms, all over she was shining faint silver. She thought her skin had a barely noticeable shimmer as if slow currents of silver grains were moving over it. Just missing the end of her tongue she snapped her mouth shut.

"What in Hades is it?" she managed.

"We have seen this before," Hosni reminded her in a strangled voice. "It means you, slut though you may be, are beloved of the Sun God – "

" – I can't be."

Mikhail raised his arm, pointing. "The bird-despoilers, they're flying off."

Well, at last something's going right –

The Egyptian sounded awed. "It must be that they are afraid of you."

The warrior shook her head, wiped back hair almost dry from bathing. It flopped again, heavy and salty as she went to her sword's sheath by the sea and bent over. Finished sheathing the weapon, she picked up and pulled on her vest. She stepped into her kilt.

"I don't see how they can be," she said, coming back to the others.

If only she couldn't see the scarcely visible silver light flowing sluggishly on her arm. Unease twisted her insides and she felt cold droplets of sweat on her face, sliding down her. She was a warrior who didn't believe in magic-looking stuff. *Why me?* She shook her head. It was the pool and surely anyone who went in it could have got the same effect… If only she didn't feel that somehow it was meant for her alone, but it was crazy, imagining such things. She wasn't that special. Zona went on feeling the chill perspiration sheathing her all over, salt on her lips.

"Look!" Mikhail had the same near-reverent voice as the diplomat. He was pointing again. "One's flown up there."

The warrior felt her insides turn over slowly, and more perspiration was dripping off her, an icy skin.

At any moment she'd be ill – she couldn't be, not here and now! Panic twisted greasily. *What's coming now?*

- I just don't want it! She knew something was on

the way; one of the flying monsters had indeed stayed behind while the others fled. It was perched on a crag high over the bay. As the tattered wings spread out behind it, the blood-red eye of the sun balanced on the cliffs lit them like wet soot. The thing was about to speak to her, she knew it, but that was crazy. *This whole thing –*

The sound came, a glottal croak. She fancied she saw filth spew like a fine mist.

"I am Celeano, first among the Harpies. I would speak with the one among you known as Zona."

The warrior steeled herself. Although dry-mouthed and all the rest, she straightened her back and moved forward. At the same time the envoy said unnecessarily,

"Here she is."

A short, heavy silence followed, the air seeming to close in stiflingly on her. Until the harpy part spat, choked and grated some more. Zona only just managed not to pinch herself. *Surely I'm awake but this can't be happening. Birds don't talk, they just don't!*

"Warrior Zona, my reason for being here is to speak with you."

"That's why you have fouled and excreted in our supper, is it?" Hosni demanded. "Merely so you can speak to the slut who travels with us?"

The warrior waved Mikhail to silence, glowering at the Egyptian. "Let's hear this out."

More spitting and grating, with accompanying showers. "It is well that you do, for time is short."

"How so?" she asked.

"You have been anointed by the gods and you should already be in the city," choked the bird. "Listen to me well."

Fluffing its wings with a harsh whirring sound, the harpy resumed. "There is a queen in a new city – "

"I bet that's Carthage," the envoy said. "It is why I'm here."

"And soon won't be," muttered Mikhail in a low voice. "If you keep butting in."

"You are a fly which feeds on what my donkey leaves, less of a matter even," the Egyptian told him.

"Stop it you two!" the warrior snapped. "We need to hear this, remember?"

Celeano said, "The queen is in dire need of you, Warrior – "

"The slut?" the diplomat said disbelievingly.

"I'll run you through the gizzard if you call her that once more," Mikhail growled. "It's offensive, untrue and I've had enough; she is our comrade, has already saved us all from bandits."

"Yet she goes stripped as the commonest slut in all Egypt, carries weapons, presumes herself our equal!"

"And so she is – her warrior dress proclaims her freedom. If anything, she is more than equal."

Glaring at each other, the men were silent, sharing mental promises. He might be an envoy from the Egyptian court but sometimes Zona thought the slight, dark and moustached diplomat had a death wish. He could be so obnoxious and Mikhail would add up to more than two of him. Even without her own temper added to the mix it was surprising he'd not been flattened long ago.

The harpy grated into the silence. "Only the woman warrior can do this."

"But I am Hosni Sulamain Al Sabrahim Pebekkanum, Chief of the Chamber, Ambassador for His Highness – "

" – Yeah, yeah," broke in Zona and Mikhail together. "And did you mention 'Chief of the Chamber'? I forget with all that – "

"Chamber Pot," said the Trojan with relish.

The Egyptian scowled as their odd messenger went on. "You must hurry or the queen will be lost, and there is more."

"More? And how will she? – " It was Mikhail again.

"Precious one, favoured of the gods."

"You mean me." Hosni drew himself up, clasping his robe.

"No, it means her," rumbled Mikhail.

"How can this spewer of filth know such things?"

"I guess the gods work with what they've got," the warrior put in drily. "But you've a point; I'm not favoured by anyone."

"See?"

"You have a shine on your skin and clothes." Celeano ignored the Egyptian. "It was put there by

Aphrodite and Athena, and I must hurry on."

"Please do, sprayer of dung," jeered the diplomat.

Once more the harpy took no notice of him. "Even if the gift of the gods enables you to save the queen, there will be much grief. Hera demands satisfaction and though Aphrodite and her brother Ares the war god favoured Troy, she will have it. Don't forget she is Zeus' wife and powerful. The one who fled the blazing city like a thief with his haul may be at the new city when you get there. If not, he will have come and gone, sneaking off in darkness."

"Is this Carthage?" asked the Egyptian.

"Just so. As I have told you, he may have left his poison which Zona must draw and moved on. He is clever with words and will deceive many. There will be battle as a result of his wrongs and, Warrior Zona, you must be there to help the Cheated King."

Mikhail looked amazed and horrified at the same time. Even Hosni was silent a while. Shaking her head, the warrior stood, neck craned as she studied the bird-thing on its high crag. She had her arms folded as if protecting herself or trying to deny what the creature said. Yet one more silence wrapped the beach except for wind and sea, the wail of a gull. Mopping her sticky hair behind her shoulders, she wondered again, *Why me? Surely someone else, Mikhail for instance, could have been chosen for this.* But the harpy had spoken of gods, Aphrodite and Athena. *Those two together? Ares?* But gods? Who could ever account for how they worked? If they would only stay out of ordinary people's affairs. Life was tough enough for most men and women without immortals meddling. But she had the silvery shine… She'd been 'annointed'. It was no good wishing it had not happened and she firmed her jaw. Like it or not, she'd better do something with it. *I guess what they all want. At the start of this, all I wanted was to drift and get myself together. I don't need this, but the stuff Celeano's saying…* There was no getting out; it seemed she had to step forward, do what she could to minimise or avoid a lot of suffering. *As if I haven't dished out enough in my past.* She caught herself taking the step, still gazing upwards.

"One more thing." The voice from above was a rasping gurgle. "Another pursues and is drawing closer. Beware."

CHAPTER SEVENTEEN

✣

IN SPITE OF their vigilance against the one who pursued them, the trio made good time, beginning the day after the harpies.

That first day the travellers went inland from the bay and the wider sea. For some time no-one said much. It just seemed a good idea to put some distance between themselves and the place where the harpies were. Zona could find no reason for thinking so but she thought the bird-creatures were sea beings.

The first day of trekking westward the sun shone out of a cloudless sky. The heavens deep blue, with odd white gulls, there was a salt-laden sea breeze but it faded to puffs and the air grew rapidly hot. Each time she looked at herself, she found her skin shining. Of course it was perspiration – but what if it was something else too?

With nobody saying anything, she found she'd even have welcomed some Egyptian posturing, complaints about his long-suffering donkey. Mikhail was joining in the silent thing. She guessed the men were trying to come to terms with the bird monsters which shouldn't have existed or been able to fly, let alone speak. She was herself, and it wasn't easy. In her travels and fighting the warrior had seen some things... but this, with the faces of women? *If these guys hadn't seen them as well, I'd think it was this sun,* was an idea which kept surfacing. The creatures, she'd barely registered at the time, had stunk when they dived at Hosni's cooking. *A bit on my mind just then, like the message they came with?* Her mind worried at that like a cur with a bone trying to get the marrow. *OK, I'm a warrior who happens to be a woman, and we know what that's like in a male world.* It still didn't explain why she was picked, apparently by gods, no less, to shine like she was hot, and then some. As if that wasn't enough, there were Celeano's words, *and we're back there again... What are we going to do about them at Carthage? There's also this guy trailing us. So we've already decided to go after Aeneas,* and here her thoughts were circling some more. Why her?

The first day the trio kept riding late towards the setting sun. The harpies' message chasing at her heels, Zona was eager to cover a lot of ground.

After a brief lunch of jerky and sips of water, the weather had also clouded up, though it stayed hot. Though travelling stayed easy through broken hills and gullies with sparse grass and brush, they all carried on sweating, even the horses and donkey.

Slight relief only came when they stopped to camp during a shower of warm rain.

The next morning the wind had risen, blowing in gusts off the now-invisible sea, but the sky was clear with large, ship-like white and grey clouds. Although Zona and Mikhail didn't speak much, the Egyptian diplomat was back on form. Even so, once more they made good progress, climbing by midday into hilly country.

On the third day it was the same, although the weather served up grey skies and heavy air. Slouching comfortably in her saddle, the warrior asked herself, *Could this be North Africa's winter? Whatever.* She reached back, wiping perspiration from between her shoulder blades. *There has got to be rain or a thunderstorm soon.* It didn't happen. With her and Mikhail riding together and the Chief of the Chamber behind them, they wended upwards through rocky gullies and no water fell. *Perfect bandit country,* she kept thinking but, although she stayed watchful, there weren't any cutthroats.

What they ran into was a patrol from Carthage.

She was in the lead as the trio plodded along a rocky pass. Only a few hardy, spiky-looking bushes grew out of crevices in the rocks, some bigger than them, through which the travellers threaded a way. With the bottom of the pass littered by rock-falls, a few patches of sparse grass eked a life. Above, the sky was thickening, darkening, and the air was closer. Sweat chafed under Zona's vest and she caught herself yet again wiping back her hair to mop her brow. *It has to rain!* Progress through the blocks and piles of stone went on being slow; even the Egyptian stayed quiet. As the sticky heat and thunderous skies weighed on the trio, buzzards floated overhead, appearing to drift nearer. Nothing seemed likely to improve the warrior's mood and she had a tightening band of pain round her brow.

Up ahead the pass narrowed, bending away to the left out of sight. *If there are any bandits, if it was me, I'd lay a trap round here.* She swiftly debated her choices. *Go back, sneak up and over them?* The snag with that was if there weren't thieves, the travellers would waste a lot of time and effort… She winced at the pain in her head. *Celeano said we must hurry… What about sending Hosni forward as bait? No, I'd never hear the end of it.* At first it was nevertheless a tempting idea. If bandits didn't kill him and run when they saw her and Mikhail… *But he's such a pain in the ass.* A deep sigh followed this. *What's with me? I have to go and get scruples.* Reaching back, loosening her sword in its sheath, she rode slowly, even more watchfully.

Round the bend, seven men on desert horses

spread in a line blocked the pass.

The man in the centre indicated with an upraised hand that the travellers should stop.

Before anyone else could react, Hosni drummed his heels on his donkey's sides. Looking back reproachfully, the creature ambled to meet the riders. The man in the centre swung off his horse.

Like his fellows, the burly man was clean-shaven and wore a skull-shaped bronze helmet. Leather tunics, breeches and boots went with simple but well-made bronze breastplates. All the men had swords sheathed behind them, long daggers at their waists. At their saddles were fastened bows with quivers of arrows alongside. *Well-armed men, these.* If the soldiers were Carthaginians, the city appeared to have access to plentiful supplies of copper and tin, people able to make and work bronze, even if it hadn't been there long.

"I am Hosni Sulamain Al Sabrahim Pebekkanum." The envoy greeted the new arrivals with a sniff. "Chief of the Chamber to and Ambassador for His Majesty Pharaoh Ramses III, beloved of Amun, Ma'at and Ra, Powerful One of Egypt, Ruler of Heliolopolis."

"Who would ever guess?" asked Mikhail under his breath.

Zona rolled her eyes. "Yeah. Here we go."

The soldier who'd dismounted enquired of the Egyptian in a version of Phoenician, "What's all that supposed to mean?"

The envoy climbed off his donkey. Maybe it was because of the heat. More likely it was sick of the way he treated it. The animal reached for a mouthful of the back of his robe. Jumping forward as if an arrow had been shot at him, the man clutched at his butt. He still managed to retain his hauteur. *No doubt of it, that's impressive,* thought the warrior. *But oh oh, any time now.*

"I have told you," the ambassador declared in the same language. "I am on a mission from Pharaoh Ramses III to Queen Dido – "

"Far as I'm concerned," broke in the trooper, "you three are bandits. An unlikely looking bunch, I'll give you that, but we get a lot here, some even weirder and scruffier than you, pal. Now what do you say to that, whatever you say your name is? Would you like to know what we do to bandits?"

The little diplomat stepped aside from a fresh assault by his donkey. Perspiration-glossed and in his grubby robe, he drew himself up.

"You are the dust of the desert," he replied. "I would hasten to wipe you from the soles of my sandals. Spawn of an eagle and buzzard, it is you who are less

than filth."

Oh, that's done it. Not wanting swordplay or arrows flying around if she could stop it, the warrior vaulted from her saddle. Behind her Mikhail's saddle leather creaked as he too climbed down.

"You think so, huh?" The swarthy man who'd been insulted was scowling. "How about this then, you with the fancy name and the tongue of an asp? We are a patrol from Carthage sent out by Queen Alissar against the scum who infest these hills. That's folk like you."

There was a short, heavy silence. Zona heard birds singing in the brush nearby. One even flew out before returning to it, as if the bird knew something was coming down. A warm breeze gusted round her shoulders, her face and ruffled her hair, blowing strands across her eyes. She pushed it back. The sky had part cleared. Broad lakes of blue had opened among rafts of cloud and, though still hot, maybe the air was a little fresher. It was hard to believe, if she hadn't seen it before, that people could die any moment because of a careless word. *And Hosni calls himself a diplomat.* Keeping her hands well clear of her blades, she sighed – and here he was at it again.

"You are the leavings of a dung beetle." He sniffed noisily. "I, Hosni Sulamain Al Sabrahim Pebekkanum, do not listen to such maundering. If you are who you say that you are, where is your commission?"

"I am Captain Khaled of Her Majesty Queen Alissar of Carthage's army. You are my prisoners, bandits. Think yourselves lucky I don't execute you right now."

The ambassador stared at the captain and his men as if they'd been left by the beetle he'd spoken of. He sniffed again, then cleared his throat like he was freeing himself of them.

Any time he'll spit and then –

"When I have concluded the treaty my Pharaoh offers your Queen, lice, I shall take you and your ruffians back to Egypt in chains. In Heliopolis the Beloved of Ra shall judge you. If he is merciful, you will be boiled or burned alive. Before your ashes are scattered in the streets for beggars to tread and urinate upon."

"Hey Captain, we don't have to listen to this." One of the troopers drew his sword.

"Let's see... Boiled or burned, then pissed on," drawled the captain. "Not much of a choice... Nah, I don't think so."

Zona drew her own blade, though she didn't aim to use it, except in self-defence. With the gods' blessings this should be over soon with nobody hurt beyond sore heads. She ran lightly to meet the Carthaginian queen's men.

One was slightly ahead of the others. Trilling a war cry, she leaped. Her boots cracked his chin and he fell. Another kick took a soldier in his groin. The man choked and gurgled. His eyes goggled while his face went purple. Colour fled it as he turned dust-shaded and shiny with sweat. His knees unhinging, he sank, went on gurgling.

Jumping over him, the warrior moved among the others. An elbow in the ribs sent one reeling. She dropped her sword; it wasn't going to be needed. Catching them by helmet flaps, she rammed two heads together with a long, ringing clang. The men collapsed as she let them go. *Should leave two for Mikhail. He ought to be able to take them –*

"Stop!"

The order shouted in Captain Khaled's voice changed the surviving combatants into statues. Zona turned her head, looking behind herself. The officer gripped Hosni by his scruffy hair. At the Egyptian's throat a sword blade winked cheerily in the sun's light. She sighed. *Wouldn't you just know? Trust him!* That wasn't fair but her feelings were scrambled by the fight. Holding out her hands to show she'd no other weapon, she turned slowly to face the Carthaginian captain and his prisoner.

"What now?" she asked evenly.

"Stand still!" barked the captain. He jerked his head at Mikhail who was looking infuriated. "You too, drop your weapons."

She took her knives from their sheaths, bending to

draw one out of her boot. They fell in front of her, a blade clattering on a stone, giving off sparks.

"Come on Mikhail. You heard the man."

She was tempted to let the Carthaginian officer finish Hosni. Since she'd rescued the envoy from his bandit captors he'd been nothing but trouble. The same idea was in Mikhail's features but she couldn't quite do it or let him. The warrior wasn't the bloodthirsty chieftain she'd been; now scruples weighed on her.

Slowly, with clear reluctance, Mikhail undid his sword-belt and let it fall. His other weapons followed.

"OK, so what's next?" He repeated the warrior's question, grating it out.

The two men whose heads had been cracked together were carefully, wobblingly, getting up. They gripped each other's shoulders to do it. Holding himself, fat drops of perspiration rolling down his cheeks like tears, the man with the kicked privates was also on his feet. Although groggy, these guys were tough, she had to give them that.

"You are prisoners of the Carthaginian army," Khaled informed him. "You will be taken to Carthage for trial and execution."

"Your city has no army," sneered the Egyptian diplomat. "Our intelligence reveals you're all mercenaries."

"Unfortunately for you, that is not true," answered the captain stolidly. "Many in our army do fight for pay. Had you met them so rudely, you would all have been put straight to the sword, after their fun with the woman. But we are professionals."

"Sure is nice to know I'll be taken care of," Zona told him ironically. "And what's the fair trial for?"

"Silence!" he ordered.

She did as she was told but thought fast. If her memory was right, the Egyptian had said at one of the night campfires that most of the Carthaginian army were hired men. Various Arabs, others and Numidians. *Only the core of it – their light cavalry? – are professionals like these guys. Can I play on that; how loyal to Queen Alissar are they?* She had precious little to try. Yet it was her experience that real soldiers had an inbred sense of fairness. *I'll do just about all I can, whatever comes up, to tap into it.* She winced at herself. At best the thinking was feeble but right now there didn't seem much else. *Maybe I can play the helpless female. No, that's not gonna work. I am pretty much a warrior. I'm not the fluttering eyelashes type. I've already beat them up, and anyhow I don't want to give them ideas...*

For the time being there didn't seem to be anything to do but go quietly, watch and wait.

CHAPTER EIGHTEEN

✜

THE CARTHAGINIAN troopers were too good at what they did.

Zona tried appealing to them as one warrior to another, their sense of fairness. Maybe they hadn't got one because it didn't work. She was utterly unable to dent their stony masks that way. These were Punic troops, as good as or better than any she'd known. If the notion of a proper trial had any traction with them, none of the men showed it. From snippets she'd picked up listening to them, she couldn't blame them. Those bits spoken in pidgin Phoenician she understood over the days of the trek to Carthage were quite a lot. The area was thick with bandits. Only the troop's presence and the reputation of the city's army kept the thieves in hiding. That and the fact that they must have figured neither the soldiers nor their captives had anything worth stealing.

One evening she tried feminine wiles on the man at the campfire after the others had turned in. The watchman was unimpressed. Maybe it was because the Carthaginian captain had promised crucifixion to any man who let her or either of her companions escape. More likely it was that, warrior and ex-outlaw as she was, she never had wiles to start with or had lost them along the way. Although she tried, the warrior knew she was making a lack-lustre job of fluttering her lashes. Breathy sighs with a heaving chest were no more effective.

She might have gotten on better if the Egyptian diplomat hadn't queered her efforts. He was the one who kept trying to get away. When he was caught repeatedly she couldn't believe he was meant to be an envoy from his king. Attempting to bribe the captain of their escort, he'd nothing to do it with except promises the man didn't believe. Zona and Mikhail wondered too how it was he misjudged the apparently incorruptible officer. Maybe bribery worked in Egypt but not here.

After Hosni's bungled attempts to turn the captain the Carthaginians tightened up. The prisoners weren't allowed to talk to each other or any of the troopers. At all times they were kept tied and watched closely.

It was a grey, heavy and close afternoon when the party reached Carthage. Hands lashed behind her back, roped to her saddle, the warrior itched with trickles of perspiration she couldn't reach. The air was still and unmoving with not the faintest of breezes. Her head ached, she was hungry and thirsty because the last stop allowed by the captain was too long ago.

She knew the sea and the end of the journey had to be close. Salt was in the sticky air, feeling like it rimed her skin and hair, the only birds raucous seagulls. Soon the travellers' bonds would be exchanged for some sort of prison cell – if they were lucky. After that would be a kind of fake trial, followed by crucifixion. From what Khaled had said of Carthage's new form of execution, how you hung till you couldn't breathe, it wasn't something to be looked forward to. To finish it all, she'd still no clue what the charges against the companions were to be.

They were sweating along what had first been a canyon, then a long, winding valley out of the hills. Flies, stinging midges and hornets were around so that she and the mounts kept shaking their heads, the horses and donkey swishing tails. It seemed to be getting hotter, more stifling.

The escort took them round a bend they'd been approaching for some time. The ground rose ahead. They rode up it and gazed across a wide, cultivated plain at the city.

As the party drew rein, the cloud layer opened. Golden late afternoon sunlight stretched all over the plain and the city. The sun was going down behind the city and its shadows reached far across the plain where Zona saw farmers leaving their work to plod home. A lone gull wheeled and cried over beige towers before veering to fly away squawking. A high, thick wall encircled Carthage and was the same colour as the towers inside. The sun turned it all to amber except for the palace, temples and other public buildings in the inner, walled citadel. With pride glowing in his voice and eyes one of the men called it the Byrsa. These structures shone dazzlingly white and cream-coloured. It was as if they'd been constructed up there of salt, and beyond shone the deep blue sea.

"Carthage!" sighed the captain rapturously. "Has our queen not built with magic?"

"A city like any other." Hosni's voice was dismissive.

His comment earned him a slap round the head from one of the escort. Swaying on his donkey, his cheek swiftly reddening, he cried out. The warrior clenched her fists but could do nothing more – for now.

"Show some respect!" barked the soldier who'd struck him.

Raising a hand for another blow, the man was red-faced, sweating. From behind the travellers came a barely audible snicker.

The officer stepped in. "Leave it, Omar. We are near Carthage."

"So?" the man asked. "Sir?"

"Soon they will get justice."

Zona had heard remarks like that more than enough during the journey. Once more she didn't like it.

"Justice, huh? And exactly what is it we're supposed

to have done?"

"Charges to do with you being trespassers will be framed when we arrive," Khaled informed her. "I have told you this."

"'Framed', you say? I don't believe you have anything against us," Mikhail said to him.

The captain gave him, all the travellers, a haughty look but made no reply. Even the Egyptian was silent, restricting himself to a scowl. The weather was changing. A light cloud layer was crawling swiftly over the sky, black thunderheads massing in the west. Hot gusts of wind carried the salt and wash of the sea to the warrior and the birds were muted, knowing something was on the way. After the single wailing bird, there weren't even any gulls. It was hot and clammy again, seemingly a common thing in North Africa, at least in its winter. Later there might be a storm but more likely it would stay as it was – oppressive, forbidding. She blinked at the stinging salt of perspiration, licked more from her lips, and wished she could wipe it away elsewhere.

Holding their silence, the travellers and their escort crossed the agricultural plain to landward of Carthage. Slowly more impressive, the beige walls, presumably made of local stone, rose on up, looming. Towers were behind them, in the walls at regular intervals. A line of tall crosses outside followed the wall and the warrior pulled a face, thinking of crucifixion. On a few of the nearest were the dark shapes of skeletons, part-decayed bodies to which flaps of leathery skin clung. The smell of putrefaction came her way and crows sat over and near the remains.

Drawing nearer behind its walls on a hill was the glaring white of the Byrsa citadel, its towers and buildings. As the troopers and their captain shepherded the companions through the neat fields, olive groves and vineyards in which a few labourers or slaves still worked, their path angled west. They eventually rode in deepening shadow along the wall. Early after capturing the trio, Khaled had boasted that Queen Alissar had built all this in seven years. Zona was sceptical but couldn't help being impressed as well. So too were Mikhail and the Egyptian envoy, even if as reluctantly as her.

Clearing her throat, she broke the silence. "Where are you taking us, what's next?"

The captain smiled expansively, more relaxed now he was almost home. His white teeth shone under his helmet in his lean, swarthy face.

"We shall enter through the Utica gate, then turn right to the Byrsa." Grinning as he lifted his helmet to wipe more sweat, he said to the Egyptian, "Filth such as you may not see Queen Alissar but you will make the acquaintance of her jail, before we crucify you – "

Mikhail cut across him, " – What about this trial then?"

"Oh yes," drawled the captain. "The magistrates. A formality only. Then I shall spit on your remains!"

"Pharaoh Ramses III will punish you!" the envoy said hotly. "Your ashes will be scattered in the streets of Heliopolis, defiled by camels."

"We'll see."

A new silence wrapped itself around the group, sifted over them like some of the ashes the Carthaginians had been promised they would be. The Utica Gate was near; the wall towered against the grey sky. The warrior thought it was easily four men in height. Barred by two spear-carrying guards, the double gates of bronze-banded, studded black timber were open. They rose to nearly the top of the wall and a stream of donkeys, horses and rough-clad people carrying loads on their heads went in. The guards likely knew many of the farmers, their robed women and children in breechclouts. The soldiers allowed the people in, most likely going to their homes for the night. Except for the last wagon which was briefly searched, even a merchants' train was allowed through the gate.

It was different for Khaled and his prisoners. One of the guards stepped in front of the captain's mount, holding up a hand in a sign to stop.

"Captain, sorry about this," the bearded man started in a deep voice.

The officer's eyes flicked over the man, his uniform and weapons, his equally hirsute companion. Zona saw approval come and go on his features.

"Don't be, Rami," he said easily. "I'm pleased to see you doing your job well."

Looking grateful, though he swallowed, the guard saluted. In spite of her predicament, the warrior liked how Carthage's army looked. Even when she went against them, she'd found them well disciplined. To have built an army and city like these – supposedly in seven years – Alissar was clearly a person to be reckoned with.

"Uh, the prisoners?" the guard Rami asked.

"For the Byrsa cells," replied the captain. "Our magistrates will hear charges that may include trespass on our land, assault upon an officer and troopers of the Queen's forces. Probably they will bring more."

Zona was aware of the guards staring at her vest and kilt, loose hair and physique. *If I wasn't a big girl, I'd be embarrassed*

"This one?" The guard who'd previously spoken nodded at her, clearly appreciating her muscled limbs. "A warrior? But – "

"A dangerous one, and don't forget Queen Alissar's one too." The captain sounded proud. "It may not usually be a woman's path but can be."

Zona added calmly in the Punic tongue, "I'm Greek, these others are Trojan and Egyptian, and if you don't stop staring I'll cut your eyes out."

The guard flushed but waved them through the

gateway. "Go on in, Sir, and can I watch this one's execution?"

"If you're not on duty, yes," the officer said.

"You wish," the warrior said.

Zona wouldn't let them see she was rattled by repeated talk of her execution. A warrior never let an enemy see the burrs under her armour... Surely there would be some kind of a trial, at which she could speak. *Khaled kept on saying... Hosni seems to think the Carthaginians are civilized, worth dealing with. It's why he's come, for a treaty with them to put down Arab bandits.*

One of the troop pulled her off her horse, first cutting her bonds to the saddle. All the men were now on foot. Someone came and led the mounts away. As the group passed through the gateway, she saw stables built against the thick city wall. Lina disappeared with a soldier at her head and the warrior felt lonely, seeing her go.

The prisoners were escorted along a street of packed clay and some eighteen feet across into the city. It went between single story buildings also of clay but with gravel mixed in which the warrior guessed were dwellings. Bearded men of all ages and robed women thronged the streets. Children in ragged shirts or breechclouts watched the party from doorways or from behind their mothers. A gang of bold urchins kept pace for a while, hurling insults but the soldiers ignored them and they fell behind. There were questions from a few adults but no more notice was taken of these.

Their route went through market places and some streets with stalls. The aromas of herbs and spices mingled with those of fish, vegetables and refuse. Gulls wheeled, shrieked and mourned over the stalls, children and dogs ran about, getting underfoot and being shoved aside. Merchants' voices, others from the crowds of their customers were raised as most haggled over prices. As Zona and her companions were herded on, the ground rose steadily and the Byrsa citadel towered closer behind its walls. Over its central tower flew what she took to be the queen's banner. Merchants sold pottery, both artistic and useful, glassware, objects of tin, copper, bronze, silver and even gold and jewels. Though she'd never seen it before, there were stalls piled with what the warrior knew were carvings of creamy ivory. She'd heard Carthage was developing swiftly as a trading port but she'd never seen such richness and variety of things. The Trojan captain walked beside her trying not to stare and even Hosni looked impressed. Most of their guards were boasting about the city's accomplishments and she figured they'd good reason. She and Mikhail listened quietly, looked everywhere, hoping to learn something which might help them escape, but the Egyptian suddenly spat on the ground.

"Donkeys' udders could produce better!" he hissed.

Khaled's face darkened with annoyance. His sword rasped from its sheath. "You'll take that back."

"Eat your testicles!"

Yet again since she'd first rescued him Zona marvelled at the diplomat. She didn't believe in kissing butt but this… So the captain might be only a soldier, an inferior to the Egyptian, but he'd got the travellers hog-tied. *Just a little discretion? I don't even know Hosni's been told or remembers what that means.*

"Very well," the Carthaginian rasped. "You three will get your wish and meet the queen. She herself will condemn you. She will order the punishment you need, rather than magistrates who can do too little."

CHAPTER NINETEEN

✦

THE TRAVELLERS didn't spend long in the Byrsa dungeons. Soldiers took Zona out.

Their incarceration was less uncomfortable than it could have been. The cell into which the three were pushed wasn't large but it held them easily. It even had a rough wooden bed with a straw mattress. Zona would have guessed it held fleas, lice and other bugs but it didn't smell much except of mildew. The prison cell had glistening walls; although it wasn't damp, it was chilly. A slop bucket in the far corner from the bed had probably been emptied recently; the air was clear of flies and only mildly rank. The prisoners weren't chained or manacled. They had yellow light which threw shadows wavering on the walls from the guardroom where six men sat playing at dice. She'd taken note that the bearded soldiers were armoured in leather and had sheathed swords and daggers. Sharp-looking spears were racked beside the doorway. Although her reputation wasn't known and wouldn't put them on alert, the warrior thought the soldiers were unlikely to fall easily to tricks. Escape from here was not going to be easy.

The Trojan captain and the Egyptian diplomat sat on the bed while she paced the cell. Khaled had gone on with assuring his charges that bad things would happen to them. As he and his men brought them here, the Carthaginian officer had talked eagerly of tortures. If he had his way, the envoy would be first. The remarks about donkeys' udders and what the man should eat had stung him badly... Down a short corridor from the guardroom and their cell came a wash of heat, light flickering on the stone walls, low ceilings and floors. The torturers were getting ready. They would draw out confessions to whatever crimes the Carthaginians charged their victims with – before the trials and executions. *So maybe there's no point shackling or chaining us. We might as well be allowed to take it easy before they start in*

She tried looking at things more positively. *If only we could gag Hosni!* The snag was he saw everyone else as inferior to himself. Her lips quirked as she paced. *After all, I'm a slut. What was it he said for Khaled or one of his guys to do? Oh yeah, eat...*

Another turn at a wall and she strode back again.

Zona wheeled and did the four paces back. That was the trouble with long legs; there wasn't any more room. Whirling, she retraced her steps, turned and was crossing the space once more. Watched in silence except for the guards' voices, the rattles of the dice and the roar of the torturers' fire, she fell into a rhythm. Even the Egyptian stayed quiet. Maybe he and Mikhail were expecting her to come up with something but her mind was blank. Time passed. She went onto the floor to vary her routine and did press-ups, then sit-ups.

An argument broke out at the end of the guardroom which was out of sight. She might be a warrior but Zona's heart beat roughly at visions of what was on the way. Until she realised it came from the far end, not the corridor with the torturers and their fire. One of the voices was breaking as well. She gripped the barred window at the top of the cell door, listening. *Might we get out of this after all?* Both the men were off the bed and listening too.

"But I come from Sabblooton, the Queen's High Chancellor and Wizard himself," the youthful voice was insisting. "He says the matter is urgent, vital!"

"Well, you tell that Chancellor of yours," growled one of the guards at the entrance out of sight, "that they're Khaled's. The little one in particular has been most insulting. He's annoyed, is the captain, and he's the one we answer to. So it's the irons, racks, knives and hatchets, whatever they do down there, starting with the woman. Then, once they confess, it's crucifixion for this lot. The captain, he's gonna watch it himself."

"But only the Queen or sometimes a magistrate – "

The boy's voice rose and broke.

"There's ways round that, boy. Now you go on back and tell ol' Sab they're already with the Iron Men."

"But! – "

"Hey!" Zona tried to shake the cell door bars, grabbing her chance. "It's not true. We're still here."

"Take no notice of her," the guard said, "or I'll paddle your ass with the flat of my blade."

"But I *must* see her!" The messenger boy's voice was breaking again, nearer the cell. "The Queen herself commands it."

"If you're lying and it's just that idiot chancellor behind this – "

The messenger appeared outside the bars of the cell door. He was wiry, looked normally full of mischief, like the urchins she'd seen on the way to captivity, but serious now. He had a moustache and beard which were like sparse grass round his swarthy features. When he caught sight of Zona his eyes lit up, the worried expression melting off his face.

"That's her!" the boy explained. "My master Sabblooton told me a goddess had put light round her."

The guard's voice had moved off, mumbling incomprehensibly. She saw one of the group playing dice in the guardroom stand and approach the chancellor's messenger. The lad appeared frightened but held his ground.

"Come on then, whelp," grunted the big man. "Give me the message."

"It, uh, isn't a message. My master says the thing is of the utmost urgency!" Close to tears, the boy jabbed at the warrior with a finger. "She must come right now or all is lost, our building over the last seven years, everything. Carthage will be lost!"

"Nah, calm down, boy. We've got old 'God Aeneas' to take care of things. Why, any day now he'll be king."

"No! You don't understand, Aeneas is gone!"

It seemed these words hit everyone, even the boy himself, like a thunderbolt from Zeus. Zona closed her mouth on what she was about to say, was aware her comrades were there from the bed to flank her. She was bitterly disappointed, as well as surprised. She'd hunted Aeneas so long, had let herself believe he might be somewhere close. Even though she was a prisoner on the edge of torture and execution, *somehow our time of reckoning is near.* Now he'd slipped away again. She clenched the door's bars in frustration – *and what was it Celeano said?* This was likely why she was here –

Hosni spoke up. "It is me your Queen wants, not the slut."

As she glanced at him, Zona just about held back a grin. *Looks like he's forgotten the harpies.* The boy answered and the Egyptian scowled at his reply.

"Who are you?"

"I am Hosni Sulaimain Al Sabrahim Pebekkanum, Chief of the Chamber, Amassador from His Majesty Pharaoh Ramses III of All Egypt, Powerful One of Ma'at and Ra, Beloved Of Amun, Ruler Of Heliopolis."

"So?" The urchin looked puzzled.

Zona laughed, she couldn't help it. The envoy turned a glower on her that was meant to freeze her bones but made her chortle harder.

"Be silent. Know your place," he gritted.

"Know yours," she retorted. "It's me they want, not you."

"You are indeed the one we need," the messenger confirmed. "I was told to find the woman with amber, lion-like eyes."

The ambassador fumed but could say nothing more. *The boy's moved by magic, the gods or whatever, or so his boss would have it.* Zona started laughing once more, then stopped herself. *This is serious.*

All the dice-playing soldiers crowded up to the door. Their sergeant rubbed a bristly chin; it could hardly be called a beard but he pulled at the hairs. "You say that the queen wants her, and that fancy boy with the gold armour has disappeared?"

The boy swallowed, big apple bobbing in his thin neck. He'd a sheen of perspiration on his face. The warrior wondered that he'd brought no written note – until she recalled how things were. The men could likely not read, and this was a crisis situation. If they might have read there was probably no time to have written anything. *Which means - what?*

"I think you guys had better let me go to the queen," she said.

"If you think we're letting you wander round the palace," one of the troopers grunted. "Right Sarge?"

"We'd be joining the queen's eunuchs," agreed the sergeant. "If we got away with our hides on."

Swallowing again, the boy wrung his hands. "But she must come, every moment is vital. There is one more thing as well. Sabblooton says he thinks the woman with amber eyes is a warrior."

The sergeant laughed derisively. "That Chancellor thinks *he's* a warrior!"

Zona groaned to herself. *Not another like Hosni. There can't be two.* Aloud, she tried being helpful. "Why don't you guards escort me? And I'm unarmed."

"I must see Queen Dido," said the envoy.

"I'll stay here as a hostage," offered Mikhail. "That way they'll know you'll behave."

She looked at him gratefully and he dropped his eyes. She had an uneasy twinge, not for the first time. *Just what are his feelings?* She was almost, but not quite, sure they were no more than the loyalty of one comrade to another. *I know I've never done or said anything to encourage him... but what if?* She was bad for men; they tended to end up killed around her – and as for what the Trojan was offering... *I can't let him do it.*

The sergeant dealt with her problem. Pointing at the Egyptian, the man glowered, almost crossing his brows. "Not that little horse fly. He stays, you both do. Only she has been asked for and only Yellow-Eyes goes."

He gestured a man with a bunch of keys to the cell door. Zona let go the bars and stepped back while the soldier found the right key and opened the door. Mikhail and Hosni watched.

The Trojan spoke up, his voice plaintive. "You're going to leave me with Hosni Sulaimain Al Sabrahim Pebekkanum?"

Zona's lips quirked. "You'll live."

"Come on, Yellow-Eyes." The trooper with the keys motioned her out.

She came through the door with the swift fluidity of a cat. Before the man could react, she gripped his nose and twisted.

"The name is Zona, not 'Yellow-Eyes'."

Grunting the man swiped at her. His eyes watering, she knocked his fist aside.

"Zona, OK?"

"Let's go," ordered the sergeant harshly.

It still sounded as if he was trying not to laugh. A low snicker did come from one of his men.

With the sergeant and three of his men around her, Zona walked the length of the guardroom and went

up the prison corridor. It was cut from the rock of the citadel's foundations, the stone appearing to weep in the light of the torch one of them carried. The air was cool and smelled rank. At the far end she could hear the torturers' fire being blown higher with bellows, the sound of men's voices. *Well, at least I'm away from there if only for a while.* Repressing a shudder, she thought of the Egyptian and Mikhail. *How can I get them out, there's got to be a way.* As they passed a cell, a bleary-eyed man who could have been a drunk thrown in there to sober up gripped the door's bars and watched. Let out of the prison by another soldier with keys, their feet tramped as they followed a new corridor. The walls were still stone, unadorned except for occasional torches in brackets which gave off smoky light and their shadows. Underfoot the floor was earthen, packed and dry, although Zona could hear water drip somewhere out of sight. At first the tunnel went downwards, the chilly air smelling of earth and the torches, but soon it angled up. Nobody spoke; there was only the dripping, the sounds of marching feet and their trailing shadows. *It's like there's our ghosts with us –*

The party came to, opened and closed a thick wooden and studded door. The dark, heavy timber thudded ominously behind them.

Soon they were in more corridors, these likely giving off into living quarters, maybe for palace servants. A greater number of torches were throwing out brighter light and there were tapestries on the walls. Closed, polished doors were to right and left. *Yeah, I guess this ain't army barracks, swankiest I've ever seen if it is.* Finely dressed people passed but all held their eyes away and no-one spoke.

A large man in deep maroon and purple robes was there.

He was bald, torchlight glistening on his scalp, the triple jowls of his clean-shaven face. Dark, intelligent eyes looked out of folds of flesh. He had a hooked nose and the skin of his head and neck merged seamlessly. As he looked Zona and the guards over, a smile came and went on his rosebud mouth. It didn't reach his eyes.

"Ah, so you've brought her." His voice was deep and smooth but sounded worried. "Not what I'd expected but... light, amber eyes, yes, this is her."

The sergeant rasped, "Chancellor, Wizard Sabblooton, can she truly help you?"

"I can only hope but she is as in my vision."

"What of our queen?" the sergeant asked, sounding anxious. Zona realised that until then he'd been hiding it. "I've heard things. Will she see her?"

The fat man who smelled of some spice or other dry-washed his hands. Powder flew from them. "If only she will but – "

" – What's going on here?" cut in Zona. Folding her

arms, she waited.

Sabblooton went on, but to the sergeant, not her. "The queen has ordered a great fire built in the central courtyard, her favourite garden, you know. Nobody is allowed in there; she says she'll light it herself. It'll ruin her best fruit trees! As you know, ah, she has not been herself since Father Aeneas and the Trojan fleet left."

"I have heard of mood swings and threats," the sergeant answered soberly. "Now many of us in the army curse the day those people showed up and Queen Alissar sent out a hunt for them."

Zona's brain ran quickly and smoothly.

Dido ordered a fire lit; oh Gods, not a pyre! But there was Celeano, folk keep on that I shine... Aeneas and his folk likely ratted her out some way, maybe strung her along while using Carthage to re-supply themselves – to go where? She's been having mood swings, making threats. I don't like this. The gods alone knew what the threats were or who they were made against... *Aeneas? It would fit...* But right now the important thing was to hurry. *I'll take all this up with Aeneas when I catch up to him.*

She gripped the chancellor's plump shoulders. The guards moved to restrain her but she ignored them.

"Quick! Take me to that courtyard," she snapped.

"But - "

"What do you think you're doing?" the sergeant

demanded. He tried to pull her away but she shook him off.

"You're going to lose your Queen Dido. Now move!"

The men started spilling questions.

"Lose?"

"But what? – "

"What are you saying?"

The sergeant cut them off. "She says it's urgent, let's go!"

"Sarge – "

"Sabblooton here thinks we need her. If she's stringing us along, she can always be flogged later, before we hand her back to the torturers."

Hearing that, remembering the fire the torturers were stoking, Zona felt sweat all over her. She hoped the men didn't notice, that Mikhail and Hosni weren't already having the artists of pain attend to them. *If they are, I'm gonna get even, first with the torturers, then Aeneas because this is all his fault.*

They hurried along three more bends in the corridor which was increasingly plush. Stopping at a bronze-covered door, the warrior rapped on it. Although he'd wanted her there, from the look on his sweat-shiny face, Sabblooton was opening his mouth to object, but then closed it. No answer came from behind the door and Zona knocked again.

She could smell resin-laden smoke leaking round

the door, see a few grey tendrils. Flayed by urgency, she found herself sheathed in more perspiration. Every lost heartbeat could mean disaster. She tried the door. It wouldn't budge.

The warrior spun on Sabblooton. "Key!"

"I – "

"Now!"

The Chancellor dug in his robe, fumbled and came up with a bronze key. "These gardens are the queen's restful place where she comes - "

Zona thrust out a hand and he dropped the key into it. More smoke was visible and the smells of burning were stronger. He and the guards watched as she turned the key in the lock. The thing stuck and she threw her weight on it.

CHAPTER TWENTY

DEIPHOBOS heaved a sigh of relief.

After too long at sea the ship he'd stolen had lowered its sail and was rowing into port at the 'shining city.'

It had been far from a smooth trip. Not that he thought travel by sea often was but the prince was in no mood to be reasonable. Though still a bulky man, he'd lost weight during the voyage and his jowls were scruffy with beard. Like the rest of the ship's crew, his salt-stained, sweaty clothes hung on him limply. As far as possible, he tried not to think about the bath and slaves, the rest of his life, he'd lost at Troy. *Ah, Miriam, so I'd have had to torture you to death soon. You knew too much, but ah…*

If he was ready and able to appreciate his good fortune – which he wasn't – Deiphobos might have realised how the gods had favoured him. He not only found some men to work the ship and escape the burning city. One heavily bearded guy almost as big as himself knew about sailing. When they got through the enemy disguised as Greek troops and boarded the ship they found the fleet pulled up on the beach and untended. Everyone was at the killing, rapine and loot, the sack of Troy. Theo captained the ship. He whipped the crew into shape and the prince was smart enough to let him get on with it. Nothing mattered any more except escaping and catching up to Zona.

Everything was her fault.

Before she appeared and meddled he was a prince of Troy. He'd got all a man could want. Until she came and tore it all out of his hands. He never thought of how he'd plotted with Odysseus and slimy Thersites to bring the city down so he could possess Helen and be king himself. It was Zona who took it away, ruined his life and cast him adrift as an exile. She'd pay, *and it'll be exquisite, every moment.*

He scowled, heavy brows knitting. *It started right after I got out of Troy.* The sea was calm and sunlit, sparkling, from a blue sky as early morning fog and cloud broke up. A lovely day for sailing with a light, salty breeze, so Theo said, but Deiphobos couldn't enjoy it. Even before the Greek warships on the beach sank from view while the flame-ripped smoke of Troy rose in dark clouds, his belly rebelled. The meal he'd so carelessly eaten at the feasting and celebrations of the previous night came rushing up… The Greek plans and his own were in place. *It looked as if they were gone but I knew…Odysseus was up to something…* He shuddered as he recalled the start of his voyage.

First came that icy sweat, like after a special night's drinking and play. It made his clothes stick to him clammily. There was bile in his throat, flooding into his mouth. *Will I ever get used to it, knowing I'm gonna be sick? Such a stink, up your nose, and the taste, after it starts! It's enough to make a guy drink some more – if only it had been that – just to get rid of it.* He sighed heavily. *And then it comes again – more'n a few times.*

That morning Deiphobos had barely made it to the side of the ship, pushing two men roughly out his way. He leaned far out, so much so that he almost fell and one of the men he'd shoved had to grip his scruff. Blue, scarcely choppy waves heaved near his face. He could smell the salt of the water. One wavelet slapped brine into his mouth – which brought up food that heaved in lumps astern. He stared at it floating, and more followed. His eyes swam, his nose and mouth were full – and his belly went on shooting out food and bile. *I wondered if it would ever stop. Felt like I'd been stabbed in the gut and still it went on. All Zona's doing, she's hated me since we clapped eyes on each other!* It was like Deiphobos saw her face rippling in the sea. The Greek spy Mikrekros used to say he was obsessed by her. *Pity he's not here now so I could kill him a second time.*

At last, with the sun a great red ball trailing blood over the water, Deiphobos was empty. Sweating and hollowed out, he slumped on a bench. Even the thought of the food and wine he'd thieved with the ship made his insides churn. All that was left him was his hatred of Zona. *That's one more thing to be added to her account,* he went on reminding himself. When he caught up to her, she'd die slowly, not in a duel. *I'll build a rack, stretch her on it. Such wonderful tortures. A knife blade heated in a fire'll be tame. She'll be naked, of course.* About then he'd catch himself licking thick lips and drooling. *I'll savour each moment...* and he kept himself going by thinking things like that – in tight circles, round and around.

He'd been through a rough time since leaving Troy. His stomach was still fragile but it was getting better. When the sun's lip was eaten by the sea, he was even able to sleep.

Until the storm.

Wind racing over his slumped form woke him. He sat up blearily, rubbing crusted eyes and rain spattered out of a black sky, then fell in a cold wall. His belly was up and frisky – and gods, there was more in it. Deiphobos leaned once more over the side of the ship. Out of the night, a huge wave crashed into him. Only Theo's hand at his collar saved him from going overboard. For that and the earlier time in due course the captain and his crew would die. Nobody saw the prince in such a state and told of it.

Shaking his head like a wet dog, flinging droplets into the sheets of water that poured icily onto him, he blinked stinging salt out of his eyes. A fresh wave pounded the ship. Deiphobos coughed, spluttering, and another was there. Someone, several people, were shouting but in the shriek of wind, deluges of rain and roaring waves, the prince couldn't make out the words. Too full of his own woes, he didn't care anyhow.

Lightning walked across the sky, glaring through all that water. *I'm finished, I'll never get out of this!* Deiphobos cowered in the bottom of the galley, hands over his head, eyes squinched shut. A roll of thunder built, drumbeats stuttering, merging into a crash like the air would split. Someone was whimpering. *It's me,* he realised with acid shame, *and, yeah, these guys have to die!* When he dared look again, the ship was broadside on to mountainous rollers. A gigantic wave reared, hung over the boat and he grovelled in water sloshing around in the bottom of the hull. Men were babbling. *They're pleading with Poseidon,* and his voice was joining in. The wave thundered over them. Somehow it didn't sink the ship which lurched in it like a drunk thrown from a bar.

More lightning sizzled though curtains of rain; in its flare the sea was heaving like a giant cook stirring a soup. Even before darkness like Hades flapped back, thunder was a shattering blast.

With all the crew including the fugitive prince of Troy joining in, the ship's bow was dragged to face the storm. Wind howled, flinging rain, spray and monster waves at them. Lightning flashed, thunder rolled and boomed. Hours crept by like a man in quicksand trying to run through a nightmare. Deiphobos had never been so wet, cold and terrified in his life. He went beyond tired, just dragged at an oar or bailed water as he was told. Blisters rose on his hands from rowing. They burst and he barely noticed it happen.

Through it all his thoughts burned on in him. He was a prince, the Heir and ruler of Troy; no way should he be in this galley with rough men in deadly peril. *Yeah, Agamemnon and Odysseus crossed me, but... They snatched and ripped up my kingdom, but it was Zona's fault, damn her!* He forgot the wooden horse which brought them into the city. In any case, the state he was in, Deiphobos would have found a way to blame her for that. *I'll fix up something special for her, all right. I'll invent a torture, lots of them, just for her.* He used visions of her in his hands, naked, glistening with sweat, twisting, lurching and howling with agony. First he'd take his pleasures, at length and painfully. *I'll spoil her every way I can think of.* The pictures were something to cling to, drive him on through the night.

When light finally seeped from the eastern horizon the sea was still heaving. The prince was too wrung out to be thankful for the dawn. If he had been, he might have been grateful that at least he'd finished being sick. His eyes grainy, the inside of his mouth tasted like a troopers' privy. The sometime King of Troy ached everywhere but he was alive. In spite of it all, Theo and his crew had brought him through. *Zona didn't win this one.*

As the morning sullenly worked across the waves, they were gradually shrinking back to normal size. By the time a muggy, cloud-wracked day was in place, the prince and his crew didn't have to bail water so much. There was even time for a sip of wine and a share-out of jerky they'd found in the bottom of the ship. Soon smiles appeared on bearded, care-worn faces and tales began to be swopped of the men's bravery and escapes.

The break wasn't to last. A stiff wind blew up out of the west, making it impossible to use the sail. Groaning wearily, everyone, including Deiphobos when he was glowered at for just sitting, took up oars. As he rowed he told himself, *yeah, I'll make these men pay.*

If he thought he was tired before, he was wrong. This was exhaustion, and then some. His blistered fingers and palms hurt with every pull at his oar and his back was nearly locked with pain. He even had a headache. The prince had never guessed he'd got the muscles which howled all over him. He ached so much all he wanted to do was sit and cry. His butt felt like it was being rubbed to butcher's meat each time it shifted with rowing. The sips of wine he'd taken and the one mouthful of salt-soaked jerky a millennium ago weren't even memories. Deiphobos' mouth tasted as if a rat had sneaked in, been killed and was rotting in there. When a man yelled there was an island ahead he didn't take it in properly. His existence was the hot, cloudy sun, the cursed wind that kept the sail down, sweat sting in his eyes, and rowing. Those things and the pain. Once a shower fell violently and he scarcely noticed it.

The man yelled again, hoarsely. - *If he does that once more, I'll hit him with my oar.* "Land!"

"Pull harder!" ordered Theo. "I shouldn't be surprised if there are currents. We need to go in fast."

"What?" croaked Deiphobos unbelievingly.

"Pull, my prince, like your life depends on it!" roared Theo.

He's gotta go, maybe with Zona. Gritting his teeth, the Trojan prince found the strength to row harder with the other men. Sweat poured off him, he was certain his back creaked and popped with each oar-stroke. Yes, the captain sitting placidly at his steering oar would pay for this. *He'll die all right; I'll do him myself, love it.* The shattered bones and screams, there'd be blood and innards as well. *This is one more thing to be marked up to Zona!* ... His mind went on with the pictures of a few of the things he'd do to her. *I'll fill her so full she'll burst – with melted lead.*

The prince was so caught up in his visions, he only noticed the ship come ashore when its keel scraped gravel. Men jumped into a line of surf and he climbed stiffly after them.

Cold seawater shocked him all the way back, slopping into and over his boots, up his legs. He stumbled up a slippery beach of shifting pebbles. There was the sound of a snigger, though wisely no-one smiled. *Time I wrenched back command from Theo.*

"Right, you men," he barked. "Pull the ship up out of range of the tide. I shall go look for food and water, and we'll camp on this beach. Get to it."

The island on which the ship had made landfall was rocky, a mountain beyond the beach and scrubby growth. With a clearing sky, the air was hot and he went on sweating. Ahead past a gently sloping, shingled beach was a dry-looking valley that cut up the side of the mountain. Seagulls wheeled overhead quietly on spread wings. The only sounds were the hush of surf, the grunts and muffled curses of the men pulling up the ship. Flies and midges of the stinging type homed in on Deiphobos' perspiration. A hornet whined, zipping past his nose; he slapped at it and missed.

He glowered round the beach, empty except for his men and the ship. The sky burned, now deep blue and a lone gull drifted over him, its shadow flitting up the valley. With a grunt, he ducked a second hornet and began walking after the shadow.

The valley was V-shaped, soon rising steeply. The heat seemed worse, sticking his garments to him until they were ready to be wrung out. As he climbed, his temper frayed. The valley turned in a bend, another was a good distance up, and the climb was steeper. Gravel and stones were slippery underfoot and Deiphobos cursed steadily. As well as fat blue flies, midges kept pace and were still the biting kind; the prince swotted at them repeatedly and swore savagely. Hornets carried on swooping at him as well. *This is all Zona's fault. I'll get her for it, see if I don't.* Halting to mop his face, he just about kept his footing on the treacherous slope and glared around. Now the sides of the valley were mostly bare earth and rock, only a few scrubby olive bushes and wisps of dried grass clinging there. It snaked behind him and he was nearer the top than he expected. *That'll show the bitch.*

Almost toppling on more loose stones, the prince

struggled on up. *I wonder if I'll find anything worth this when I get to wherever I'm headed. Might as well find out, and I need to bring something back to put Theo in his place.* He'd told the men he'd discover food and water, and so he would. *I'm boss here and Zona's not gonna stop me.*

Reaching the bend, he paused to gasp for breath, mop sweat away and out of his eyes. His coarse hair was sodden and flopped back as he looked round some more. The valley went on steeply, inhospitably behind him. Another bend was above. On his right a little way up a fresh, wooded but narrower valley curved sharply to meet the one he was following. With the corners he'd rounded, the sea was no longer visible and everything looked barren and dry, even the trees to his right.

At a scuttering and clatter of falling stones, the Trojan ruler looked up and ahead. A brown, wiry goat with arcing horns was jumping up the valley on his left to vanish in brush. *Food, and Zona made me not see it until too late.* Lips peeled back in a snarl, Deiphobos climbed on.

He reached the top of the valley at last. To his left a crag leaned his way cutting off the sun a bit though his shadow was still black in front. Grateful for the rock's shade, he stopped to mop sweat and catch his breath. His pants had worked up the crack in his butt and he

pulled them out. Irritably, he slapped at and waved off insects. On his right woods crowded towards him, narrowing the way upwards.

The prince slogged on a little more to round the outcrop.

At what he saw she'd done next, he stopped, jaw hanging. Spit slid out his mouth and dripped onto his front and he didn't notice. His clouded brain shuffled around. *Where did she get this, how did she manage it?* Then he just stared, neck cricked back.

The guy had to be at least, likely more than, four times as tall as somebody like Hector, twice as broad. Since the crag had cut off their views of each other, the giant's mouth was dropping open too. The overhang had likely saved Deiphobos' hide but he was in no shape to appreciate that.

He went on looking up, and up. His mouth opened further, then closed and nearly sheared his tongue before falling apart once more. In the dry heat it seemed to creak but he couldn't say anything. All the sweat on him, sticking his garments to his skin, went cold. The prince's insides turned to hot liquid.

Details started to burn into his mind. The giant wore a ragged grey shirt, equally dirty and patched brown pants tied with a rope around his massive waist. His features, what could be seen, were tanned mahogany over a wild black beard, hair escaping and stringy under a shapeless hat. Pale, yellow-white eyes fastened to the intruder in his domain. When he closed his mouth, Deiphobos saw the ragged stumps of brown teeth. They were the length of a good dagger but that wasn't what turned the prince's legs to pillars of water. It was the massive club as thick as a warrior's thigh which the giant gripped in a knotted fist. The Trojan's heart thudded in his throat like a cavalry charge.

"Aaaaahhh," came from somebody. *Who's that?* he wondered. He didn't recognise the thin, reedy voice. "Aaaaaaahhh… "

Curse her, it was me! He was sweating, drenched with it, all over again.

"What are you doing on Cacus' land?" the huge man boomed. At the sound of him, three gulls flew up screaming in the hot, blue sky.

"C-C-Cacus?" the Trojan prince managed. *Yeah, that was me.* Everything had the too-clear, graven quality of nightmare. *If only I was dreaming this.* "B-b-but Hercules k-k-k-killed you… "

Cacus grinned, showing the horrible teeth. Deiphobos caught a gust of the giant's breath. *Oh gods, I can be sick again!* "I played dead, as you soon will be, little man. I think I'll roast you tonight. No-one steals my goats."

"B-b-but? – "

Club swishing back, the giant moved.

How can he be this fast? –

Deiphobos threw himself back and rolled. The tree branch crashed down, scattering rocks, chips of wood and stone. Deiphobos scooted back on his rear as the colossal man wound up for a fresh hit.

Bleating, scrambling to his feet, the prince ran.

CHAPTER TWENTY-ONE

❖

AENEAS leaned back on his seat at the stern of a Trojan ship.

It was part of the fleet he was leading up a broad river a peasant had called the Tiber. After a few minor difficulties mainly concerned with Carthage's Queen Dido, he was well pleased with how things were going. 'Godly Aeneas' was on the way to setting up his kingdom.

The problems he'd extracted himself from were all linked to the queen. He congratulated himself on getting out so easily.

At first Dido and her new city were just what he'd been looking for. After his 'visit to the Underworld' where he said he'd spoken to the goddess Aphrodite and his dead father Anchises, he returned in the morning to his folk. He told all about it, gave them the story he'd made up during the night, said great things were on the way. The gods planned a shining destiny for his Trojans and they couldn't fail, provided they followed him and did just as he said. There would be a new home for them in a distant land – ruled by him, of course.

When he'd finished addressing his people, they boarded the ships and sailed on. They didn't need to go far; round the next headland was Carthage.

He'd never hoped for anything like this. Even in a fever-dream.

The blue sky was only slightly less deep than the turquoise sea. The water was calm with not a ripple, even the always present gulls silent. The sun burned on the back of his neck but Aeneas didn't notice himself sweat, or smell its odour.

Across a wide bay was the city. Either this was a naturally occurring good place to build or the people had dug themselves two harbours. Both were shielded by a tower and packed with ships. Shading his eyes under a hand as he peered, Aeneas thought one fleet was of warships, sails furled and oars shipped. The other harbour contained gaily coloured vessels which were merchants. So this was a city with good trade links. *Perhaps I can find a way of taking it over for myself.* Eager, he licked his lips at the prize before him. It looked rich, domes, towers and buildings gleaming in hot sunlight. *So much easier than founding a place of my own.*

As his ship was rowed closer, a breeze wafted and fell away. Aeneas could smell sewage, like with any place where there were large numbers of folk in heat like this. There were also the scents of herbs, spices, a lot of other stuff. He picked out various animals, the smells of things cooking. Over the water had also come the voices of merchants bargaining, children, arguments, who could guess what else.

The ship was rowed still closer. Aeneas shouted out an order for the merchants' anchorage. *It's a good idea to keep away from the warships till I know more of this place.*

It was easy to guess where to make his start. The shining citadel which towered over the rest of the city would do just fine. Aeneas sighed happily. That was where the place's ruler was, the person to whom he'd put on the best show in arriving that he could. *Flags and stuff, and then some. I wish. If only I'd not been at sea quite so long.*

Even though the merchants' harbour was crowded, Aeneas' fleet discovered places to tie up. *Another sign I can use to show the gods are with me.* The docks were swarming with people from all known parts of the world. Black faces and torsos sweated along with brown and paler, even a few yellow. He guessed the black men were Nubians, though some were darker than any he'd seen before. All manner of clothing, some of it voluminous and brightly coloured, was there. People were loading and clearing ships, haggling for every kind of goods, including different fruits piled high on stalls. Every language Aeneas had heard in Troy before its siege merged into a babble of voices, and there were some which were new to him. Pickpockets, children and dogs were among the crowds, the latter sometimes cuffed on their heads or butts. Everywhere the smells of the market, the odours of herbs, spices, cooked meats, people and dogs were stronger. After disembarking, he stood a few long moments simply enjoying it all. It seemed forever since the great trading city of Troy had fallen. Aeneas felt sharp pangs of regret and homesickness bite in him, and was surprised to feel his eyes prickle.

With Dares, Achates and three other men he started walking, headed for the citadel. The rest he left behind with the ships which they were to keep an eye on. Some at a time, they could haggle in the market but were to stay out of trouble. When they left the docks the streets he walked through were wide, of packed clay with clay-built dwellings. More stalls and crowds thronged around the travellers, adding aromas to the heavy air. The sky had clouded over. It felt as if he walked through warm soup and no breeze moved. Yet it didn't rain. The wet season was some months away and thunder merely grumbled in the distance.

The city appeared well laid out; Aeneas thought it fell into four sectors. He followed the streets upwards, pushing through crowds. Gradually he passed more opulent dwellings, many of them set back from the roads with uniformed guards at the gates to extensive grounds. Towers and domes, some gilded, suggested temples, although he'd no idea what such a mixed population might worship. It didn't matter to Aeneas. *Maybe I can use some strong gods and goddesses to help take this place.* He drew nearer and the gleaming tower of the citadel reared higher over him. A strange flag hung limply against the murky sky and crows flapped heavily over thick, encircling walls. The street up to it had widened. He saw helmeted, uniformed sentries at the closed gate.

Steepening, the sharp hill up the final approach was set with marble steps to make the climb easier. Sweating, Aeneas and his men began to go up. He realised he was not as fit as he'd thought and time stretched out before they confronted the sentries.

Crossed spears barred the way. The swarthy, bearded guards had a strange language he'd never heard before.

Irritated, Aeneas turned to his men. "Anyone understand this?"

Dares answered. The man had evidently been to more places than Aeneas knew of; he wasn't just a killer. *I thought I knew all about him; it's a drag I didn't but I guess it's useful too.*

"Sir, it's Punic, a bastardised form of Phoenician," the huge man answered.

"Can you speak it?"

"A bit, Sir."

Aeneas bit his lip. He weighed the fact that he'd

need an interpreter, at least until he learned Punic. *I know a little Phoenician; maybe it won't take long. For now, though I'm going to look merely human, not 'God Aeneas.'* A long sigh. *It can't be helped. It'll look worse to my people if I can't understand enough to get around.*

"OK, Dares, tell him we want in." He pointed to the man on the right.

His burly interpreter came out with some words, only a few of which Aeneas picked up. Unfortunately while he didn't quite bunch his fists, Dares looked and sounded grim. In reply, the guards didn't look friendly, scowling. The man addressed grunted a reply and both spears stayed crossed over the entrance.

"What did he say?"

Dares turned his large, scruffy head. "In brief, Lord Aeneas, he said, 'Why should we?' and 'Who says so?'"

Aeneas took a deep breath, drawing on his patience, dredging up diplomatic skills. *Why does this have to be so hard?* In the heat, sweat was still plastering his clothes to him, a headache like a badly fitting helmet clamped on his forehead. He was thirsty, hungry and tired from the long walk up the hill. Polydamas would have done this well, maybe even knowing the language. Aeneas briefly regretted killing the other general in the fall of Troy. *Guess I'd no choice, though.*

"Tell him who I am, the titles people have given me on the trip here," he gritted.

The hulking man dropped into reverential mode, as much as he could with his gravelly voice. Aeneas heard his name in the rush of words, and waited for an answer.

It came at once, a stream from the guard. A second time Aeneas could only pick out words here and there and heard his own name afresh. *Maybe it's a good sign –*

"Well?" the Trojan leader asked.

"Uh, Lord Aeneas, do you want the word-for-word translation or just the main part? – "

Another flash of impatience. *Steady, this is not godly behaviour, and it'll get round the ships if I'm not careful.* "Come on, just give it to me."

"Uh, Sir, he said, 'My ass and your face, a perfect match,' and 'No way, shirt lifter.'"

"He said *what*?"

"Lord Aeneas, he said 'My ass and your face – '"

Looking thunderous, Aeneas was close to losing it and forced himself to think. *It's gotta be something good, show these peasants who's top dog.* The insults, everything else, boomed in his head. He needed time to come up with something, but it had to be now.

When he spoke his voice was calm. "Why is he being like this? What do we need to do for these people?"

Face congested, Dares spoke quickly and angrily. The guard stormed back, shaking his spear, and his companion moved silently to back him up. At length

Aeneas' massive trooper and the guard were silent.

"Well?" Aeneas still managed to use the mild tone.

"It's to do with his queen, Alissar's her name. Most people like him and me fight for various reasons. With me, I just like to kill. Oh yeah, loyalty, patriotism, standing with the guy next to you in a spear line. For him it's her, and only her. His pal here is the same. Nothing to do with collecting their pay; little though most soldiers get, that drives a lotta men. Neither is it protecting families, buddies, anything like that. It's all her, this Alissar."

"So what do we do? Fight? I'm not backing away."

All were silent, the two guards truculent and menacing, Aeneas and his men thinking hard. The Trojan didn't want to get into the citadel with slaughter and mayhem. If he and his men weren't killed or jailed, it might send the wrong message. It wouldn't do to let Dares or Achates off the leash… In any case at the thought of his own possible death, it sent a chill of panic rippling over him, deep into his bones and insides. The 'God Aeneas' couldn't end here at this gate before his plans had properly begun to develop. So pointlessly. But weren't all deaths this way? A man spent his life working, scheming and manoeuvring for top prizes – and then nothing! Ever again. Just nothing, no seeing, hearing, tasting, any of that. Just nothing, forever more, even for him. Once again he felt the clammy grasp of deepest fear; it wound around his guts and threatened to clog up his breath. This was something he couldn't duck and weave out of, no-one could – *and what in Hades has got me like this – now of all times?* He was the 'God Aeneas'. *This can't happen to me, other men, yes –*

A woman spoke from behind him. Aeneas felt his heart stutter, cold sweat bursting all over him. *What now?*

"What's going on here?" she asked in a light voice.

Aeneas was surprised she'd spoken in his own language, then pleased. *This could mean things'll be OK, my breakthrough at last. I'll see these soldiers punished. Fancy thinking they'd keep me out. She talked to me and my men, not the guards. I guess she heard me and Dares exchange words with them as she climbed up here. If she heard what they called me – yeah, they're for it!* He took a deep breath, feeling his heartbeat steady as he calmed himself and got set to begin talking.

Clearing the gateway, the guards snapped to attention.

"Queen Alissar," they barked. "We live to serve!"

"At ease, faithful warriors."

Aeneas and his men turned slowly to see the owner of the bewitching voice.

Yeah, play it right, I'm in!

She was of medium height, lean, almost rangy, with honey-coloured hair tied back from her face, held in place by wooden pins. Her clothes were a workman's shirt hacked off at the shoulders, a matching pair of worn brown pants and boots. The woman's face and muscled arms were tanned from the North African sun and winds. Grey eyes regarded the strangers thoughtfully, and a smile broke out that made the near-harsh lines of her face beautiful. Aeneas was entranced and reminded himself to go carefully. She was a means to an end, nothing more.

Alissar moved, holding out a hand. He took slim, warm fingers in a strong grip, and there were calluses on them and her palm. *What kind of ruler is this?* flashed through his mind. *She just might be harder to con than I thought.*

"Alissar, Queen of Carthage," she said in that voice.

For a moment Aeneas couldn't answer as his feelings lifted giddily. Then his mouth unlocked. *What in the name of the gods is happening here? Now to impress her, I hope.* "Aeneas, general of Troy. Some term me 'God', 'Godly' or 'Pious'. Simple folk, you know, but I guess I have brought them through some stuff."

She smiled again. It was dazzling, making her tired, dusty features light up as if from within.

Gods, what's with me? I don't need this!

"Well, God Aeneas, you and your mortal escort look tired. Care to come in for refreshment? I've been with our crew building the library, but now I must go to Apollo's temple. If you can wait while I pray and give thanks for good labour?"

Aeneas grinned back. *This is good, maybe I'll go with her, polish the god image.*

"Why don't I come as well? All the travelling we've done – "

"OK."

On hearing himself Aeneas winced. He sounded like a teenager on the point of getting his first girl in a barn loft. *I gotta take this steady, stay in control.* Yet he couldn't seem to help himself. She wasn't anything like what a queen should be, and her people, certainly the gate sentries, appeared to love her. The city of Carthage looked prosperous. *I've landed on my feet here. I bet I can do something with this. Yeah, looks as if I don't need to sail any further, this is it! All I need do is string her along, then get her out of the way when she's off guard.* That last bit had to happen, in spite of his corkscrewing feelings. He wasn't here to share power with anyone, not even her. *Yeah, enjoy her for a while, get everyone to trust me, then take her out.* Whatever went down, this was win and win all the way. At the very least, he'd use Carthage to give his folk a break from travelling. They needed to repair ships, renew supplies, drill fresh crews where necessary before moving on. *Should be a walk in the park if I play her right.*

"Yeah, let's go." He was smiling broadly.

She returned it, and put a hand on his arm. It was

so artless, unaffected, and he knew she'd fall to him. "We call this citadel the Byrsa."

"OK." Another smile wreathed his face, stretching his lips.

One of the sentries opened the heavy, bronze-clad gate they'd blocked. It swung easily on its hinges. Aeneas felt so good he thought maybe he'd let these men escape punishment. After all, they were just doing their job and it would create a good impression. He'd befriend them, a lot of people – at first.

He and Alissar passed into the Byrsa.

CHAPTER TWENTY-TWO

✥

ZONA threw the bronze-coated gate open, sent it crashing against the wall behind it. Even though she'd expected something like this, her lion's eyes widened at what she saw.

A moment later…

Because the place was full of smoke it took her that long to make out what was happening. Torches around the walls flared and sputtered with the draught from the door, adding their smoke to heaving clouds.

Open to the cloud-wreathed sky it looked to be a rectangular courtyard. Buildings, likely part of the palace, surrounded it and the warrior stood in the sole entrance. She could just about make out trees at either end, flowering bushes with them. In better light she'd probably have seen benches, a path for strolling through more flowers to the sounds of fountains and songbirds.

Any chance of doing that was stopped by the huge fire – *no, it's a pyre. Not hard to guess what's going down here.* The pile of branches, planks of wood and kindling nearly filled the garden. It was higher even than the surrounding buildings.

Crackling, spitting and hissing in a roar, flames were springing up the pile of brush and trash. A platform was balanced on top. Long, honey-coloured hair whipping around in the blasts of hot air, flames and smoke, a woman stood. Zona could see she looked annoyed, as if interrupted. *You ain't seen nothin' yet, sister,* zipped through the warrior's mind. The woman was holding a sword, gripped two-handed with its point resting on her chest. Abruptly, her features twisted, crumpled and shone with tears.

Zona ran a few steps into the garden. A yell burst from her throat. "Nooooo!"

She leaped at the side of the pyre, making it rock as she slammed into it. Coughing from billows of smoke, eyes streaming, she climbed fast. Zona went up like a mountain goat, digging fingers and boot toes into holds wherever she found them. The pyre thundered over her, flames licking its sides. More smoke coiled up in fresh updrafts. She went on, hacking and gasping for breath as she climbed faster. Whatever might be with the woman up there, *she doesn't deserve this.*

Near the top Zona whiplashed and cartwheeled to the platform. Hoping her aim was good, she kicked at the sword. *Got it!* She connected, the impact jerking through her boots. The sword flashed copper, bronze-red as it spun away and down the pyre. A scream of rage greeted her strike. She came upright. Seizing the woman by her shoulders, she held on, stopped her jumping after her blade.

"You don't really want to do that." Zona's voice was just audible over fire sounds.

"How do you know what I want?" the woman she'd saved raged.

Oh boy!

"Not too many folk want to gut themselves on top of a bonfire. Why don't you tell me about it?"

"You wouldn't understand! There's nothing to explain. Anyhow who are you?"

"Let's just say a girl from your dungeons," answered Zona drily. "And 'nothing to explain.' How many times have I heard that before? As for who I am – "

"You have no right here!"

"Well, I like it better than your torturers' attention."

A loud crack, splintering noises, were followed by a series of bangs. Flames and sparks rushed into the space around the two women facing off. The blonde who was lean in a diaphanous robe and greased with perspiration looked as if about to hit the warrior who shook her head slowly. *Queen or not, she better not try it. I'll punch her out.* The warrior who was as hot as the other looked stood with her fists on her hips. She flipped her hair back over copper-shiny shoulders with a toss of her head. As she did so, the platform tilted with a long creaking like an old, drunken man.

"Looks as if it's a good thing I am," Zona added.

"Can we take this somewhere else?"

"No!"

"Come on, hold my shoulders. I didn't risk my neck up here for nothing. I could have let your torturers take care of me. Oh, and I've two pals in your jail. One's an Egyptian diplomat come to see you, other's a Trojan army captain. You owe them too."

"I hate you!"

Why aren't I surprised?

"Yeah," Zona answered. "Hold onto me."

Scooping the queen – *She has to be, to be like this, and Celeano* – she ran a few steps and jumped off the heap of blazing trash and brush. Coughing, she fell through banners of fire and smoke. Her body jarred right up into her bones as her feet hit the ground. Its heat searing through her boots, skin stretched and dry, hair brittle, she ran.

At the entrance to the fire-filled garden, Chancellor-Wizard Sabblooton, the sergeant and his men waited. Still holding their queen, Zona barged through them and kept on. Swirling veils of acrid grey and white smoke gradually thinned. Behind them were the men shouting questions, gratitude and relief in their voices.

Stopping, she put the queen down. Sabblooton and the other men caught up. The fat man red and shiny-faced, jowls wobbling, they all went down on one knee before her.

I don't want this.

"Get up!" Zona couldn't help sounding exasperated.

"H-How can we, we thank you for saving – our beloved queen?" gasped Sabblooton.

"You did your bit with the magic – "

" – Your Majesty!" the sergeant breathed, his men echoing him.

Brushing two-handed at sweaty, draggled hair, the warrior rolled her eyes, then addressed the Chancellor-Wizard. "You can do something for me. The two men who came to Carthage with me? Turn them loose."

The queen was looking at Zona as if she was a low form of life, something she'd tread underfoot. A worm of unease slithered inside the warrior and she felt her skin turn cold all over. Dido had been on the point of suicide. By rescuing her, she might well have made an enemy. *Why can't I just stay outta this kind of stuff?* Yet she knew she could not have stayed away, and it was why Sabblooton had sprung her from jail. *Then there were those damn harpies… I just wanna keep away from gods an' goddesses, weird stuff.* The coldness went on, sinking inside her.

"All right," Dido said at length. "Release them and have them brought to my chambers. Now, all of you – go!"

She fixed Zona with a look from which icicles grew over the warrior. So short a time ago this queen was ready to give everything up and end her life. *Looks like she's forgetting that already. Oh, oh, I think.* Abruptly the warrior was conscious of her smoke-stained kilt and vest, her straggly hair.

"You," said the queen. "With me."

Maybe I should bend the knee to her, she is a queen. Rebellion came alive, and Zona was bridling at the woman's tone. She wasn't used to being ordered about by anyone, *and what happened to some thanks here?* When she'd headed up a band of cutthroats it was she who was boss, and people kneeled to her. *If I let them live.* She was tired and scratchy, first from coming into the city tied to her saddle, then the dungeons and her near meeting with torturers. After that came her rescue from suicide and flames of this ungrateful, volatile brat of a queen… *But maybe I oughta cut the woman some slack.* Both of them were laved with drying sweat, wild haired and streaked with soot. It was still hard to do. Zona reminded herself that her comrades were being freed and lowered her head. *Play it right, and maybe I'll get a bath from this as well.*

"Lead on, your majesty."

Dido gave her a searching look, as if she couldn't believe this acquiescence from the fierce-looking, black haired warrior. With a shrug she began walking and Zona came with her.

Soon they turned corners nearly doubling back on themselves like a snake. Zona thought the place would make good defensive positions. Some general had a sound hold on tactics when he built; the palace and Byrsa told the same tale. While the highest place in Carthage might be one of privilege for big guys, it would be easy to hold against any opponent.

A set of bronzed double doors was in front of them. *The real deal,* passed ironically through the warrior's mind. Dido practically had to lean on them to make them part. Zona resisted pushing too. *I don't think this queen would be pleased by having to be helped out.*

The doors opened to a long, high-vaulted hall. The floor was marble, two-foot diagonal triangles of black and white. The half-dozen-man tall walls were panelled to her own height in dark, polished timber. Above that were painted scenes of martial glory but also of everyday life. She recognised pictures of Achilles, Hector, Odysseus and the man she was hunting. Evidently her reluctant hostess knew of the battles for Troy. *And there ain't one pic of me.* The high, flat ceiling was exquisitely done with more artwork of gods and goddesses in Olympian surroundings and at play in pristine fields. *Whoever painted these must have spent an age lying back on scaffolding.* Running down the hall were three long tables of polished dark wood with matching benches. The hall was a bustle of activity as servants worked to lay out plates of fine china, cutlery of silver and gold with crystal wine glasses. *Some kind of banquet's on the way. Gotta hunch I and Mikhail won't be there. Hosni might get in though.* Down the right-hand wall were three huge fire pits ready to go when it started.

At the end of the hall they climbed three steps to a dais that went as far back as the main chamber was wide. Another long, dark table with high-backed chairs crossed it. The walls and ceiling of this annex were painted with more figures of gods and goddesses. Here too servants were preparing the High Table, though they looked to have nearly finished.

The queen opened an inconspicuous door at the back in shadows behind the table. They passed into a room which looked a place to relax. Although the walls were painted as well, the ceiling was lower and plain. Here were chairs and well-placed side tables. Dido threw herself into one of the chairs, sprawling in it while Zona stood by the door.

"Oh, sit down," the queen snapped.

The blonde woman looked hot, dirty from the fire, and sulky. Zona crossed to a chair opposite her and sat.

She gave vent to her damned-up feelings. "You have got to be crazy!"

"I beg your pardon?" That came icily.

"All this!" The warrior turned in her seat, indicating the hall, sweeping out her arm.

"My choice." The queen gnawed at her knuckles.

"Crazy!" the warrior repeated. "And the way I heard

it, you built this whole city. What is wrong with you?"

There was a long pause in which the air seemed to vibrate with tension. At length the answer came through clenched teeth.

"Aeneas."

"Might have guessed *he* was involved."

Dido looked at her, grey eyes like stones. "What's that supposed to mean?"

Getting up, moving around while she gathered words, Zona sympathised. As soon as Aeneas' name was spoken she'd felt her emotions change. Shaking her head, she flipped back sweaty tresses of hair, paced some more, then halted.

She faced the other woman, planting her hands on her hips, fixing her with a 'look' of her own. *Xan used to say I did specials. I reckon I could do with some now.* She stilled the pain that turned in her at thoughts of her lost friend.

"Only that I'm looking for him; he and I have some stuff to settle," she said. "And I bet he told you, reluctantly of course – "

"You leave him alone!" Then Dido gave a fleeting smile. It was there and gone like the sun peeking in and out of clouds. "How did you guess that?"

"Uh huh," murmured Zona. "And I know him."

She drew a breath, vest straining at the front. *Better get this over with. Hope she doesn't give me back to her torturers.* "Listen. At Troy he ratted out Troilus."

"That's not true! He tried to save him."

Zona came back to sit in her chair facing the queen. As the woman looked about to surge at her, she said gently. "I was there, Alissar, I saw it. Aeneas wanted the Heirship for himself. You should have seen him in King Priam's throne room. He and his pal just about held back from killing the old man... Listen, will you? Aeneas did nothing when Achilles did Troilus, just a boy; the kid didn't have a chance, but Priam had made him Heir. Go figure. Aeneas is clever, and that's one of the things I have to go over with him. I bet he spun you a web of stuff about being a hero at the fall of Troy."

"He carried his aged father Anchises out on his back. He looked for his lost wife Creusa everywhere. Then he had to save what people he could – "

" – Yeah, I just bet. Listen to me. He killed his father and wife, and where was his pal Polydamas? He murdered him too, and they were nearly joined at the hip. I'd believe anything of that man."

"That's not true!" Dido flared, but with less conviction.

"Well, I've no way of proving any of it – yet." Zona leaned forward, hands on her knees. She fixed the queen with an earnest look. "But I'll get the proof, you'll see. He's up to something here, and I bet you fitted right in with his plans – whatever they are."

Collapsing back in her chair, Dido made a disgusted

sound in the back of her throat. From the look on her features it was at herself. She spoke in a low voice the warrior almost didn't catch. "I was such an idiot – I was in love with him."

Everything was made clear, all that had occurred. Zona reached over and squeezed the queen's fingers with her own, then let them go. Her heart contracted in sympathy. *Boy, have I got some catching up to do with him!*

"Uh huh." She sighed, then her voice was steely. "One more thing I need to go over with him about."

"Why should you care?" Dido sounded dispirited. She passed her hand wearily across her face, then bowed her head. "We threw you in jail. You said about torturers."

Another sigh pulled at Zona's vest. Her tone was ironic but hard. "Let's say it's my quaint idea of justice. You were going to kill yourself because of this guy, right?"

The other nodded but didn't reply, looking shame-faced. A silence fell like cold dust sifting through the air. The warrior decided it was time she took control, shifted the talk onto different trails. *If I don't hurry and grip this thing, who can guess what she'll do? I like her, abrasive though she can be, and that's Aeneas' fault. She's like bronze-making, hot copper and tin running every which-way.* Although Zona thought the queen was normally a strong person, she didn't like the idea of being a nursemaid. *Xan might have done it but me, uh uh.*

"So what do you want to do next?" she asked, and added, "I'll help, whatever it is."

She shook her head, as much at herself as anything else. *What did I just let myself in for? But I can't stand back from this, and what has Xan done to me?* "But there's one thing I won't do. If you try to throw yourself away again, look for me in the way."

Dido smiled. "I think I just about get that."

She paused, then went on, "We're doing a banquet for one of the Libyan kings, Iarbas. As for that unspeakable – he up and left me! Sneaked away with his fleet at night. I bet he was planning it all along, re-supplying his ships and everything. Aeneas, you, you – I'd like to get an army together and go after you – wherever, however long it takes."

Zona grinned fiercely. *This is more like it, the kinda stuff I do.* "Let's do this. What about Iarbas, you called him? Will he help?"

Dido looked thoughtful and the warrior felt more hopeful. *She's starting to think like a queen.*

"I never wanted to marry him, though it's what he wants. I'll never marry again, not after Sycheas, but I've kept him aboard."

"Strung him along, huh. Nice bit of statecraft."

The queen went on with reflective. "It was one bunch of Arabs I didn't have to suppress. Yes… He might be interested. Especially if we agree that any plunder he takes stays his. Yes, he might."

"Good, already we're making progress. Uh, I hesitate to say this, but one of the guys I came here with. Hosni this and that. He's an Egyptian diplomat…" Zona stroked her chin. "He's nearly driven me crazy, unless he's a better diplomat than I think."

"I don't think much of Egypt, haven't had a lot to do with them," the queen told her slowly. "I don't know… but maybe. And I'll try anything."

"Spoken like a fighter."

Dido grinned mirthlessly. "You don't want to get on the wrong side of me."

The warrior still decided she'd watch every move the woman made. *This is one unstable person, unless my arrow misses its mark.*

Her own survival, that of her comrades, might depend on how she could ride Dido's moods.

CHAPTER TWENTY-THREE

✛

DIDO'S BANQUET for Iarbas was under way. The heat in the crowed hall was fiery.

Zona almost didn't feel like herself because she wore a long, forest-green dress. It was thread-strapped, leaving her shoulders, chest and arms bare, and she was grateful for that. The glossy thing was also cut so low she only just stayed in it. *Thank the gods I'm not like a lot of the other women, covered in this heat.* Held up only by the thin silken ties, the dress's sole adornment was a triangular cluster of silver flowers just below the plunging neckline. She had on no jewellery though her hair had been teased into shining curls by servants with hot tongs. In the oppressive hall which was loud with voices and eating, smells of roasted food, incense and torches, it was a thoroughly practical dress for which she mentally thanked Dido. *I reckon the hair's already coming out of its curls though.*

The warrior was cauled in perspiration, as was Dido to her left in jewel-encrusted royal purple. With her dark hair, bronzed skin and build, Zona was magnificent in her borrowed dress. *I'm good with*

this, even if it is odd, she told herself yet again. The queen had put on a gracious face with her finery, was charming and witty to Iarbas seated on her left. Nothing hinted at her emotions. After a long, hard day the warrior matched her in too many glasses of excellent wine. Everything, helped on by strolling minstrels, roared and swam together.

Otherwise Deiphobos would never have gotten close.

Surely nothing can go wrong here, and Alissar's chatting that Arab up well. Politics!... It's OK to have fun. Hosni and Sabblooton were on her right, eating and drinking, trading stories and jokes. Maybe the little Egyptian in his maroon robes was a better diplomat than she'd guessed.

Another visitor being fêted was the slight, lithe Camilla with her Volscian horsemen. At the right time Zona aimed to bring the short, black-haired rider and the laughing queen together. Dido needed someone to anchor her, and the tawny-skinned Volscian in her silver and grey might be just the person. Where the queen kept switching from one mood to another and back, the rider seemed more placid, good-natured, humorous and even tempered. *Better than me for stuff like this anyhow. Another thing too...* Zona wasn't sure how she was going to tie him down when she caught up to Aeneas but the cavalry could be useful. *For now, though, I'll play it as the dice fall, enjoy the company, food and wine.*

Taking a chance because the banquet was unexpected fun, she leaned in to Dido. Catching the woman's thyme perfume, she sniffed appreciatively. *And if I'm not careful this great lady thing could grow on me.*

"So what's your story?" she asked. "How come you built all this? The painted hall and the rest..."

The queen looked at her and arched an eyebrow. "How do you know I built anything?"

"This guy named Khaled and his boys who took us, the guards at the dungeons, let's say they bragged about it. Way I heard it, you practically built Carthage with your own hands. So how come?"

"You don't want to know all that." It came with a bleak expression.

"Alissar, if I didn't want to know, I wouldn't have asked."

The queen looked at Zona as if trying to see inside her. They were enclosed in their own silence, like a bubble sealing them off from the sounds of the banquet.

"Well, do you want to talk?" asked the warrior, disliking the defensive tone which seeped into her voice. *And do I really wanna hear this? Something tells me it's gonna be bad.*

There was a new, longer silence, that sensation of being on their own some more. Finally Dido broke it.

Her face was torn with bad memories. "OK, you keep asking, so here we go. Though what you think will be achieved by this, I don't know."

"Sometimes it just helps to talk." *Is this really me, not Xan?*

"Yes, well, where to start." A grin came and went. "I guess the beginning's as good a place as any, that's what I bet you'll say."

"So? Stop messing with this, Alissar."

The queen gave her a part hostile look, an equal share of sulkiness, until she relented. "Seeing as how you made me go on living, I suppose you can hear this."

Zona waited, elbows on the table, chin cupped in her hands.

Dido spoke reluctantly in a low voice. As she did so, she kept worrying at her hair, loosening it from its diamond-studded band.

"I grew up in the city of Tyre west of here. Some term us Phoenicians, others Tyrians. King Matten was my father."

"But what about you?"

"It doesn't matter. We're all Carthaginians now and we speak Punic, an offshoot of basic Phoenician. My childhood was a normal princess's."

Zona smiled at the irony, liking it and her companion.

The queen went on, looking rueful. "My brother,

it's all because of him, Pygmalion."

"What did he do?"

"What didn't he do? He was always greedy, right from when we were small. The best sweets were always his. He had to climb highest in the trees. Our parents tried to hold the ring but some of the things he did when neither was around. Let's just say Pygmalion was spiteful."

Dido stopped, looking guilty and dismayed. She worried at her hair and Zona reached out to gently stay her hands.

"Little brothers can be like that," she observed. *I ought to know, mine was bad enough. Still, he grew out of it - before he was killed. I miss him so!*

"He wasn't my little brother, he was my elder. Anyhow, when we were eighteen and seventeen our father died after a hunting accident. A wound in his leg that went bad. Mom couldn't take the loss, so the doctors said. There was nothing they could do and she followed him to Tartarus. Pygmalion and I became joint rulers of Tyre. Now I'm not so sure he didn't have something to do with Mom's…"

Halting as if for breath, the queen went for her hair once more. Zona stopped her.

"Thanks." Dido bit out the word. She looked round the increasingly lively banqueting hall. "Where was I?"

"Telling me about when you were growing up." The warrior hooked a shoulder strap back from where it had slid down her arm. She was a little too big for this dress the queen had loaned her so it was odd it wasn't tighter. *What the hell? Me an' dresses just don't get along, I guess. Better keep her off her mother awhile, if I could figure out how. Xan always did this kind of stuff so much better.*

"So what happened next?"

The Carthaginian monarch drained her golden goblet of wine. At once a servant was there, refilling it.

"You don't really want to hear all of this; a real weepie of a story."

"If I'm to help, I think I need it all."

"Why should you – help? We threw you in jail."

"Your guys, that Khaled, were keen on their work." Zona shrugged. The strap slid down again and she pulled it back up. She nodded her head in the direction of Hosni. "I guess he upset them. Told 'em to eat their nuts or something. So, Alissar, I'd like to help, if you'll let me, and I've a stake in this too, remember."

Dido shook her head, as if not able to believe her.

"Come on, give." The warrior smiled encouragingly. "What's the rest?"

"Well… Pygmalion didn't change, not on the inside, but he got smoother, better hiding what he was at. When our mother's body was given back to the gods, he and I inherited Tyre as joint rulers – have I already said that? I married Sycheas, as he was High Priest. He was older than me and I didn't love him, but I guess it creeps up when you're not looking out for it." The queen firmed her voice, quickly looking away, then back to the warrior. "Yes, that changed; he was so kind, and devoted to me. Nothing was too much trouble for him. So in time I loved him."

A sigh hit Zona. *Why couldn't I have met somebody like that, instead of low-lifes such as Maron. I reckon the gods aren't fair, but who can tell about god types?*

"Yes, he won me to him, and it was politically sensible. Our marriage joined Crown, half of it anyhow, with religion." Dido shook her head, maybe at herself. "He was a good man, too good for me. Together we took on the child sacrifice customs of Ba'al."

"You wanted to wipe 'em out?"

Looking distracted, grief-torn, Dido worked on her hair again.

Zona smiled. "That's gonna look like birds have been fighting."

"What? Oh yeah. Doesn't matter, though, what does?"

"What happened to Sychcas, your brother?"

"Yes, Pygmalion," confirmed the queen savagely. "One of these days… Oh, who am I fooling? For a while we were happy, till my husband vanished. I really will never marry again – but that was what I convinced myself of before that rat Aeneas. I was ready to give him everything. And now look at me!"

Seeing the queen's face ready to crumple, the

warrior thought some more. *Maybe it's OK I never did meet a guy to steal my heart. What's the point? It turns people into mush. This woman nearly killed herself over it. Yeah, I'm glad I stayed focussed.* She waited for Dido to get herself under control and go on. She gazed at the sea of cheerful, flushed faces in the hall around and below her. She met the eye of the grey-clad Camilla seated and laughing among her men. *They seem a pretty tight bunch. I wonder whether I can do anything with them.* The next day she'd see – when she'd slept on it and had a clearer head. *There's the rest of Alissar's story too.*

The queen broke their short, grim silence, rasping, "Pygmalion! To think he's my brother. He murdered Sycheas, or had it done. For a while he managed to hide it from me when I kept asking. Told me Sycheas was off on a hunting trip after lions. I, ah, guess I wanted to believe it, think he was all right. How could I have been such a fool?"

Zona thought once again of the times she'd known men. They tended not to do very well around her, to end up dead, like Maron whom she killed at Troy. *I reckon he did ask for it, though.* She shuddered at the memory of a young girl raped by the bandit chieftain. *But even him... It seems a man can make a woman think anything.*

"It happens." She laid a hand over the other woman's. "When you're in love the way you were, you always want to believe the best."

Dido worked at her hair some more. Tendrils of her carefully arranged style were beginning to pull loose. "I should have guessed. I knew what Pygmalion was like. Listen, Sycheas didn't show up but after several days the temple began to smell. My brother ordered it cleaned out and the stink went... A few weeks later my husband was washed up by the sea with a thin rope embedded in his neck. He'd been garrotted."

They were silent a long time. Both Zona's straps had come adrift and she pushed them back up. *This dress is cool in here but* - passed through her mind. With it was the question: *What do I do now?* The silence between her and the queen felt as if it shivered on in the hot, rowdy hall. The woman had been through so much, first with her creep of a brother, then Aeneas. *Maybe it's no surprise she tried to kill herself. She'd just have been getting it together when that slime came to her door.*

At length, clearing her throat, she scooped her own hair behind her shoulders. She took comfort in its tickle on her skin, its cool weight.

"So, uh, what next?" she asked.

The queen sighed hard. "When Sycheas was found my *brother* pretty well gloated. I rallied some people I knew could be trusted; we took what treasure could be packed along on horses and camels and ran. I expect Pygmalion let us go because he'd got what he wanted – the crown of Tyre. The army was his; he'd probably packed it with his own men, and we were going to be no trouble. But little does he know! It's why I built this city. We're going back – after I've dealt with that snake Aeneas."

Zona was disturbed, jangled up. *I can see me in her.* Once a young girl had left Thebes to find Maron and punish him. Behind her lay her parents and brother in their ransacked, torched house. By the time she caught up to the bandit at Troy she'd recruited a feared band of cutthroats. She would have been consumed, hollowed out by hatred if not for the lost Xanthia. Now she reached out impulsively to grip the queen's hands so tightly the woman freed them.

"Alissar, I can guess how you feel. But if you give in to hate and anger you'll end up like me."

"What's wrong with you? You seem OK to me, and I have to tell you, Zona. You're either with me or against me. No middle way."

"I, ah, think I get that," said Zona slowly. She changed the subject. "This city, all of it, how did you build it in, how long?"

"It's seven years since we got here from Tyre."

Zona shook her head in astonishment. "You're kidding, right? It's not possible, all this?"

"Everyone did a bit – "

" – and you think your people don't love you?"

"They don't, not anymore; I've neglected them too

much, left them to get along on their own. It's one of the reasons I must die; I can't bear having betrayed them, lost them. So many folk gave up so much following me out of Tyre."

"Where Pygmalion would have slaughtered them, everyone not loyal to him." Zona swept an arm over the banqueting hall. "These people don't love you? Give me a break!"

"Well… " Dido pulled a face, raised a hand to her hair, then let it fall. "The snag with you is you notice too much."

The warrior laughed.

If only she'd seen what was going to happen next when it was coming. Before, for that matter. She should have recalled Celeano's warning but, guard lowered, she was enjoying the feast, and focussing on Dido.

It began with a minor disturbance in the middle of the hall. Sharing a rare instant of mirth with Dido, she didn't see anything wrong. The hall was getting more excitable and noisier as food and drink were steadily put away. Near the back a bunfight was going on with a lot of pushing and shoving. No-one took any notice when the man stood unsteadily in the middle. He was dark, burly, dressed in a blue robe, not much different from anyone else. Nothing about him showed that he'd killed the wearer of the robe and stolen it earlier that day.

Zona was alerted by a flash of steel in candle and lamplight. The man's hairy arm came back for the throw of a dagger. As his hood fell back, she saw a perspiration-slicked, red face. Shock rooted her in her seat. *This can't be him! But how – The guy should never have got out –*

But it was the man himself. Astonishment, the wild idea she was dreaming, kept her in place. *What's he got against Alissar?*

As the dagger left the assassin's hand, Zona's limbs unlocked. Lurching sideways, she grabbed the queen. Dido landed underneath as they crashed from their chairs. She was too winded to speak. The dagger drove into the wooden panel behind them and stood quivering. Dido's eyes widened.

"You saved me, again!"

"Not now. It may be me he wants. Stay down."

The warrior scrambled up. Looking for the killer, at first she couldn't see him. *He's in the middle – somewhere.*

Tearing at the long, constricting skirt of her dress, she felt the shoulder straps give. The whole thing came off in her hand. Tossing it aside, she sprang to the table. Diners shouted in alarm, throwing themselves out of the way.

Zona scanned the hall. *Where is he?* Surely he'd not escaped already. *It ends here, pal –*

There was a commotion at the back of the hall

close to the nearest exit. The banquet in full swing, most people didn't notice him or care what he was doing. They weren't even properly aware of the tall, broad-shouldered woman on the high table in only a loinband. When she yelled for someone to stop the attacker, her voice was lost in the noise of the meal.

Zona leaped, hurtled to the table below. She kicked off her high-heeled sandals for easier running. With a crash of breaking glass and crockery, she landed, bare feet in some kind of glutinous dish. Yells and screams burst out around her, spread down the table. The food was a cold sweet, made of fruit and wine, splattering up her legs. *I can smell the wine.* Knocking aside, crashing through glassware, silverware and gold, she raced along the table. As she went more people cried out, several getting in her way. A few tried stopping her but she pushed them aside.

She was gaining on Deiphobos. *This time he won't escape.* Zona was on the point of a flying leap to bring him down. Yelling a war-cry, she put on more speed.

A man rose in front. Beefy, with a red and sweating moon of a face, wearing gaudy robes and jewels, he reached out with both arms.

Skidding, the warrior ran into him. The big man cursing, they fell with a crash.

CHAPTER TWENTY-FOUR

"What in Hades did you do that for?"

"I, uh – "

"I nearly had him!" Zona raged.

Eyes afire, mouth a thin line, she hauled herself free of the tangle with the burly man.

By then a crowd of angry and scared people hemmed them in. To give him credit – *Not that I feel like doing it* – the big man whose name was Yusef Abdullah was sorry for what he'd done. As she listened to his apologies, the warrior thought, *It doesn't give me Deiphobos though.* He was even more regretful when Zona explained through tight lips that she'd been chasing a man who was after her or the queen.

Someone she didn't see properly in the crowd handed her a silver-thread shawl. Zona wiped at the mess on her legs, bits of meat, fruit and other things falling off as she rubbed herself elsewhere. Scrubbing at her tangled hair, she realised what she'd done.

She held the ruined shawl out. "Sorry."

It went back into the crowd and she apologised once more. Until it struck her again that Deiphobos had escaped.

That guy's slipperier than a seaweed-slimed rock. Zona hissed in annoyance, then let it go. *A time'll come when we meet again, you snake.* Because she knew that it was her the prince wanted, not Dido.

New frustration claimed her. In case he was somewhere close enough to hear, she yowled, "Deiphobos, you're mine! I'm coming for you!"

Though she hadn't seen the woman approach, Carthage's queen was beside her. She needed to get better control of herself but, warrior though she was, Dido wasn't the only one rattled. Where had the prince come from, how long had he been stalking her? *Seeing how I left him in Troy, I guess it's fair enough he wanted me, but even so...*

Dido was holding out the dark green, satin-shiny dress. The warrior climbed into it, holding it up with one hand.

Grey eyes shining with tears ready to fall, cheeks wan, the queen looked desolate. Zona couldn't help her harsh voice; she was still annoyed.

"What?"

The queen flinched as if she'd been whipped. Zona was irritated afresh. *Is she a queen or isn't she? What in Hades now?*

"Now my people want to murder me," Dido said in a low tone. "I know I've neglected them since Aeneas left but I didn't think I'd been that bad."

"This isn't about you," Zona said tightly. "That man was out of my past, he wanted *me*."

The queen went on as if she'd not heard. "I really don't know what point there is in me being here. I can't marry, so no heir for me – "

"Alissar, I killed the last man who took me on. *You* talk about no prospects? Come on!"

A pale copy of a smile followed this. "Well, look at you."

The warrior glanced down at herself and back up. A grin came and went. She was dishevelled, hot and bare-shouldered, still holding the dark green dress in place.

"Yeah, look at me."

She turned wholly serious again, reaching out to grip Dido's shoulder. Her dress pooled at her feet but she ignored it. "Never mind the heirs. They'll come in time; you're young, attractive – "

"Nobody wants me. I might as well not be here. You shouldn't have broken in on me."

Zona shook her gently. *What in Hades can I do with her?* Everyone watching and listening had drawn back in a circle, and people were just there, making no attempt to intervene.

"I know you've been through a lot." Zona just about masked irritation, desperation too. "I suspect you only told me a little but that's the craziest thing I've heard yet. 'Nobody wants me.' If that's the case, why did Sabblooton yank me out of a jail to save your ass?"

"He was scared – "

"Grow up Alissar!"

"Why you! I'll have you thrown back – "

" – No you won't."

Dido sighed so heavily the warrior thought she'd split something. *Moody, difficult queens - why me?* She thought of how her lost blonde friend had got on so easily with Helen and held back a sigh. *Xan's not here, there's only me. She's off somewhere with Helen, Andres and Rupros making a new life.* So she, Zona, simply had to do the best she could.

"Your people do care for you, Alissar," she told the other woman quietly. "You owe them, so shape up."

She pointed at a tall, dark-skinned man nearby. He'd short black hair, a hooked nose and pencil-thin moustache and was watching avidly.

"He wants you. Look at him."

Dido put on a smile, then lost it. "He's Iarbas, ruler of the Arab tribes to the south. You met him before the banquet started, remember? And maybe it's you he's more interested in."

"I do have all my wares on show," Zona observed drily. "If I can't get a man, looking like I do now, I never will."

She picked up and held the dress again. *So nice, this dress. I enjoyed playing lady awhile. Such a shame I wrecked it. Still, I guess that's me.* Things like it were not for her, and she had been acting fast to save them both from an assassin. *Except it was really me he was aiming at.*

"But no, it's not me, it's you. I know these things," she finished.

"Yeah. I suppose I have to admit it. He thinks of an alliance between Carthage and himself, if I'm worthy."

"Well?"

"Well what? And this is hardly the place to discuss politics." Dido flashed a grin and the warrior was grateful her mood appeared to be shifting. Maybe if she could be steered along trails of practicality... "And with you like that."

Zona returned the grin. "Yeah, you could be right, and I'm sorry about the dress. It was beautiful, far more than I rate."

"You did rather fill it." As they began to walk, diners cleared a way for them. Dido held out an arm to her companion. "Here, give it to me."

The warrior relinquished the dress, passing it over and attracting stares as she did so. She coolly acted as if she didn't notice them. The queen stopped. She did too as Dido held up the dress and inspected the damage. "It's only the straps that have given. I'll have a seamstress fix this."

They began walking in step again, the queen carrying the green dress over an arm. Reaching the steps to the High Table's annexe, the two women began to climb them.

"I so want to catch that lying, cheating – " breathed Dido.

"So do I, and now I've a little more to go over with him."

"You don't have to do this for me."

"Oh yeah, I do." Zona paused before the door behind the High Table they'd gone through earlier. People at the table stopped talking, craning round to watch. "And I've a feeling that when we catch up with Aeneas, Deiphobos will be with him or not far behind. Mikhail is training with your army. I think we'll need every man of them before this is through, your navy too."

The queen stared at her. "What?"

"I don't know for sure but I'd guess Aeneas is planning something big. I'm sorry but I think he was just using you and Carthage from the start. I have said this."

Dido looked flattened. "But we were nearly married! Once we took shelter in a cave from a storm…"

"I know this guy. I'm sorry, really I am, but yes… Well, I'm sorry."

Dido breathed. "I'm coming with you, wherever you go. I want to be there. When we get him, I'll hand him to my torturers."

"He's mine – "

" – That's what you think."

Zona sat, back propped against the wall of a Carthage dockside bar. On the rough table in front of her stood an earthenware pitcher and mug of cheap, sour wine. The place was busy with stevedores crowding in for their lunch breaks and the noise from the jostling crowds was a loud roar of voices. The hot air was full of the odours of wine like that in front of her, fried food, vomit and sweaty bodies.

Some men with palm branch fronds worked in the corners, near the door but it didn't make any difference to the fug. Although she was back in her strapless warrior's vest and kilt, the clammy air pressed in on her. Her hair was limp and damp behind her and the bench she sat on was glued under her thighs. Rising behind her shoulder the hilt of her sword showed she was a warrior, not to be messed with. For that reason, because of her stern features and cold amber eyes, her table was unoccupied, even in this press.

She was finding her detective work hard. This was hardly one of the best bars in Carthage but surely, trawling round such places as she had been for three days, was going to yield something. Aeneas with his fleet had sneaked away in the darkness of night. Deiphobos had covered his trail but sooner or later someone would talk. *I hope.* Zona blended, although female warriors weren't the commonest sight there.

A few men always moved her way and she bought drinks freely with cash supplied by Dido. Near-suicide behind her, the queen was very focussed on Aeneas. *I wouldn't like to be him when she next speaks with him; I don't think it'll be love-talk,* thought the warrior.

She's hunting him however she can think of. There's gonna be war soon as well. Though determined to adopt no further liaisons with any man, Dido had a policy of forming alliances with the Arab tribes and even some bandits in the surrounding country. Iarbas was key to this. She made a treaty with him which included the supply of Arab troops if Carthage went to war. *She's a smart pol, all right.* He got trade advantages with free access to the city's growing merchant fleet and a promise of protection for his traders by the navy. Messages went out to other Arabs and soon leaders were coming into the Byrsa. Some men, including Iarbas, were dangled promises which weren't quite of marriage, and all joined the alliance.

Dido proved a canny leader indeed. *She's even done a deal with Hosni, seems to get on with him. More than I could ever do,* mused the warrior. Once he and Mikhail were freed from prison untortured and his dignity was soothed, the little Egyptian proved tough but fair in negotiations. Showing herself tireless, the queen held those while concluding treaties with the Arabs. It secured her eastern flank with a friendly and powerful Egypt and kept the Pharaoh from eying

Carthage too closely. *She hopes, but I'm not sure how far you can trust those guys. Maybe she doesn't...*

A third alliance got Camilla's aid with her Volscian cavalry. The queen started out flattering the dark woman but didn't have to offer much. It only proved necessary to tell the story of Aeneas' treachery and running out on her. As well as joining up with Carthage, the horsewoman had friends in Latium north across the sea and brought along promises of further aid. There was a king called Turnus...

Mikhail carried on training the Carthaginian army which was formed largely of local people and surrounding tribes who came along as mercenaries. As soon as he'd gotten out of jail, the Trojan captain wanted to return to soldiering. *He's gotta be loving every moment of what he's at. I've heard some good stuff.* Tired of wandering, oppressed by his time and deeds as Aeneas' captain of guards, he threw himself into training and drills of the soldiers, welding them all together. Zona sighed, and looked into her mug. *Wish I was with him, this spy stuff isn't me. I guess maybe I'm jealous... He's a good recruiter too, even brought Nubian horsemen aboard. Ah well...*

Joint battle plans were developed with Camilla, Arab chiefs and Iarbas. Throughout the city, forges were busy as bronze and steel swords, spears, axes, bows and arrows were made. Mainly recruited from Carthaginians, the navy was being expanded, though its training was outside Mikhail's remit. As a shipbuilding programme gathered pace, more and more warships were launched.

Queen Dido was soon going to be strong enough to go to war against Aeneas and Deiphobos, whatever forces they managed to assemble. *All we need do now is to find them,* brooded Zona. *Enter me.*

Making it last, she sipped at her mug of wine, managing not to wrinkle her face. *Sure have had better than this.* She considered the rangy stevedore who approached her table and sat without being asked, his back to the wall like her. Ruffled brown hair thinning in the middle. A black skullcap was plonked down with a drink and pastry which smelled dubious. Brown and fair whiskers stubbled his cadaverous face and he wore a loose blue shirt stained by lots of somethings with brown, baggy pants. He'd a black patch over his left eye; the other was a milky blue. He introduced himself as Sadique and the swarthy, middle-aged guy didn't say much else. Both of them sat gazing into their drinks, slouching more comfortably on the wall.

"Good ship this morning?" she asked. *I'm not gonna get much outta this one.*

"What's it to you?"

"Just talking."

They were silent a while in the crowded bar and each of them sipped drinks. The stevedore slurped at his again and wiped his mouth on a wrist.

"'Nother trader out of Latium," he said at length.

Zona creased her brow in puzzlement. She took a fresh bite from her pastry which didn't taste much better than it smelled, like his. Her butt was still adhering to the splintery wooden bench. Almost expecting to hear herself peel from it, she held back a grunt of displeasure when she moved cautiously.

"Where's that?"

Sadique squinted at her, then pointed with the hand gripping his mug. Even over the noise from the bar she heard the wine slop in the bottom. "North, 'cross there, leastwise that's what crews from there say."

Good eye narrowed in suspicion, he leaned sideways and hawked at the floor. *I'm not going to look,* the warrior told herself firmly as she tried not to flinch.

"Why d'you wanna know?"

She pretended to sip more wine. *This is such a waste. How do I get rid of him?* "Just making talk"

"Yeah." The guy growled slowly. He considered her, the milky eye glazed over. She couldn't guess what he'd already had but drink was starting to get to him. Like her the stevedore was sweating, droplets in his stubble. *I'm ratty-haired, none too clean myself. On the other hand maybe he likes what's there. Perhaps I can trade on it – a bit.*

Sure enough – "What'll you give me," he enquired.

"Depends. What do you want?" She fluttered her lashes outrageously.

He bent over and spat again. Once more she nearly looked at the floor. A harsh cackle which might be laughter followed.

"Y' couldn't keep up with me, girlie."

He's gotta be kidding but she didn't reply.

A new silence dragged itself out. Sadique pulled at the contents of at his mug, tilted right and spat some more.

"Drink's gone."

Sighing to herself, the warrior signalled to a harried-looking barman. She laid a coin on the table and the pair waited until fresh drinks were fetched. She let the bar's heat, stinks and noise wash over her, and started again.

"Where were we?" *and why am I still bothering? This guy's not going to have any more for me than the others I've talked with.* Zona was increasingly frustrated, aware the trail was going cold.

The worker had a long pull at his fresh drink, wiped his lips on the back of his hand. Leaning right, he appeared to think of sending another gob after his previous one, then changed his mind.

"Merchants from Latium," he muttered, "From up north ya know."

"You said that." *At this rate, I'm going to hit him.* She somehow held onto the shreds of her patience and pointed north. "From there, you said, right?"

He peered at her and his good eye glazed a second time. She began to think she ought to have worn something more covered up, but this was her normal warrior gear. *And whatever he's got to say isn't worth fighting him off.*

"Somethin' goin' on up there," he mumbled.

Maybe I've got it wrong; this might be interesting. "Yeah?"

The next thing the dockworker said was even more worth her time. "What I hear, Latium's a fine, rich land. Least it's why this prince feller wants it, I reckon."

"Who?"

Sadique leaned over to look at her some more and she caught his breath, avoided scrunching up her face. His belly gurgled and he quieted it with a deep slug of wine. That done, he leaned right again. *Why does he drink the stuff if he just gets rid of it this way? Maybe he's fed up with me, knows he can't bed me and is trying to put me off. He's wrong; I may be about to hit paydirt here.*

"I dunno," he grunted. "But ole Gebril, the guy I sometimes drink with, he reckons this prince is from Troy way. Least he was high n' mighty 'nough to be somebody royal."

Sadique rambled to himself and Zona contained her irritation at him. *This looks like it, the real breakthrough I've been after at last.* She made herself wait while the dockworker sank more wine, lurched over and sent a new gobbet at the sawdust covered floor. She leaned in and could just about catch his voice, though not the words. *Don't let him pass out now. He's gotta get back to work, man's a sot but maybe he knows what he can take. I hope.*

To her relief, he slurred more loudly. "Though way

I heard, folk were sayin' he was a kinda god... Crazy stuff like that... Now we got this sect..."

"*What?*"

"Yeah, s' what I said, girlie. I reckon it's 'bout how he's a god, dint I say?"

It's him, at last I'm getting somewhere. I've got to be –

CHAPTER TWENTY-FIVE

✜

THE DOOR of the bar slammed open.

As Zona looked that way, a broad line of hot sunshine cut through the shadows, blinding her a moment. Sadique put his hands flat on the table to push himself upright and she pulled him down.

"What?"

"Trouble."

Standing, she reached behind her shoulder to draw her sword. With a soft hiss of steel through the leather scabbard, it came into her hand. As people saw her, a hush spread out around her like ripples from a stone dropped in a pool.

Three men pushed through the bright doorway. Standing, looking round the bar, they cut off most of the light. All were bulky, clean-shaven, hard-eyed men. Dressed in regulation Trojan uniforms, they were armed with swords, knives and spears. *Maybe they're some of the guys Mikhail's working up,* but she knew at once that it wasn't the case. For close-up fighting as this would be, the men stacked the spears by the door. Separating, they advanced into the bar, space clearing for them. It was wholly quiet now and splitting up would give them room to use swords. They didn't yet draw but their eyes under their helmets flicked all around.

Oh, oh, passed through the warrior's mind as she stood relaxed, prepared for battle. *Whoever they are, why can't they just leave these people alone?* The bar was full of ordinary workingmen at lunch, nothing more. *Got to face it, though. Maybe it's me they're after. But same question: why?*

"What's the matter with you?" grated the centre man. When he turned his head, Zona saw he had a healed scar down his cheek.

"Carry on with your fun," he added. Pointing at the warrior he said. "You, with us."

She answered quietly, "Who says so?"

"Never mind that. Come here."

"You want it, you got it."

Zona ran lightly forward. As she did so, she cut backhand at the scarred man. It was a hard blow. Starting behind her shoulder, the steel flashed in sunlight, whistling down. As it came she howled a war cry. Unnerved, the soldier parried instinctively. Zona's sword wasn't there. Switching it between hands, she thrust forward, weight behind it. He nearly fell over his feet, tripping back. She followed up, regaining balance. Her blade whacked his helmet. Mouth forming an astonished O, he crumpled soundlessly.

The man on the left was coming with an overhand blow. Zona swayed outside it. As he tried for a backhand, she stepped in and kneed him before his blade swept round.

His mouth opened and shut with a click. *I think he bit his tongue.* Colour washed into, then fled his cheeks. Collapsing, he started to fold and she banged his helmet with the flat of her sword.

One man was left. Making no attempt to fight, he turned, breaking into a run. The warrior bounded to get him but he ducked and slipped away.

Her sword came after him. It sheared the back of his neck. Emerging from his mouth in a spray of blood and shattered teeth, the blow pitched him to his front.

After all this time trying to get something about Aeneas, where he's slipped away to, I get buckets full of it. First there'd been the aggravating Sadique, now these three, the fight she'd not been wanting. There might not be anything to connect them directly to her quarry but Zona's instincts were talking to her. Especially with how the men had worn Trojan gear.

Watched by the bar's patrons in a silence through which a bird's sigh would have been heard, she sheathed her steel, having first wiped it on a fallen man's tunic. Moving to the one who'd been in the middle, she bent and slapped his cheeks.

Stirring, moaning, the scarred trooper didn't fully awake. Hunkered beside him, impatiently she slapped his cheek again. His eyes opened, filmy, staring. As they cleared, he pulled himself up.

Zona grabbed his scruff. "Where do you think you're going?"

The man looked at her sullenly. *He's not going to talk much, at first.* She disliked what she was about to do but didn't have much choice. *I need to learn what he knows fast.* At any time more like him could show up; for all she knew someone might have slipped out to fetch them. Wherever he was, Aeneas would be getting further away each breath she and this man took. If her hunch was right as well, Deiphobos had linked up with him or would do soon. Once, as a bandit chief, she wouldn't have hesitated – and she'd have killed the trooper afterwards but now... She tried once more.

"Why don't we start with something easy? Who are you?"

No response.

"Come on, you and your pals wanted me. Now, here I am."

Still no answer.

The warrior sighed. *I can't avoid this; it's gonna be messy.* If only Xanthia's voice wasn't an insistent whisper in her mind. *Ah well.* Her fingers moved quickly into an Egyptian nerve grip at his neck.

With a gasp he jerked away but she held onto him. His eyes bugged and colour flooded his features blood-red. An instant later he was white, glistening with sweat. The man began to judder, heels drumming the ground. Still crouched by him, she watched coldly, then loosened the nerve hold.

"So who are you guys?" she repeated.

Still pallid, the soldier glared at her but said nothing. His companion, the one she'd kicked, was stirring. Hauling the man nearer by his collar, she used a different nerve hold to put him to sleep.

Her fingers wiggled at the man she was trying to question. Getting her meaning, he lost the trace of colour he'd regained.

"Well?" she asked.

"My name is Coulash," he choked. "The man you killed, he doesn't matter now. The other of my comrades is Sarnir."

"Strange comrades if they don't matter, and…?"

He was silent again. Once more Zona flexed her hands meaningfully. "Must I?"

"We are soldiers of an elite order."

"And what does it do, this order?"

From behind her were mutterings, although she couldn't make out words. However, it wasn't hard to guess from the tone that the workers were angry, eager to get even with the order, starting with these three men. Whatever else they were, Coulash and his men hadn't been part of Dido's regular forces. If they had been she would have known.

A man growled, "Stake him out for the ants, birds and jackals. Don't waste time on him."

Kneeling more comfortably next to her prisoner, she turned her head. Looking threatening, a mass of the bar's patrons crowded her and the soldier. She guessed from the arrogance with which the three men had started in on her that the workers had stuck enough of them and their order. She returned her attention to her captive, fixing him with icy eyes.

"You were telling me about this order of yours," she prompted.

Coulash gazed at her sullenly. His eyes shifted to the watching crowd and defiance crept into them.

The warrior sighed. "Next time I may not take the hold off."

"Then I shall tell you nothing."

"Gut him," said a different man.

"Or I could vary it. You'd come out of it able to speak but otherwise like a baby. Unable to move, fouling yourself and dribbling. I'd be surprised if anyone round here fed you. They'd probably expose you at night for lions, and the rest at daybreak. Like to bet on it?"

Coulash glowered some more, then began to force out words. "We are the Order of Purity's servants. It has been established by the God. We are proud to do the God's will."

"Uh huh."

Now he'd started talking, the man went on. Eyes glowing, he seemed to puff up with pride, his voice vibrating with it.

Another fanatic, Zona thought wearily.

"His will is that the members of His Order remain in Carthage. Much work has to be done showing this city the light."

"Oh, oh," she said ironically.

"Do not mock!"

"Sorry."

He glared at her. "This is a heathen city. Our instructions are to purify it."

"You said that, about showing the light."

"All must be converted to the worship of the One True God, may His name be ever praised! Heathen cults like that of Ba'al must be stamped out. Practice of abominations such as the sacrifice of children shall be cleansed away in the righteous fire of His wrath!"

An unexpected pang of sympathy for the Order cut into Zona's mind. Since she'd rescued her, Queen Dido, supported by herself, Camilla and the Volscians had all worked at moves against that practice. At crucial points, however, Dido drew back. The cult of Ba'al was powerful in the city, growing in numbers and influence. *But who in their right mind would want to sacrifice babies?* Many nobles were members or supporters of the religion – at the least until it came to giving up their children. In some cases it was said that babies from slaves or bought children were offered to the god. *It figures; big guys would squiggle out of it if they could.* Whatever the truth there, Dido knew she needed the cult and its wealth to fight Aeneas. There was only so much she could do against the religion, *but now here's a new bunch of zealots, and they're agin' it. Tricky for her, or is it?*

She knew one thing. *I can't show these OPs any sympathy here and now. I need to find out more about them, their connection to Aeneas, where he is. That comes first, but maybe then me and Alissar can deal with them. Set 'em against Ba'al's people? Yeah, she could go for that.* The two religions could fight themselves to a halt, crush child sacrifice with no responsibility attaching to the queen. But first…

Could be a different approach might do it here. She didn't like Coulash's fanaticism any better but forced herself to a quieter tone, acting reflective.

"Maybe we can help each other."

He glowered. "You have killed one of my men, and are not properly submissive. As a woman should be."

She tried, and failed, to keep irony out of her reply. "Sorry about that, but you guys started it."

"You are not a proper woman."

"Don't know what I am then, and I thought you wanted to tell me about your OP thing, convert me."

"Purity is what we are about, of mind, body, what a man eats and drinks, the air he breathes, the way he does his duty of making children, how he worships the God."

Maybe at last we're getting there. She wrinkled her brow. "What's the God's name?"

"Surely even you, an ignorant, depraved woman knows? It shows how much remains to be done. Our task is just beginning."

Zona was irritated by his automatic assumption of superiority for the male. *I've been told I'm not submissive, don't know my place. He got that right! And I killed one of his men, knocked another out, I'm unnatural, a warrior.* A sigh. *Guess I'm a hopeless case.* Either Coulash was an especially revolting, bigoted specimen or the OP thing was way out of line. *But we all hate child sacrifice... And mustn't forget what matters here is getting a lead on Aeneas.*

"So this God I should know and bob to, what's his name?" she prodded.

"He is all-Mighty, as high as the sun and moon, lower than the bottom of the sea. He is in each bush or tree, every flower or blade of grass. You see Him in each rock, all sands, the flight of every bird or insect. When you take to the sea – "

"Each time a camel grunts or spits, it's him, huh? Must be quite a guy." She'd not been able to stop herself. Zona was getting tired of the rant; this man was so like fanatics everywhere. *It might have been better to have kept that grip on him.*

Coulash looked at her like she was a cud the camel she'd mentioned might have spit. Irritated, she pushed hair back where it had fallen across her eyes and waited but he appeared to have dried up.

"So what's his name?" she finally said, "and I have asked before. How about we move this on?"

"You are a woman! – "

"He's noticed."

"– and a freak who plays at what men do. You are not fit to hear His name or to tread the earth where He goes."

"I'm glad you brought that up, where he is, and in case you've forgotten, Coulash, I'm the one who beat up you and your men. Now give or – " She worked her fingers threateningly. "Name and place, please."

"You don't scare me," he grunted.

"Oh? I should."

In spite of her threats, the warrior was frustrated over again. The man had gone on extravagantly about how his boss was a god and all but had actually told her very little that helped. *I've more than an idea, though.* So she tried an arrow shot in the dark. Coulash wasn't as tough as he liked to act because his face drained of colour, sweat-greased, eyes dark and staring.

"He's Aeneas, right?" she purred at his ear, leaning in to him.

"We could have told you that," said a gruff voice from the crowd.

Zona was irritated, sitting back on her heels. "Then why didn't you?"

"We were enjoying you with him," said the man. He added, amid a chorus of yesses, "Hey, you gonna put that hold on him again? It was fun when he was choking, and blood started leaking out his nose."

"Not if he answers right." She stared at her prisoner from chill eyes. "Well Coulash? It's another question: where is he?"

In spite of his fear, the man was silent and once more Zona felt frustration grow. *I can't just wring it outta him; once I might have done but not now.* She sighed. *In the old days I might have used more than the Egyptian nerve hold. Sometimes this being different is a real pain.* Trouble was there was a large part of herself which was bone-tired of things like putting heat on someone, of battle too. Her sword had killed so many, the latest person one of these zealots. *Once I did stuff like this because it was necessary, even instinctive. These guys had to be stopped before they brought others along. Now I don't even know how well when it comes to it I can fight for Alissar against Aeneas.* She realised that what she wanted most of all was an end to things like this, to find somewhere peaceful alone in the sun. *I'd be a farmer, hang up my sword for keeps…*

The soldier jerked her out of her thoughts. Maybe he'd thought he noticed something about her he could play on.

"So?" He was yielding nothing.

Zona tightened her grip again. "You're going to tell me where he is. Now."

Same reply, which was none at all. She sighed, a second time leaning over the man.

His nerve broke but it came with a last snatch at bravado. "God Aeneas is in His Holy Place where all His servants will one day go."

A voice spoke up from behind the kneeling Zona and recumbent Coulash. "We going to see him choke some more? Why don't you do that thing with your fingers again?"

"What about it?" the warrior asked the zealot. "Or shall I just let this crowd have you? They don't seem to have too much affection for you. Been collecting stuff for your god from them? And I still don't hear what I need."

"God Aeneas is in the Holy Realm of Latium," the man rasped. "He is preparing the way for His followers, so much good that will do you."

I know that place, from somewhere. Then she had it... *When I was a pirate, commanded a ship. We were carried by a storm to there.* The country was fertile, with olive groves, scrub and forests. Savage cave dwellers lived near the coast, although she and her crew didn't see them but heard stories... Fishermen captured by her men spoke a language that was strange to her.

I learned it; no guessing when it might be useful. It could get me out of a spot one day. Dragged before her, the fishermen had said they were from Latium which was ruled by the benevolent King Latinus. He was a peaceful man who'd tolerated the cave dwellers as long as his people were not molested. Sadique had spoken of Latium, a prince…

"We'll just have to see, won't we?" she murmured.

CHAPTER TWENTY-SIX

❖

IT WAS A HOT late summer day with the sky a clear, deep blue and no cloud in sight. A brisk, clean wind, loaded with salt and blowing off the sea offered good sailing.

In vest and kilt, Zona was bronzed in the crystal light. She stretched, enjoying the sun and sea. The warrior was pleased that finally she, Dido, Camilla and the men of their war fleet were sure where they were sailing – Latium.

When Zona told her of Aeneas headed for Latium and being thought of as a god, the queen had been excited at being finally able to get after him, contemptuous of his pretensions. *I guess I can see her point of view. That her former lover should adopt the guise of a god. It takes some beating.*

Dido had scoured dockside bars, the loading docks themselves, for any person who knew where Latium, the place he'd gone and disappeared to was. Neither mercantile, naval moorings nor haunts held anyone who knew the answer, though the name of the mystery land was known. Finally at Zona's suggestion she called Carthage's merchants together and quizzed them. *Yeah, people traded with it and some knew how to go there. So here we are, going to war. The voyage is dangerous, with unpredictable seas. Even the ship she's aboard mightn't make it back but does that stop her?* The warrior couldn't entirely blame the queen. Revenge on the man who'd betrayed and abandoned her was getting close.

Hands on the sun-warmed and smooth rail she leaned against, Zona looked around the naval harbour. Loading of the warships was going swiftly ahead, nearing completion.

Just along the quayside from her ship, the last of the Volscian cavalry had boarded with their mounts. There was a great deal of stamping and whinnying and she could smell the nervous horses, along with the other scents of the port. *A few sailors are gonna be kept busy swabbing decks,* she observed wryly to herself. Infantry were well advanced with their loading – crack Carthaginian units along with mercenaries, Arab, Greek, Nubian and other troops.

Merchants, many offering their wares from stalls, customers and pickpockets crowded the dockside. As well as stepping through ropes, nets and other seafaring clutter to get aboard her ship, she'd had to thread her way with Lina through traders shouting their wares, how theirs were best.

It would have been a slow process boarding her

ship with the restive horse even without all the noise and smells. *Lina just didn't like the idea of ground which moved under her hooves,* she mused. *I guess I can't blame her.* Head close to hers, she spoke to the palomino reassuringly, did a lot of stroking and rubbing her neck and ears before they tried the gangplank. Lina snorted, pulled back and jerked sideways before only cautiously trusting her warrior companion and following at her heels.

In early afternoon the ship, along with the others of the fleet, raised anchor, cast off its lines and set sail. Amongst the traders, soldiers, pickpockets and others a crowd of well-wishers had built up too. The whole city knew of its queen's brush with a pyre, why it happened and her fixed aim of revenge. Every sort and age, all races of people known had turned out to see her and the war fleet off. *She may have been right, though somehow I doubt it. Could be these folk were put out when she hid herself away and brooded. Her words, not mine, and I really doubt she was right.* Now it seemed the whole city waved and cheered while flowers were tossed at the ships like rain.

Soon Carthage had fallen below the horizon, appearing to sink into the waves which rolled up from astern. A stiff breeze cooled the heat but it quickly veered and was in the wrong direction for sails to be used. To the soft rumble of oars in rowlocks, the rhythmic swish as they dipped into the water, the crews rowed steadily. Soon drums thundered out over the sea to set the pace. It kept the few gulls which came along hoping for scraps wheeling high and crying raucously. The sun sparkled on the waves, the air blowing salt and men began to sing.

Keeping formation, such as it was, the ships sailed on. Gradually it clouded up, great shadows flitting over the sea. Strengthening, the wind shifted direction again to blow from the south-west. It was enough in the right direction for sails to be raised; crews rested as the ships speeded up.

Later as the sun westered, sinking and laying gold across the sea, Camilla stood beside Zona as she stared across the water, thinking. Although so far it was going well the expedition weighed upon the warrior's conscience. She wasn't happy over Dido's motive of revenge and felt responsible for turning the queen. About all that could be said for it was that it was better than victimhood and suicidal depression. *I'm sure if only Xan was here, she'd have thought of something better.* Zona reckoned that she'd taken the easy way out – of warrior stuff and vengeance. *I should have done something else, not just grabbing one of her mood swings and building on it.*

"So what's wrong?" asked the dark, slender woman.

Zona sighed. "I don't know."

"Yes, you do. Come on, talk to me. I'm told I make a fair listener."

Zona thought. *I know she's too damn smart, but maybe she's right as well.* Since they met the two hadn't spent much time together. The Volscian cavalry leader was busy drilling her men to fight on horseback and afoot with various weapons. Zona had spent a lot of her time with Dido, turning her and working to keep away thoughts of suicide. She'd helped with the alliance that kicked this trip off, as well as searching docks and bars for Aeneas. *Yet, whenever we ran into each other we talked easily enough, maybe too much so, perhaps because we're both fighters. Yeah, we're that all right.* As well as being warriors, both were riders, easy with a lot of weapons. Zona had commanded brigands, Camilla her Volscians, inspiring near-fanatical loyalty. Camilla's ready humour and knack of poking fun, including at herself were reminiscent of Xanthia. Even so, for some reason, she didn't keep making the warrior miss her lost friend.

"Go on, try me," Camilla urged. "I only bite in battle."

Zona hesitated. *I've gotten used to a life on my own – well, until Mikhail and Hosni. Do I really want this?*

Chewing at her lip, she ran her hands back through unruly hair. *This sea air; it's like a Harpy's.* She winced as she recalled the bird-women. *Hosni never let me forget 'em.* "It's just that this whole thing's down to me."

The other woman had on her normal black

sleeveless jerkin and leggings. She held her elbows, then rubbed brown arms. "How do you get that?"

"I talked Alissar into it."

A mock-puzzled expression came, the dark eyes dancing. "Oh, you mean when you saved her life? Yeah, I'm sure someone told me about that, in a bar here or there."

Camilla waved as if dismissing a troublesome fly. "One or two other little things."

"Yeah, well."

"Well what?"

"Camilla, I'm not happy about her being so much out for getting even."

"You got her to live. Don't ask too much of yourself, and don't forget this as well. Every man here is a volunteer. It's not just about you, what you have or haven't done."

"I don't know... I guess. What about you? What are the Volscians doing in this?"

Camilla grinned, and ran her hands through her short hair. "We like to brawl, bit of rough stuff. Volscians have been known to get into the odd barroom scuffle."

"Come on, though." Zona leaned in towards her, then pulled back. *I mustn't invade her space, I have no right.* "How about you? We've never had time to get into that."

Camilla grinned again. It was girlish, engaging. *That sure sucks you in.* "It started out with trade. We heard about this new city – Carthage – in North Africa. Nosiness as well, I guess. Well, we had to go see, and we little girls and boys did want perfumes, herbs, spices, silk and stuff. It was – where was I?"

Zona pulled a face. *Let's try this.* "About to fill me in on child sacrifice. I never knew how far you were – "

"Yeah, yuck! Turned out Alissar didn't like it any more than we Volscians did, and guess what?"

"She couldn't do all she wanted herself against the Ba'al cult because they're too powerful and she needed them. Lots of wealthy people belong, and so on."

Camilla dragged her hands back through her hair, looking frustrated. "Has anyone ever told you about your bad habit? Stealing all a girl's best lines."

"You're not going to like this then." It was Zona's turn for a grin. "How's this for a guess? It kinda follows."

"What?" came with knitted brows.

"It's not hard," said Zona ironically. "Alissar couldn't move openly against the Ba'al people. She told me – "

" – But we could!" Camilla jumped in, punching the air. "We could, and did we ever want to! Burning babies alive, can you begin to imagine it? Of course we were nothing to do with the queen. Oh, the whole city knew we were staying at the palace but she didn't have any say in what we did. We were free agents. If any of us were caught she could protest she didn't instruct us, condemn our unruliness. If she was even asked about us."

"Bet you enjoyed yourselves."

"We did. I told you what we're like. And not a man in my troop didn't want to hurt the Ba'al priests."

"So you – "

"What didn't we do? We wanted to shut that cult down and were well on the way. Me and my men roughed up priests, kicked them around some, made their robes dirty with something other than babies' blood. When they were taking kids for their rites, we were there watching, ambushed them and took the babies home. Naturally we were masked, just bandits, you know. Would you believe?"

Zona guessed the other's next words. *Yeah, I would –*

" – Some of the parents were angry, we'd screwed with the god's will, but most were so relieved. And we climbed up on the roofs of the temples, you know they have holes up there for Ba'al's fires. Guess what we dumped through those holes when priests were stoking up their blazes? Let's just say it smelled!"

"I bet Alissar was well pleased with you guys."

"Oh she was! One time she laughed so hard I was certain she'd split something – but then Aeneas came."

Always Aeneas. Just wait till I catch up to him. Zona didn't say anything but waited quietly for the rest. It wasn't long coming.

"I never did trust that man," Camilla said slowly. "I'd guess he couldn't have been more smiley, utterly charming in fact, but... The first time I clapped eyes on him was at a welcoming banquet to which the Volscians and I were invited. You should have seen his finery! Anyhow, by then we were pretty thick with Alissar. Not for long afterwards; she had no time for us, called off our games against Ba'al's people too."

The warrior sighed, glad she wasn't in love herself. *That could easily have been me if I hadn't known what I do of him.* She recalled Troy, and winced at herself. *He's got something with women all right. No wonder Alissar was so easy a mark.* At present the queen appeared better and improving but what might happen to her when the expedition caught up with Aeneas? *I've got a real bad feeling on this.* Maybe Zona ought to have kept out of things but it was hard. *There were the harpies, Celeano, then in Carthage we were prisoners, and... I guess it couldn't be avoided. Prophecies, gods stuff, this isn't me! Oh, I couldn't stay out. I like her, admire her grit. I couldn't stand by and let her kill herself over that pond scum.*

"Get in line." The Volscian had apparently guessed her thoughts. "Yeah, he was good-looking, have I said that?"

"Sort of, but never mind. And when we catch him, he's mine."

"We'll see, and Alissar really pushed out the boat

for him, not like for poor little me!" The rider pretended to look woebegone and Zona laughed.

"Zona, you should have seen her banquet hall! When that man tried for you, that lot of finery was nothing."

"Deiphobos, and I've some things to go over with him."

"Tapestries, polished timber, lamps and torches everywhere, the place was magic. Gold and silver, crystal glasses; Alissar got out the best dinner set all right. There were musicians, tumblers, fools, you name it. The food, well, I've never had ambrosia but if I had… " Camilla shook her head. "She hung on every word he said, looked as if she wanted his baby right there. I don't know… "

I do, thought Zona grimly. *And oh Aeneas, just you wait…* She had another, chilling thought. *What if gods are somehow mixed up in this? But they can't be, can they?*

"I know what he's like," she said. "And I guess it's just how love takes you."

"We should have been able to do something. I feel so bad, and I always knew that behind the smile was a stinking privy."

"Don't beat yourself up about it. When a woman's like she was, there's not a great deal you can do. A girl in that space doesn't listen too well."

"At least you saved her life!"

"For now."

A fresh silence fell between the two women. It was filled with the sound of rolling waves, thundering drums and men shouting out rowing songs. Zona could smell salt mixed with their perspiration. It stirred nostalgia with memories of when she'd commanded her pirate ship.

"You know, Zona." The Volscian's face was crinkled as she narrowed her eyes against the low sun. "We've talked around this but it changes nothing. I'm so mad at him; basically me and my men are just here to take him apart."

We don't need to settle this now, but I'm not bowing out. The warrior raised her hand to slap palms with her. "So am I."

In a spray of foam, a vast head burst from the water.

It was black, glistening and wedge-shaped. Three times as long as the galley Zona and Camilla were aboard, it showed rows of sword-like teeth. Opening its mouth wider, the blue-eyed monster screamed at the ship that rocked in the waves it threw up. The warrior flinched at the gust of its breath. *Like the battlefield I bet we find when we come up with Aeneas.* Seeming miles of the thing unwound from the sea, slapping more foamy waves at the ships. Men were crying out in alarm but they seemed distant, in a different place. *This is a nightmare, can't be real. I've never heard of anything like it before. Maybe it's survived from a time before men down on the seabed.* A fresh shriek sounded hungry. Ships were trying to back up, some men jumping in panic over the side, all resemblance to any formation lost. Everywhere screams, waves and spray blotted out the sunset.

As she dived into the sea, Zona shone with white light.

CHAPTER TWENTY-SEVEN

DEIPHOBOS slouched at a grimy table in a dockside bar. Arrived in Carthage at last, he was scowling into a mug of cheap, sour wine.

Even after the business with Cacus from which he'd scarcely escaped with his hide, the trip here was slow and hard. Now he burped heavily and stared around the bar which was dimly lit by smoking torches. The air was thick with the smells of wine like the swill he was drinking, vomit and the stale rushes on the dirt floor. Sweat was in there too, *likely mostly my own,* but he didn't care. After arriving in the 'shining city', he'd fallen on hard times. *So when I landed, I took Theo and the crew for a little drink. After that, when their guard was down, I was going to figure a way to do 'em. I wasn't careless, left a coupla men aboard on guard. How was I to guess they'd not be enough?*

When he and the rest of the crew got back, the ship was gone, the two men on the dock with their throats cut. With it had gone the treasure he was able to steal from Troy – which wasn't a lot but better than nothing. After that of course Theo and the rest of the men deserted.

He slurped his wine moodily, then rubbed a bristled chin. His bloodshot eyes gazed round the bar like a trapped rat's. Digging for his purse, he emptied it out, counted the few coins there. *Nothin' much but better'n empty.* He'd stolen them from an old woman trading fruit down the road and round a few corners. He'd snatched a meal from her stall too. *Wasn't much but a coupla oranges made a kind of meal.* Deiphobos' belly rumbled emptily and on bad wine. *It was such a long way off what I had in Troy…Ah, marinated songbirds' hearts.* At least he'd been able to outrun the merchant as she hobbled from behind her stall. *Old bitch, yellin' like a pig got ready for the spit.* In spite of her shrieking, he'd lost himself in the crowds along the docks, and now here he was.

The prince – *Yeah, I was at home before I was king and Zona ruined it all* – sighed heavily. Draining his mug, he looked blearily round himself. It wasn't his suite at the palace but he was lucky to be here. A servant passed and he grabbed the man's arm.

"More wine," he ordered thickly.

"Who says so?" growled the man who was as unshaven and smelly as Deiphobos himself.

He slammed some coins onto the table. "This does."

The other man in his greasy leather jerkin and pants tucked the cash away and vanished in the noisy, crowded bar. Deiphobos snuffled round his mug after the dregs of his wine. *Better make room for the next drink.* He supposed luck had been with him, even though it didn't feel that way. His thoughts turned once more to Cacus the giant. He'd done well running down to his ship on the island's beach. *A tactical retreat.* He forgot his panic, shouting till he could only whisper as the crew got it to sea. *They didn't seem to get the need to move their asses till Cacus hove into view with his club. That shook 'em. I never saw guys shift themselves so fast, and then Cacus caught the last two.* Deiphobos shuddered, seeing it again as the men were whisked into the air screaming. It would be a long time before he forgot the sounds of pulped bone, saw their heads bounce down the beach and the sprays of blood. When the giant finished, the crewmen were just red stains sinking into the sand – except for the three joints Cacus took with him. Once more the prince shuddered at his memories. *It could have been me!* As he vanished over the hill they'd raced down, the giant started chomping wetly on a joint, spitting out pieces of bone.

The servant was there, plonking his wine onto the table, slopping wine over the rim of the mug. *Cacus...* If he could only stop dreaming, jerked awake to the stink of his own fear, his rough pallet wet with it. *I'm too imaginative...Even now I can feel those brown teeth rip...*

Hastily Deiphobos slugged at his drink. He glared

round the bar and several sets of eyes avoided his. *Probably deciding if they've the nerve to rob me,* he thought. *They better not.* Although he was alone since the others had scuttled away when the ship was stolen, he still had sword and knives. *If they try, I'll carve 'em into pieces.*

His thoughts ran in a circle to the source of all his troubles – Zona. *Those inhuman cat eyes, black hair free to her shoulders.* The shoulders were broad and bare, as were her shapely, muscled arms, long legs. At the vision of her, thoughts of what he'd do to her, the prince felt himself growing excited. *Black warrior vest and kilt. No doubt of it, she's unnatural.* He wouldn't admit she was favoured by Ares. He shied away from it; Deiphobos would have been paralysed by fear if he had confronted it. *How else did she wriggle through the battles outside Troy? She damn near saved Hector's skin when he was fool enough to go against Achilles.* The prince sighed noisily but had to accept it; catching Zona was the whole of his life. Somewhere deep inside he felt dirty, slimy, but he couldn't help it. She'd taken everything. Now here he sat, alone in this pisshole bar – almost broke, like the drunk snoring in a puddle of booze just across from him.

Deiphobos was awash with self-pity but he was too drunk to care. He swigged more wine, and his cup was nearly empty again. He'd find a way to get even, love each moment of it. If he could just get a handle on where she'd gone.

I did get a lead on her, at Alissar's banquet. He'd been so near to killing her there. *I heard it in a place like this; it was all over the city.* Everyone was talking about how she'd rescued the queen, the big party for new allies of Carthage. His mouth twisted bitterly. He was perspiring freely, chest hard with discomfort. It had been an extremely narrow escape.

Getting into the feast wasn't hard…

In another bar he plied a corpulent merchant wearing the robe he had on with drinks. *When I figured he was hammered enough, I just offered to see him back to his swanky home in the citadel. All easy as falling off a log that far.* Ordinarily the guy would have been suspicious but he was drowning his sorrows, having just lost a ship laden with spices to pirates. He was grateful for the concern of his new friend, seeing nothing wrong. It was easy for Deiphobos to steer him into a back alley.

The fat man stopped, swaying on his feet. Maybe it was the smell of the place which got through to him, or the buzz of flies. *It was the kind of place a man can find in any city, even the 'Shining' one.*

"Wha' we doing?" asked the merchant.

He never got an answer. In the darkness the prince moved swiftly. A blow from his dagger handle sent the other tottering.

" – Wha'?"

Deiphobos hit him again. With a grunt the merchant pitched forward. He landed with a splat face-down in the muck of the alley. Working quickly, breathing hard through his nose, the prince divested him of his blue robe. *Didn't want to get blood on it.* Smelling of the guy's perfume, it fit more or less. If only the garment wasn't too messed up by the mud; he was holding his breath because some had to be there. It couldn't be helped; he'd just have to do his best to clean the garment. Anyhow most guards at banquets didn't pay that much attention. *They'd simply assume I had a right to be there.* A flash of inspiration: *I decided I'd tell the truth, just not all of it. I'd say I got drunk and fell over before going to the jamboree. But it never came up... Maybe they thought it was a new perfume.* Even now in this dive with rotten wine, Deiphobos grinned savagely.

Rolling the merchant over, the prince slashed his throat. Adroitly, he jumped clear of the fountain of blood that followed. A stench which came as the man voided his bowels made him wrinkle his nose. *The guy wasn't going to be talking. When he was found several days later as he began to stink badly, they'd have thought thieves did it.* The guards wouldn't even bother to investigate; in the kind of unsavoury quarter he did the crime, things like it were always happening.

The Trojan prince was pleased to find it was as easy to get into the banquet as he'd hoped. He simply walked into the palace, then the hall with a throng of other people. The queen was so revered by her folk that they didn't seem to think security was needed. No-one suspected an assassin might be after the warrior who'd saved Dido's life.

There she was – at the High Table right beside the magnificent blonde Dido. For once Zona wasn't in her black vest and short kilt. She looked stunning in a dark green, shimmering dress. With silver flowers on the front, it was otherwise classical, leaving her top bare. *Soon it'll be even darker – soaked by her blood,* he thought with satisfaction.

Except it didn't happen like that.

He was back towards the hall's entrance at a long table crowded with increasingly happy diners. *Perfect!* He'd let people get even more drunk and silly before he struck. That way not too many would notice what went down until it was too late. *And the doors were near enough for me to escape easily. It wasn't a perfect scenario but it should have worked. You always gotta leave some things open, flow with it.* As long as he threw his dagger well and fast all should be well.

Zona ought never have suspected anything until the knife was in her. *Curse her, she's got to have magic eyes!*

Even as he stood to throw, she was dragging the queen aside, down behind their table. Cursing – *it was already too late to back out and I might hit something*

– he threw the dagger.

It missed! He stood, mouth open and stared.

The warrior was up, leaping from the High Table to the long one where he sat. Dishes and cutlery crashed over in all directions, china, glass, gold and silver went flying, part eaten meals splattering the diners. While he carried on gaping, she'd torn off her long dress. With other people, some yelling while others got out of the way, he went on looking. *As she stormed along the table, she was so, so Zona!* Another thing, her form was outlined in silver light. Part of him just wanted to give up and let this Fury have him.

He was only given a way out when a large gaudily clad man stood and reached into her path. She was so close. Deiphobos saw muscles flex in her belly and long legs. There was the reek of his fear – and Zona was going to jump at him. His insides nearly let go. It would be all over any time. *Not this way, it wasn't meant to be this way! –*

She and the big diner were tangled up. With flailing limbs and the guy swearing, she and the big man were falling into a crowd, behind the ruined table –

Deiphobos unfroze and ran…

Now, sitting in the bar wrapped in cold sweat at the memories, he drained his cup and looked for more wine. He needed to be careful or he might end up like the trader in the blue robe – but those images! *Just a little more.* He looked muzzily around the packed bar for a servant. At last he spotted one and signalled the man over. The guy was big and overweight, muscled arms tattooed all over in a sleeveless jerkin. His baggy cutoff pants were held up with a rope and, when he arrived, still rattled by his memories, the prince started off wrong.

"Got a face in there, do you?" he rasped, "In that Hydra of a beard. What do you use for a mind under that black rug? What took you?"

It was the wine talking, had to be. *She can't reach me here.* Would his nerves ever settle?

The man scowled. "Money, Donkey Face!"

Deiphobos was grateful this wasn't worse. He counted change out but the guy's heavy brow knitted further.

"You know, as insults go, that lacks – " the prince began.

The server clicked his fingers. The bar had quietened, every customer looking, and Deiphobos guessed what it meant. *Seen or heard of enough spots like this; I know how it goes.* With a sigh, he pushed back from the table and headed for the door. *Did she ever make me screw up!* He'd lose his money but it couldn't be helped.

By the time he was half way there a huge bald man with a shiny tattooed skull was beside him. The guy wore a sleeveless jerkin and cutoffs like the wine man. He was tattooed wherever dirty skin showed, and he smelled worse. His arms were bigger than one of the Trojan's legs. He was smacking a fist as heavy as Cacus's in the palm of his other hand. Deiphobos kept walking; he reached the door. The giant stopped with his fist and politely opened it, squeal of hinges, muggy air and outdoor smells. With another long breath, the prince went through.

It was then the bouncer kicked his butt.

Letting out a ripe curse, Deiphobos flew. With a splat and applause from the bar, he landed face-down in mud and something that smelled worse. When he propped himself on his hands to wipe it off, it dripped to the front of his already wet robe.

This has got to be the worst yet. Sticking his fingers down his throat, he ejected the wine, and that went down him. The stink didn't help and his innards roiled. This was so far from his life as a prince, briefly the ruler, of Troy, he found himself snivelling into the mess. *Maybe I really should end it all, right now. I'll never catch Zona, and she scares me anyhow.* Kneeling over his vomit and whatever else was in the mud, he thought she'd eyes in the back of her head. *I'd better throw myself in the sea, keep right on going.*

No, he wasn't about to give up, not this way, and help came to him.

At first it didn't seem so because someone grabbed his hair and yanked back his head. He felt cold metal as a knife blade pressed across his throat. Now that it had come to this, Deiphobos was surprisingly calm. *So here we go. Tartarus I'm coming.*

"Here's my problem, friend," said a mild but phlegm-laden voice. "Do we understand each other? You're wearing a nice blue robe, although it's seen better times. Interesting to speculate where you got it, might even be yours, I suppose. But my problem is whether or not to kill you to get it. Can you help with my dilemma? Alive or dead, what's the difference?"

"You can see why we call him the Philosopher," broke in a wheezy voice. "He's always with the questions. Me? I'd just cut your throat and be done."

"Ah, but you're always too quick, Hakim," mused the Philosopher from behind the prince whose hair he still gripped. "You miss so much in life because you're too quick to get all there is in it. Cutting his throat would get blood on this really quite fine robe. I take it we're all agreed we want it, right? Right. Granted it looks and smells like he's been sick and has wine down the front, but it washes out. Now blood, it would ruin the thing and it's really quite fine material, worn perhaps but very nice. I like that particular shade of blue."

"Don't cut me then," Deiphobos choked. "Problem solved."

"Be quiet a moment, please," drawled the knifeman. "I'm thinking."

"Like I say, he's always at it," grunted Hakim.

"It's what makes us different from the beasts, I'm always reminding you," the killer behind the prince told the other man. To Deiphobos, he added, "And I guess you'd better take the robe off before we get into this any further."

The Trojan's head was still being dragged back. It hurt and made talking hard. "No, I'm guessing you'll cut my throat if I do."

"There is the possibility. Of course we could just hit you and remove it ourselves. But we like people to co-operate with us – we are after all part of the human family."

A new voice spoke up, also out of sight to the prince. This one sounded high-pitched, too eager. Deiphobos didn't like what it said and felt his insides curdle.

"Yeah, let's cut him," the man said.

"I've something to tell you," gasped the Trojan. *It's worth trying, anything is.* "You need me."

"And we have you," pointed out the Philosopher, holding the knife at the prince's neck. It dug in a little and as he felt blood trickle panic washed over him.

"I don't mean that way," he said quickly. "How about letting me up?"

"No. You're best to go on kneeling where you are. Convince me."

"Why lissen?" asked yet another new voice. It was deep enough to have come from the Underworld. "Let's just take his robe, cash too. Cut him and away, same as usual, yeah?"

There was a pause during which Deiphobos was careful not to move. Mud and stuff was cold on his aching knees, soaking through his robe. There were the smells of the place, close air too. *This might be the last thing I feel. Me, the ruler of Troy. Ares, help!"*

"I'd like to hear him talk first," decided the Philosopher.

This is it, my chance. Deiphobos swallowed nervously, brain racing, and felt the knife blade in his skin again as his throat bobbed. More blood ran warm and he bit down on his terror. He began to sweat hard, and he could smell it. As if he'd ever stopped since the gang had taken him. *In Troy I was reckoned a politician, talker before a fighter. Where's the talk now I need it?* This was one of his most challenging situations yet. On his knees, the thing which stank not far away, the Philosopher's hand in his hair pulling back his head, a knife poised to finish him off. Panic once more surged from its hole, black tentacles writhing close. Somehow he forced thought to come.

His voice shook, was too high, but he couldn't help that. Words tumbled where there had been none before like a stream in a Spring torrent. "As I said, you need me; don't get me wrong, you're a good group, work well together. Your leader, he certainly is a philosopher, has brains but you need more even than that."

"Such as?" Two men spoke, the high and the low-pitched. Neither sounded friendly.

"Well, there you have it, the kernel of it," Deiphobos gabbled. *If only he'd move the knife!* "You guys are doing well enough but only in a small-town, dockside kind of way. Sharing ideas with your leader, well, all of you, we can reach for the heavens. Just think of it!"

"Talks pretty but I still say we cut him," growled the deep voiced man. Like the rest, except the Philosopher who was silent, likely thinking, he was too fixed on the idea.

Deiphobos was warming to his own talk, the flow of ideas it brought. *Maybe I* can *do this.* With these guys under his control he could catch up with Zona, rebuild himself.

"I can give you a whole city, not just a bit of one," he said.

CHAPTER TWENTY-EIGHT

❖

SOON AENEAS would have the woman he wanted.

He'd tried to get her in a more peaceable way. It wasn't that such an approach was better; it was simply less wasteful. Even after all the people who'd joined up or been 'recruited' by his sergeants, the Trojan fleet wasn't strong. It had lost a lot of ships on the trip from Carthage to Latium. Those who came through the voyage were too often tired, hungry and thirsty, wasted by seasickness. *When three of the scouts I sent out returned with news of ol King Latinus, Queen Amata, their fort, I thought I'd struck it rich.* He knew he'd got to visit, pay his respects, see for himself. *I smelled out a whole lot of possibilities.*

He'd called on Latinus with all ceremony. There was a princess, Lavinia, and she was slender with good hips, dark haired with deep brown eyes. Her features were delicate, finely cut, and she was demurely robed. She showed proper respect to her parents and the newcomers when they were introduced. *I was pretty sure she'd know her place as a wife, do whatever I*

want when I snap my fingers. Not like Alissar! His previous wife Creusa whom he killed when Troy fell was too strong-minded as well and independent. *Then there was Alissar. She was all over me. We had some sizzling sex in that cave when the storm trapped us hunting. I thought I'd never get the smell off.* She was willing to give him everything, including herself all right but... *Like Creusa, she thought too much, and her bottom line was Carthage, not me.* He'd thought of sharing the Carthaginian throne with her – until it was time to dispose of her of course. *That would have been hard too; she was so damn popular with her people. As it was, I tried to let her down lightly, spun her a tale of Apollo's commands.* If only it worked, but Aeneas had his doubts; the woman was too smart. He could do without her bringing an army with that navy of hers before he'd properly fortified his position in Latium. After all, especially here on the Tiber's bank, he was 'God Aeneas.' He couldn't be shown up to have any weaknesses, let alone lose what he was building. Maybe she wouldn't be vengeful, although his neck prickled each time he thought of her. Dido could solve the problem by taking it hard and killing herself. *She was gone enough on me; it's possible.*

Just then Aeneas wasn't in his Tiber place. He was looking down on Latinus' fortified palace and city. It was late night and most of the lights were doused. There was no moon and, though it was too warm, the night was ideal for what he was going to do. Soon it would be time for him to move with his squad, *and Lavinia's really a fine idea; this is worth what risks there are.*

If it wasn't for her mother Amata, he, the hulking

shadows of Dares and Achates with the rest of the men wouldn't be here on this hillside.

Dares was a bull of a man. Huge, bearded and living only to kill, he'd not been an obvious choice for this covert mission. Same with the bald, clean-shaven Achates. Yet the giants could move silently when needed, *and they'll have my back*. The rest of the men were picked Trojan soldiers, good for this type of thing.

Amata. His mind ran over her. *Another goat-headed female, still handsome though. But it seems my life's cursed with them… It makes Lavinia so promising. She comes with a rich dowry and I can bend her any way I like.* But her mother! Tall, dark with strands of silver in her mane, she had a pleasantly laugh-lined face, and old Latinus listened to her.

He'd been easily able to sway the king, an aged dodderer. *A bit of 'Father Aeneas' having a tough time since escaping Troy but blessed by the gods stuff did it.* He threw in about doing the will of Apollo and the guy was his – to do with as he liked. Lavinia was almost his, Latinus' previous contract with the Rutulian king Turnus easily dumped aside. Aeneas convinced the old fool he was able to buy Turnus, but then Amata had to meddle.

He pulled a face in the darkness. *She's not only powerful; she's a hell of a wife and mother.* She wanted the best for her daughter who was in love with Turnus.

The mother set out strong arguments, including the fact that he, Aeneas, was an unknown and the love thing. The queen also kept reminding her husband that they had contracted to give Lavinia to Turnus and the boy was hot-headed. *Why can't women simply know their place and shut up?* Aeneas thought sourly. But there was more. *There would be. Do the sun and moon shine? She went on like water dripping on stone.* If Latinus broke their agreement – dowry had already been paid – there was no guessing what the young king might do. There could be a ruinous war, and breach of this contract was dishonourable. She wouldn't hear of it. *So the old bastard listened to us both. He kept me dangling with worthless promises and leaned toward his wife. The old goat!* But Aeneas couldn't keep a grin from twisting his lips. He couldn't help it; he admired the king's diplomacy.

At length I knew I couldn't mess around any longer, not if I wanted Lavinia. As well as doing what she was told, she'd bear fine sons to carry on his dynasty. Also with all the delays and excuses, Amata could be sending secret messages to Turnus alerting him to what was going on. *The gods take her, I wouldn't put it past her at all.* If that happened, from the sound of the man, it might be war, and Aeneas preferred to be stronger before it came.

As he lay with his squad on this hilltop something else made him shiver. *I haven't thought of her in a long time but now she's here...* It was enough to make him believe in his carefully nurtured mystique of 'God Aeneas', his links with other gods – like Apollo.

Why think of her now, for the gods' sakes?

Zona...

At renewed thoughts of her, fresh chills ran on him, puckering his skin everywhere, ruffling his hair. He felt his stomach tied in knots as a vision of her took shape.

...The dark hair falling behind her shoulders which were broad, her arms shapely but strong, palely tanned in that vest of hers. She was so tall with powerful thighs and long legs revealed by her short black kilt. A sword rode behind her. *It's rumoured to be of the new metal steel, a gift from Hepheastus.* Most of all it was her stern face, those unearthly lion eyes. *She's coming, I know it, for me...*

Aeneas shuddered yet again. Telling himself not to be so silly, he rid his mind of the idea of her with a jerk of will. Her bangs and the eyes were the last to go, like a ghost which kept sticking around. *She's coming... for me.*

What's wrong with me? She can't be anywhere nearby. The warrior didn't even know where he was. They'd fought on the same side at Troy; there wasn't anything against him driving her. Then her words rang in the vaults of his mind... 'You and I haven't done with this, Aeneas.' They'd never gone over the killing of Troilus by Achilles. He'd taken good care to avoid it, but still... *No way can she know about Creusa, Anchises or Polydamas, or how I dumped Alissar when I'd got all I needed from Carthage. Zona's not on my trail.* She might not have survived the fall of Troy, the Greeks would not be happy with her after how she tried to help Helen... *Except there's her skill in battle. I wouldn't care to be on the wrong side of her,* and if anyone got out of the burning city to track him it would be her.

It was time to focus on the task ahead. But then he couldn't avoid thinking how his lies about talking to his father in Tartarus, speaking with Aphrodite, the whole 'Father', 'God' Aeneas thing would stick in Zona's craw. He wiped cold droplets of sweat from his brow without noticing and tried to reassure himself. *She'll never catch up to me; if she does I'll welcome her, then arrange an accident.* He could lay on a feast, one warrior greeting another, and poison her. Some tinctures could empty a person from both ends painfully for days – and there was a nice idea. *Just like it's bad food doing it. There's bound to be a witch or healer somewhere who can cook me a suitable potion.*

Once again he tried to clear his mind and get focussed. The final torches below had been snuffed, except those used by sentries on the city wall. He wormed on his belly over the hilltop, out of sight of the skyline. The squad came after him, Dares on his left, Achates his right. The star-crammed sky behind them and no chance of being silhouetted, he breathed easier.

Standing but bent over it was possible to go faster. Although Dares had scouted the land by day it still wasn't easy. The descending ground was broken, rocks, bushes and small twisted trees hardly visible in the starlight. Additionally the squad needed to be as silent as they could. There were two gate guards, others on the walkway at the top of the wall with its crenulations.

He'd not gone far before Aeneas realised he wasn't as fit as he had been at Troy. *There I spent days on battlefields; since then I've been sitting on my ass either in ships or at Carthage, and that was an easy life. I so enjoyed sinking into a hot tub at the end of the day.* Now a short downhill run was making his thighs shudder, flare with pain – and his back. Any moment he could be stopped by cramp; he could sense it getting ready to strike with paralysing speed. His breath whistled, breathing ragged, he could feel and smell the sweat pour off him, salty in his eyes and stinging. *I spent too much time in soft living with Alissar, not enough training with my men. When this is over that has to change – and they expect 'Father Aeneas' to lead from the front.*

At last the squad reached the wide plain before the city. That was good; there was some relief from this routine, less chance of being spotted; no warrior shapes against the skyline. Even so they needed to step more carefully; it wouldn't do to fall over anything unseen, and the pace was slower. The ground was rough, with potholes but they soon came to a dry, rutted cart track and went more easily. Wiping perspiration from his face, Aeneas started to become aware of night sounds.

Apparently from every bush there was the persistent strum of cicadas; an owl also twitted and by the high-pitched squeaks which also sounded bats seemed to be around. Small animals, likely the owl's prey if it found any, scuffled in calf-high dry grass and spiny bushes. Once some creature ran over his feet. Aeneas practically yelped in surprise but at least he and his men were able to walk upright. Until they were within a hundred feet of the city walls and were forced to worm on their bellies.

The wooden wall of Latinus' city reared above, cutting an uneven line against the massed stars of the night. Two guards were outside the gate, almost certainly with others inside.

By craning back his neck, Aeneas could see more atop the walls, shadows outlined by the stars. He steadied his breathing. *Here we go.*

He and his squad were only a few yards from the gate. The air seemed to have gotten colder, and even the owl was silent. He looked up and clouds were rolling across the sky. He winced. *We don't need to do this in rain and mud.* Then: *Is this more of me getting soft? Maybe that kind of weather will give us cover, keep guards' heads down.* Once more he mentally cursed Amata. *The old guy would have handed over Lavinia and a parcel of land, if she hadn't stalled, kept me waiting.* It couldn't be long before Turnus the Rutulian king arrived to claim his bride. Aeneas went over the politics again. It was why he and his men were here and he steadied himself some more. He couldn't let Turnus beat him to the prize but he reminded himself he wasn't just risking his hide on this raid but war as well.

Once more he wiped at sweat, hating the way his clothes smelled and stuck to him. *The gods know I'm not a coward.* He'd gone through the Trojan war, often in the hottest fighting. *There was that time Zona saved my neck…*

It's only nerves, same as before every fight I've been in. Nothing to do with her, and I'll take care of her if I have to… But his sweat had dried, an instant layer of cold salt he licked from his lips. His mouth more dusty than the road, his insides cramped to a hard, cold ball. *The other side of nerves,* he told himself, *is I can see everything with knife-sharp clarity, smell it all too. Come on, Zona, bring it on!*

Aeneas stood, put his hands to his mouth and hollered, "Over here. Stone-head morons!"

The two gate guards peered through the darkness;

he could practically feel them squint as they tried to see into the shadows.

The men were good; they didn't come running but unlimbered bows.

From a quickly shifted position, Aeneas yelled, "I'm here!"

Again the guards stared into the night. Even though he felt raindrops, Aeneas decided that now he didn't mind the weather. He was glad of the clouds, their extra blackness. *I feel like a pimple on a man's ass, as it is. Big, red, glowing like a beacon.* Moving to a new place as an arrow swished past his head, he wanted to hurry and finish this. *That guy nearly hit me; it was too close.*

He called out a third time. "Can't catch me, couldn't even catch a cold."

The squad had crept into position while the guards were diverted. He saw the huge shape of Dares rise, just caught the jut of his beard. A crack came through the night as Dares broke a man's neck. There was a gurgle, stink too as the soldier voided his bowels. At the sounds, the other gate guard spun. A member of the squad took him down, a knife blade gleaming as it thudded in his back. Aeneas heard the limp body fall forward. *A good start,* he exulted.

Voices sounded from the other side of the gate. More troopers. With luck they'd include men from the top of the nearest sectors of wall. *A bit more luck and they'll open the gate.*

Ares blessed the Trojans. *While the men outside are good, these are sloppy.* Things were helped along by the moans of the guard who'd been stabbed. There was nothing like a man who sounded in trouble to bring his buddies running.

As Aeneas, '*God Aeneas*', he thought, hurried to join the rest of his squad, the gate opened. Hinges creaking and squealing covered the sound of him drawing his sword. His other men also had weapons gleaming in their fists.

The gate was all the way open. Men crowded behind it and he shouted, "Go, go, go!"

Dares, Achates and the others leapt forward. Aeneas came behind them. Blades rang and clashed as the two sides met.

The fight was quick but messy. *So far, so good,* and everything depended on speed.

Aeneas saw, heard the action in vivid flashes. Dares' great blade swept in a circle. Someone went to scream, stopped as his mouth opened. The burly Trojan's blade cut his neck as if there was no bone. Gore jetted, spattering Achates who was also there with a blood-stained blade. Dares kicked the head aside, going after someone else. One of the squad gutted another man, leaving him crying, curled round pale entrails. There was a ripe stench with it.

A man towered over Aeneas, on his toes as he

struck down. Their swords met, raining sparks. The metal rang as, grunting, the soldier fought him. Now that combat had begun he was no longer fearful, felt nothing. At last he turned the other's blade. Lunging forward, he crashed his sword into the whiskery face in front. He heard the lower jaw crunch as the soldier wailed. Teeth and blood showered as his blade went on to stick in the man's skull. When he yanked it free, more bone cracked and the body dropped.

As quickly as it started, the fight was over. His squad were wiping and sheathing blades. He did the same and was surprised, pleased by how steady his voice was.

"Well done, men. Let's go."

Dares grinned, white teeth flashing in the tangled night of his beard. "They were too easy."

"Well, we'll just have to try and do better next time."

Once more Aeneas was pleased with himself. The relaxed speech fitted his voice. *One more addition to the legends of 'God Aeneas'* – which was why he was on this raid himself. The god took what he needed or wanted, and nobody stopped him.

After he and his men had changed into some of the least bloody of the guards' uniforms, Aeneas led the squad at a jogtrot. Before going on, they cut the throats of any men who weren't already dead. Hopefully the uniforms would give them a little time till the alarm was raised. They might even hide their identities after they took Lavinia. *Folk'll only be able to say men dressed as guards took her, maybe to a safe place.* It was certainly necessary because unruly men, bandits and the like were loose in the city.

The squad made its way along darkened streets. The clouds had broken up and starlight was just enough to see where they were going. Occasionally the packed mud was slippery from rain that had sprinkled it during the fight with the guards inside the gate. Aeneas and his men still made good progress, meeting no-one, and soon climbed a hillock to the palace gates. Out of view of the two guards, he waved his men to a halt.

"What?" Achates' voice was a low rumble.

"I'll handle this," the Dardanian replied.

"You mean I don't get to kill anyone," Dares grumbled.

"Let's try my way first."

Aeneas pulled a face in the darkness. He killed when necessary without compunction but the huge Dares and Achates did it for the sheer pleasure. *Right here and now, bodies at the palace gates, I don't think so.* If there was a better way that would give his squad more time before they were discovered, it was worth a try. He marched towards the gates.

The guards saw him. Because of his uniform and manner, they came to attention.

"Evening, men," he said pleasantly.

"Sir!" answered the guards, then one added, "Ah, password?"

So it was finished before it was begun. Fortunately Achates hadn't gone with the implied order to stay back. *He and Dares will hear about it later.* For now Aeneas was grateful they'd sneaked along in the shadows by the wall, one each side of the gates.

Visible as no more than a hulking shape, Dares reached out into the gates' torchlight. Big hands and hairy, muscled arms came from the darkness. Catching the head of the man who'd talked last, Dares twisted it. The man's neck snapped like a chicken's and the killer let him fall into his stink.

The other trooper had his sword out and swung with it. Achates wasn't there. His blade punched into the man's leather armour with a thud. It was wrenched upwards, gleaming wet in the torchlight, with a soft tearing. Insides flowed with blood. Before the man could utter a sound, Achates cut his throat. More blood spouted. The air stank like a butcher's shop as the soldier toppled. Achates wiped his blade on the body and sheathed it.

"We're better now," the huge men announced as one.

Aeneas nodded at the cold-blooded killers. *I'll let the dressing-downs slide,* he told himself. *For now at least.* It couldn't be denied the men were useful, fiercely loyal. *Let's keep it that way. Might be more prudent to reward them for a job well done.*

"Let's go get Lavinia," he said.

CHAPTER TWENTY-NINE

IT WAS A BRIGHT summer morning when Zona and Camilla's ship pulled over to the bank of the Tiber. The majority of Dido's fleet having been scattered by a storm a day out from Latium, only two others followed their ship. On the decks three hundred Volscians thronged around their horses and were nearly all the forces there...

Zona couldn't recall all that happened after she dived into the sea with the snake-thing. However, it was clear in her mind that the fleet's losses were bad.

There was a lot of screaming, much of it from the blue-eyed monster. Surf was everywhere, salt and making vision blurred. Thrashed up by the creature, the spray glittered white in sunlight and the water was cold as she cleaved into it. All around her and the thing, it flared deep blue with sunlight running over waves that were soon full of other warriors splashing around, hurling spears. Blood began to stain the water pink.

Over her the sea beast towered, dark, wet and

coiling. The darting, wedge-shaped head seemed all bad breath and teeth like spears. Wielding her sword, Zona never knew how it was she lived through the fight. She was yelling, hoarse, her voice lost in all the others and the monster's shrieks.

Until, inexplicably, the serpent was gone...

The river was wide, placid, with scarcely a ripple on the surface in the lazy flow of its current. It was dark and clear and the warrior hadn't been able to see the bottom as she leaned over the side to look. Insects, including spectacular green and blue dragonflies, darted over the water while birds swooped after them. It was mid-morning, heat building in shimmering waves. Her vest and kilt were stiff, the leather cracking from swimming in salt water. She could hardly wait to rinse them and herself in fresh. The garments were also sticky with perspiration. Later it was going to be oppressive; even the dark-featured Camilla was shiny-faced.

The ship nudged into a wide mud-bank with a few rocks. Some of the crew jumped ashore; lines were thrown to them and they snagged the ropes around a leaning tree's trunk and some rocks. All the vessels were drawn from the water, gangplanks run out.

Some time later, after lunch Zona ate in the saddle alongside Camilla, as the sun was lowering, flooding everything with dusty, coppery light, they met trouble. With Volscians three abreast behind them, the two women were riding a forest trail at a walking pace. An evening breeze was starting in the leaves round them. Birds sang and flitted, making foraging runs before night took over. Shadows were deeper under the trees, lengthening on the trail ahead. Soon it would be time to find a campsite which could take three hundred men and horses.

They continued to walk their mounts along a shadow-pooled trail. Suddenly there was total silence. The air hot, clammy with even midges keeping away, Zona reached back to draw her sword.

"What?" asked Camilla, then, "Ah."

"Yeah. It's too quiet."

Still in silence, hardly swaying the brush under the trees, dark shadows advanced. *To move so easily through such rough country... I don't even need guess at it. They live around here, know these woods.* Zona's mind speeded up. What might be done with this?

One thing she could do.

"Camilla, there may well be spears or arrows in this. Space your men out and dismount them."

The dark woman saw her point at once; they'd make smaller targets.

"Spread out, dismount!" she called back down the lines.

Her cavalrymen swung from their horses. Unsheathing swords, they stood next to the beasts.

"We can't fight in that forest. We'll have to wait for

the enemy to come to us," she muttered.

Zona flashed her a grin. "Riiiiight."

People were sliding out of the gloom. In the fast, jerky flashes of battle, events hotted up.

Only a few arrows, a couple of dozen spears flew. There were also chunks of timber, a hail of rocks of all sizes. The cavalry were able to stop most of what came with shields. They stood their ground, trained mounts with them; angry yells and curses burst out under the trees.

As they went on shouting, people sprang into view. At their appearance, the soldiers moved forward, closing into tighter lines. Zona yelled to their commander.

"Stop your men, these are just farmers!"

"Shields, flats of blades only." Camilla sent the order down her lines.

Yowling, the attackers came on, a few with swords, most with knives, hatchets and hammers.

Just as Camilla ordered her troops to lock shields and push them back, the farmers crashed into the lines.

Zona clouted a large, whiskery man in tunic and brown pants with the flat of her sword. She saw a similarly dressed teenager hare off under the trees. As the man dropped an axe and buckled, she pointed the child out to Camilla.

"I'm gonna catch him, find out what's making them do this."

Not waiting for an answer, the warrior sheathed her blade and took off. She crashed through brush. Somersaulting over more, higher growth, she shrieked a war cry. Face white, eyes huge and dark, the boy looked back. Seeing her leap a bush, closing fast, he put on a spurt.

The pair raced on, leaving the sounds of battle behind them. As she swerved, dodged and jinked through undergrowth, Zona began to enjoy the chase. Reddening evening sunlight flickered through leaves above her as she ran. She caught a glimpse of light silvering her arm. *It's gotta be sunshine. It's nothing weird.* Not even breathing hard, she tumbled and leaped more bushes and saplings and whooped again. She was very close to the boy. Hearing her, somehow he found more speed.

He vanished.

A yell burst from the ground.

Zona careered to a stop, arms flailing to keep her balance. She leaped over the pit he'd fallen into.

It was several feet wide, three big men's depth. The bottom was fixed up with sharpened stakes. It looked like a hunters' trap; she could see dark blood coating some of the stakes. Crouched in the bottom, her quarry had been lucky to miss them, and his white face showed he knew it. Panting, dark eyed, he stared upwards.

Stretched on the edge of the pit, she reached down.

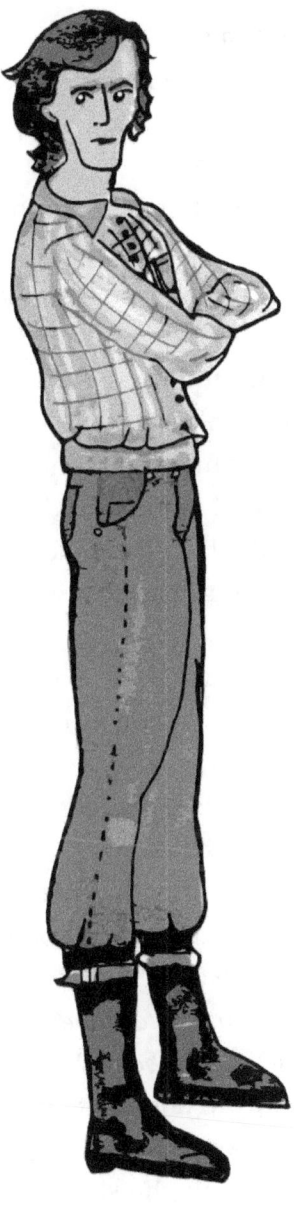

"Take my hand. Jump!"

"No, you'll – " The teenager's voice sounded on the verge of breaking. He backed away until he came up against an earthen wall.

The warrior couldn't help sounding exasperated. "I'll *what?*"

"K-k-kill me, like those men are doing to the rest of my people."

"Don't be silly. Jump, take my hand, I said."

"I'm too young, please don't – "

"I'm not gonna hurt you." Zona worked at patience. It was looking as if something bad had gone down with this place, the lad and his folk. "If I was going to injure you, I wouldn't have chased you. You'd already be dead."

"I was getting away. You don't want anyone left alive to talk about what you've done."

"Uh huh."

She could sympathise with him; the old Zona would have done exactly what he was saying. Clearly her rep had got to Carthage's trading partner Latium. The boy had heard of her, and she felt a pang of sorrow like a dagger blade. She was never going to be free of this kind of reaction, *no matter where I go or what I do. I guess I'll keep trying anyhow. What else?* Standing, she unbuckled her sword and let it fall. Her belt knife and the one in her boot followed. Since he was looking at her side of the hole, he should be able to see her disarmed. *Now I'm in just my vest and kilt; surely that ought to get through to him.*

"Better?" she asked softly. "Now let's get you out of there."

The boy looked up, black eyes holes in his bone-face. Zona lay on her front again, and reached down into the pit.

"For the third time," she said, "And what do I call you?"

The boy hesitated, then: "It's Nantes, and I can't reach you."

Zona stretched some more, feeling it in her shoulder and arm. "I've also said to jump. Grab my fingers, Nantes."

Silence met her again from below.

"Jump!" she called.

A scuffle was followed by a thump, but no weight hanging from her arm. Once again she heard Nantes leap but felt nothing.

"I'm stuck," he admitted. "Can't reach you."

"OK. Wait there."

He sounded alarmed. "What are you going to do?"

"Come down to you."

"You can't! The stakes, I don't know how I missed them."

"I'll be careful."

Zona picked out a spot where the sharpened stakes were a bit wider apart. Watched by Nantes, she checked out distances and angles. When she jumped, the teenager gasped. She moved to a wall of the hole and crouched.

"On my shoulders," she ordered.

"What are you up to?" Nantes cowered back. "You're down here to kill me!"

Not again. Once more Zona found herself clinging to her patience. *It's slipping away like I'm trying to grip an eel. Gotta do better than this. This boy, though. And what have he and his folks seen to make 'em like this?* It was scarcely the behaviour of people who should be attending to lands and crops.

"I've told you; if I was here to kill you, I'd have already done it. I wouldn't have joined you in this trap. You'd simply have been left here and, with that fight going on, no-one would have missed you until too late."

"Ha! – "

"If a big cat had found you? Now get on my shoulders."

The boy went on watching her doubtfully. He approached one step at a time.

"Come on, you're no weight. I can do standing up real easy."

Nantes looked at her leerily some more. Those broad shoulders, black hair, the unearthly amber eyes. From the way he was looking, was she rimmed with silver? *It seems lighter in here, but that has to be my imagination. He's gotta be scared as well. I said about lions.* At last he climbed cautiously onto her. She didn't let out a sound as she lifted him, standing to do it, gripping his ankles. *I daren't; if I do, he'll spook.*

As Zona held onto his ankles, his rough-soled sandals scraped her. *That's gonna leave marks,* and she wrinkled her nose at what came off them with normal feety smells. *He's probably trodden in something it would be better not to know about.*

"Can you grab the rim?" she asked.

"Not quite."

Zona muttered under her breath, wincing as he climbed onto her head. *Great! Now my hair's gonna stink.* As the boy's weight lightened, she sighed.

"Wait – "

"Uh huh," she growled.

Flexing muscles in her shoulders and arms, she boosted him up.

"Now I can," he told her brightly.

"Good," she gritted through her teeth. Bending her knees, straightening quickly, she tossed him out of the pit. Grabbing the lip, Nantes scrambled all the way from the trap. Zona sized up the distance and leaped after him. Backs to a large oak, they sat beside the hole.

"So what's this all about?" she asked.

As new fear bloomed in his eyes, he stared at her suspiciously.

A long sigh, *and I'm sure I can smell it in my hair, whatever it is.* "Not that *again,* and I just got you out of there. Another thing: What was it you stepped in?"

He took off a sandal and sniffed its sole; trying it with the other, he grinned. "Sorry, I was herding goats earlier this morning."

"Great," she muttered, and then pointed at the hole. "Don't you think I deserve a little explanation?"

"We do some trapping in the woods."

"I just about figured it out, and I don't mean the trapping."

"Wild pigs, you know."

"And you." She grinned at him.

I may not know what to do with kids, but I think he's starting to trust me. Which was good because she'd also found she liked him.

"You're a goat."

She groaned to herself. *He's the age where kids think this kinda stuff is funny.* Zona rolled her eyes and started again – *and I've got to get to a pool, stream, anything I can bathe in!*

"And you, and why are you so frightened of our men and me?"

"You don't need me to say!" he burst out.

"Try me anyhow."

There was a fresh silence, the longest yet. Evening midges and flies hung round her and she slapped at them, wiped mess off a shoulder. Zona pushed hair out of her eyes, then wished she hadn't. *Nantes' goats seem especially strong, but surely they only eat normal pasture.*

"They like olive trees, all kinds of stuff," he smirked as she rubbed her fingers on her kilt. *Why in Hades' name did I do that?*

"You let them eat olives?" she asked, her expression pained. "But shouldn't you be doing that?"

Once more he smirked. *It's time we changed the subject,* she decided, and prodded at him.

"Nantes, we need to push this along. Camilla and I gave orders nobody was to be killed with a sword, spear, arrows, anything like that. But men can lose their heads in battle. It shouldn't but it happens. So I ask yet again; what's this all about?"

"You're not with that man and his army, really?"

"I don't know what you're talking about. Why don't you give me some more?"

Another pause, then: "He came with a lot of soldiers, people like you, only men. Folk from neighbouring villages went out to meet them. The soldiers killed everyone, had their way with women, though our girls didn't want it. Children younger than me were hit against walls till their heads cracked open. All this happened after the soldiers had forced people to lead them to the villages. The soldiers laughed while people were killed, drank wine, ate and took what they wanted. They burned all that was left. So we decided to fight when you came. Our men were sure you were more of the enemy. It's foolish to trust anybody now…"

Zona felt her heart clench with sympathy. *And once Nantes would have been right about me.* Her eyes were prickling and wet; she licked salt from her lips. *I owe Xan so much, it can never be repaid.* Something familiar burned within her and she was grateful to recognise a warrior's anger. Once it would have taken her on a path of blood-soaked vengeance. *Now at least what I want is justice for those innocents. Thanks again, Xan.* Zona had a good idea of who was likely behind this but first she had to be sure. *But surely there can't be two like him; maybe I'm getting close.*

"Do you know who they were, what their leader was called?"

The teenager screwed up his brow, trying to remember. He spoke slowly, looking appalled.

"I think one of the old men they missed because he played at being dead told my father something. My father, he's fighting now, and ah, what was it the man said?"

Zona waited, containing her impatience. *This kid has been through so much but maybe he'll recall soon.*

Nantes' features cleared. "One of them might have been 'God' something or other. Or was it 'Father'? I don't remember, not properly. He was so horrible, killing, all that blood! I *hate* that man! I wish I could tell you who he was. Shall you kill him, please, please?"

The boy started to cry, looking both annoyed and ashamed of himself. Zona gathered him into her arms, rocked him gently as she smoothed back his hair.

"Don't you worry," she said softly. "The name will come, and, yeah, I aim to take him down."

I know who he's talking about, all right.

Killing to hide his tracks was so much his style.

CHAPTER THIRTY

✣

ZONA and Camilla led the Volscians across an open, rolling plain at an easy canter.

The plain was wide, dry and scrubby though the morning had started out as if it might rain. Low, a sheet of grey, the sky had felt as if pressing in. Just riding, the warrior felt perspiration's cool tickle under her vest and her skin was glowing. Sweat itched in her hair and she licked salt from her lips. What with Nantes' goats, she was really praying for a bath, a pool somewhere. It wasn't going to happen for a while. The only breaks in the landscape were twisted olive trees, a few of the goats and a range of hills to her left, the north…

At least she and Camilla had managed to stop the fight between Nantes' people and the Volscian cavalry. Being the youngest person there and as he called out to his father, Nantes helped. *In fact,* Zona repeated to herself, *He did it.*

The boy had climbed with her into the lower branches of a tree that just about raised them above the combatants' heads. Both of them yelled at his father until the man saw his child was safe. From there Camilla added her voice, *and together we stopped the fight...*

As they rode on, slowly the cloud layer thinned and it got lighter. A cool breeze puffed. It seemed the birds turned up their singing as well. The troops ate jerky and drank water in the saddle and kept riding. Zona recalled that it was her doing – *I knew we were getting closer to Aeneas all the time. Camilla agreed, and he's got more murders we need to talk about.*

The day moved towards and then way past mid-afternoon and nothing happened. The last clouds had long burned away and the sun struck down like a smith's hammer.

No moisture left in the land, dust rose around and hung in the air behind the column as they rode three abreast. In the growing heat the birds had fallen silent. All that could be heard was the clop of hooves, creaking saddle leather and the skrees of buzzards floating high above. For a long time nobody spoke; in the heat and dust which worked inside clothes and caked lips, it was too much effort. Occasionally a soldier would slap away one of the many flies or hornets which plagued everyone, clear a throat or cough at dust.

As time wore on, Zona was increasingly frustrated. Aeneas' men were mounted but the Volscians were pushing on as hard as they could. *We ought to be gaining but there's no sign of them. Maybe Nantes was wrong about where they struck. We just had to take what he said; it's not as if we know this country.* In the heat it was easy enough to make a mistake, and he was upset, recalling someone else's account of a massacre, not even telling his own story.

In rising irritation, the heat and insects, the warrior finally muttered that she'd take the point. Camilla grunted in reply, looking tired and out of sorts, and Zona kicked her horse ahead till the column was left behind.

At a fast walk she rode until the troop was left some distance back; she couldn't see their dust clouds when she turned her head. *Alone – finally. Camilla's very OK but...* The sun beginning to lower in the brassy sky, the shadows of rocks and olives were darkening, stretching out. Zona stopped to take a swig of tepid water from her skin bag which she returned to her saddle. Perspiration was sliding down her face, shining on her skin. Blinking it away, she stared at the near-flat but gently rolling horizon.

A wind took that moment to puff and fade. It was the first of the early evening breezes, welcome on her hot shoulders and face. It also swirled dust, wiping away whatever sign there might have been for her red-rimmed eyes to pick up.

She huffed in annoyance and tried again, this time

shading her eyes from the westering sun with her hand. *I'm just as hot as can be; I don't need this.* Sweat went on slipping down her; she could smell the goat-stink in her hair and longed some more for a bath. *And there it is again.*

I really don't need this.

Except that this time there could be no mistake. It was a far-off dust cloud.

The warrior squinted – and salt ran into her eyes. They stung, watering, and she blinked, then rubbed at them, trying to see better.

The view cleared again. She sighed. *Yeah, it's that dust cloud, bigger, and we're getting closer.*

Of course she'd got to see who it was. *No guessing what I could find out. And me and those Volscians; we're due a break in this.*

She didn't want to ask this of Lina. After their hot, dusty day, the palomino was tired like her – but Zona knew it had to be done. *He could know something Camilla's gotta have.* She pushed the horse to a steady canter. The other rider was flogging his mount but their courses were still drawing together. Soon she ought to catch him.

Lina's gait was smooth and easy. Zona began to close on her quarry faster. *Surely he's gotta notice us, but so far I seem in luck. This guy has to be blind or riding with his eyes shut. What's more, looks as if he can't hear us either. But maybe he's just very sure of himself. In which case he's due a shock soon.*

As Zona rode closer, she made out details. Like her, the rider didn't wear a hat. Head and face shiny with the heat, he was black, clean-shaven and as bald as a bird's egg. *Guy's crazy; he'll get sun-struck,* and maybe that was why he seemed so oblivious. He looked to be wearing a kind of sleeveless jerkin with baggy, sweat-stained grey pants tucked into calf-length boots. She fancied she could smell his sweat as well.

She could also see that he was well armed. A great sword rode in a sheath tied at his saddle, bow and arrows on his wide back. A long knife was sheathed at his thigh. *Bet there's a spear the other side of his horse. The man's ready for trouble or prepared to make it. Suits me, the way he's riding that horse.* She could see that the animal was lathered, wild-eyed and foaming at the mouth. The wretched beast was set to founder at any moment.

Drawing alongside, she called out in the Latian tongue. "Pull over; your horse is about done."

The man didn't answer. Instead, showing the whites of his eyes, he reached down. Even as he came up with a spear, Zona knew what he was about. She leaned low over Lina. Head almost touched by racing hooves, she felt the spear's wind as it passed over her. Drawing sword and knife, she snapped upright.

Wielded two-handed, the rider's blade met hers with a crash. Shock travelled up her arm, into her

shoulder and jarred her teeth. Sparks waterfalled. As they galloped together he struck again.

Zona took the blow on her sword. The result was the same. Her arm, shoulder and teeth ached.

This guy ain't gonna be easy –

The next time she turned her wrist sharply. The greatsword flew out of the bald man's grip. Letting off a string of impressive curses, he jumped from his horse after it. As he went, he drew his knife. *Almost as big as a sword,* and it glittered red in the setting sun.

The warrior was tired; it flowed through and over her. For an instant it was all nearly too much. *I so can do without this – but there's Aeneas.* The man's behaviour told her loud and clear she'd got to know what he was at, where he was from and going to.

At least he's baled off his horse. If we carried on like we were doing it or Lina was going to be hurt. Then I'd have had something with him, no mistake. Both mounts had been ridden hard, his probably like hers all day. Neither one deserved likely fatal injuries. *I'm gonna need Lina later as well, it isn't hard to figure that out.*

Leaping from her saddle, she slapped her mount with the flat of her sword blade. She and the other rider faced off.

"Why are you like this?" she gritted. "Who are you?"

His upper lip curled. "I am Tawfik Mishra, messenger from the God Aeneas."

Zona sneered back. "I might have known."

"You are a woman!"

She arched a brow. "You noticed."

"You are not fit to use a man's weapons and you do not dress properly."

"Well, Tawfik, we'll see about the fitness bit, and as for what I wear, I fight in these things because I'm comfortable with myself."

They went on facing up to each other. Zona held Tawfik's eyes and was cold at the fanaticism, hatred and intolerance she saw. He began to pace slowly around her. She turned with his circling and waited. She was looking out for the slightest movement that was wrong, the flicker of an eyelid. *Anything to signal an attack on the way.*

Tawfik swung his two-handed sword at her. The blade whooshed in the hot air, sunlight winking along it. She swayed out of the way. Tawfik came on with a backswing. Again she leaned aside. *So now we're back to watching, and is he rattled yet? Maybe.* The bald man was sweating while Zona stayed cool.

She held her blades down at her sides. A smile twitched her lips but didn't reach the ice of her eyes.

"Come and get me."

The big man roared. *That's meant to put me off? I think not.* It showed the even snow of his teeth in the stretched mouth.

He stormed towards her. The two-handed sword

came up in an overhead cut. It would have cleaved her if she'd not waited till the last moment to step aside. Tawfik snarled as he wrenched his blade from the ground. Zona waited for him calmly. She was irritated by his contempt for her, *and who does this guy think he is?*

In a flurry of ringing blows they duelled. The sinking sun lengthened their shadows which danced, tangled and came apart beside them. The light reddened fountains of sparks, sweat on their faces and Zona's limbs. The man went on showing himself to be good; *it's time to end this.*

I need to provoke him, break his focus. As the thought came, the warrior's boot turned on a loose stone. Her opponent landed a clanging blow that tore the sword from her grip.

Zona wiggled her fingers to clear the numbness. Taking a blow on her knife, she threw the dagger away as it broke. A couple of backward somersaults followed. A roll to her feet. She grabbed up her sword as Tawfik rushed in.

Swords locked at their hilts, the pair were gasping, chests pressed tightly.

"Why are you doing this, what is it you want?" she rasped. *OK, so I've already asked him, doesn't matter, he never answered properly anyhow.* "Who are you? And I don't just mean your name, I've got that."

"You must know by now. I am one of the best in our

army. You are unnatural, an offence to the God, and I shall kill you, woman."

"We'll see, won't we?" Zona answered softly.

She darted out her sword, leaping back. A red droplet appeared on the man's ear lobe. He thundered again, charging her. His sweating face was twisted, eyes black. She used her feet, moving away, blade pointing down, held at her side. He yelled once more, incomprehensibly. When he pivoted after her, almost languidly she flicked her blade at his other ear. As a red bead appeared, he stopped, looking at her incredulously.

"Ready to quit yet?" she enquired pleasantly.

A storm of curses in Arabic followed as he threw himself at her some more. *I can't understand him, but never mind.* Right then she was being kept busy defending herself. She'd aimed to put him off. *Guess I did that.*

"I am a member of the God's army!" he panted, "You shall die! Such a thing in a woman, it is against all gods. The God Aeneas commands it!"

"Uh huh."

This level of fanaticism so fit. *What in Ares' name has Aeneas done to his men to get them like this?* The names, titles she'd heard attached to him in Carthage... Dido had hissed it once, as in, "Wait till I catch God Aeneas! I'll give him God!"

The messenger went for a roundhouse blow at

neck height. Zona squatted but it ruffled her hair. While Tawfik was off balance, her own blade flicked out. The man lost his sword but grabbed it up again.

She moved in on him. Another drop of blood was there, this time at his throat. Tawfik's eyes goggled as he looked along her outstretched arm to the sword point at his neck.

"Hand over the weapon," she ordered.

Her voice didn't give him room to refuse. Before he'd guessed what he was doing, the sword went into her free hand.

"On your knees," said the warrior. "Hands behind your head."

Tawfik went onto his knees, hands clasped behind his neck. His face showed mingled surprise and resentment. *It's like he's pissed at himself, and I guess that's not far out. After all, I'm just a woman, and I got the drop on him.* Sheathing her sword behind her shoulder, she went on one knee beside him. Tawfik's dagger pricked his neck when she picked it up.

"Why don't you tell me about yourself properly?" she suggested. "I got that you're Tawfik Mishra of the God Aeneas' army, but I bet there's more."

"You'll get nothing from me."

"Oh?" She leaned into him, the dagger piercing his skin. More blood ran. His eyes were wide and scared and he was sweating hard. "We'll see about that, Tawfik."

"There's nothing to tell."

"Try me anyhow."

Tawfik sucked in a breath. His throat bobbed and some new red trickled but he was still full of bravado. "Do your worst. I am not afraid of you, an unnatural creation of demons. You are an abomination!"

"One who has you at her mercy. You set great store on being a man, Tawfik. I think I'll start cutting there." Zona trailed the point of the dagger down him. "What do you think?"

Perspiration rolled down his grey face in clear droplets. His bald scalp shone with it too and he was breathing heavily. He looked on the edge of collapse. Zona would never have done such a thing. *But this Arab scum doesn't know that.*

"OK then Tawfik." She was deliberate in her repeated use of his name; it would help intimidate him, *and it saves on me using the knife. I hope.* "Let's get started."

With a quick move of the razor-sharp blade, she slashed his pants; they pooled at his knees. Tawfik's mouth opened and closed, like something flopping in the bottom of a boat, but no sound came.

"Pardon, Tawfik?" she enquired sweetly.

Gobbling some more, he still couldn't speak.

I'll wait him out.

"Anything to say?" she asked finally. "Surely you must have a few words in there, or do you like the idea of becoming a eunuch? Come on, Tawfik, talk to me."

Another silence closed over them like cold, clammy drapes, and the man sweated, panting. His eyes flitted both sides like someone looking for aid which wasn't going to come. Tossing the knife idly from hand to hand, Zona went on waiting.

Finally, swallowing, the messenger gasped out words as if his throat was too dry. Like a beaver's dam bursting in a flood, they came gradually, then in a torrent.

"You know... I am in... Father Aeneas' army. I am a messenger from him to the fortress in Latium, the Lords Menestheus and Serestus who command there. That is in Aeneas' promised land of Latium, I said."

The warrior didn't want to halt the stream now it had begun but she had to know more. She pushed back her hair with the point of the dagger and shifted to ease her legs. "What's the message?"

The Arab looked rebellious. She toyed with the knife again.

"Must I, Tawfik? The rest."

His throat worked, sweaty features twisted with hate. "My message from the God is not – "

Zona couldn't help irony. "God, huh?"

"He *is* a god. He has communed with his late father in Hades; he has spoken with other gods, and the goddess Aphrodite!"

"You mean he's told you about it?"

"Of course he has, all the gods are with us!"

"The message? You still haven't told me." She ran her finger along the edge of the knife and cut herself. "Nice blade."

"You are a she-wolf!"

"Thanks for the compliment. The message?" Zona gestured with the dagger. In another move, she cut his underclothes and he gulped. She also saw him flinch and he perspired a bit more. *That oughta get him talking, surely.*

The sun had almost gone down. In a fiery bed of colour, it was a huge red ball, flooding the plain with deep orange light, making his features look as if covered with blood. Behind an old olive tree, it outlined twisted branches and leaves in soot, throwing a jumble of shadows on her and the Arab. "It's getting late and I'm hungry and thirsty. That makes me impatient, Tawfik."

"It is simple."

"Good. Clue me in."

"There is going to be a war."

"Why?"

"Father Aeneas has a worthy bride, Lavinia, daughter of King Latinus and Queen Amata of Latium. Many fine sons will be bred upon her. All should be happy, but no. Some king of the Rutulians, Turnus by name, wants her back or to have revenge. Bah!"

Looking interested, Zona sat back on her heels. "Your God Aeneas snatched her, or did he talk Latinus round?"

"Nobody denies God Aeneas. So we took her!"

"I see… "

"The god is assembling allies. Now we have them, many allies. We have King Evander for the Arcadians, also his son Pallas. Separate divisions under each. Then there is Tarchon with the Etruscans but the God leads all. Many men will walk and others ride. As ever, the god has done well by us, and victory is certain."

"How do you figure that? Why pick Lavinia and not get someone else? He's starting a war, Tawfik."

"God Aeneas takes who or what he wants!"

Zona sighed. *I can't let this happen. It's the war between Greece and Troy over again.* A lot of innocent people who didn't know Lavinia, couldn't care what happened to her, were going to die. *Just so Aeneas can set himself up as a king. He missed out being Heir at Troy so this land will suffer instead… Not if I can help it.* Aeneas' bloody progress, the war and its destruction, had to be stopped.

If she could just find a way to do it.

CHAPTER THIRTY-ONE

✧

IN A STIFF BREEZE Zona sat on her horse. It was a cool but sunny morning. Though the sun kept vanishing before coming out again from bars and lumps of clouds, she thought later it would be hot. In these southern, partly rocky and wooded hills, the air was usually at least warm. Birds sang from trees, a buzzard tweeted high overhead and she ought to have felt at peace. The breeze, increasingly blue sky and a comfortably full stomach from breakfast, *it all shouts you're OK – so...*

There was of course the fort.

I suppose I've got to give it to him. Aeneas hasn't been here long but he builds fast. So he'd used wood; it was the most plentiful, easiest material in these parts. *Then I guess there's the few things involved in kidnapping another guy's bride-to-be, starting off a war and recruiting allies...* What a pity the Dardanian couldn't put all that energy to something good.

The fort sprawled widely on a hilltop in front of her. It was the size of Dido's palace and a half again. A moat had been dug round the foot of the hill with the fort behind it, an outer palisade just inside the ditch between it and the buildings. At intervals along the walls were towers, each around four times the height of a man. In the centre of the main building was a citadel with walkways connecting it to other towers, and from it a banner snapped in the breeze.

Now she was closer as she kneed Lina on, she saw more fully the swathes of woodland that had been cut to put up the place. The ground was clear as well for a long way round the moat, except for the right flank which was protected by the River Tiber. *Maybe it ain't surprising I don't feel so good with all this,* and there was more to disturb her. She couldn't help sizing the fort up with a tactician's eye. *Aeneas is going to be hard to get outta here.*

Once over the moat with its bed of sharpened stakes, an attacking force would have to take the palisade, and cavalry wouldn't be much use. The infantry would then have to run up the long slope behind it. Camilla was on Zona's right, her contingent of Volscian cavalry behind her but their losses could be horrible. *No way, we're taking this with horses,* Zona thought sourly, and it was getting hotter. *We're going to have to wait for Turnus and his boys.* She was regretting her confident words to Tawfik when she'd let him go. *I really am too soft these days; I couldn't take him out like I should have...* The fort might answer to Mnestheus and Serestus but, according to Tawfik, another had recently been put over them with higher command – no less than her old enemy from Troy Deiphobos. She told herself, *it's why I let that rat Tawfik go instead of killing him.* She'd given him a fresh message: 'To Deiphobos from Zona. I'm here for you, so you'd better run while you can.'

"Well, let's keep on scouting it out, I guess," she said to Camilla.

The last of her misplaced sense of well-being had gone at thoughts of Deiphobos, memories of his assassination attempt on her at Carthage. *And I will get to him in time.* Zona was thoroughly fed up with how the ex-prince kept popping up in her way. *Yeah, Carthage, and he was sliminess itself at Troy. He can't get enough of me, and it's so returned, Deiphobos... You're gonna have so much you'll choke on it, I promise.*

She added, "Might as well say what we both know. This fort is going to be hard to crack."

Camilla flashed her a smile.

Some guy should have swept her off her feet long ago... But I dunno. There was still a lot Zona didn't know about the woman, other than her riding, spears, the good job she'd done for Dido at Carthage. She also reminded herself that it was none of her affair. *Camilla's lovers or lack of 'em is her business alone.* She still couldn't help liking the Volscian leader, though, feeling curious about her.

"I agree." The dark cavalry rider turned on her mount. "Rest the men, captain," she said to the officer behind her. "Me and Zona will go on alone; we'll be back soon."

The two women rode slowly right, looking up at the walls; the ditch was deep, steep-sided outside the palisade, and there were those stakes. Zona could see the heads of soldiers up there, plumes on helmets fluttering in the wind. Feeling chilled as she saw Camilla hug a cloak round herself, the warrior rubbed her arms. The breeze which had blown over them faded. *Not that the wind's any big deal; soon we'll be in combat, and that'll be warm enough. But I wish we could stop this; it's gonna be a bloodbath. If only I could see a way. Ares has got to be yukking it up.* The snag was she could see it how Turnus did. *The way Tawfik said, Turnus had a marriage contract, and here comes this snake and kidnaps his bride.* She shook her head. There had to be a way to negotiate this, but Aeneas wasn't going to give up his captive, and nothing else would do it.

Then there was the Tiber flowing close to the steep hill on which the fort stood. The river was smooth and dark but it was wide and deep, with treacherous currents. The water was a natural defence, or so the men in the fort thought, and there was no moat or palisade beside it.

Zona frowned at the river. "We could use a fleet of small boats. Under cover of darkness."

"Yeah, I wish too," agreed Camilla. "But likely our ships would be spotted by any sentries worth their pay. Any ideas yet?"

"I wish. I think we'll have to just storm it," Zona said. "Let's ride on back."

At a walk they retraced their route; as they went, Zona kept eying the stockade. Suddenly she stopped and pointed at the timbers.

"Over there, a weakness in the way it's been lashed together. See it?"

The other rider squinted. "Ah yes, we attack there, right?"

"I think so. It'll help if we can mount a diversion, thin out the numbers there. Hmmmnn."

A rider came galloping up. He was absurdly young with dark eyes and a good tan. Dark hair flopped over his brow; breathlessly he shoved it back.

"The Lord Turnus and the Rutulians have come. They are setting up camp and my lord bids you attend him."

Zona didn't like the abruptness of the summons, *but maybe it's the way this lad puts it.*

Aloud she was unable to keep irony from her tone. "Does he now?"

"My lady, the request is for Camilla of the Volscians. Who are you?"

"Doesn't matter." She kept her voice dry.

Camilla spoke. "Where I go, she does. She's my friend and partner."

Well now, Zona thought. Aloud she said, "You'd better lead on."

They rode slowly back along the fort's outer palisade and ditch. The main gate was approachable over a causeway and looked to be of heavy timber studded with bronze. In spite of the messenger and his summons, they paused to study it. *That's got to be well defended.* Once more the warrior marvelled at how well Aeneas had built in the little time he'd had since coming to Latium. *Or maybe he found this place or stole it.*

When they finally got back to the Volscians, they found things very different. Having arrived with his Rutulian army, Turnus had taken over the place. Already he pretty well had the cavalry under his command. Camilla seethed as she saw what was going on and Zona felt for her.

The rise where they'd left their troops was swiftly being turned into a large army camp. Rows of brown-skin tents had gone up. Men were cutting wood for fires which were already smoking, hauling water up the hill from the river at the bottom, digging latrines, all the varied tasks of an army establishing itself. Some were drilling under bull-voiced sergeants, among them Camilla's people. Shooting glances the rider's way, Zona was glad she wasn't Turnus or any of his commanders. The thin lips and black eyes were bad news.

They were conducted by the young messenger to what the warrior took to be Turnus' large command tent. *Reminds me of my own times as a bandit, always making a show.* Outside the black and red Rutulian flag snapped in a rising wind.

In a hesitant but proud voice the boy asked the two women to dismount, adding that their horses would be cared for. Once they were out of their saddles, he asked for their blades, and ran into trouble.

"Nobody takes my sword," Camilla answered stiffly.

"I guess I'm with her there," drawled Zona.

"You cannot enter His Majesty King Turnus' presence armed." The messenger nearly stuttered in his anxiety. "It is forbidden."

Zona saw him redden and felt sorry for him. *I'm still not going to give on this.*

"We'll see," she answered.

Nobody saying any more, all three of them met each other's eyes. Camilla was already riled by the take-over of her men and the warrior knew she wouldn't stick much more. With herself it was the old thing; she wasn't going to be intimidated. *We're gonna know where we are here, and it's where I want to be. I don't blame this lad for what's happening, I guess it's just rules; bad luck for him he's in the middle.* Giving way simply wasn't her style; right from the start she was going to be treated as the warrior she was, an equal.

"You tell your king," she said quietly, "that it's the warrior Zona and Queen Camilla of the Volscians here."

"So I'm a queen now," said the dark woman wryly. "That could be useful."

To the young man she added, "And ask King Turnus what he thinks he's doing with my men."

Following another, shorter silence, the messenger lifted the flap and went into the tent. Voices sounded, quick and angry, especially the deeper one, but the words couldn't be made out. It finished with a loud roar.

"Bring 'em in, bring them here, whelp!"

If the man's voice was meant to cow its listeners, it failed. Camilla's jaw squared, her dark eyes hot. *Oh, oh,* thought Zona. She felt her own annoyance simmer and the two clasped arms. When the messenger came out the tent as if he'd sat on an ant heap, she was sorry for him again.

"You may enter," he said unnecessarily, "If you will follow me."

The tent was lit by a cluster of four candles on a desk made out of three planks of rough timber. Although daylight could be seen through the hide walls, shadows pooled around it. A tree stump held the desk up and Turnus sat on another. A couple of

scrolls, a pen and inkpot were on the desk which was otherwise clear. The king had a large drinking cup; a few chairs could be seen in the shadows. But for them the tent was empty, as sparsely furnished as Zona's had been.

King Turnus didn't invite his guests to sit and she wasn't surprised. He was a huge, blond-haired man, black-eyed and clean shaven, though his craggy features were stubbled grey and white. With one clamped round the earthenware drinking pot, his hands were like black-haired sides of beef. As he looked the women over, his thick lips curled.

"What can I do for you, ladies?" he boomed, then added slyly, "Nice."

Zona was at once irked by the man's attitude, his indolent sprawl behind the desk. *I hope he falls off his log,* went through her mind. She reminded herself to give him a chance. *He is the wronged party in this. But maybe I can see Lavinia's point if she doesn't exactly rush his way.* Aeneas was a snake but could be he was the better man, *but what a choice!* It made seeking peace, if there was any chance of it, more important – *and never mind these two; innocents are going to die if I can't do it. Maybe I can figure a way to let Aeneas keep the girl, but then I've got a few issues with him…* She reminded herself of how Aeneas had treated Dido, and it helped a bit. Also 'God Aeneas' had snatched Lavinia from her parents' city; she'd not gone with him of her own choice – *whatever she might feel now.*

Camilla barrelled in. It wasn't the most tactful thing she could have said, but it was hard not to sympathise.

"How dare you take over my men?"

Turnus raised a bushy eyebrow. "Have I? Who would they be?"

"You know well enough," she snapped.

He sighed loudly.

That sound's all, 'This is a bit of a nuisance but let's see if I can humour the girl.'

"My army's growing nicely now. Perhaps you can give me a hint? And forgive me but I don't." Turnus leaned back, clasping his big hands behind his neck. "I do have allies, you know, as well as my own Rutulians. On my council I have, along with my father Mezentius, Lausus, my brother Aventinus, the twins Catillus and Coras, and Evander of Arcadia. Each man has brought his own troops so I do get trouble keeping track of which contingents belong to which general. I should say 'belonged' before they committed their men to the cause. Surely you think it is just; I have to get Lavinia back, punish this thief who has so grievously wronged me – "

"You could have asked me." Camilla sounded mollified but still annoyed. "I was out scouting for you, Turnus."

He cracked his knuckles. "King, if you please, wench."

Somehow the Volscian cavalry leader kept herself on a tight leash. Maybe it was the 'wench' that grated with her now. *It sure does with me,* Zona thought acidly.

"King Turnus," Camilla said through her teeth, holding her elbows over her front defensively – *Or should I make that 'aggressive'?* "They are highly trained Volscian cavalry, and you have them drilling under your sergeants like raw recruits. What next – digging latrines?"

"Someone's got to do it. Surely you see that." Even if he thought he was being soothing, the king's voice was like rolling thunder.

"I don't deny that – "

"Well then." He cracked a few more knuckles. Zona almost winced at the noise. *Why does he have to do that?* Appearing to recall his manners, Turnus waved expansively to the walls. "Have a seat, ladies, do. I'll call for cups, you shall have wine. You must be tired and hot after all the, ah, scouting out the field."

Camilla wiped her dark, hot brow with the back of a hand. "I want my men back under my command."

He grinned at Zona, for the first time dealing her into the talk. "Have you been scouting too? Of course you have. Silly of me to overlook it, but a man has so many details to remember. And you are?"

"Zona. Some call me Princess of Troy."

"Oh, *that* Zona. Even in Latium we have heard of

your, ah, doings." Turnus raised his voice in a bellow. "Orderly! Bring two more cups, some refreshment for the ladies!"

"If I might suggest." The warrior wondered at herself being so diplomatic. "Maybe you'll do better to deal with Camilla's problem first."

"She is rather like a donkey – following the same trail," he agreed.

Camilla flushed, even under her dark tan. "I want my men. We're leaving."

Getting to his feet, joints crackling, Turnus picked up two more chairs which turned out to be tree stumps when dragged to the table. A frightened-looking boy in soldier's uniform bustled in with a tray containing two cups like the king's, some bread and cheese. There were crisp looking onions too. Putting the tray down on the desk, the boy saluted and left, drawing the tent flaps closed after him. Turnus poured wine from the flagon that had been brought too. With Zona seated next to the Volscian leader, he gave them brimming cups.

"A rough red but quite good," he remarked. "Now where were we?"

Zona sipped and found the wine as he said.

Camilla said, "My men – "

"Oh that."

Turnus waved a hand dismissively. He sat, took a long drink and wiped his mouth on the back of his hand. A discreet though rumbling burp came after. "Yes, you've got them, just the way my other generals have – "

" – Thank you."

" – But naturally everyone's under my command."

Zona listened and watched. He was genial enough but *he disturbs me, there's too much - arrogance for want of a better word.* She drank more wine and put the cup down on the desk. Her hand could have been steadier. *Got to watch how I go with this stuff on an empty stomach. And I can't see these two, and me, working together. He rubs Camilla up pretty near every time he breathes, me too for that matter.* The tent was hot with sunlight blurred through it and chill trails of perspiration ran down under her vest. Almost mopping her brow, she stopped herself. *No way can I afford to display weakness to this guy.* A long sigh which she muffled. *Yet we gotta work together somehow, all of us have the same interests.* She and Camilla had a reckoning to come with Aeneas who'd got an army, a fort and was bringing reinforcements. The agenda included vengeance for Dido. The man before them also had an army and was ready to fight to get Lavinia back. *So I guess I have to go on trying…* But diplomacy had never been one of her talents. The silence drew out as they all waited for somebody else to speak first.

"Maybe for now," Camilla said tautly.

Turnus leaned back, reached up to clasp his hands behind his head once more. A third time he began to crack his knuckles. A broad, easy smile came and lingered.

"Good, so we're all happy together," he boomed. "Now, what have you two busy little girls dug up for me?"

He was so patronising Zona wanted to hit him. *Wonder how many times I'll have to rein myself in.*

Instead she found herself talking.

CHAPTER THIRTY-TWO

IT WAS EARLY MORNING when the attack on Aeneas' fort began. The sky was partly covered by wedges of violet and grey cloud but there was plenty of blue as well. A stiff wind gusted cool spatters over her skin though Zona was hot in the sun each time it faded away. Cloud shadows chased over the Rutulian army as it surged forward.

Zona was running next to Turnus and carrying her sword. She wore vest and kilt though the king/ general had tried to persuade her to put on armour like his own. Preferring the lightness and speed of movement her things gave, she'd refused. *I can see under his helmet he's already hot and we've a way to go.* With a sunset-red face, he was glistening, sweating heavily. His bronze chest plate, long gauntlets and greaves flashed in sunlight as he ran. *No doubt about it, though; it's impressive and I guess as king he thinks he's got to cut a figure.* Yet like so many men she'd treated on battlefields for their wounds, he was going to cook in the weight and tightness of the metal he carried. Turnus had his sword, a huge two-handed weapon bouncing on his shoulders as he ran. *I'm so glad I'm no king or whatever, don't have to put on a show. Still he's a big boy; he'll cope, and I'll help out if he needs it.* In his right hand he wielded a huge, double-edged battle-axe over his head. Among the crowd of his leather-jerkinned soldiers with swords, spears, bows and arrows she ran on but...

Her thoughts turned fleetingly to Camilla.

In spite of leading a mounted assault, the woman she liked increasingly wasn't going to have an easy time. *When we scouted these defences a couple of days ago, we saw the weak part of the wall as the key.* She and Camilla had argued with the king and his officers that there, up on the right, should be the point of attack. *Stubborn – a donkey's easy to move compared to him!* The king wanted the attack there to be a diversion only, the main attack being here at the central gate and tower. Its purpose was only to draw off Aeneas' forces, leaving the gate exposed.

Still prickly over his arrogance and condescension, Camilla disagreed, as did Zona, and made it known hotly. *I had to do diplomacy again – me. It's almost enough to make me wish Hosni was here. Maybe not, though... Camilla had the idea that her Volscian cavalry was not number one for Turnus, and I have to admit she was right there.* As long as the horsemen drew enemy infantry away from the main gate, he didn't care if they were chewed up. It was the traditional view of horse soldiers all over again. *He said he knew of me – and I used them well, including at Troy, but to him they're not important. She said he's arrogant plenty times. Yeah…*

Zona mused again on the debates *It's what Turnus called them, shouting matches is more like it. And I'm really fed up with being peacemaker.* Having been first with Achilles in Asia Minor, then the Amazons, she knew the value of cavalry and couldn't stick Turnus' obtuseness on the matter much longer. *I so wanted just to side with Camilla. She's right, and we both want a reckoning with Aeneas. Do we really need these men?* A sigh even as she ran. *I guess we do, to make sure Alissar's avenged for him running out on her and how she nearly killed herself, and there's Lavinia, how he stole her. There's Troilus, the way he did nothing while Achilles butchered the kid at Troy, and the rest.* And, of course, they couldn't get to Aeneas without an army.

The trouble was Turnus' ideas were OK. His strategy was good; the plans he'd argued for could easily work. Aeneas was on his way with reinforcements. If they struck quickly, the Rutulians and Volscians would escape the nutcracker jaws of the fort and those advancing forces. They'd drastically cut the enemy's numbers and demoralise the men left by eliminating the fort and its defenders.

What they ended up with was a compromise. The Volscian cavalry would be backed up by Rutulian infantry to give it a bigger punch. Zona reminded herself, *Hey, it could work.* The snag with the idea was that committing infantry to Camilla's assault weakened the forces at the main gate. *I guess like all staff meetings its compromise had to happen and it's a gamble, same as all plans like this. We're soon gonna see if it works. If it doesn't, Turnus will likely have our heads.*

Marked by dust clouds, the clash, yells, screams, cries and whinnies of a cavalry battle, Camilla's forces were already in combat. If they weren't thrown back this had to work; *Turnus' men can't screw up. He'll likely find a way to blame us if they do.*

Zona slid into the moat, avoiding stakes, with Turnus and other commanders. At first like them she went down at a kind of stumbling run, holding her sword over her head while they sheltered under heavy shields. Waving, then casting spears at the palisade, Rutulian troops poured around and after them. They were met by spears in return and steady volleys of arrows. Although they took increasing casualties, the infantry pressed on to the stockade. From the fourth row back they carried ladders which were thrown up against it.

Zona, Turnus and his officers went quickly up from the crowd at the foot of the stockade. Shouts and cheers from the men below rose with them. Spears, arrows and other missiles picked off warriors, pitching them screaming among the attackers.

Near the top of the ladders Turnus looked her way, eyes goggling, mouth sagging.

"What?" she snapped.

"You! You're – "

"What?"

"Can't you see it, the light?"

Not that again. Still, whatever it was, it proved helpful last time when Alissar tried to kill herself. Looking at an arm, Zona saw familiar skin and muscle but she was sheathed in a film of light. *Spooky,* but she was no closer to understanding what it could be. As at the other times it showed up, all she could do was go with it.

She swung off the ladder. Palms slapping the top of the wall, she vaulted the last couple of feet. Light slid over her. *I can see its flecks move on my arms.*

Keeping low, moving smartly right, she avoided a spear thrust. An axe came her way. Zona shuffled, squatted under it. Turnus was over the wall with her. Others were scaling it all along its length. Unsheathing her sword where she'd put it to climb, she closed with the spearman.

He blocked her, swung with his shaft. She feinted, cut once more, but he was at her again. *He's good.* She fell back. *I'll leave myself open; look like I've made a sloppy mistake.* The man came on. He stabbed out and the warrior wasn't there.

Slipping inside his thrust, she saw alarm leech the colour from his face. Beads of sweat popped on his brow. The man expected a journey to Tartarus any moment. Spinning her sword put him off some more. Zona cracked him on the helmet with the flat of her blade. His knees unlocked as he grunted. He collapsed at her feet.

Two more soldiers were behind him. Drawing her knife from its boot sheath, she stepped to meet them. *This is gonna be hot.*

Swords clashing, raining sparks, they engaged. *These two are good, like the guy I just clouted. No surprise; I'm up against Aeneas' trained Dardanians.* Of course 'Father Aeneas' would have gotten the best of his men out of Troy. Even in battle her mind flitted. *Maybe they're Polydamas'. Odd I haven't heard of or seen him. Maybe he's gone his own way.* But then she recalled that 'God Aeneas' had murdered him, and she remembered Mikhail at her fire seemingly another age ago. *I wouldn't put anything past Aeneas.*

The man on the left lunged. Zona got her sword in the way. A roll of the wrist made him drop his blade, clanging on the platform they fought upon. Somebody else shouldered into the place in front of her.

He rushed her, fists wheeling in looping arcs. She dodged inside them and her knee jerked up. The impact jarred through her kneecap but it was worse for the soldier. His face went dark, then whiter than a high cloud. He goggled. His mouth opened and shut, opened and closed once more but no sound came. As his knees folded, he was sweating hard. Collapsing before her, the trooper made keening noises.

That just left the third man, or would have done but for others shoving to get past him. With a roar he sprang, blade raised, flaming with sunlight.

Turnus was there, swinging his great two-handed sword roundhouse. It thunked into the man's neck. Before he could scream, his head lifted off on a gout of blood. Droplets splashed Zona's front, warm on her skin. She tasted iron as she licked her lips. Staring, the head fell and rolled off the platform. She kicked the rest of him after it.

"Thanks."

"You're welcome," he growled. "Let's go get Aeneas."

"He's not here. If you remember, the messenger Tawfik said – "

"When we take this fort he'll come."

She grinned, wiping blood off her cheek. "You could be right. Let's go."

The other enemy troops were keeping back after what Zona and Turnus had done. It couldn't last. Too many were pushing up and would press them forward. She spared a moment to sheathe her dagger and take the king by an arm.

"Just one thing. When we catch up to him, he's mine."

It came out as a roar. "He stole my wife!"

Turnus' heavy blond brows were knotted. His sword was dripping blood by his side, point to the decking. He looked as if he might use the blade on her.

She shook her head slowly. "Mine I said."

"We'll see!"

"Yeah, we will."

Brushing damp, ratty hair off her brow and cheeks, Zona sighed in exasperation. "We don't have time for this. I'll say it once, though, and fast. I feel with you but he's done a lot more than take Lavinia. He killed a Trojan Heir, little more than a boy. No-one knows for sure about his wife and father. His partner Polydamas? He's never been spoken of by anybody all the time I've been trailing this guy. Oh, wait a moment... There was Mikhail, the guy I was with. Aeneas murdered his partner Polydamas, same as those other two. He was at Carthage – until he sneaked out. Queen Alissar would have killed herself over him if I'd not been busted outta jail to interrupt. Luckily Sabblooton, her High Wizard and Chamberlain, cared for her enough to fetch me. So yes, I can see how you feel. And now there's a war on. 'God Aeneas' is mine, Turnus. It's justice for a lot of people, got that?"

He stared at her thunderously. An enemy shuffled forward. The Rutulian king lunged with his sword, wrenched it up and free. There was a soft tearing sound. Crying out as he held in viscera, the soldier reeled back, tangling up others. The pale, greyish coils wafted a stench, looped round a man's feet.

"This isn't over, Zona."

"Fine. Now let's go."

There was a new pause among the attacking troops. Zona took advantage of it by leaping from the palisade, running a few steps to keep her footing. Turnus thudded behind her. As she began to charge up the long, grassy hill to the walls at the top, others were coming too. She could hear Turnus panting, laden with heavy shield, armour and weapons. As strong sunshine beat down out of a turquoise sky only the slightest of breezes blew. *Thank the gods for my vest and kilt.* She was sweating, perspiration rolling, too busy running to whisk off pestering flies and midges. Even with the yells from the fort, the answering shouts and cheers around her, she heard the whine of a hornet close by. It was a long run, even for her and she was breathing hard. *My things won't stop all these spears and arrows, got to trust the gods for that. At least I'm not roasting in armour and helmet though – damn hornets!*

The leaders slammed into the shelter of the main wall and gate. The Rutulian king was red-faced, grunting for air beside her.

"On to the next stage," he gasped. "But this is the hard bit. We still haven't properly worked out the how."

Soldiers had massed around them. Too many were hit by spears and arrows fired by men leaning out over the wall. Rocks and other missiles came from above as well. *No buckets of hot water yet.* The slopes up to the wall were strewn with bodies and wounded men. The losses were already heavy. *There has to be a way to stop this.* The smell of hot troops was thick around her, and men cried out with pain and thirst down the hill.

"I have," said Zona, because it was really rather obvious. "I'm gonna call him out. If he's any honour at all, he'll come fight me, if he's in there. Otherwise the fort commander will. We can stop this, a one on one'll do it."

The king was a hulking, glowering mass looming over her. She saw him clench his fists, mouth a white line in his features.

"It will be me."

"Don't let's start that again."

Turnus raised his hand, saw her expression and dropped it. Under his bronze breastplate his chest visibly rose and fell. Perspiration dripped off him, shone in droplets in his stubble, and the whites of his eyes showed.

Man's got a temper all right.

"It's me does this, I have the right!" he roared.

"No you don't!"

Zona leaped into the space before the gate. The king of the Rutulians grabbed to hold her back. His fingers dug in a shoulder but slipped from shiny skin as she wriggled free. Her move had shocked the fort's defenders so no-one fired an arrow or threw anything. As she stood with folded arms, booted feet apart, the light round her seemed to hot up.

"Who commands?" she yelled. "Is Aeneas skulking here?"

Silence.

The noises Turnus' men were making as they rushed up to cram against the wooden wall seemed to fade. Nobody was shouting and the cries of the wounded appeared to tail off. *I guess it must be the heat, because I'm hyped up.* Birds were silent, none appeared to be flying; no wind blew. It was a moment locked in time.

A deep voice rang out. She was only a little surprised.

"Zona, Bitch of Troy!" It was mocking, jeering. "I'm here for you!"

"Deiphobos."

"I'd have liked 'Father Aeneas' to be here for this." He was putting on regret. His smile was broad, the coarse voice oleaginous as he peered over the wall. "He should have been able to watch this. I'm coming out, Zona, and this time you won't escape me."

She was recalling what Tawfik had said and smiled back easily. *This so needs doing. The world will be a much better place when we're done, and maybe...*

"Bring it on, Deiphobos. You on me, and if I win the fighting stops. It ends here."

"You wish!"

Almost immediately the main gate was flung wide and Deiphobos swaggered out. He hadn't changed a lot during his travels. His burly frame was clad in a flashy version of a soldier's armour and boots. The heavy features were perhaps a little thinner. Coarse black hair flopped over his brow – *but is he starting to go white or am I seeing things?* – as he broke into a run towards her. In his right hand the ex-prince carried a sword, a dagger in his left. Seeing that, Zona stooped to draw her boot knife.

In his eagerness to close with her, he left the gate open behind him. Turnus seized his chance, waving men forward.

"Go, go, go!" he roared.

A tide of troopers saw him and speeded up, rushing the last of the way up the hill. With Turnus at their head, men poured from by the wall, cheering and shouting. Now facing off to Zona, the prince glanced at them but otherwise took no notice. *He reckons when he kills me, everything will be all right. We'll see.* She decided to rile him; it had worked before when

Troy fell, and she knew all about his temper.

"Pretty sloppy, don't you think, Deiphobos?" she drawled.

Curling his lip, he glowered. "I know how you work. Getting your opponents off balance. It isn't going to do it for you here."

She pointed with her sword at the battle which had now moved inside. "I'm right, though. I don't know what Aeneas was thinking leaving you in charge. Like putting an eagle to watch over lambs. Nah, that's not fair to the eagle. He is a noble bird. I should have said 'like a buzzard or a carrion eater.' Like a crow."

With a howl Deiphobos sprang at her. As he came, his sword was raised. It fell, audibly cutting air as she swayed aside. His dagger slashed upwards to gut her.

Zona stepped from the dagger stroke. She eeled away from the sword's return cut. Kicking out, she swept the big man's feet from under him.

Politely she waited for him to scramble up. As spittle shone at his lips, his eyes were rolling, showing their whites.

"You, you!" he choked, hefting sword and dagger.

Her blades scarcely raised, she went on apparently taking it easy. "What? I guess I don't make the sun shine for you, but what?"

"Because of you!" He leaped at her and she pushed him back. "You have thwarted me at every turn, Zona!"

"Oh, you mean when you murdered Paris?" she

asked lightly, but there was steel in her voice.

He attacked with sword and dagger again. Her blade licked out to send his knife spinning away. Chest heaving, he went after it. Zona tossed her own dagger aside.

"I only need my sword to take you." Her smile was all teeth.

"You're on the way to Tartarus," he grated. "If Hades will put up with you. And it's going to be bad and slow, Zona. I promise you that."

"We'll see."

Blades angled, they circled. Deiphobos was grinning half crazily. Just before he rushed in, his eyes flickered.

With a screech of steel, she met him. He'd one of the special steel swords. *Wonder where he got that?* Their blades locked, he was panting, his breath meaty in her face.

"You took it all from me, Zona. I was a prince of Troy, its Heir, then King, but you ruined it all. Couldn't stay out of stuff that wasn't your affair. Now I take my revenge!"

"Dream on."

With a slither of swords, they came apart. He cut at her, an overhead sweep. She backed away. He cat-footed on, raining blows from every direction. Yielding ground, she countered. *I'd forgotten how good he is, need to keep him off kilter.* He was strong too, hammering at her guard. Face red and sheened with perspiration, he started his manic grin again.

She shook her head. *Try some more distraction.* "Looks like you landed on your feet, Deiphobos, but soon you're gonna be on your ass. I'd guess – as usual, too much good living. You can't keep this up for long."

Boring in with a sweep that would have chopped her in two if it had connected, he snarled. Stepping back, she felt the wind of it. *Time I attacked but first a bit more.*

"You're in a mess, Deiphobos." *Keep using his name. Shows derision and it'll make him madder.* She jerked her head towards the fort which was on their left. It was full of the sounds of battle – roars, shouts, screams. "Aeneas left you in charge. You lost your head over me; I guess I should feel flattered. As usual – and look at it. You screwed up. He won't be a happy man when he gets back from wherever he's at. If you weren't such a bottom feeder, I could feel sorry for you."

Deiphobos snarled some more. "I'll give him your head. He'll like that, promote me in his army… Time'll come when I'll get rid of him – "

"What's keeping you? Slowing up, are we?" she purred.

In a fresh attack he rushed her. This time she didn't back up but moved into it. His face white, the prince changed a swing to a stabbing move. Caught by surprise, Zona was only just in time to slide away from it.

She leaned forward and her blade flickered. His throat torn, he showered blood, then it jetted over her. Deiphobos looked at it as if he didn't believe it was his own. This was the sort of thing that happened to others, not him. She wrenched her sword free, widening the hole in him. Terror flooded his eyes as he reeled, choking on blood.

"Ghrryaa – " he bubbled as blood coursed between his lips.

"I'll make this quick," Zona said. "Which I bet is more than you've done for a lot of others."

She went forward, sword arm extended. Her blade pierced his leathers, finding seams around his breastplate. As it plunged into his side, Deiphobos gargled blood and fell.

CHAPTER THIRTY-THREE

✛

THE NEXT MORNING Aeneas and a large army came ashore to the battlefield. They were in a fleet of high-prowed, beaked warships and made up of the allies the Dardanian had recruited while he was away. Aeneas wasn't the first to wade ashore through shallow water; a lot of his forces were ahead. He brought Tarchon and his Etruscans as his biggest contingent but a lot of other peoples had sent troops as well – just as Tawfik had told Zona.

It was a cloudless day, the sky shining blue. A shrieking, fighting cloud of gulls swooped around the ships which were jostling ashore as if the gods were angry. Maybe Poseidon would burst from the surface of the water flourishing his trident with a roar. *Anything to stop the coming slaughter,* thought the warrior as she watched the Trojan's allies storm onto the beach.

Around her and her horse were Camilla and the Volscian cavalry. Turnus had split his army. The infantry were to carry on with the siege of the fort which had managed to throw them back the previous day after

Deiphobos' death. Camilla's horse would repel the river-borne attack. Able to see what he was thinking, Zona was still uneasy.

Maybe Turnus is still in shock after his narrow escape from the fort, she thought. *He should be thinking better than this but as usual he wouldn't listen.* At first he and the men whom Deiphobos had let in when he left the gate open made good progress. It didn't last. A Trojan officer, Pandarus, forced the gate shut behind them. Although Turnus killed him in the fighting, the officer sent so many against him that the Rutulian king had to jump for the river to escape. The men he left behind were butchered, heads spiked along the ramparts.

Dividing the army's a gamble. Zona thought their full numbers should be here to throw back the invaders into the river. Then the whole army could turn on the fort, as long as Aeneas was repelled quickly.

Like other mounts in the cavalry, Lina tossed her head, eager to begin. Next to her, in sleeveless leathers, Camilla mopped short, dark hair from her brow. Near-black eyes shone as her dark face was split by the white of her smile.

"Now at last, if he's with this fleet, we get even for Alissar. We'll drive them into the water, chop up those left."

The two women sat on their mounts and went on watching the landings. After a while Camilla pointed at the mounted leaders coming their way. The men wore fancy armour which flashed in the sunlight.

I bet Aeneas says some god made him his armour, Zona told herself sourly.

"I know some of these men," the Volscian said slowly.

"Yeah, Aeneas," answered the warrior dryly. "And he's mine."

Camilla seemed to ignore that. "Look, the big one, that's Abas… " She picked out several more leaders. "Aeneas has certainly done well getting this lot together."

"He's a good talker, always has been."

Camilla mimicked Turnus' arrogant growl. "Change of plan."

Zona grinned. "What? And that was good."

"Well you know we were meant to hold back, let plenty of them ashore before we strike. I reckon a beheading strategy here. Take out the men on horses in showy armour, what do you say?"

"Works for me."

"Let's go then. You have the riders on the left; I'll get the ones on the right. Our horsemen then just sweep up their troops."

Zona pushed Lina to an easy canter. Camilla on her right, the Volscian cavalry drove forward behind them. Gradually the pair drew ahead. The sun went on being golden out of a cloudless sky. Air flowed over the warrior's shoulders, around her like she was bathing in warm, crystal water. The pounding of hooves, yells from the riders woke all her love of battle. It was hard to credit that in moments they would mix it in a mess of men and horses.

As she rode closer, the warrior drew her short spear from her saddle boot. She couldn't see Aeneas but the large guy her comrade – *When did Camilla turn into that?* – had said Abas was a target.

She hurled her spear in an arc. Flashing in sunlight, it plunged towards him. The range was extreme but Zona was sure of her aim. Hand and eye worked without her thinking about it.

Punching through the big man's neck, the spear emerged in a shower of blood and he tumbled from his saddle. His feet caught in the stirrups and Abas was dragged as the creature bolted.

Other riders copied her. Spears whooshed through the air but many fell short. Leaning down in her saddle, she drew her knife. Sighting carefully, she threw it. She heard it whistling as it flew, even over the thunder of hooves, the cavalry's yells and answering shouts. The dagger went in under the arm of a man in bronze, decorated armour and he fell.

With her and Camilla still leading, the cavalry crashed into Aeneas' troops. Everything became the struggle. Flashing limbs and blades ran with sunlight, tangling together. There were the screams and wails of men fighting and falling, whinnies and howls of horses. Blood flowered; she smelled its coppery-iron stink mixed with the riper stench of entrails. The heat was ramped up.

Two soldiers were coming at her. Zona kicked the spear out of one's grip. Sensing what her rider needed, Lina sidestepped the other man. Horses behind her trampled down the spearman as he shrieked in agony.

At first the battle went well. The Volscians tore into the enemy infantry, brushing them aside. Shouts, war cries and screams reverberated in Zona's ears. Choking clouds of dust fogged out anything more than a few horse's lengths away. More stenches of blood, gore and death were there as men and horses collapsed in masses. It seemed that everywhere were smashed bones and gaping, bloody wounds. The old Zona would have gloried in the charge. *I hate this now.* She was all too aware of the fragility and intricacy of life. The ease with which it was ripped away in battle, the little regard with which it was held sickened her. Life was the gods' gift but it was destroyed almost casually. Through the battle her anger against Aeneas grew. He'd caused this war and she vowed afresh that he would pay. In the carnage she hunted 'Father Aeneas' but grew increasingly frustrated as she found no sign of him. She recalled his prudence in battle when he and Polydamas were generals for Troy. *Yeah, trust him to keep well back.*

It started to get harder to push on. Soon she saw why. The Dardanian had always been a clever soldier, and he was doing his thing now.

Men were advancing slowly up the river's broad, muddy beach and they had their shields overlapping. Zona had seen this tactic at Troy, and it worked there. Behind their lines curving with the beach were high-prowed ships. From beached vessels and others in the shallows, men crowded gangplanks, some leaping straight into the river. *How many troops is Aeneas bringing?*

Zona studied the developing situation. The enemy front line was anchored at each end by river bends. It wasn't an obvious place at which to land troops but it was clear why Aeneas had picked the spot. She thought of her and Camilla leading their cavalry at the lines. *We might be able to punch through but the losses would be high.* Same if they tried to attack either end of the shield lines. They would lose a lot of horsemen to the river. More warriors were disembarking all the time and could attack on the flank. Even as they came ashore, these men were also forming shield walls. *I hate this but seems like there's only one real choice here. I think we bit off a little much coming against this army, but we told Turnus…*

Grim-featured, she looked at Camilla who returned it. The Volcsian's hair was wild around a sweat and dirt-smudged face. The leathers clung to her perspiration and battle stained, her sword red along its blade. Zona was using her own sword to get tangled hair out of her eyes. Her chest was heaving; the fighting was some of the toughest she'd done in a long time. The way it was going didn't improve her mood.

"We've gotta back up," she growled.

Camilla sighed. "With those four ranks they have – "

" – All with closed shields."

"I'm sorry, we should have hit them earlier – and I so want Aeneas!"

"Yeah, well don't forget Turnus had a hand in this plan. As for Aeneas, he's mine," Zona said. "I've been after him since Troy. I've told you before."

The other woman sighed. "Never mind that for now, I guess. If we get the chance I'll fight you for him later. And I'll say it again – I'm sorry."

"What for?" Zona asked sharply. The bitter ashes of pulling back grated on her mind. "I'm meant to be the one with the rep. I should have told you to get out of this sooner."

"If only we had some foot soldiers of our own," the cavalry leader lamented.

Zona wiped perspiration from her chest and arms. This interval for them couldn't last. *It's time we got on - withdrawing.*

"This is Turnus' fault. If he'd not left us here out on a limb. He thinks he's going to take the fort. We both told him before this started he should never have split the army, or at least have given us some infantry. But no, mule-headed!... 'If you little girls are any good, you should be able to roll back the ships' men.'" She reverted to her own voice. "If he calls us 'little girls' again... You were at this morning's council, you heard him. Ha!"

"He'll want our hides for this," said the Volscian soberly. "But we can't lose any more time."

Standing in her stirrups, she shouted to her nearest commander, giving the order to retreat, adding that he should pass it on. Over the crash and screams of the fighting, Zona yelled it too. Slowly, nothing like fast enough with the enemy pressing forward while more came ashore, the order was passed on. Reluctantly, then ever faster, the Volscian cavalry began to disengage.

When they linked up with Turnus and the infantry the king was throwing a strong force at the fort. The clamour of the struggle was deafening and fighting looked to be by ghosts appearing and vanishing in dust clouds. Zona saw that once more they'd taken the stockade. Strewing casualties, having crossed the open rise, the infantry were hammering at the inner walls. At first Turnus didn't see the returning cavalry or the linked shields coming after them like a bronze wall. He was co-ordinating and leading an attack on the central tower which had caused him so much trouble the previous day.

It reared over the rest of the fort, its flag still flying and wreathed in dust clouds. Full of Aeneas' men, it was still connected to the walls and their walkways by its network of gangways. These had to be stronger than they looked and the tower gave views all over the battle. Spears, arrows, stones, any missile to hand, rained from and at the tower. Scalding water was also thrown at anyone who got close enough to the wall. As everywhere else, there were yells, screams and dust as waves of men came at the wall, only to be thrown back amid heaped wounded and bodies.

Turnus still hadn't seen the approach of Zona, Camilla and the Volscians. Brow drawn into a scowl, he was looking grim but fierce. Under his helmet his face was red, glistening with perspiration. He appeared to have been aged by the war and his features were dirty, cut by deep lines round his mouth.

Catching sight of Zona as she dismounted, he glowered at her. "What are you doing here? The cavalry should be defending the beach, as we agreed at our meeting earlier."

"Have you seen what's headed our way?" she countered. "I don't think so."

"I don't see anything. Only your supposed cavalry." He turned his back and flung at her, "Now get back and do your job."

As Zona, Camilla and the nearest Volscian riders watched him in amazement, he called for a torch.

Dismounting too, Camilla burst out, "You're mad!"

Turnus wheeled on her. "What did you say?"

"I said you're – "

" – When this is over I'll have you crucified. Like the Carthaginians have started doing with their criminals. It's a very special penalty. I'll look forward to watching it."

"You won't!" Zona snapped. "The Volscians are independent allies."

"And not for the first time I think we might be mistaken there," added Camilla. Silkily. "Maybe Lavinia's better off with Aeneas. Even after what he did to Alissar, he can't be such a thug."

His eyes hot, Turnus' mouth was a straight white line. "This isn't over. We'll pick it up later, I promise you that."

Somebody thrust a torch into his fist. With an overarm pitch he tossed it at the tower. Trailing sparks and aromatic smoke, it lodged in the tower's side.

Golden and scarlet flame leaped and billowed up the wooden wall. Coughs and screams burst from inside. The tower lurched away from the fire which was spitting, crackling and gusting up sparks. *The gods help those men in there; that tower's likely resinous pine.* It was as if a lot of folk inside had crowded across it, away from the blaze. Gangways collapsed, wrapped in flames and the Rutulian troops cheered hoarsely. The whole thing lurched again, with fresh cries from inside and fell. More howls and cheers broke from the army outside the fort's walls.

The Rutulians surged at the walls. Arrows, spears and rocks cascaded down at them. Men fell shrieking into the dust and roil and were trampled but they pressed on. Ladders were thrown against the logs and soldiers went up them. Zona wondered if maybe this was going to work. *Turnus may not be such a show-off idiot after all.*

The gate burst open.

At first nearly hidden by smoke and dust, men boiled out. Brandishing swords, spears and axes, with smoke-rough war cries, they charged the Rutulians. Sheets of arrows flew over them from behind. Around Turnus, Camilla and Zona, soldiers fell wailing and shouting.

With a roar, the king punched the air towards the stampede out of the fort. Adding their voices to his, men sprang that way.

Then the army from the ships got into the fight. The Rutulian forces were in a swiftly closing trap.

Camilla acted.

With a scream to the Volscians, she leapt into her saddle. Jumping onto her mount, Zona was beside her. The cavalry's losses against the massed shield bearers were going to be bad. All those men had to do was hold their lines but the horse riders no longer had any choices. Yet there was one thing they could do; Camilla likely knew what it was but this was too important to take any chances.

As the cavalry tried to get up their pace in the little distance they had, she leaned in her saddle towards her friend. *We'll be lucky to work up a good trot,* which made this all the more vital.

In the clash of battle Zona yelled out: "Close up, hit them in a mass! It's our only chance."

The Volscian commander added her voice. *She's seen the need for this.* "Keep going, smash on through."

Bunching together as they managed a canter, the horsemen neared the locked shields of the Etruscans. Even over the other sounds of battle, Zona heard hooves pounding as dust enveloped them all. Pushing Lina to the front, she smelled the tang of horses and sweat. *Just like old times,* passed wryly through her mind. Spears and arrows took down riders and horses into screaming, threshing heaps but the Volscians pressed on. *Turnus was right, damn him. We shoulda done this earlier.* She shrieked encouragement to the riders. Camilla was next to her, face alight with the rush of battle as she unlimbered her spear and short axe.

The two sides met.

Horses and riders bellowed, as did the men Aeneas was bringing to battle. As the infantry started to buckle, weapons clashed. Riders poured into gaps while foot soldiers sought to plug them. At other points in the first line, more horses and men were brought down in howling tangles. The air was thick with dust, heavy with the stenches of blood, viscera and death. It was one of the worst, bloodiest fights of the war so far.

Somehow Zona and Camilla stayed mounted and, as she fought, the warrior noticed her arms. Splashed with gore, they shone faintly silver. She didn't have time to wonder about it; all she could do was note it there and go on.

Three men right ahead were trying to link shields over a fallen comrade. Zona pushed Lina among them, the man yelling as he was trampled. She heard bones crack and winced. *If only this weren't happening.* Two staggered back, avoiding her while the third cut with an axe. She caught it on her sword, feeling the impact ring up her arm, and the horse barged into another trooper.

With a flick of the wrist she disarmed the axeman. As he lunged with a spear he caught up, her sword took him in the throat. Blood spattered her. Goggling, choking, he collapsed.

The injured man had somehow pushed himself to his feet, gripping a sword two-handed. Lina kicked him; he dropped the weapon, moaning as she rode him down.

In the brief lull she saw Camilla. Enemy riders were pushing through the infantry. *However many troops were there in those ships? I guess more came.* Circling in a ring where men had given ground, the Volscian battled another rider.

Both wielded axes. The big, clean-shaven man flourished his over his head. White teeth showed in a grin, splitting his tanned features.

"A woman on a horse!" he boomed. "What is this? It is I Orsilachus come to take your head, wench."

"Oh yeah? Prepare for Tartarus yourself, warrior. Have your coin ready for the ferryman."

Camilla sawed her reins. Her bay horse turned into a smaller circle inside the big man's. They struck with their axes, blades ringing over the sounds of surrounding battle. The woman was first to recover from the impact and swung again. Her blade went straight and fast at Orsilachus' perspiration and dust streaked face. His eyes widened as his colour drained. He got his axe in the way just in time. He looked as if he'd liked to have run if he had the chance.

Rising in her stirrups, Camilla rained blows at armour and bone. Her blows were turned by the leather armour – until one went straight through. Orsilachus let out a high cry like a child's. The axe wedged in the bone of his shoulder and was twisted free. He sounded as if he was begging for mercy but Camilla hacked on.

As she chopped at him blood and gristle flew. A strike stove in his helmet. Face twisted and coated with blood and grey stuff, the man gurgled, sliding from his mount.

Camilla punched the air with her gory axe. She screamed in triumph.

Must remember to stay good with her, Zona thought.

More soldiers came at her. She wheeled her mount to meet them. It took hard work with her sword against spears and axes to break free. When she did, three were down, one sitting as he held in his innards with both blood-soaked hands. The others retreated. Zona went after them one at a time and cut them down.

Looking round for more opponents, she saw Camilla again.

Afoot the other woman duelled a fresh trooper. Zona saw her mount was held by one of her men. Her opponent was mounted; he was big, or maybe the armour over his leathers made him look that way. It was bronze, showy. *Looks like an officer –*

He was also laughing, his brown, clean-shaven but stubbly face wreathed in a smile. The Volscian leader calmly awaited him with sword and shield. The guy set his heels to his horse to ride her down.

CHAPTER THIRTY-FOUR

ZONA cried out a warning but it was lost in the crash of the fighting. She leaned over her horse's neck, beating with the flat of her sword to force a way to her friend. *I'm not gonna make it.* Someone slashed at her with an axe from the side. She had to take a moment to block it. Another was lost as she cut at him backhand. Her blade severed his neck above bronze armour. Gore splashed her as she wrenched at her sword while his head fell. Her blade was lodged in the spine; she had to twist it to free the steel of the corpse. Next Lina's footing almost went as she trod down a body and a man shrieked. A few paces on the horse slid in innards. A hand reached blindly, grabbed the horse's leg and nearly unseated her rider.

Wiping her hair away, blinking at salt, the warrior forged on. She was still too slow to be able to help.

"See how I've fooled you, silly woman!" crowed the enemy rider, pounding at Camilla. "I, the Ligurian son of Aunus will take you down. Your head shall adorn my spear. Fancy you thinking you could beat me from on foot. Silly woman!"

Camilla was still waiting for him. His long spear lowered, the Ligurian charged. He was thundering across a cleared circle, almost on her at a gallop. Waiting to the last moment, she dodged.

Watching, Zona's heart was in her mouth, beating hard, and she was dust-dry. *I wish it was me doing this –*

The mounted warrior blundered past Camilla, dragging his foaming, sweating horse in a tight turn. With quick footwork, she moved in on him. Seizing the horse's reins, she yanked the animal off balance. It crashed onto its side, the rider only just kicking free. As the horse struggled up and charged through a watching crowd, the man drew his sword.

The Volscian let him use it to climb to his feet. When he attacked she met him with her blade. They swopped a flurry of blows. If not taken up with more warriors, Zona would have worried for her afresh. Again as she fought clear, she saw that she was afire with light but once more didn't have a chance to think about it.

Wrapped in dust, the heat seemingly worse, the battle swayed one way, then another. Men yelled war cries, shrieked in agony. Horses whinnied and screamed. The smells didn't bear thinking of but Zona compared them to hot sewage. Darkening the air still more, javelins and arrows rained. It seemed every man sought death by iron-tipped weapons to claim honour and glory in the carnage, and Zona was part of it. She went through the enemy as if Ares himself was protecting her.

Slowly the Volscian cavalry were pushing their opponents back. Zona was beginning to hope this might go the Rutulians' way, as long as Turnus held on at the fort in the rear.

Caught up with men at each side, another in front, Zona didn't notice the spearman. With the Volscian leader close at her right, Camilla didn't see the guy either. Looking for an opening, he was on foot circling round them.

Neither woman saw the spear arc into the sky. They didn't spot it on the way down.

It punched through Camilla's leathers, knocking her off her horse. Stuck in her chest, it was covered in gore. She was coughing up more as it kept pumping when she slammed into the ground.

Zona spotted the man who'd thrown the shaft. She was later to hear that his name was Arruns but names weren't on her mind right then. *I'm gonna kill him, I'm gonna kill him! If I had a choice it would be* so *slowly.* Then rage blotted everything out. With a cry that was part howl, part snarl and shout, she hurled her sword. The point went through his throat, smashing his voice box so he could only whimper as it tore the back of his neck. It practically cut his head off, leaving it flopping in bloody streams on his shoulder. Fountains of blood erupted from the stump of his neck and his mouth but not enough for Zona. Engulfed in grief and fury over another friend lost, she wanted to kill him again. Flaming with her need for vengeance, she'd no trace of changed Zona left.

Flinging herself out of her saddle, she took the blood-soaked Volscian in her arms. Rocking her gently, she was crooning to her wordlessly.

Camilla was pulling feebly at the spear shaft. The point lodged in her ribs, she couldn't shift it. Her face was white and turning grey, dark eyes losing their shine as she sank into everlasting blackness.

Lips now only bubbling red, she breathed, "I love you, sister, comrade. Get word to – to Turnus, pleeeeaaase… "

Guessing a lung was pierced, if not the heart, Zona threw back her head and howled again.

Through tear-blurred vision, she noted that her hands and arms were burning white. She couldn't feel any heat but the light was blinding. *It's been here so often – not now! What does it want?* Then Dido's pyre came to her, but she'd learned mainly to ignore this light thing since then. It seemed to come and go at random. Deep inside she knew her mind was all over the place, so how could she know anything about it now? Zona's reeling, spinning mind flashed back to when she'd first seen this glare happen. *Did someone speak in that pool? I'm imagining it.* But the light was spooky, inexplicable; things like this didn't happen to an ordinary, practical warrior. *Now, though, what if?...* Maybe it was a thing given her especially for this. The notion was crazy but so was the whole thing.

No more thinking on this. Very gently, trying not to hurt the other woman, Zona worked the spear loose. After it came a rush of dark heart blood and the blade grated on ribs. Chewing her lips to hold in emotions she could no longer allow herself, she tore open Camilla's jerkin.

Blood still flowed out the jagged wound. She'd never seen so much while a person lived, and the Volscian was unconscious. Zona wasn't a follower of Asclepius or any god. She'd seen too much suffering, dealt out a lot, and none of it made any sense. She didn't trust gods; they had their own agendas which folk like her could never fathom, but she prayed now.

Not knowing what else to do, she put her palms on the wound. Blood flowed over her hands and soaked her wrists. *At least her heart's still working; has to be - there's so much.* If only this would help.

White light brightened, flared even more. As it ran down her arms, pooling on and round her hands, it blotted them out. Full of grief, anger and frantic hope, Zona worked on. She had to save this woman, impossible though it looked.

When the injury knitted together, she didn't see;

everything there was dazzling light. The warrior had fought hard for hours. Then had come her burst of fury at the man who did this. Swaying with exhaustion, she held her hands in place and poured out light.

It was Camilla's voice which got through to her. Feeble, it was still clear and firm.

"What?... "

Zona carried on letting the heatless fire slide down her to the wound's site. She was putting all she had into this, still praying. It *had* to work.

"What?" said the horsewoman more strongly. "Where am I, is this Tartarus?"

Sounds, sights and smells of the battle raging around them flashed back. While being a conduit for the light, Zona had shut them away. She clutched the other gently to her chest, taking care not to crush her. Light spilled over them both, though it was fading, job done. A thousand and more things needed to be said and jumbled up her tongue.

"No, you're not there," she said brokenly. "This is the middle of a battle."

"Huh?"

"I've never believed until now but I prayed. I think a god healed you. There was a spearman, I killed him – "

"My poor Zona!"

"When Xan left, I wasn't going to let myself care about anyone else. People die round me!"

"Ssshhhh."

They clung to each other, giving and receiving comfort. Zona could scarcely believe what had happened, didn't ever want to let her friend go.

"You are a real princess of Latium," Camilla breathed into her hair. "How could you do this? I was dying – "

"I don't know about that," the warrior answered uncomfortably, still holding the reviving woman. "And, as for how, it just seems to have happened. That light, I'll never be mad at it again."

She looked round the field, seeing the battle a second time since she'd begun healing. As the fighting came into clearer focus, she saw that most of the Volscian horsemen had retreated since their leader fell. Only the leader's three trusted lieutenants – Tarina, Tulla, and Tarpeia – were there to keep the enemy off while Zona healed. *Camilla and they had such fun trashing Ba'al's temples -* She couldn't avoid an upspring of contempt for the others. *They might have seen their commander hit but surely they ought to have avenged her. It was left to me!* Zona wasn't sure she liked being called Princess of Latium if this was what its people were like.

Camilla had seen the same as her. With difficulty, gasping, she tried heaving herself up.

"My faithful three." Her face, chest and arms were sticky with mingled perspiration and gore. "And you men. Only you few left?"

The dark-haired and complexioned Tulla answered. "The Volscians saw you fall. Thinking everything was lost they withdrew. The Rutulians are falling back as well."

"They turned tail and ran!" Zona said harshly.

Shame-faced, Tulla nodded.

"Not you, though," Camilla panted, "Not Tar and Tarp, these faithful men with us. I must, must – "

Zona held her firmly but gently. "Take it easy. It'll come."

She gave thanks to God, gods, whatever. By a miracle she'd never start to fully grasp, she had her friend back. Whatever happened now, she wasn't going to risk losing her a second time. She wasn't certain the white light would be there again or that she'd be able to call it up. A second time she might not be able to restore Camilla.

"Let me deal with this while you get your strength back," she said softly. "Camilla, I do armies; they're kinda my thing."

A man was on one knee beside the two women. *It must be urgent for him to have got past our people shielding us,* thought Zona. *Oh, oh, I reckon.* He was wild-haired, eyes rolling as he panted out words.

"Lady." It was unclear which of the pair he was talking to. "The Rutulians are in retreat, leaving the field quickly – "

"We know they're quitting," Zona answered

sardonically.

"Lady, the Lord Turnus is down."

"What?" both women burst out. They were echoed by Tarina, Tulla, Tarpeia and their men forming a wall of swords round them.

Motioning her friend to stay down, Zona rose. She put her hands on her hips. "What happened?"

Taking a deep, ragged breath, the messenger rose to face her and began to talk. "It happened fast. Turnus and the enemy commander, 'God', 'Father', 'Pious' Aeneas, he calls himself. In the midst of the hottest fighting they found each other. Turnus was in a chariot but he jumped down. Why in Hades did he have to do that?"

The man closed his eyes. The expression on his smudged features said he was reliving the events, battling his memories. He rubbed a hand at short, grizzled hair.

"A wide space cleared, how it does for such fights. We, the Trojans, everybody around watched. Gods, I wish I hadn't! But, even although I had a bad feeling on this, I couldn't look away."

He was a veteran and was facing up to Zona, in spite of her hipshot position and cold eyes. The man dragged in a deep, shaky breath and tears stood in his eyes.

Seeing what she looked like in her mind's eye, she said calmly, "Take it easy, soldier. I know you've had a rough time."

Barely audible, he whispered, "We're finished."

The warrior laid a hand on his arm. "Take it easy, I said. Just tell it as best you can."

"Right." Another breath which was part gasp. "There's not much, then we must run."

"We'll see about that." It was Camilla, her voice thready.

The messenger began once more. "They started in with spears. Both missed. So they closed up and went at it with swords. Their shields crashed and they fought. Turnus was the bigger man but 'Father Aeneas' held him off. Well, they carried on, back and forward, but then Turnus must have seen an opening."

"And?" Camilla leaned forward and Zona went onto one knee to hold her. More colour was in the Volscian commander's cheeks but she still came over weak. "And?"

The trooper wiped at his slick face. He left a new smudge on his brow and looked haunted.

He spoke fast but succinctly, as only a soldier could of such events. The women leaned forward, Camilla held in Zona's arms.

"I'm not kidding, right. He, Turnus, leaped straight into the air. His sword came down with enough power to hack away a tree, an old, twisted olive nearby. It met Aeneas' blade with a shattering sound, and that's what it did, broke off right near the hilt. Turnus stared at it like he didn't believe it. Then he started to back off, but slowly… "

"Go on," said Zona.

"Two men were there with him, standing in the front of the Trojan watchers. One man was as bald as a boulder, the other had a beard. Turnus was big but they dwarfed him. The bald one, he said something like 'You want me to take him, Father Aeneas?' Aeneas, he said, 'I've got this, hand me your spear, Achates.'"

By then a wide ring of surviving Volscians was leaning in, engrossed by the story. Tulla, her companions Tarina and Tarpeia were bunched together. Zona noticed there were even some Trojans leaning in. *Soldiers love a good story, specially if they're on the winning side. This is a catastrophe for the Rutulians but even so… And this guy is good. Maybe after the war he should take it up…* Realising he was the focus of attention, the guy cleared his throat and warmed to his tale. He drew it out, almost grinning as he looked around, doom-laden though his words were.

"Get on with it, Virgil." Tulla sounded impatient.

"OK… Achates gave over his spear, a thing like a tree. Aeneas threw and it went through bronze armour to pierce Turnus' thigh. He couldn't stand, not with it sticking out of him like that, and he crashed down. Next thing Aeneas is standing over him with his sword. Turnus, he begged for his life. It was pitiful to see and hear but that bastard drew it out, just standing there.

Unman anyone it would. When he'd had enough listening, he simply said, 'You lose.' With him lying there and trying to shield himself with his hands, 'God Aeneas' plunged his sword in his chest. He put his foot on Turnus to wrench it out and roared like a bear, and that was all."

The silence which followed was deep, the noises of battle appearing to come from another world. The sun was still hot but the shadows of the watching men and women lengthened; the afternoon was drawing on. Zona could hear buzzards and looking up she saw vultures drift over the battlefield. *Nobody else might but those birds are going to do well after this is over.*

Aware of men and horses starting to break round the island of quiet, she gritted, "This isn't over. He's mine."

"I have to go soon. If I live I'll record all this," the soldier said. "But Lady, he's got Achates, and that other monster Dares with him, and the things I saw him doing. He was loving it! Those guys are as horrible as each other. Are you sure about this?"

"Yeah, I am."

Camilla struggled in her arms to rise. "I want him! I owe him for my men, and Alissar. She's my friend too."

Zona held her back. "I have to do this, me. You know it. And you're getting better, though you're not there yet. Rest. I'll take him, and I have the right – "

" – Zona!"

The warrior was gentle but firm. "Seems like we both want a piece of him, but you've got to recover, and this won't wait. I don't know just what I did to heal you, but I've said I don't think I can do it again. You can't even stand yet, and he's got those two guys. Don't do this to me, Camilla."

There was a new silence. The soldier Virgil took the chance to fade into the watchers. *I guess this is one thing he won't record,* thought Zona dryly. She didn't blame him. Even if he could tell a good story, he was only an ordinary soldier and this kind of stuff was over his head. The sounds and reek of combat were more immediate as the Rutulian retreat washed around the little group faster. The Trojans who'd listened to the words about Turnus and his end were gone, maybe to warn Aeneas. She needed to act fast. He was *not* getting away this time.

When the Volscian looked defiant, she went on, "I'll take him. I promise I'll get justice for all the people he's hurt and killed, all the ruined lives. I swear it."

"All right, I should think you will." Camilla gave in to the facts of her condition reluctantly. "But I want to hear it all, every detail."

With a relieved smile, Zona got to her feet. She reached down and they clasped hands. "You will."

Camilla went on holding her fingers. "I never thanked you for saving my life – "

" – No need."

"There is for me. And one other thing; I'll stay now; I've no real choice. But, Zona, once this is over, however it works out, I want to be with you, go where you do. If you'll have me."

Zona was so engulfed by emotion she couldn't speak at first. Her throat closed like the hollow in a reed, her eyes blurred and prickled. *How can anyone want me, the things I've done, and there was what I did to that man over Camilla.* The thing she was setting out to do; Xanthia would be horrified but this had to be, and there was more.

"Your place is with your folk," she got out.

"No it isn't. Except these faithful few, they ran when I fell, didn't even check to see if I was still alive."

"You shouldn't be; your wound was pretty bad."

"Tarpeia, Tarpina and Tulla can lead the Volscians, what's left of them. Will you have me, Zona?"

Two warriors sharing promises, they squeezed each other's fingers. Dark eyes met and held amber ones.

Zona's voice was fervent. "Yeah."

"Take care of yourself, you hear. And don't forget he's got those two men."

She grinned. "I'll do my best, and they're just a little bonus."

Saying no more, she released Camilla's hand and went to find Aeneas.

CHAPTER THIRTY-FIVE

✤

IT WAS SOME TIME before Zona found the Dardanian.

Forcing a way through retreating troops as the evening drew on was hard going. They made such a press of men that, although trying to flee quickly, they slowed themselves up. It wasn't so bad a retreat that they were leaving wounded comrades behind, and those slowed them further. Some of the men hauled themselves along – slowly. Where there were gaps, loose horses got in the way, panicking and going all directions.

It was hot, dust reddening the low sun; shadows danced and writhed together everywhere and Zona was bone-tired. Having been healing Camilla after fighting most of the day, she was thirsty and irritable. It seemed every muscle ached; the next day if she lived they would punish her. *I'm maybe getting a little old for this stuff*, she kept telling herself.

Yet she couldn't give up. Camilla was her sister in a way she'd all but forgotten since Xanthia left. She'd promised her justice and a full account of this. She kept on reminding herself of the many things she had to settle with Aeneas. Now he was somewhere near they wouldn't wait – and if she wasn't careful he might evade her again.

Even so, if only she could be allowed to rest, for a couple of moments. Gritting her teeth, she forced herself to shoulder a way on. If she said 'excuse me' one more time!

At last she caught up to him.

This is quite the scene, she couldn't avoid thinking wryly.

Aeneas was backlit by the falling sun, his shadow long in front of him. Squinting, she could see that he was the same deceptively slight, dark man. His face was maybe a little thinner. He was riding a fancy, gold-coated chariot with what looked like black horses which were also throwing distorted shadows. *Trust him to make a splash. Still, I guess, seeing how he's 'God Aeneas', he's got to go for it, comes with the title.* She reminded herself none of that meant he wouldn't be a tough opponent; he'd not have slowed up and she'd seen him in action at Troy. He wore a soldier's leathers but they were shiny with polishing and sweat. His corselet was plated with gold and bronze, glass or diamonds. The helmet he had on was crested with purple – a colour difficult and expensive to get and adopted by kings and Emperors. Of gold, it flashed and winked in sunlight when he moved his head. The cloak he wore was also of purple and gold-clasped.

'Pious Aeneas' carried a gold-plated bow. On seeing Zona he took aim at her. The bow stretched until its tips almost touched. His left hand was against the arrow point, the right and bowstring back against his chest. She saw the arrow released, heard it whirr and ducked out of its flight path. Aeneas' face creased in annoyance.

Flanking his chariot, one on each side, were two colossal men, their shadows long and black. Leathered and armoured as they were, both seemed to disdain helmets. The one on the left had scruffy, dark hair and was shaggy-bearded, his companion bald as an egg.

Aeneas waved them forward.

The bearded one reached her first. His sandaled feet came off the ground as he leaped. A large spear was thrust out before him.

Swaying inside his strike, Zona stabbed out. Someone had returned her sword after she'd thrown it and killed Arruns the spearman. Its point thudded into the giant's belly with her weight behind it. The steel cut through the tough leather and slipped into him. The man looked at it in amazement as she jerked it up to open him. Pulling it smoothly out, she stepped aside from the rush of innards and blood. As she smelled him, she wrinkled her nose. He crashed to the ground, throwing up clouds of dust, pieces of earth and grass. Coiled around his wound and the mess, he was whining.

The bald, clean-shaven man swung a long sword.

"I, Achates, shall avenge my comrade Dares!" he roared.

"Yeah, yeah."

Zona ducked under the whooshing blade. A long knife, almost a sword itself, was in his other hand. It nearly gutted her as she fell back.

Dust slipped under her boot. The warrior was on her back, winded by her fall. Stones dug into her shoulders and she saw faint silver on her skin through dust. Achates stumbled over her feet, cursing. *Some words there, I must remember* – Her legs straightened as he fell. His momentum added to her kick. The big man thumped down behind her head. There was a sharp crack as something broke. When she rolled clear of the rush of Aeneas' chariot and climbed to one knee, the huge warrior stayed down, groaning. The sounds he was making faded rapidly.

"You and me, Aeneas," she drawled.

The Dardanian was pulling his four black horses into a close turn.

"Very impressive," he replied, and his voice changed, "And what's that?"

She looked at an arm. It was perspiration and dust-streaked. She was unsurprised, grateful too as she saw the silver radiance glow brighter.

"Just a little something, especially for youuuu!" she

cooed, and went on, "You *are* meant to be a god, and all."

After that Zona kept quiet. She sprinted at him. *Get him off balance if I can.*

As he gaped, she grabbed the side of the chariot. The muscles knotting in her shoulders and arms as she wrenched at the still turning vehicle. Zona threw her weight into it. When she pulled a second time, the chariot tilted onto a single wheel, its horses screaming. Zona heaved once more as he slashed at her with his jewelled sword. With a crash, the war car overbalanced, throwing her clear. Aeneas cried out in shock and alarm.

He'd also been thrown out. He was on his feet, moving toward her, blade raised. His swarthy features were reddened, mouth a thin white line.

Rolling clear, she bounced to her feet. Swift cuts at their traces freed the struggling horses.

A space was rapidly clearing round them as fleeing men slowed to watch. Zona confronted 'God Aeneas'.

His voice was quiet but murderous. "That was my ride."

She shrugged. Her tone was light, amused. "Oh."

"So, Zona." He hefted his sword, advancing like a cat.

"It's been a while. Last time was at Troy. But I'm here to get justice for all the people you've killed and wronged, starting with Troilus. Remember him? You stood by and let Achilles butcher him. Then there's Alissar. Almost killed herself – over you because you ratted her out."

"You left out Creusa and Anchises. They were in my way, so I removed them, Polydamas too – "

She nodded. "Oh yeah. Mikhail, your soldier told me about them."

It was his turn to shrug. "Why am I not surprised? He weaselled out on me. And you will say there were a few more, but none who didn't need to be removed."

Slowly they were pacing round each other, appraising, looking for ways in. Zona was relaxed in a sword-fighter's stance, as was her enemy now his anger had cooled. His face was impassive, along with the dark eyes. She was watching for the slightest change in him that might signal an attack. The circle of spectators had thickened. Massed shadows fell into the fighting circle as the scarlet ball of the sun went on sinking into layers of dust. The sounds of battle and the Rutulian retreat muted, the only other sound was the slide of the combatants' feet.

"Oh yeah, I can see that," Zona drawled. She was still sizing him up, the coming fight pending. She kept talking to prolong this stage, increase the chance of finding a chink in him. "And you said about Polydamas; but you guys were always so tight."

"He'd have got in the way. Scruples, you know."

"Uh huh."

Aeneas came on slowly, watching her as closely as she was him. *I need to be careful with this guy. He's as slippery as a fish on the line.* He was a lot more than the urge to rend and destroy, brawn like Dares and Achates, his tame thugs.

"Way I heard it too was you snatched Lavinia when Turnus was set to marry her and started all this." Her tone was conversational but the amber eyes narrowed. "Is that true?"

He tried a prod with his sword. Still watching him, she moved back.

"You shouldn't believe all Turnus said." He smiled like a hunting cat. "Oh, all right. King Latinus was pretty well with me but her mother Amata kept being awkward, strung me along. Mothers never approve of prospective sons-in-law, do they?"

"So you grabbed Lavinia?"

"Dares and Achates helped. You just killed them, you know."

"I do."

"Anyhow, with a few others they helped bring her to the right man."

"Hmmmmnnn."

Zona tested him. As expected he moved away from her strike.

"That wasn't bad," he conceded.

"More where it came from. So what are you doing in Latium, other than this war?"

Aeneas returned her smile with one like a snake's grin. They were still circling each other, both watching for an opening.

He started a swift exchange of rushes, feints, and they returned to their positions. Their swords were tilted up, ready to begin again. Blood-red sunlight ran down Zona's blade.

He was breathing hard. Although the sun had pretty near gone down and dusk was everywhere, it was still hot. Perspiration dewed his forehead, gleamed through the dust on Zona's chest and arms. Under it silver light was still shining.

"Where were we?" he asked easily. His brow furrowed, then cleared. "Ah yes. My plans. I'm going to establish an empire that'll last a thousand years, the greatest ever."

"Small change. Heard that stuff before."

The warrior was pleased to see him flush. Maybe, after all, she could get to him, put him off balance. *It's worth trying; press on with it.* "So what was wrong with Alissar and Carthage? Seems to me you'd a lot to look forward to there. They've harbours, a growing navy and merchant fleets. It wouldn't surprise me if they command the seas in years to come."

"There's nothing wrong with Carthage," he said as if discussing some minor difficulty of the day round a campfire. "Your take on it isn't so far from mine."

"So why all this?"

"Alissar. She had this annoying habit of thinking and doing for herself. I need somebody who'll do as I say, and Alissar *is* Carthage."

"Wouldn't Creusa do for you? Oh, I forgot. You had Mikhail kill her."

Aeneas made a face behind his sword. "Too Trojan, boring, provincial. I was going to do Ascanius as well but Mikhail said he could be useful, and I saw that. And don't forget: Lavinia brings me Latium, then sons, the first building block of my empire."

"Shame you won't see it."

He saluted with his sword. "I was going to say the same to you. I've taken the trouble to explain all this. Now it's time I killed you."

"We'll see who takes who, Aeneas," she said quietly.

"It's such a waste," he continued with mock regret. "You could have worked with me, had it all. Together. You'd have made a splendid empress. Such fine sons, all that."

She murmured. "All that wishing."

"A problem, I'll admit, but it was more than just hopes."

"Me, your queen? Dream on. And you talk too much, Aeneas."

In a kind of dance-like slide, he moved towards her. His sword whistled at knee height. Zona jumped it. Blurred by speed, a backhand came for her head. She countered. Showering golden sparks which lit up the dusk, their blades clanged. After that blows came at her from all directions. She blocked, ducked, dodged and weaved, only just kept him out. He was even better than she remembered. Her swordcraft was honed too but only a multiple backflip put distance between them.

A moment later they were together. Chests pressed, sword blades locked. The warrior was grateful to see him breathe hard, sweat on his face. This was costing her as well.

"Well, who's the best?" he kept his voice easy but had to work at it.

"You should know the answer to that."

He shoved her back, swords parting with a screech of metal. Off balance, she managed to kick his chest as she lurched. Aeneas recovered but she was attacking. He only just managed to deflect her cuts.

They finished up a short way apart, gasping. Zona's chest and arms were shining. She could feel the prickle and tingle of light. *Unless it's sweat. If not, maybe it'll put him off, and the energy boost is useful.* Once more she decided to try and rattle him. Against a man like Aeneas it might not work but she reminded herself, *like me he's tiring.* She'd do footwork, let him chase her. *It may not work but same thing...* She had to do something to break the stalemate.

"Give it up," she said crisply. "You can't win. I promise if you go on with this, you're gonna die badly."

He sneered. "I'll take your head, decorate my chariot with it. You've overreached this time, Zona. You'll be a fine start to my empire. Princess of Latium, they call you. More like 'Died of Latium.'"

"I told you about your so-called empire. You'll never see it."

He rushed her.

Sword pointed down and held at her side, she flitted out of his way. Leaving it to the last moment, she smiled lazily, feet moving like a dancer's. Snarling, he pounded at her again. Once more she floated out of his charge.

"Careful, Aeneas," she drawled. "You're starting to lose it."

"I know your tricks, Zona." He was glaring, truculent. "It's not happening with me."

She tilted an eyebrow, sword still at her side. "Oh?"

Eyes glittering, he began to stalk her. She kept backing off, keeping just beyond his reach, swaying aside whenever he swiped at her. Some of the watching Trojans started to barrack Zona's tactics. At length Aeneas shouted at them to be quiet.

When it came, the end was swift.

From the ring of spectators someone pushed her.

Zona fell onto her knees in front of him. The sword flew out of her grip to land most of the width of the circle away. Aeneas raised his blade over his head, prepared to deal a death blow.

"Here it comes, Zona," he rasped.

She did the only thing possible.

Diving at him, she seized his legs and yanked. With a shout, almost drowned by the roar from his men, he lost his balance. As he teetered to regain it, his sword flew off to land not far from hers.

Toppling, Aeneas pulled out a knife. When he hurled it, Zona rolled. He fell next to her and they both grabbed for the weapon stuck in the ground.

Together they got their hands on it. Rolling, they struggled for it. She got a knee between his legs but he gripped it with his thighs before she could damage him. Aeneas was on top, features shiny and dusty, glaring into her face. His weight crushing down on her, she just about held onto the dagger's slippery handle. One at a time he started to unlock her fingers. Soon she was holding on with only two. Fighting to breathe with the sweaty pressure of him, she jerked, whiplashed herself. Grinning crazily, Aeneas hung on.

"I'll be the man who killed Zona!" he crowed.

"That's what you think."

Desperately, she let go the knife. Hands freed, she slapped his ears. Aeneas grunted in pain. As he swayed upright, the knife stroked her shoulder. Doing a final coiling up, Zona struggled with him; the man was much stronger than he looked. *Will nothing put him down?*

Snatching the dagger, she buried it in his cheek.

Blood ran down his face and he blinked rapidly. When she hung onto the weapon, it came her way.

"Bitch, whore!" he screamed.

Zona was aware of commotion from the watching men. Some were pushing forward while others held them back. There was a lot of shouting but she couldn't make out words. If they tore her apart, at least it would be quick, and she'd take 'God Aeneas' with her.

She cut his throat.

The big artery was severed. Utter disbelief in his eyes, he shrieked again. Blood fountained and she only just got her head aside. Even so, she was blinking salt from her eyes, rubbing as she fought to see. In moments he would bleed out.

"You!" he gargled, mouth running with blood.

"I'm sorry," she croaked, "it had to end like this. I tried to say you were going to die bad."

"You, y! – "

Pumping gore, he collapsed in her arms. Zona laid him aside as his heart and bloodflow slackened. His sphincter let go and she gagged at the stench.

She was weary in every muscle and sinew. Zona didn't feel anything but numb relief that it was over. She'd put down a man who would have been a tyrant but at the cost of giving in to her darkness. Because under it all, a wild exultance sang.

Although she didn't realise it Zona was an awesome

sight. Blood-soaked, her dark hair was tangled, matted round her face and shoulders. Her high cheekbones and her chin had dark, glistening splotches. Gore ran down her arms, the front of her vest and kilt heavy with it. Even her legs were splashed. If she'd not seen so many battlefields, Zona would not have realised there could be so much blood. Only her amber gaze was unmarked.

Yells of 'kill the witch!' and 'Vengeance for Pious Aeneas!' sounded in her ears. Men were surging at those who held them back. She'd be slaughtered very soon.

A voice rose above the clamour. "Zona's not our enemy! She fought at Troy!"

Another replied, "I saw her take on Achilles."

"She tried to save Hector!"

"She's fought bravely; leave her be."

Somebody else shouted her name. In moments others had taken it up.

"Zona, Zona, Zona!"

The shouting mingled with a surge of cheers.

Seems like I might live after all, she thought. Instinctively, she fetched and waved the two swords over her head. The cheering rose and swelled. Zona went to Aeneas' body and laid his blade on his chest, his fingers clasped on the hilt. The acclamation grew louder and men were throwing helmets into the air. She could have had this Trojan army, have taken it where and to what she liked. That wasn't for her; it was her past.

Goddess or god-blessed or not, the white light which had helped her kill Aeneas was with her again. She was grateful but didn't want to think of it further. Zona clung to the belief that she was just an ordinary warrior. She wondered if she'd ever understand the light, and why her. Weary as she was she'd leave it for later, and likely still wouldn't grasp it. *Maybe it won't appear anymore, and how do I know? Let it be – for now at least.*

In any case there were other things to do, and she knew the first one.

Zona sheathed her sword. Turning, waving to the troops a last time, she went to find Camilla and her future.